shadows OF YOU

THE LOST & FOUND SERIES

CATHERINE COWLES

This is a work of fiction. Names, characters, places, and incidents are either the products of the author's imagination or are used fictitiously. Any resemblance to actual persons, living or dead, businesses, companies, events, or locales is entirely coincidental.

Editor: Margo Lipschultz
Copy Editor: Chelle Olson
Proofreading: Julie Deaton and Jaime Ryter
Paperback Formatting: Stacey Blake, Champagne Book Design
Cover Design: Hang Le
Cover Photography: Wander Aguiar

For Elsie
Thank you for immunity necklaces, serial killer jokes, epic voice memos, and, most of all, your friendship. I'm eternally grateful to have you in my life.

For everyone who has felt like they don't fit.
Your magic is in your uniqueness.
Find the people who see your light.

shadows
OF YOU

Prologue

RAIN POUNDED AGAINST THE WINDSHIELD IN A STEADY drum that only seemed to accentuate the thumping rhythm in my chest. I glanced in the rearview mirror, taking mental stock of the vehicles behind me.

Red Acura. Navy sedan. White Honda minivan.

It was the navy sedan that had me on edge. Cars that blended tended to be the ones you needed to watch out for.

I slowed at a red light, one hand slipping beneath the neck of my T-shirt. My fingers eased over the angry, raised skin. Even months later, the flesh there still twinged. I wasn't sure if there was still a wound somewhere under the surface or if it was just phantom pain—ghosts of what had happened still haunting me.

A bubbly laugh broke through my thoughts. My gaze shifted back to the rearview mirror, taking in the source of the sound. My girl grinned, her tiny mouth full of spit bubbles and her first few teeth poking through.

For her.

That was why I was doing all of this. Because she deserved everything good in the world. And I was going to make sure she got it.

Pressure built behind my eyes. "For her. I'll do anything for her." I muttered the words over and over as if to build up my belief in them.

A horn honked behind me, and I jolted, gaze flying to the rearview mirror. It was the navy sedan. Some hurried businessperson behind the wheel.

It would've irked me under normal circumstances—that rude impatience. But now, I felt nothing but blissful relief. If he'd been following me, he never would've honked, wouldn't have drawn attention to himself.

I eased my foot off the brake and placed it on the accelerator. "It's a brand-new adventure," I told Lucy as though I'd actually believe it if I said it enough.

She banged her little fists on the car seat. "Ba!" she said in emphasis.

"I'm taking that as excitement." Or she simply wanted her toy ball.

I flipped on my blinker and made a right-hand turn into the mall's parking structure. Plenty of cars were doing the exact same thing I was. I couldn't help but investigate each one, trying to read if the soccer mom or elderly gentleman had ulterior motives.

Rolling down my window, I grabbed a parking ticket. "Lower levels. P4, section C." I whispered the words to myself over and over. I'd memorized Evan's instructions the past three days as I packed as much of our belongings as possible while still following his dictates to "*keep it light.*"

Traveling with a toddler meant you could never keep it light. I drove my sedan to the basement levels, fighting a shiver as darkness descended. Sure, fluorescent lights guided my way, but lights could fail.

"Maybe we can get a kitty at our new house," I told Lucy.

She blew air through her lips in answer.

"I'll even let you name him."

I had to focus on the happy. The silver linings of everything we were facing. It would be the only thing to get us through.

Pulling into an empty parking spot, I gripped the steering wheel, unmoving. Blood roared in my ears as my palms dampened. I could do this. I'd already been through hell; the last thing I needed was to stay here and subject myself to more.

Shutting off the engine, I let out a whoosh of air. I climbed out and rounded to open the back door. Bending, I unhooked Lucy's straps as she chattered away in mostly nonsensical sounds, punctuated by the few words she had in her vocabulary. She slapped a hand against my cheek, and a laugh bubbled out of me. That light expulsion of air almost sent me into a fit of sobs.

Keep it together. Just a little longer.

It was the same refrain I'd been telling myself for months. But it was the only thing that got me through. That, and Lucy.

My throat burned. Soon, I wouldn't be able to use the name she'd had since birth. That felt so incredibly wrong. But safe was more important.

Footsteps sounded behind me, and I whirled. A little of my anxiety eased when I saw the familiar face. "Evan."

His name sounded more like a rasp of breath than actual syllables.

Light brown brows pulled together. "You okay?"

Another laugh burst free, but this one had a hysterical edge. "Okay is the last thing I am."

I was leaving behind everything I'd ever known, every person and my entire support system.

Evan reached out and squeezed my shoulder, revealing the gun and badge at his hip. "You're going to be just fine."

I nodded, resisting the urge to bite my lip.

He released me and handed over a folder and a set of keys. "New identification. The name changes are sealed. No one will be able to track you."

I flipped open the file. My gaze landed first on Lucy's new moniker. Cady. My older sister and I had always loved the name. It was John who hadn't been crazy about it. And John always got his way.

Anger flared, hot and deep, but I shoved it down. I couldn't let it take hold, not when I needed complete focus for the task at hand.

I pulled a driver's license out of the folder. The picture was the same as my Mississippi license, but I guessed cops had access to that sort of thing. Only this one said my home was in Washington state. And that my name was Aspen Barlow.

My gaze shot to Evan.

He shrugged. "You said you always wanted to live in the Pacific Northwest. It was the least I could do."

My nose stung. "Thank you," I croaked. Those words didn't come close to encompassing what I wanted them to. Not for the officer who had seen me through the investigation, the arrest, the horrible trial, and everything that followed.

Evan's expression went from gentle to the official one I'd seen more than the rest. "You can thank me by staying safe. No contact with people from your old life." He handed me a cell phone and a set of car keys. "Text when you get in. Say, 'Is this Joey?' I'll know you're safe. Then don't contact me again unless it's an emergency. Map and address are in the station wagon."

I nodded, adjusting Lucy, no…*Cady* on my hip as I handed him my keys and cell.

"There are enough vehicles coming and going from here that you should be safe, but I put a wig and sunglasses in the vehicle just in case. Car seat is ready to go. Don't stop until you're over state lines, at least. Your face is still making the rounds on the news now and then."

That anger flared to life again. People had a morbid fascination with others' suffering. Maybe it made them feel better about their lives. Maybe it was that car-crash phenomenon. No matter the reason, it kept me from finding any sort of safety.

"I won't stop until we've gotten some distance."

Evan nodded. "Check in on the regular."

I moved on instinct, giving him a quick hug. "Thank you."

"You'd better get going." He patted my back. "You've got this. It'll be the fresh start you two need."

I swallowed against the burn in my throat, nodding but not trusting my voice.

Evan studied me for a moment and then dropped his hand. "I'll get your stuff."

I headed toward the station wagon a few spots down. Opening the back door, I got Cady situated while Evan loaded our bags. I slid behind the wheel and picked up the black wig. It was so different from my vibrant red hair, but I guessed that was the point. Pulling it on, I slipped the sunglasses into place.

Evan watched as I carefully pulled out of the parking spot. The gas and brake were stickier than my sedan, but I'd have plenty of hours to get used to the vehicle.

I lifted my hand in a wave that Evan answered. Then, swallowing hard, I headed for the parking garage exit. The mall's structure was already filling up on the higher levels, and I was thankful for the cover. I'd learned the hard way that you never knew who might be watching.

I held my breath as I pulled out into the sunlight. I didn't release it until I was two blocks away. My lips moved in a muttered prayer—maybe a mantra. "Please let us be okay. Please let us be free."

But if there was one thing I knew, it was that John's fingers had a far reach. And they could steal the breath right out of your lungs.

Chapter One

Aspen

FIVE YEARS LATER

"**M**AMA!" CADY YELLED, FLINGING HER ARMS WIDE as she ran out of the elementary school. "It's snowing!"

Her glittery, off-brand Uggs weren't exactly protecting her from the wetness, but this storm had come on unexpectedly. In our small town nestled in the mountains of Washington, getting the occasional dump in October wasn't unusual. Sometimes, we even got some in September. But we typically had a bit of warning.

Cady spun in a circle, tipping her head back and trying to catch snowflakes on her tongue.

My heart squeezed. She was everything good in this world—a walking, talking beacon of hope. "Come on, Katydid. Let's get going before your nose freezes."

Cady's best friend, Charlie, laughed. "Dad says it takes at least a couple of hours for frostbite to set in."

I pressed my lips together to keep from chuckling. "Good to know."

"See you tomorrow," Charlie called as he ran toward the SUV with the police emblem on its side.

I waved at his dad, Lawson, behind the wheel. He lifted his hand in answer.

"Can we make snowmen when we get home?" Cady begged as I hustled her toward my station wagon.

"Depends how much snow we get."

But given that a good three inches were already on the ground, I had a feeling we would be in snowman city.

I opened the back door for Cady, and she slid in. "I'd say there's enough for snow cones already."

Her green eyes lit up as a grin split her face. "Can we make mine strawberry?"

"What do you think?"

"Strawberries and cream!" Cady yelled and held up her hand.

I laughed and high-fived it. "Let's go home, and then we can get started."

I just hoped my station wagon would get us there. I needed to replace the tires. I'd known it months ago but thought I'd have time. Unfortunately, an early dose of winter waited for no one.

Climbing behind the wheel, I started it up and turned on the heat as high as it would go. Cady chattered on and on about her day, but I stayed focused on the roads. The elementary school was on the outskirts of downtown Cedar Ridge, not too far from The Brew, the coffee shop and café I managed.

I followed Main Street through town. Usually, I let myself take in the quaint tourist shops, restaurants, and the gorgeous lake that peeked out from between the buildings. But not today. Even five years into my life in Cedar Ridge, I still wasn't used to driving in the snow.

"It's so pretty," Cady said with a sigh.

My hands loosened on the wheel a fraction. "It is."

Something about the blanket of white stretched out around us was incredibly peaceful. It reminded me how much I loved living here. But it was more than the beauty that surrounded us. It was the people. Even though my friends here might not know my past, they loved and supported us with everything they had.

My gaze flicked to the rearview mirror as I turned onto the road that would take us out of town. My habit of watching who might be following at any given moment had proven impossible to break.

I shifted my focus to Cady. "What do you think? Winter wonderland walk?"

She beamed. "Yes, yes, yeeeesss!"

"I don't know. You don't sound excited at all."

"I'm excited!" She bounced in her seat as if to accentuate the point.

"Okay, I guess we can go."

The typical ten-minute drive to our house at the base of the mountain took almost twenty, given how carefully I drove. I was thankful I'd gone to the supermarket yesterday because I had a feeling we might be holing up for a day or two.

The moment I pulled to a stop in front of the farmhouse, Cady was unbuckling her seat belt. "What about the goaties? And Mabel and Phineas? And—"

"I got them all in the barn before I picked you up," I assured her.

"We gotta let Mabel out later. She *loves* the snow."

I grinned as I slid out of the station wagon, my boots disappearing into the snow. One of our donkeys was crazy about fresh powder. She would zoom around her paddock like nothing you'd ever seen. But it was hard to get her back inside the barn afterward.

"Tomorrow, when the storm has stopped," I told Cady.

She bounced on her toes. "I wonder if the ducks will like it."

"They might."

A customer at The Brew had told me about a mama duck with a broken wing on their property. She was worried the duck wouldn't be able to protect herself and her babies from predators. So, I brought her to our place. Now, she was set up in the barn with a heat lamp and a play pool in one of the stalls. My hope was that the wing would heal with time, and then she'd be able to be on her own again. But until then, she and her babies had a safe place to stay.

Cady raced through the snow and up the steps, jumping from foot to foot on the front porch. "Let's go!"

I laughed as I headed to join her, my gaze going to the tiny piece of wood I'd left jammed into the screen door. It was still there. I might not have been able to swing a fancy security system, but I'd learned ways to keep us safe.

Snagging the wood chip, I placed it on the windowsill and opened the three locks on the door. Cady was inside before I could blink. A deep woof sounded, and our dog bounded toward his best girl.

"Chauncey!" Cady giggled as the three-legged pup licked her cheek. "I missed you, too."

"Come on, buddy," I called, letting him out into the snow to do his business.

By the time we were back inside, Cady had donned her bright pink snow gear. I winced as I took her in. The pants were a little too short, and the jacket a bit tight. It looked like I would be doling out cash for new gear before the winter season hit us full steam. Sometimes, I could get two seasons out of Cady's gear if I was lucky. But she'd had a growth spurt this year.

Cady shot her gloved fist into the air. "Winter wonderland walk!"

"Let's go." I grabbed a pair of gloves and a hat for myself, and then we headed back out. I locked the door and shoved my keys into my pocket.

Cady launched herself off the porch steps into the snow. "I'm flying!"

I hurried down the steps, caught her around the waist, and lifted her into the air. Cady's laughter caught on the air and swam around us. *This.* This was what I'd fought for. I hadn't regretted leaving our old lives behind for a second.

Cady's giggles died away. "Mama," she whispered.

Something about her tone had me on alert. My gaze shot in the direction Cady was looking, and I stilled.

A deer limped along our drive, headed away from the house.

"She's hurt," Cady whispered, tears filling her voice.

My heart clenched. That was obviously the case, and as I

squinted, I could just see what looked like wire wrapped around her chest and leg. A million curses filled my mind.

"We gotta help her," Cady begged. "It's so cold."

My nose stung, imagining how scared the poor deer must be. Usually, they traveled in groups, but I didn't see any signs of other animals around. They'd probably left her behind because she couldn't move fast enough.

A burn lit along my sternum. I knew what that felt like, to be alone and scared, not having anyone at your back.

"Come on," I said to Cady, hustling her back up the steps.

"We gotta help her," she argued.

"I'm going to, but I need you to wait inside." I didn't want Cady to scare off the doe as we approached.

To her credit, she didn't argue, simply followed me inside. I entered the kitchen and grabbed the apple half I planned to cut up for her after-school snack. "I'm going to lock the door after me. Don't answer for anyone. Promise?"

Cady bobbed her head up and down. "Hurry, Mama."

I didn't wait. I slipped out the door and locked it behind me. The deer had already made it down our long drive and was heading up the two-lane road. I cursed as the wind picked up in a loud howl, sending the snow flying.

I hurried to catch up with the doe, slowing as I got closer and trying to examine the wire around her. I bit the inside of my cheek. It was digging into the poor deer's flesh. This might be out of my wheelhouse.

Pulling off my glove, I retrieved my phone from my pocket and searched the number for Fish and Wildlife.

"Harrison County Fish and Wildlife, this is Andrea. How can I help you?"

"Hi. My name is Aspen Barlow. I live in Cedar Ridge on Huckleberry Lane. I'm following a deer with some wire wrapped around her pretty badly. Do you have anyone who might be able to help?"

"Ma'am, do *not* approach the deer if it's injured. They can react badly when cornered."

"I'm not trying to corner her. I just want to help her," I explained.

I'd fallen into rehabilitating animals over the last several years. It seemed like they found me more than I found them. It had started with Mabel. The farmhouse's previous owner hadn't only taken poor care of his property; he'd neglected his donkey, as well. He'd mentioned just putting her down when he moved out, and I'd hurried to say I would take her.

I hadn't had the first clue how to care for a donkey, but the internet had taught me most of what I needed to know. It had taken time to earn Mabel's trust. She was the one who'd taught me not to corner an animal who was scared or hurt. I had gotten a nasty gash courtesy of a kick from her when I got too close, too quickly.

The woman on the phone sighed. "My officers are only responding to emergencies right now due to the snow."

Annoyance flickered through me. "This deer is suffering. That's not an emergency?"

"The public isn't at risk from an injured deer."

Meaning she would've responded to a call about a black bear or a cougar.

"Ma'am. Please. She's hurting." My voice nearly broke as I spoke. I couldn't leave the doe out here alone in the cold.

The woman sighed, muttering something under her breath. "I can try one person who might be out that way, but I can't make any promises. Where are you?"

I rattled off my approximate address, and she hung up without another word.

My teeth began to chatter as the wind picked up again. It was the kind of cold that hurt your skin. I didn't want to think about what the temperature might've dropped to.

The deer trembled, looking over her shoulder at me.

"It's okay, girl. You're not alone. I'm gonna get you fixed up in no time."

She started walking again, limping on her bad leg.

"Just stay put. It'll be easier on both of us."

The doe didn't listen.

"I get it. You're determined. Been living like this a while?"

She kept right on walking.

I followed her, wondering if I could just grab the wire and free her. I worried the inside of my cheek as I studied the metal imprisoning her. I thought I might be able to get her out if I got my fingers under a specific corner.

I made a clucking sound with my tongue as the wind howled again. The deer halted, glancing skeptically at me.

"Here, girl. Want some apple?"

She sniffed the air and took a step closer.

"That's it."

Another step.

"This apple is super yummy."

A little closer.

The doe strained her neck.

A deep voice cut through the wind. "What the hell do you think you're doing?"

Chapter Two

Roan

THE WOMAN WAS GOING TO GET HERSELF KILLED. STANDING in the freezing cold in a jacket that wasn't nearly warm enough and a hat with some sort of damned pom-pom on the top. And was that *glitter* woven through it? Sparkly shit didn't do anything to keep you warm.

There she was, bending over, trying to get an injured animal to come to her with an apple. The second she tried to pull that wire free, the deer would lose its mind and probably kick her in the head. She'd be lucky if she got out of it with only a concussion.

The woman whirled around, her red hair flying as her eyes went wide—eyes so green they were a sucker punch to the gut. I sucked in a breath.

The moment I saw true fear in them, I wanted to kick myself. She covered it quickly, taking up a stance I recognized as one ready for defense. I instantly took a step back. I should've expected it, been used to it by now, but it still grated. "I'm from Fish and Wildlife," I gritted out.

A little of the tension bled out of her. "Oh."

Then annoyance filled her expression. "Then you shouldn't be barking at me for trying to help a deer."

"I didn't bark at you."

She arched a brow. "Pretty sure you came storming over here looking like the abominable snowman and growling like one, too."

I scowled at her. "I was trying to stop you from getting yourself killed."

"I know it's a risk, but she's hurting and alone. I wasn't going to leave her to suffer."

A muscle in my jaw twitched. "A cornered animal, especially when they're in pain, will react badly. Deer's hooves can be lethal. Especially if they connect with your skull."

"I can move quickly. I know how to escape an animal lashing out."

"Civilians trying to interfere," I grumbled. Just like Marion Simpson, who refused to stop feeding that damn bear she'd practically adopted. "Do you know how much paperwork I'll have to do if you get dead?"

The redhead gaped at me. "Did you seriously just say that?"

I shrugged and turned back to my snowmobile—the same vehicle she'd been oblivious to as I approached. A fresh wave of annoyance flashed through me. Wandering around after a deer in a whiteout was the height of stupidity. Not being aware of your surroundings was even worse.

Bending, I grabbed my kit from one of the snowmobile's side compartments and assembled the tranquilizer gun. It had only taken a quick glance to see the deer would need medical attention.

I turned around, eyeing the doe, who was trying to make her way through the deepening snow. Poor girl. I lifted the tranq gun, and the redhead threw herself in front of me.

"Don't shoot her!"

I let out a string of curses. "What the hell are you doing?"

"Stopping you from committing deer-i-cide. I won't let you hurt her."

A fire blazed in those green depths, one I had to admire begrudgingly, even if the woman was risking life and limb.

"It's a tranq gun," I growled. "The doe needs medical attention."

"Oh."

"Yeah. Now, move out of my way so I don't miss my shot."

The redhead moved back, and I aimed. The dart hit true. The deer jerked, then stumbled into the snow.

The woman didn't wait. She rushed over to the doe, sinking to her knees, not giving a damn that she wasn't in proper snow gear. "It's okay, girl. We're going to help you." She positioned the deer's head on her lap, stroking her cheek.

Something about the gesture tugged at a place deep in my chest. I bit the inside of my cheek to distract myself from the sensation. Grabbing my medical kit, I made my way over to the fallen deer.

"It looks bad," the woman whispered.

She wasn't wrong. The old, rusted tomato cage had cut into the doe's flesh, and the injuries looked infected. "These cages are a recipe for disaster. Deer stick their heads in, trying to get the tomatoes, and they get stuck."

The redhead worried a spot on the inside of her mouth, making her cheek pucker. "I never thought about that."

"Most people don't." I grabbed a pair of wire cutters from my kit, quickly freeing the doe from the cage. The wounds looked angry. "I need to get her some real medical care."

I looked at the road. I didn't want to take her into town. The ride would be too long.

"I've got a barn she can stay in."

I glanced back at the woman, arching a brow in question.

"I take in injured animals sometimes. One more won't be a problem."

Of course, she did. A bleeding heart, through and through. "You'd need high walls so she doesn't try to jump out."

"I've got a stall like that. It's not a problem."

I searched out her property. I could just see the barn in the distance. Even from here, I could tell it needed some serious work. I cursed. "Fine. Stay here."

"You could say *thank you*," she muttered.

I moved back to my snowmobile and grabbed the stretcher. It only took a minute, but when I returned, the woman was shaking.

"You need a better coat."

She sighed. "My coat is fine."

"You're shivering."

"I don't usually make a habit of sitting in the snow."

She needed a coat made for this climate, not one with little decorative stars on the sleeves.

"Can you help me roll her so we can get the board under her?"

The woman nodded. "Aspen."

"Huh?"

"My name is Aspen."

I simply grunted in response. I didn't want to know her name. I already knew too much.

She muttered something under her breath that I couldn't make out.

"On three. One, two, three."

We shifted the deer and slid the board into place. It didn't take long to strap her down. I hurriedly backed my snowmobile up to the site and connected the stretcher.

I glanced at Aspen. "Get on."

Her eyes went wide. "With you?"

"You want to walk all the way back?"

A shiver racked her, and she shook her head. So very carefully, she thrust a leg over the vehicle's seat.

"Hold on to my waist."

My words were low, gravelly, but she obeyed.

The contact nearly made me jerk. Even through layers of snow gear, there was a burning heat to the woman's touch. *Danger.* The message flashed over and over in my mind as I slowly started down the road.

My back teeth ground together as I made the turn into Aspen's driveway, and she gripped me tighter. As we slowed in front of her old farmhouse, she let go, and I released the breath I'd been holding since the moment she gripped my waist.

Aspen quickly climbed off the snowmobile just as the front door flew open, and a little girl ran out. "Mama!"

She charged down the steps as fast as her snowsuit-clad legs could carry her. She looked like a pink glitter snowball.

"Cady," Aspen chastised gently. "I told you to wait inside."

A guilty look passed over her face. "I know, but—" Her words cut off as she saw the deer at the back of my vehicle. "No! Is she—?"

Aspen quickly wrapped her daughter in a hug. "No, Katydid. She's just sleeping so we can help her."

Tears welled in the little girl's eyes. "Promise?"

"I promise. We got some help from Fish and Wildlife. We're going to make sure she's okay."

The little girl's gaze cut to me, so much like her mother's, it froze me to the spot. "You're going to help my mama save Bambi?"

Fuck me. I couldn't say no to that face or the damn deer.

Chapter Three

Aspen

I SAW THE MOMENT THE BURLY MAN SOFTENED. EVEN THE hardest-hearted didn't stand a chance against my Cady.

"Yeah. I'm gonna help her," he muttered.

I couldn't stop my lips from twitching. The man didn't miss the movement, and it turned his reluctant agreement into a scowl. It only made me grin wider.

Cady wiggled to get out of my hold. "Thank you, thank you, thank you! What do we do now? I want to help. I'm a real good helper. Right, Mama?"

"The best helper in all the land," I agreed.

The man frowned. "I think it's best if you keep a bit of distance, just in case she wakes up."

Cady bobbed her head up and down. "I can do that." She glanced up at me. "Do you think she needs a blanket?"

I shook my head. "We've got straw and heat lamps in the barn."

The man, whose name I still didn't know, raised his eyebrows in surprise. I was going to start calling him The Grouch in my head.

"You've got heat lamps?"

I nodded. "We have some baby ducks that need some extra heat right now. And we've had baby goats, too."

Cady filled him in on our menagerie. "We've got ducks and goaties and donkeys and a pony and an alpaca and four cats and a dog and an emu and—"

The Grouch's jaw dropped. "Did you say an *emu*?"

My cheeks heated. It did sound a little out there when Cady listed them all like that. "There was a guy over in Brookdale who thought it'd be fun to have one as a pet but didn't realize all that went into caring for one."

The Grouch shook his head. "Let's get her inside before the snow gets worse."

We had at least a foot already.

Cady tugged on my hand. "Think I'll get a snow day tomorrow?"

"You just might."

She squealed and spun in a circle. "I love snow!"

I laughed, grinning at Cady. She was a constant reminder of everything I had to be grateful for.

The man cleared his throat. "Over there?"

I jerked my gaze to him. He'd already unhooked the stretcher from the snowmobile and had hold of a tow rope.

"Yup. I can help you pull her—"

"I've got it," he clipped.

"Alrighty, then," I mumbled, leading the way toward the barn. My skin itched, feeling just a bit too tight for my body. I wasn't used to having people in our space. Only the few friends I truly trusted or when it was strictly necessary. This qualified as necessary—an emergency, even—but it still made me twitchy.

Cady bounded around us, chattering away about all the animals, sharing their names and funny stories about them, and how they'd come to live with us. The man didn't respond once, except with the occasional grunt, but Cady didn't seem to mind. She just kept right on talking.

I hurried ahead to open the barn door. The animals lifted their heads at the sound. Syd, our deaf pony, just followed the others' lead and turned toward the door. He let out a whinny, and Cady hurried over to stroke his nose.

The man tugged the deer into the barn aisle. "Which stall?"

"Far back right has the tallest door."

He didn't respond, just dragged the board and doe back there. It didn't take him long to unhook her and lay her on the hay.

Cady pressed into my side. "She's hurt."

I wrapped an arm around her. "That's why she's here. So we can help her get better."

She looked up at me. "Did someone hurt her?"

My ribs constricted. I walked a delicate line with Cady, never wanting to lie to her but also knowing she wasn't ready for the whole truth. Still, she knew enough to understand that sometimes people did bad things.

The man's gaze lifted to Cady, sensing something deeper in her words.

"Not on purpose," I hurried to assure her. "She got stuck in something from a garden."

Cady nodded, a little of the worry leaving her expression. "We gotta give her a name."

I tweaked Cady's nose. "Good thing I know the perfect person for the job."

She giggled. "I'll start thinking."

"Shouldn't name her," the man said.

My eyes narrowed on him. "Everyone deserves a name."

"She's not a pet. If we do our jobs right, she'll be going back into the wild."

"She can have a name in the wild," Cady broke in, not put off by his brusque tone in the slightest. "I name all the animals that are around. There's Rita, the turtle. Juliette and James, the deer. Carson, the chipmunk." She tapped her lips. "Sometimes, I forget what I name them because there's lots and lots. But I just give them new names, and I don't think they care."

The man stared at her as if he didn't have the first clue what to do with her. Then he pushed to his feet and pulled out his phone, tapping the screen. He held it to his ear and waited.

"Yeah. I got an injured deer out on Huckleberry Lane. Got caught in a tomato cage."

Silence for a beat.

"Got it free but looks like an infection."

More quiet except for the animals all around us, making sounds of curiosity or bids for an early dinner.

"Yeah, got some in my kit. Will do."

The man glanced at me. "Can Dr. Miller come out here tomorrow to take a look at her?"

I stiffened. I'd heard there was a newish vet in town, but it hadn't been time for Chauncey's checkup since the doctor had arrived a few months back. I was sure he was perfectly nice; it just meant more strangers on my property. I licked my suddenly dry lips.

The man's gaze narrowed on me, assessing that slight bit of hesitation.

"Sure. Give him my number." I rattled off the digits, ignoring the sweat gathering at the base of my spine.

The man read them out to the vet and then hung up. "Miller said he'll call you first thing tomorrow."

"Okay." The single word caught in my throat, and the man didn't miss it.

"You got anyone else helping you with all these animals?"

I stiffened, feeling the Taser I always carried in my pocket. "We can handle it."

He just shook his head. "Miller wants the doe started on antibiotics. I'm going to give her an injection now while she's out. He'll give you pills tomorrow. Probably some treats to get her to take them."

The tension radiating through me eased a fraction as he stalked out of the barn.

"He's *really* tall," Cady whispered.

"He is," I agreed. You couldn't see much of the man through his snow gear, just the fact that he was tall and clearly built. And those hypnotizing dark blue eyes.

"He's gonna help her," she assured me with complete certainty.

My heart ached as I took in the deer. The poor thing would be terrified when she woke up.

Footsteps had me looking back to the aisle. The man strode in our direction, bag in hand. He set it on a tack box and opened it.

Cady left my side immediately. "Whatcha doin'?"

The man glanced down at her. He started to frown but then seemed to catch himself. "I'm going to give the deer some medicine."

Cady watched as he pulled out some supplies. "A shot?" She shivered. "I don't like shots."

There was the faintest twitch to his lips. "I don't either."

Her eyes went wide. "Really?"

He shook his head. "Never have. Freaks me out."

Cady bobbed her head up and down. "They hurt, too." She looked at the doe. "Is it going to hurt my new friend?"

A pang lit along my sternum. She had the best heart.

"She won't feel a thing. She's sleeping right now, which is what she needs."

"I wish I was sleeping when I got shots," Cady grumbled.

The man grinned. That curve of his lips and the flash of straight, white teeth had me sucking in a surprised breath. When he wasn't scowling, his beauty was devastating.

"I wouldn't mind napping through my shots either," he agreed.

"Can I help?" Cady asked.

The man opened his mouth as if to say no but then glanced at the deer. "Sure."

I watched as he led Cady into the stall. He explained each step as he did it. The deer didn't flinch as he inserted the needle and pushed the medicine into her muscle. Then he slid on gloves and cleaned her wounds, placing ointment on the gashes.

There was a tenderness to how he treated the animal that was in direct opposition to his demeanor. The gentleness told me his cold, grouchy exterior was nothing but a defense mechanism. It was to protect the tenderness that lived within him.

"We did it, Mama! Did you see? I helped. I spread the medicine on her and everything."

I crouched in front of Cady. "You were amazing."

"I think I wanna be a vet or maybe a—a—what did you say you were again?" she asked the man.

There was that faint lip twitch again. "A Fish and Wildlife game warden."

"A game warder," Cady whispered. "That's so *cool*."

My gaze lifted to the man's. "Thank you. For helping her."

The hint of amused affection slipped off his face, and the mask came back. "It's my job."

I only smiled wider, having gotten a glimpse of what he was hiding beneath the façade. "Well, thank you for doing it."

He shifted on his feet, clearly uncomfortable. I wanted to laugh but resisted the urge.

"Call Dr. Miller if she gets worse. I gotta get going."

"I will." As he headed into the snowstorm, regret flashed through me at knowing I'd likely never see him again. Something about the man pulled at me. Something I couldn't quite pin down.

"I like him," Cady said in a matter-of-fact tone.

I pushed to my feet. "Oh, yeah?"

"I think Mr. Grizz and I are gonna be bestest friends."

My brows flew up. "Mr. Grizz?"

"Yep," she said, popping the P. "He's like a grizzly bear. Cranky after coming out of hi-hi—"

"Hibernation?" I supplied, fighting back laughter.

Cady grinned. "Hibersnation!" Her tiny features scrunched. "Maybe he's cranky because he's hungry."

This time, I couldn't hold in my laughter and pulled Cady into my arms. "You might be right. We should've offered him a snack."

Chapter Four

Roan

I STRODE THROUGH THE DEEPENING SNOW TO MY SNOWMOBILE, but I couldn't help glancing over my shoulder at the barn. My back teeth ground together. The woman was in over her head. *Aspen.*

The name fit her. As if she were some woodland fairy out of the storybooks my mom used to read to my siblings and me every night.

Whatever her name, she clearly didn't have the knowledge to be doing animal rescue. Her bid to get the wire off the deer told me that much. She could have ended up hurt or killed.

My phone buzzed in my pocket. I slid it out, seeing Lawson's name flash across the screen. I tapped *accept.*

"Yeah?"

"Well, hello to you, too," my brother said.

I scowled at the horizon. "What do you need, Law?"

"Got a missing hiker. Feel like going out?"

I let a series of expletives fly. "Do these people not check the weather?"

"His wife said he wanted to experience real mountain snow."

"Tourist?" I groused.

"Yup. From Dallas. Definitely not cut out for this weather. A small team's meeting at the Cedar Creek trailhead."

"I'm on my way. Be there in ten."

"Thanks, man. Bring good gear."

I grunted in answer and hung up. Swinging a leg over my snowmobile, I cast one last look at the barn. They were still in there. Doing what? Probably messing around with the rest of their ridiculous zoo.

I forced my gaze away and started my vehicle. Sliding my helmet on, I headed down the drive. The combination of wind and snow slapped against my visor as I flew down the two-lane road. Soon, I was turning onto another mountain pass and headed toward the trailhead.

A handful of vehicles were already gathered. I recognized all but one. And that one had a rental car plate frame. Had to be our guy.

I pulled to a stop and cut the engine. Climbing off the sled, I heard a whistle.

Caden strode toward me, my sister at his side and our other siblings behind them. "Now that's a thing of beauty. I think I might need one of those."

Grae smacked her fiancé's chest. "You've got enough toys."

My youngest brother, Nash, grinned. "I've been looking at one for this season. We could race."

Lawson groaned, pinching the bridge of his nose. "The last thing I need is to have to arrest you both."

Nash waggled his eyebrows. "Good thing I'm an officer of the law and can get out of a speeding ticket."

Our other brother, Holt, chuckled. "Somehow, I don't think Law would let you get away with that."

"I wouldn't," Lawson agreed, eldest brother through and through.

"Enough shooting the shit," my dad called from a spot at the back of his SUV. "You guys need to get going. We're losing daylight, and the temps are dropping."

The tone of the group immediately changed. Gone was the

good-natured ribbing, replaced by the buzz of adrenaline that always came with a search and rescue mission. Dad was involved in SAR long before we came along, and we'd grown up helping the volunteers, whether by working the command post with Mom or going out with Dad and his team when we got older.

"I'll be in my vehicle, working the radio," Dad said. "We start with a hike straight up the trail. Hopefully, he didn't wander off it. Got your gear?" His gaze lingered on Grae for a beat longer than the rest of us. He'd gotten better at not babying her because she had type 1 diabetes, but it wasn't a habit you could break overnight.

Grae took pity on him. "I've got extra snacks and my emergency GlucaGen kit."

Holt thumped Dad on the shoulder. "We've got it. Can you keep us up to date on the weather?"

"No problem," Dad agreed.

"Let's hit it," Holt called.

Our SAR teams were typically larger. Now that our second youngest brother, Holt, had come back to Cedar Ridge and taken over the team, it'd grown nicely. But I had a feeling he'd gone with a small, core group today because he knew we needed to move quickly.

And he trusted we all knew what we were doing. That was what happened when you grew up around SAR your entire life. Thanks to our dad, it was practically in our blood.

Grae fell into step beside me. "You were already on a callout?"

I grunted at my sister.

"I'm taking that as your very verbose way of saying yes. What was it?"

I shifted my pack on my shoulders. My siblings never stopped giving me a hard time about not being talkative. What they didn't realize was that it was easier this way. I couldn't say the wrong thing. Didn't hurt people.

"Injured deer."

Grae glanced up at me. "Is it going to be okay?"

"Think so. Got her out of the cold. Dr. Miller will take a look at her tomorrow."

She grinned. "The hottie vet, huh?"

"I heard that, Gigi," Caden growled behind us.

"It's just a simple fact."

Nash smacked Caden on the arm. "What? You can't take a little competition?"

"Oh, shove off. You can't even take it when your thirteen-year-old nephew sits next to Maddie."

Nash glared at Caden. "Drew hits on her all the time."

"He's *thirteen*."

I lost myself in my family's banter. The din of chaos was both a comfort and a torment. I'd wished for so long that I could join in instead of hovering on the outskirts. But I simply wasn't built for it. And all the secrets I hid didn't help.

"I see something," Holt called.

We all picked up to a jog, slogging through the drifting snow. I caught sight of a figure huddled against a tree. They weren't moving. My stomach plummeted.

Holt and Lawson reached the man first. They sank to their knees. Holt felt for a pulse while Lawson began asking him questions. The man's teeth chattered.

"Can you tell us your name, sir?" Lawson asked.

Holt looked up. "Pulse is slow. Likely hypothermic."

Grae pulled out her radio. "We've got him. He's alive but possibly hypothermic. Have the ambulance meet us at the trailhead if they can get up here."

I pulled the stretcher from Holt's pack and quickly assembled it with Caden's help.

"I've got hot packs," Caden said as Holt and Lawson rolled the man onto the stretcher.

Caden slid the warming packs under the man's jacket while Grae pulled out a mylar blanket and covered him.

"Let's move," Holt ordered. "I don't want his pulse getting any slower."

I grabbed hold of one stretcher handle. Holt, Lawson, and Nash took the others.

"Grae, keep checking his pulse and breathing," Holt instructed.

We made our way down the trail as quickly as possible, still traversing safely. None of us talked or joked; there was too much at stake.

As I saw the lights of an ambulance through the trees, I breathed a little easier.

Caden ran ahead to help them ready the stretcher we'd transfer the man onto. It only took a matter of minutes. The EMTs got a line running with a warming solution as we secured the man in place.

The female EMT cast me a wary look I was used to but tried my best to ignore. Fastening the belt around the man's chest, I stepped back and out of the way. A few moments later, they'd loaded him into the back and were off.

My siblings and Caden slipped right back into giving each other hell. This time, it was about Nash stealing the cookies that Holt's fiancée, Wren, had made for him. I stayed back and watched.

These SAR missions were the best and the worst. They gave me a sense of purpose. Let me be a part of my family I wouldn't otherwise have. But I still felt like I didn't fit. Like I was…other. And at the end of the day, it left me knowing one thing.

I was so damn alone. But I needed to be. It was the only thing that was truly safe. So, I slipped away into the shadows of that loneliness all over again.

Chapter Five

Aspen

MY FINGERS CURVED AROUND THE COFFEE MUG AS I TOOK in the blanket of white out my front windows. Something about it was so peaceful. As if the entire world had gone silent.

It felt safe. A cocoon of blissful snowflakes.

Chauncey leaned into my side, and I dropped my hand to scratch behind his ears. "I know. I promise to let you have a good romp later."

I'd taken him out on a leash first thing this morning, but he was itching for a run.

A sound had me instantly on alert, my hand going to the Taser I kept balanced on the window, just out of Cady's reach. My grip loosened as I took in the plow making its way up the two-lane road. The air left my lungs in a whoosh.

How long would it take for me to breathe easy again? For John and all the people taken in by his pretty façade to no longer take up space in my brain?

I had moments when I thought I'd found that. I had Cady, a cozy home, and a job I loved, managing The Brew. The position had brought me friends for the first time in years. When Maddie worked there, she'd brought Wren and Lawson's sister, Grae, into my life. It didn't matter to them that I had walls up or places I wouldn't go in a conversation. They welcomed me anyway.

Guilt gnawed at me for how much I'd hidden. Especially when they had been so open and honest about all the trials they'd endured. But I couldn't get myself to release my story. Because burying it deep had kept me and Cady safe.

"Mama?" Cady's sleepy voice drifted down the hall.

I turned, letting the gauzy curtains fall back into place. "Morning, Katydid. How'd you sleep?"

She smacked her lips as if still struggling to get her mouth to work. "Good. Are we late?"

It was past eight-thirty, so the sun streamed in through the windows. I grinned. "Snow day for you and me."

Cady's whole face lit up, her green eyes dancing the way my sister Autumn's had when we were growing up. The ache that took root in my chest was a war of pleasure and pain. I loved that I could see glimpses of Autumn in Cady, but God…I missed my sister like a limb.

"Snow day!" Cady started dancing around the living room, shaking her little booty in an exaggerated motion I did not want to know where she'd learned.

Chauncey barked and took up a three-legged dance around her.

I couldn't help but laugh.

Cady giggled as the dog jumped up and licked her cheek. "We're gonna have the best day, Chauncey! I can make snowballs for you to fetch, and we can make snow angels and a snow fort."

"Sounds like you've got a busy day planned," I said, smiling so hard my cheeks hurt. "Think you've got time for hot cocoa with me first?"

"Duh!" Cady hurled herself in my direction.

I had just enough time to set down my coffee before she collided with me. Cady's arms and legs wrapped around me as I lifted her. She buried her face in my hair. "You're the bestest."

Everything in me twisted. "I learned it from you."

"Nuh-uh. You're way older than me."

I chuckled. "Are you calling me a grandma?"

Cady pulled back, shaking her head. "You're not a grandma. Charlie and I gots to grow up first and get married. Then you can be a grandma."

That beautiful pain was back again. All of Cady's amazing dreams. Dancing ballet on the world's stages. Marrying her best friend. Becoming a mother herself.

My sister wouldn't get to see any of it. Because a monster had ripped her away from us. And we were still hiding from his reach.

The sound of an engine had me looking up from the endless pile of snow. I'd been working all day as Cady played, with only a few breaks to warm her fingers and toes. I was finally almost done clearing the driveway, but not before cursing myself for not finding a way to buy a snowblower.

The SUV crept slowly up the drive, and each rotation of the wheels had my stomach twisting tighter. "It's just Dr. Miller. You're safe. Cady's safe." I murmured the words over and over under my breath.

"Is that the vet?" Cady called from her snow mountain.

"I think so," I answered.

"He's gonna help Dory?"

"He is."

"Is Mr. Grizz with him?" Cady asked hopefully.

I bit back a chuckle. I had a feeling my grumpy savior from the night before didn't want anything to do with us and our chaos. "I don't think so, Katydid."

Her shoulders slumped as she crossed to me. "I want him to come back. I think he needs some friends."

My ribs squeezed, and I wrapped an arm around her. "You've got the best heart, you know that?"

Cady smiled up at me. "Kind hearts are the best hearts, right?"

I booped her nose. "Can't think of anything more important."

A door slammed, and I turned to see a figure walking toward us. His dark brown hair had just the slightest hint of salt and pepper at the temples. His sunglasses kept me from seeing his eyes, but he smiled warmly. "Aspen?"

"Hi, Dr. Miller."

"Please, call me Damien." He extended a hand for me to shake, his grip firm but not too tight.

I nodded as I swallowed. There was nothing but kindness in his expression, but his mere presence put me on edge. I couldn't help the way my mind worked: plotting exit strategies and looking for physical spots of weakness.

I forced my mouth to curve, but I knew it probably looked strained. "Thank you for coming all this way."

"It's the least I can do. It's incredibly kind of you to take in an injured deer."

"Kind hearts are the best hearts," Cady chimed in.

Damien tipped up his sunglasses, resting them on his head, then smiled at her. "I've found that to be very true."

Now that I could take in the vet's entire face, I saw he was remarkably handsome. A little too polished for my taste, but I'd bet he had all sorts of frequent flyers at his office, just hoping for a date.

"Are you going to help Dory?" Cady asked.

Damien glanced at me. "The doe?"

I nodded. "We have a habit of naming every creature we come across here."

He grinned. "I bet you're constantly needing new inspiration."

"We find them in books and movies lotsa times," Cady volunteered.

"I like it," Damien told her. "Do you think you can show me where Dory is?"

Cady beamed, puffing out her chest. "Totally. I helped Mr. Grizz take care of her last night. I can help you, too."

Damien's brow furrowed in confusion. "Mr. Grizz?"

"The Fish and Wildlife officer who helped us," I explained as we walked to the barn.

Damien chuckled. "Does he know she calls him that?"

My cheeks pinked. "Thankfully, no."

"It is fitting," Damien mumbled as he stepped inside. He took in our full house. The animals were restless, wanting to stretch their legs after being cooped up for so long. "You've got quite the menagerie."

"They all just kind of found their way to us," I explained.

"They have a way of doing that." He glanced at me. "Do you have any help caring for them at all?"

"We manage."

Damien's lips thinned. "I'd be happy to make house calls at no charge, and we can get you medicine at cost, possibly even donated."

My brows flew up. "You don't have to do that."

"It's the least I can do. I like to contribute my time whenever possible."

I wanted to argue, and hated the feeling of a handout, but it wasn't for me. It was for the animals. "Thank you."

"Here's Dory," Cady called.

Damien moved down the aisle to check on the deer.

"I gave her deer feed and water this morning, but she's only had that one dose of antibiotics," I told him.

The doe was shaky on her feet, her eyes jerking about.

Damien set his bag on the tack box and pulled out a few things. "I'm hoping I can avoid sedating her again. If her wounds aren't too bad, we'll continue treating her with oral antibiotics. If everything heals, we should be able to release her in a week or two."

Cady leaned against the stall. "Will she find her friends again? She was all alone."

My throat tightened. I hated the idea of the beautiful doe out there all by herself.

Damien pulled out some sort of treat and shoved a pill into it.

"Deer tend to stay on the same migratory patterns. I bet they'll find her pretty quickly."

A little of the pressure in my neck eased. "How often do I give her the meds?"

"Twice a day. Try to minimize contact as much as possible unless you want a permanent member of the family."

"We could keep her, Mama. We've got room," Cady said, eyes lighting with hope.

I shook my head. "We need to try to get her back to her family. They'll be missing her."

Cady sighed. "Okay."

Damien slipped into the stall, and the deer backed into the corner. He didn't rush her, but he watched her panic closely. He crouched low, extending his hand with the treat and humming softly.

The doe sniffed the air but didn't approach.

Damien simply stayed still. My heart hammered as we waited. She took her time. One step, then another until she could stretch her neck and nab the treat. She gobbled it down as Damien studied her sides.

Slowly, he rose and backed out of the stall. "I think the wounds will heal on their own. But she needs a full course of antibiotics to make sure we knock out the infection. I'll come back in a few days to check on her."

I wiped my damp palms on my snow pants. "Thank you so much."

"Of course. Call me immediately if she stops eating or drinking, or if the wounds look worse."

I nodded. I knew the drill.

As we headed out of the barn, I saw the sun had dipped lower in the sky.

Damien shot me a smile as he climbed into his SUV. "You've got my number. Call if you run into issues with any of your critters."

Something about that smile told me he might be interested in me calling him for *any* reason. He'd be disappointed there. I didn't have time to date. Wasn't about to welcome someone I didn't know well into Cady's and my lives.

I tried to convey polite gratitude with my return grin. "Appreciate it."

He waved and backed out of the drive. I waited until he was completely out of sight—a habit I couldn't seem to break. I was so used to identifying every vehicle that lingered and not breathing fully until my property was free of unknowns.

Cady tugged on my hand, bringing me back to the moment. "Are we still gonna go have Hartley dinner?"

I surveyed the drive and the road. Now that the plows had been through and I'd cleared the drive, my station wagon would probably do fine. I bit the inside of my cheek. I hoped so, anyway.

"*Please*, Mama? I wanna go so bad."

Charlie's grandma, Kerry Hartley, had been inviting us to their family dinner for months now. Since Wren and Maddie were engaged to two Hartley brothers, Holt and Nash, they all seemed to think I should join the crew, as well. I'd resisted, fearing the questions that might come my way if we ventured into that territory.

I looked down at Cady, seeing so much hope in those green eyes. She deserved this. A real family dinner. What Autumn and I never had growing up.

"Okay," I relented.

Cady leapt into the air. "Yes, yes, yeeeeesss!" She did a boogie dance toward the house. "We gots to get ready."

I laughed but nodded, my stomach twisting at the thought of what I should wear to a family get-together. I decided on jeans and a sweater that made the green in my eyes pop just a bit more. Cady opted for her glitter boots and a sweater with a glitter pig on the front.

Her hands went to her hips. "Mama, you need sparkles."

I laughed. "Well then, fix me up."

Cady ran back to her bedroom and returned with a glittery gold headband. "This!"

I bent so she could place it on my head. It was too small for me, but I didn't argue. I would've done anything to see that light in her eyes.

I stood, straightening. "What do you think? Am I ready?"

Cady beamed. "You look like a princess."

I curtsied to her. "Why, thank you, milady."

She giggled and ran into the kitchen to grab a bone. "Here you go, Chauncey."

He lumbered across the threshold and gently took it from her outstretched hand.

"Let's go!"

We donned coats, and I loaded Cady into my station wagon. The engine sputtered twice before it caught, and I winced. I needed to take it to the local mechanic, but I dreaded what they might tell me needed to be fixed.

Thankfully, the drive to the Hartleys' wasn't bad. People had clearly been out and about today, and the snow was already melting. That was the thing about these fall storms; the snow never stuck around. But it would leave plenty of mud for the animals to roll around in afterward.

I slowed as I approached the massive gates for the Hartley property. It shouldn't have surprised me. Grae had told me once that her father had started an outdoor gear company. It grew incredibly popular, and when he sold it years back, it left him and all his children with more than enough money in the bank. Yet all the Hartley siblings I'd met had regular jobs like the rest of us.

"Wow," Cady breathed.

I rolled down my window and hit the intercom.

Kerry's cheery voice filled the speaker. "Hartley residence."

"Hi, Kerry. It's Aspen."

"Oh, good. I was worried you might not make it with the snow. Drive on up."

A buzz sounded, and the gate began to open.

"Thanks."

I rubbed my palms on my jeans before placing them back on the wheel and continuing on. The drive wound through the trees, and I nearly gasped as they thinned. The house on the mountainside was something out of an architecture magazine.

A massive blend of wood and stone nestled into the incline. It seemed to be separated into two parts with a glass walkway connecting them. It was absolutely stunning and more than a little intimidating.

"Is this a castle?" Cady asked, awe filling her voice.

I chuckled. "Kinda looks like one, huh?"

"No wonder Charlie likes it here," she mumbled.

It wasn't as if Charlie's house—where he lived with his dad, Lawson, and his two older brothers, Drew and Luke—was anything to sneeze at. It just wasn't quite as imposing as this one.

I pulled into a makeshift parking spot next to a row of vehicles. My pulse thrummed in my neck, but I did my best to keep my breathing even.

Climbing out of the station wagon, Cady met me around the side of the vehicle. "Careful," I warned. "It might be slippery."

I grabbed the cookies I'd baked earlier in the day from the back seat, and we headed toward the porch. When we reached the steps, the door flew open. Grae's petite form barely filled the space, but her smile was ear-to-ear. "There are my girls!"

"Miss Grae!" Cady yelled, running up the steps.

Grae lifted Cady into her arms. "I'm soooo happy you're here. I've missed you like crazy."

Cady giggled. "You saw me two days ago."

"*Way* too long."

Cady ran her fingers through Grae's pale blond locks. "Your hair is so pretty."

"Thank you. So is yours. I love these braids."

Cady beamed. "Mama did 'em for me. Look at my sparkles." She showed Grae the glittery ties at the ends of her pigtails.

"Fabulous, girlfriend." Grae grinned at me. "So glad you could make it."

"Me, too." My voice wavered slightly, but I hugged Grae quickly to cover it. "Thanks for having us, G."

"You know you're welcome anytime."

We headed inside the large but welcoming home and toward the sounds of chaos and conversation. As we stepped into the living space, a dozen faces greeted us. I swallowed hard, trying to take it all in.

But Cady was already moving, shimmying out of Grae's arms and running toward a large, imposing figure. "Mr. Grizz!" she shouted, skidding to a halt in front of the man. "You're here!"

He was here. My grumpy, brooding savior from the night before was standing in the Hartley living room.

Chapter Six

Roan

"MR. GRIZZ?" NASH ASKED WITH A CHOKED LAUGH. Cady grinned at my little brother. "He's grumpy like a grizzly bear after hibersnation. Mama and I think he needs a snack."

Nash couldn't hold back his laugh this time, and the rest of my family joined him. But I was too dumbstruck to give a damn. The infuriating, tenderhearted woman from the snowstorm was in my parents' house.

As I took her in, I realized this must be the friend my sister always went on and on about. One whose name I hadn't bothered to get from G before but now wished like hell I had.

"Mr. Grizz is pretty damned fitting," Holt said from his spot on the couch.

His fiancée, Wren, smacked his chest with one hand while she rubbed her pregnant belly with the other. "Don't be mean."

Aspen's face flamed. Her porcelain skin gave everything away. I liked that. It was honest. Authentic.

She worried the inside of her cheek. "Sorry, she has a thing for animals."

Grae grinned mischievously as she wrapped an arm around Aspen's waist. "You guys know each other?"

"Mr. Grizz helped us save a deer," Cady chimed in.

"Really?" Charlie asked, hurrying over to his best friend. "That's so cool. What happened? Was there blood?"

He tugged her off to a corner of the living room to hear everything about our adventure.

Aspen shifted uncomfortably. "A doe got caught in a tomato cage."

My mom made a tsking sound as she patted my dad's shoulder. "They've got to warn people about what can happen with those if you don't have deer-proof fencing around them. How's the poor thing doing now?"

Aspen cleared her throat, but I didn't miss how her knuckles blanched. She didn't like being the focus.

"Better today. The vet came out to take a look and gave me some antibiotics for her."

Maddie let out a low whistle from her spot next to Nash. "Damien Miller?"

Aspen nodded.

Maddie grinned. "Not too hard on the eyes, that one. He's single, you know."

I scowled at my soon-to-be sister-in-law.

Nash gaped at his fiancée. "Did you seriously just say that right in front of me?"

Maddie shrugged as she leaned back against the couch cushions. "I'm taken, not dead."

Nash pounced on her. "I'll show you taken."

She shrieked as my brother tickled her sides and kissed her neck.

"There are children in the room, Nash," Lawson called from his stool at the kitchen island. He shot Aspen a grin. "Welcome to chaos."

Aspen eased a bit at his greeting, her fists loosening a fraction.

Heat and annoyance swept through me, some sensation that

seemed a lot like jealousy. I shook off the ridiculous thought. "She eating?"

Aspen's piercing green gaze found me again. She wore an emerald sweater that hugged her curves and made the color of her eyes burn impossibly brighter and the red of her hair look deeper somehow. I forced myself to focus on the ridiculous glittery gold headband in her hair. What was she, five?

"Seems to be eating and drinking just fine." A hint of a smile played on her glossy lips. "She loves the treats she gets the medicine in."

I grunted. "You're not going into the stall too much, are you?"

That smile dropped away, and I wanted to kick myself.

Grae glared at me. "Aspen knows what she's doing. She's been helping injured animals for years now."

I didn't say a word.

Grae huffed, turning back to Aspen. "Come on. I'll give you a tour of the house, and we can leave Mr. Grizz to brood."

I glared at my sister. The last thing I needed was for my family to pick up on Cady's ridiculous nickname.

"I'll come," Wren said, struggling to her feet.

"Me, too," Maddie echoed as she extricated herself from Nash's hold.

Aspen sought out Cady. "You okay with Charlie?"

The girl nodded, only half-paying attention to her mother.

My mom sent Aspen a reassuring smile from the kitchen. "I'll keep an eye on them."

"Thanks," Aspen said, but Grae was already dragging her off.

Once they disappeared, Nash turned his focus to me again. "Mr. Grizz, huh?"

"Shut up," I muttered.

"You know we're never letting that one go," Holt echoed.

My thirteen-year-old nephew, Drew, flopped into an overstuffed armchair next to me. "Putting the moves on Ms. Barlow, huh? Respect. She's smokin'." He held out a fist for me to bump.

I simply stared at him.

"Drew…" Lawson warned. "That's not how we talk about women."

"Come on, Dad, no disrespect. I'm just spittin' the truth, bruh."

"Well, let's tone down that truth-spittin', *bruh*."

Nash chuckled. "I don't know. I'm happy the kid wants to hit on someone who isn't Maddie."

Drew grinned. "Naw, Mads will always be my girl."

The amusement fled Nash's face. "Do *not* try to steal my nickname."

Drew's grin only widened. "Come on, Uncle Nash. You scared of a little competition?"

Nash launched off the couch and Drew flipped over the chair to escape him, cackling as he dodged his uncle.

Lawson just shook his head. "I swear they're both thirteen."

Holt's gaze turned my way. "What happened last night?"

I fought the urge to squirm in my chair. "Nothing. Just a typical callout."

That was far from the truth. Nothing about last night had felt routine. The green eyes that had haunted my dreams hadn't either. But this wasn't the first time I'd lied to my family. And it wouldn't be the last.

As everyone clustered in the living room for appetizers, I pushed open the door to the back patio. Grae immediately pulled away from her fiancé. Caden mumbled something about me being a cockblock.

"You act like you two haven't seen each other in years," I grumbled. "You work and live together."

Grae stuck out her tongue at me. "Don't hate. One day, there'll be someone you can't stand going a few hours without."

Not bloody likely. But I didn't tell my sister that. I simply grunted.

Caden chuckled. "That's Roan-speak for *screw you*."

Grae rolled her eyes. "I can't wait to watch him fall."

"Could be fun to witness," Caden agreed, wrapping his arms around her.

Now that the sun had dipped beneath the horizon, it was freezing. The bite of the cold was a welcome relief. I'd felt on edge since the moment Aspen walked through the door. Any hint of discomfort the frigid air brought distracted me from that.

"How are things at Fish and Wildlife?" Caden asked.

"Good."

He stared at me for a bit. "Care to elaborate?"

I fought the urge to shift in place. I wasn't good at chitchat. Normal. So, instead of trying, I turned to Grae. "Where's Aspen from?"

Grae's brows flew up. "She lives here. You know that."

"Before that," I pressed. I wasn't sure when Aspen and Cady had moved to Cedar Ridge. I only knew they hadn't been here all their lives. I'd kept a low profile the past several years, avoiding crowded, touristy spots in town like The Brew. The only things I knew about Aspen were tidbits I remembered Grae, Wren, and Maddie dropping.

"I'm not sure. Somewhere in the South. Why?"

Something about Aspen's reaction to crowds and how she'd braced when we were alone in her barn had me on edge—tweaked my radar because I recognized it. I knew what it was like to look over your shoulder constantly. It made a phantom energy that you couldn't turn off run through your system. Because you knew there were shadows everywhere.

My back molars ground together. "You don't think it's odd you don't know where she's from? What about family? Other friends?"

A need had dug into my gut. A compulsion to figure out what was going on with the redheaded beauty. I told myself it was because she was friends with my sister, and the last thing we needed was Grae in danger, especially after almost losing her a month ago. But the rational part of my brain called me a liar.

"You sound like the Spanish Inquisition over there," Grae clipped.

Caden's expression had shifted from relaxed to alert. "You think something's going on?"

I mentally cursed. I didn't want my entire family on Aspen's case. I only wanted to uncover the truth. Shrugging, I met Caden's gaze. "I just think it's weird no one really knows much about her."

A grin spread across Grae's face. "You like her."

"No," I protested.

Her grin widened into a smile. "You do. You should ask her out. She's the kindest. Super funny. Loyal. Protective."

That last word had my radar dinging again. You weren't protective for no reason. It was built into you because of an experience. Because people around you got hurt or you had been. The idea of someone hurting Aspen made my gut clench in a foreign way. I shoved it down and stared at my sister.

"Enough." The single word lashed out, making Grae's eyes widen.

"Chill, man," Caden warned.

My teeth gnashed together. The last thing I wanted was to hurt my sister. But what was new? I was constantly saying or doing the wrong thing. It was better when I was quiet, removed.

"I'm not interested in your friend. Just leave it be, G."

Her expression softened, sadness slipping in. "Okay. Sorry."

And I hated myself even more.

Chapter Seven

Aspen

I GLANCED OVER AT GRAE. SHE KEPT STARING AT ME AS THE girls holed up in the family room while Kerry had the boys helping her prep dinner. We'd gotten caught up in watching Charlie and Cady put on some cross between a ballet and a battle. I finally turned to face my friend. "Do I have something on my face?"

Grae winced. "Sorry."

A hint of worry trickled through me. "What is it?"

"Roan was asking about you."

I stiffened. What were the chances that my gruff savior was Grae's big brother? I'd heard her speak about him with affection and frustration more times than I could count. Had been curious what the only Hartley I hadn't met was like. But the fact that he was asking questions about me put me on edge.

This was why I hadn't made friends or connections of any kind since I'd left Jackson. Because it was a risk. When you let people into your life, they wanted to know about you. Your past. Who you really were.

Until Maddie started working at The Brew, I'd been content with casual acquaintances—mainly my regulars at the café. But Maddie had worked past my defenses.

Maybe it was because she reminded me so much of Autumn. Her kind gentleness and her situation at the time. I couldn't seem to keep her at arm's length. Then, Wren and Grae stormed in right behind her.

Grae hurried to fill the silence. "He never asks about people. He doesn't care to know anything about anyone."

Wren shifted in her seat, her light brown hair swishing around her shoulders. "She's right. He's always been one to stick to himself. But after what happened, it got more extreme."

That stiffness in my muscles intensified. "After what happened?"

Grae, Wren, and Maddie shared a look.

My stomach roiled. "What?" I pressed.

Wren linked her fingers, squeezing them. "When I was attacked in high school? Roan was initially a suspect."

I sucked in a sharp breath. Wren had become the focus of three twisted classmates when she was younger. They had gone on a spree one night, killing a few people and injuring others. Wren had been shot and almost died. Initially, the police hadn't been sure there was a third assailant. It had taken years to find him, and lives had been turned upside down.

The thought that Roan had been a person of interest made my stomach twist. I couldn't imagine how painful that must've been for him and his family. He might have a gruff exterior, but I'd seen kind tenderness in Roan.

"I never thought he was involved," Wren hurried to say. "I told the police he would never hurt me. But someone said they saw him near one of the crime scenes. They were mistaken, but it was a few days before he was cleared."

Sympathy washed over Maddie's face, her blue eyes shining. "People just didn't get him. Roan was quiet, reserved. Liked being out in nature more than with people."

Grae picked at an invisible piece of lint on her jeans. "He's still that way. I worry about him being in that cabin all alone. It's a battle just to get him to come to these weekly dinners. And now that Caden and I live together, he doesn't come see me as much."

I reached over and squeezed her hand. "I'm sorry you've been worried about him."

She swallowed hard, her white-blond hair slipping in front of her face. "I just want him to be happy." She looked up at me. "He's curious about you."

My hand tightened around hers. "Not like that." My words were gentle. I could see it now, a sister so badly wanting someone to take care of her wounded brother. But I knew interest when I saw it, and that hadn't been in Roan's gaze.

"You don't know—"

"I do," I said, cutting her off. "He's not interested in me, and I'm not in a place to date."

"Why not?" Maddie argued. "I'm not saying Roan is interested or not. I couldn't read that man if my life depended on it. But you deserve some happiness. I've seen the customers who come in and flirt with you. Ask you out. You reject every single one."

My face flamed. "I've got Cady and The Brew to worry about. The animals."

"Excuses, excuses," Wren singsonged. "Single parents date every day."

I released Grae's hand, my palms starting to sweat. "I'm not interested in dating, okay?"

Worry crept into Maddie's expression. "Aspen. Is everything—?"

"Mama, look!" Cady called, spinning around in some sort of pirouette.

Thank God for tiny children.

"That was beautiful, Katydid."

She beamed, running toward me and launching herself onto my lap.

I caught her with a laugh. "Having fun?"

"The bestest best time. I love Hartley dinner."

Grae smiled at my girl. "I'm so glad because you're part of the family now."

Her eyes went wide, then glassy with unshed tears. "Really?" she whispered.

Grae sent me a slightly panicked look at Cady's unexpected emotion. "Of course. We love you like crazy."

Cady blinked away the tears before they could fall. "I love you, too."

Charlie crossed to us, flopping onto the couch next to Wren. "When we get married, it'll be all official," he announced matter-of-factly.

Wren's lips twitched, and she drilled a finger into his side. "You gonna beat me down the aisle?"

Charlie grinned. "You guys are taking *forever*."

Maddie snorted. "You're ruthless, Charlie."

He shrugged. "I just tell the truth."

"Dinner's ready," Kerry called from the other side of the house.

"Finally!" Charlie yelled, jumping off the couch and grabbing Cady's hand.

They ran ahead of us as we rose and followed. Maddie fell into step beside me, getting close. "You know I'm always here if you need to talk, right?"

My throat burned. I'd almost told her so many times. The words swirled on the tip of my tongue. But I couldn't set them free. Didn't want to bring her into my mess. Couldn't risk that telling her would mean telling everyone in this house. The only way to keep a secret was if I was the only one holding it.

I reached out and squeezed her hand. "Thank you."

Disappointment flickered in her expression, and I felt like the worst of the worst. Maddie had shared the hardest parts of her past with me, and I refused to do the same. I shoved down the self-hatred and released her hand.

"Find a seat anywhere," Kerry called.

"You can sit next to me, Ms. Barlow," Drew called, shooting me a wink.

I couldn't hold in my laughter as Lawson ruffled his son's hair.

"Dial it back a notch, Casanova," he muttered.

"Here," Grae offered, pulling out the chair next to hers.

I was grateful for the offer until I lowered myself to the wooden seat and met fathomless dark blue eyes across the table. Eyes that searched deeper than any others I'd ever encountered. As if they could discover all my secrets without even trying.

I should've averted my gaze and put my mask back in place. But I couldn't. Something in those dark blue depths called to me. A pain that spoke to mine. I found that a part of me wanted to tell Roan Hartley all my secrets. And that made him lethal.

"Thank you so much for dinner," I said as I donned my jacket.

Kerry pulled me into a warm embrace. "Please come again next week. We'd love to have you."

Cady danced around me. "Yes, yes, yes! Please, Mama?"

My insides twisted. I wanted to give her this. Cady deserved to have raucous family dinners and to be surrounded by people who loved her. But the idea of exposing myself to Roan's scrutiny each and every week had me on edge.

"Let me check my work schedule. Hopefully, we can make it."

Lawson gave me a warm smile. "I know it'll make Charlie happy."

"Can we have a sleepover, Dad?" he asked.

Lawson's lips twitched. "It's a school night, buddy."

"We'll go to sleep early," Charlie promised.

Lawson chuckled. "Likely story."

His oldest son slunk by, heading for the door to the basement. Lawson clapped Luke on the shoulder. "Say goodbye to Ms. Barlow and Cady. They're leaving."

Luke looked at me briefly, and I didn't miss the shadows in his eyes. "Bye."

"So verbose," Lawson muttered with a shake of his head.

Luke just grunted and disappeared into the basement.

I sent Lawson a reassuring smile. "I don't think the teenage years are easy on any parent."

"I've got one who's going to be breaking hearts left and right and another who won't say more than two words to me."

I winced. "That's quite the combo."

Nathan came up and thumped his son on the back. "This might be payback for what you and your siblings put us through."

"We were angels," Nash called from the living room.

Nathan snorted and then grinned at me. "If we haven't scared you off, please come again next week."

"I'm made of stronger stuff than letting Hartley chaos run me off."

He laughed. "I knew I liked you."

There was a warmth to Nathan that made my chest ache. I couldn't imagine what it must have been like growing up with him as a dad instead of one who took off when I was less than a month old.

Cady waved to him. "See you next week."

Nathan smiled at her. "I'm counting on it. I want a rematch in Go Fish."

Cady beamed. "You might want to practice."

Kerry choked on a laugh. "I'll try to get him up to snuff, Cady."

I hated that I looked for him as we left. Roan had disappeared without a word after dinner as if he'd hit his threshold for people time. Now, he was nowhere to be found.

Cady chattered on and on about the Hartleys as we walked to my station wagon. I loaded her into the back seat and climbed behind the wheel. I turned the key in the ignition, and the engine sputtered. I winced and tried again. Still nothing.

My palms started to sweat. This wasn't happening. Not here. Not now.

I closed my eyes and tried again. Only sputtering.

A knock sounded to my left, and I jumped.

Roan's face filled my vision: slightly wild light brown hair, angular jaw, and piercing blue eyes. He made a motion for me to roll down the window.

I did it automatically.

"Problem?"

"This happens," Cady answered helpfully.

Roan arched a brow, and my cheeks heated.

"It just takes a second to catch sometimes," I explained unhelpfully.

"Pop the hood."

"You don't need—"

"Pop the hood," Roan repeated, his tone brooking no argument.

I ground my teeth together but did as he asked. "Overbearing, grumpy, too gorgeous for his own good," I grumbled.

Roan lifted the hood, blocking himself from my vision.

"Is he gonna fix it?" Cady asked.

"I don't know. I hope so."

"Mr. Grizz is the best," she said with a sigh.

He was certainly something.

A few minutes later, Roan shut the hood and came back to my window.

I rolled it down again.

He bent, the faint scent of sandalwood teasing my nose. "You've got some corroded cables. Need to get them replaced."

I winced, wondering how much that would set me back. "I'll take it in tomorrow. Is it drivable?"

"Give it a try."

I turned the key again, and the engine caught. The air left my lungs on a whoosh. "Thank you."

"I'm going to follow you home."

"What?" The word came out as more of a squeak.

Roan's expression hardened. "It's not safe for you to drive an unreliable vehicle home in the dark."

I bit back an annoyed retort. "It'll be fine. It never dies while I'm driving. It's just hard to start sometimes."

Roan's gaze drifted to the starry horizon as if he were searching for control. "Just gonna make sure you make it home. Should check on the deer anyway."

I started to argue, but Cady cut in. "Dory would love to see you, Mr. Grizz."

Roan's gaze shot to her, and his expression gentled. "Came up with a name, huh?"

Cady bobbed her head in a nod. "You like it?"

"Fits her."

Cady grinned as if he'd just paid her the highest compliment.

Roan glanced back at me. "You gonna let me follow you home, or you gonna make me stand out here all night freezing my ass off?"

"That's a bad word, Mr. Grizz. Words can hurt."

Roan's lips twitched. "Sometimes, a situation calls for harsh language."

I scowled at him. "Let's go before you teach my girl the F-word."

Roan simply grunted and headed for his truck.

"What's the F-word, Mama?"

Great. Just great.

Chapter Eight

Roan

ASPEN'S TAILLIGHTS GLOWED IN FRONT OF ME, A TAUNTING, aggravating reminder. Her station wagon needed more work than it was probably worth. My back molars ground together at the thought. Based on the state of her barn, I doubted she had the cash for it.

My gut twisted as I thought about her and Cady making their way around town in an unsafe vehicle. And it just pissed me off that I cared. Grae loved them. That was why I gave a damn. It sounded like bullshit, even to my ears.

Aspen's blinker flashed, and she turned right onto Huckleberry Lane. At least the snow was mostly gone on the road. The rest would melt in the next couple of days. That was good. The wildlife around here wasn't ready for winter. They still needed time to prepare.

The station wagon pulled to a stop in front of the farmhouse. They needed a garage. There was too much snow in these mountains to get by without one, not to mention they were exposed walking into their house in the dark.

I threw my truck into park and turned off the engine. Sliding out, I drew up short as Cady grabbed my hand.

"Come on! We gotta check on Dory."

Something foreign shifted in my chest. The little girl had no fear of me. It was a bizarre sensation, that innocent trust. So kind it almost hurt.

Cady tugged harder on my hand. "Come *on*," she urged.

My lips twitched. The little thing was strong, too. I had no choice but to follow.

Cady pulled on the barn door, and I helped her open it. The animals were already in for the night, making sounds of greeting. There were too many for me to identify.

I glanced back at Aspen. "How many animals do you have?"

She rolled her lips over her teeth. "I think I've lost count at this point."

I heard pigs, donkeys, ducks, chickens, a pony, and who knew what else. I shook my head.

Aspen shrugged. "Everyone needs a place to belong. Somewhere they feel safe. I like being that for them."

My gut burned as I stared into those green eyes. But I couldn't get words to form. It didn't matter. I never said the right things anyway.

I forced my gaze back to the aisle that Cady led me down.

She bounced on the balls of her feet as we reached the doe's stall. "We gotta give her the nighttime meds."

Aspen rounded us and lifted the lid on the tack box, pulling out a treat and a pill bottle. She expertly shoved the medicine into the center of the snack and then looked at her daughter. "Remember, be real quiet and still."

Cady nodded solemnly. "I will."

Her words were an adorable whisper, and she still didn't let go of my hand.

I didn't remember the last time someone had held my hand. Grae, maybe. When she was in the hospital, recovering from her ordeal last month. I shoved the memory and the fear that had accompanied it down.

Aspen slipped into the stall. The deer was edgy, pawing at the ground. Aspen didn't encroach on her territory; she simply crouched and held out her hand.

I wasn't sure if the vet had taught her this tactic or if it was intrinsic. But it worked. Aspen didn't rush the doe. She just waited as if it weren't freezing, and she had all the time in the world.

The deer approached slowly. She waited to see if Aspen would make a move, but the woman remained still. The wounds on the doe's sides looked a bit less red, even with just twenty-four hours of antibiotics. She nabbed the treat from Aspen and gobbled it down.

Aspen rose, keeping her movements steady and unhurried. Then she slipped from the stall. "She seems a little better."

"Her gashes aren't as red," I added.

Cady tugged on my hand. "They'll heal, right?"

"Won't be long now," I assured her.

She beamed and started dragging me down the aisle again. "You gotta meet Chauncey. And Pirate, if she'll come around."

I glanced over my shoulder at Aspen. "Chauncey? Pirate?"

Aspen just laughed. The sound was light and airy, something so pure it almost hurt to hear.

Cady dragged me toward the house as Aspen closed the barn door behind us. The little girl was stronger than she looked, and we were at the front porch before I had time to ask another question.

Aspen rounded us, pulling keys out of her pocket. She reached up and plucked a small wooden chip from the doorframe. My eyes narrowed on her as she set it on the windowsill. Then she opened the screen and began unlocking two deadbolts and the lock on the doorknob.

My scalp prickled. People around here didn't have three locks. Until recently, they rarely used one.

Aspen opened the door, and a deep bark sounded. A large dog with an awkward gait lumbered toward us. It took me a moment to realize the pup only had three legs.

He went straight to Cady, licked her cheek, and then ran out into the snow to do his business. After emptying his bladder, he returned and shoved his nose into my crotch.

"Chauncey," Cady called with a giggle. "That's not polite."

"Chauncey, huh?" I asked.

Cady nodded, leading us inside. "He's the best."

I took in the space. It had a lived-in feel. There were colorful throw pillows on a couch that looked as if it had seen better days. Family photos in frames that Cady had clearly decorated with paint and glitter littered the fireplace mantel. And I could just make out a kitchen with a battered table set for two.

"What happened to his leg?" I asked Aspen, turning back to them.

"The shelter said he was hit by a car. His owners didn't want to pay for the surgery." Anger flashed in her eyes.

"We saved him," Cady piped in. "They were gonna put him to sleep, but we got there just in time."

Total bleeding hearts.

Chauncey pressed against my side, and I rubbed between his ears. "Who's Pirate?"

Cady started making kissing noises, calling for Pirate.

Aspen smiled, and the action lit up her entire face. "That's our indoor cat. She's missing an eye, so she can't be in the barn with the others. Her peripheral vision isn't good enough to look out for predators."

"Three-legged dog, one-eyed cat. Do any of your animals have all their body parts?"

She shrugged. "These are the ones that have a hard time finding homes. And those that have been unwanted for so long just love you that much more."

There was that off-kilter feeling in my chest again. "I need to go," I clipped.

Aspen's eyes flared. "Of course."

"You haven't met Pirate yet," Cady argued.

My chest felt tight. I needed air.

Aspen placed a hand on her daughter's shoulder and squeezed. "Roan needs to get home to his own house."

It was the first time I'd heard her say my name. Something about the shape of it in her mouth sounded different than how I heard it every other day.

Cady pouted.

Aspen simply tweaked her nose. "How about a bubble bath before bed?"

The little girl instantly brightened. "Can I wear my goggles?"

Aspen laughed. "Go get them."

"Bye, Mr. Grizz," she yelled as she ran off.

I was already on my way to the door. My lungs felt like fire. "Lock up after me."

There was a bite to my words that I didn't intend but couldn't help.

Instead of annoyance or anger in Aspen's eyes, there was concern.

I bit down on the inside of my cheek. The last thing I needed was for her to see me. There was too much darkness there. I slipped out the door, shutting it hard behind me. But then I stopped, sucking in ice-cold air.

I waited until I heard the telltale sound of one, two, three locks. The snick of each one twisted my gut and ratcheted my unease higher. She had three locks for a reason. The need to know what that was ate at me.

But I forced my legs to move and carry me away from the farmhouse that needed serious work. I beeped the locks on my truck and climbed inside. Starting the engine, I rolled down the window. I needed air. I didn't care how frigid it was.

Carefully, I executed a three-point turn, my gaze pulled toward the house. The glow of light in the windows was just as sunny and warm as the two people inside.

They needed to be more careful. Not everyone would wander into your house with good intentions.

I gripped the wheel tighter as I placed my foot on the accelerator. I'd go for a run if there wasn't still so much snow on the ground. I needed to burn off the bizarre energy thrumming through me.

Glancing both ways, I turned right out of Aspen's drive and headed away from town. My truck took the familiar bumps in the road easily. In a matter of minutes, I was turning off Huckleberry Lane and onto a private drive.

I slowed at an imposing gate. Tiny red lights flashed, recording in night vision. Usually, each security measure eased a bit of the feral energy running through me at any given time. But it didn't touch it tonight.

Sticking my hand out the window, I typed in a gate code. Changing it every three weeks was a memory exercise of sorts. I waited a beat for the gate to swing open, then drove through. I stopped just on the other side of the fence while it closed. I needed to see the locking mechanism click before I could drive on.

I lifted my foot off the brake and started the climb up the mountainside. The drive was gravel and still dotted with snow, but it wasn't enough to give my truck any trouble.

No warm lights greeted me as I pulled to a stop in front of my tiny cabin. No one welcomed me home, not even a three-legged dog. Usually, the silence gave me the only measures of peace I'd ever known. But not tonight.

As I slid out of my truck and walked to the front door, I felt… lonely. I unlocked the deadbolt and doorknob and stepped inside. My alarm let out a series of beeps, and I quickly disarmed it, shutting and locking the door behind me.

I didn't bother turning on any lights. Instead, I let the glow from the house below guide me. That warmth seemed to reach all the way from the dilapidated farmhouse into my cabin.

I slid open the glass balcony door and stepped outside, then lowered myself into an Adirondack chair and stared at the farm in the distance. I'd never seen her close-up, not until the other night. But I'd seen that flash of red in the breeze as the woman moved to the barn, a child bounding at her side.

I'd made up a million and one stories as I saw them let animals out and call them in. But everything looked different to me now that I knew who lived there. I could no longer make up stories about the woman and her child. They were too real.

And something told me they were in danger.

Chapter Nine

Aspen

*T*HE STARS SPARKLED OVERHEAD. THEY SHOULD'VE BEEN A *comfort. Autumn and I had always loved the stars. It didn't matter if we were living in a car or a shelter or a studio apartment, the stars were our one constant while apart from each other.*

I tapped my fingers on the steering wheel and looked down at my phone.

> **Me:** *I'm here. Do you need help with your stuff?*

I'd sent it four minutes ago. I told myself I'd give her five and then go in.

John was at a business dinner, but he could come home at any time, and I wanted Autumn and my niece out of here first. My phone clicked over to five minutes to seven. My stomach cramped.

God, I hoped she hadn't changed her mind. All she'd ever wanted was a family. To create the environment we'd never had growing up. It made it that much harder for her to walk away. Even if it was the only thing she could do to keep her and her daughter safe.

I slid out of my car and headed up the front steps. This McMansion in the suburbs was never something I'd pictured

Autumn in. She had too much heart and soul. She was more the type for an old farmhouse with a wraparound porch and notches in a wood post where she'd measure her growing kids.

But John had wanted big. *He'd said they needed to keep up appearances, which meant a pristine home without a single thing out of place. I gritted my teeth at the memory as I searched my key ring for the pink one Autumn had given me. Sliding it into the lock, I opened the door.*

"Autumn?" I called.

A light was on down the hall, but everything else was dark. Too dark. Shadows danced along the walls. My heart hammered in my chest.

"Autumn?" I tried again. "Where are you?"

I heard nothing but the drip of a faucet somewhere down the hall. I moved toward the faint light in the direction of the kitchen.

A soft cry sounded from upstairs. Lucy.

I turned, heading quickly up the stairs, and moved on autopilot toward my niece's room. The door was open, the faint glow of a nightlight shining through.

As I stepped inside, I pulled up short. A figure sat in the rocker. Autumn had hemmed and hawed over what color she'd wanted for the nursery, changing her mind at least a dozen times before settling on a pale purple. But the person in the chair now was too big to be my sister.

And they were completely ignoring the now-wailing baby in the crib as a faint breeze ruffled the gauzy curtains.

"Hello, Tara. I didn't hear the bell."

The voice froze me to the spot. It was so calm yet admonishing. The familiar line John so often walked.

"What's wrong with Lucy?" I croaked, my palms sweating.

He didn't turn to look at me, just fixed his gaze on a spot over the crib. "Did you really think I wouldn't find out?"

My throat constricted, tightening to the point of pain. "Where's Autumn?"

I could barely get the words out as blood roared in my ears.

John chuckled, the sound light and airy. "I've given everything for my family. Worked myself to the bone to provide a good life." He tapped a finger on the arm of the rocker. "And this is how they want to repay me?"

"Where is she?" Hot tears filled my eyes.

He laughed again, but the sound was darker this time. "I don't know... Where's Mommy, Lucy? Where is the traitorous whore?"

The fury broke free then, forcing him straighter in the chair. The moonlight caught on his crisp white shirt. But it wasn't just white. There were red smears and splotches.

John slowly pushed to his feet. The moonlight illuminated his face. Red spattered what I could see of it.

Blood.

Bile surged into my throat.

"They're mine." His hand twitched.

A gleam of silver.

A knife.

Coated in a deep red.

John took one step and then another. "You think you can take them from me? I'll send you all to hell first."

And then he lunged.

I shot up in bed, face beaded with sweat, a scream lodged in my throat. My fingers fisted in the blankets as I struggled to breathe.

"Just a dream." I murmured the words over and over. John wasn't here. He was thousands of miles away, locked up tight.

My nightlight cast a sea of stars across the ceiling. I hadn't been able to handle the dark after that night.

I threw back the covers. The sheets and my pajamas were damp. I wrinkled my nose, glancing at the clock. Five-thirty in the morning. Too early to start the wash, but I could at least strip the bed and get cleaned up.

Chauncey looked up from his dog bed in the corner.

"It's okay. Go back to sleep."

My muscles trembled as I stood, and I took a moment to get

my bearings. I pulled the sheets off the bed and left them in a pile, putting fresh ones on. Then I tiptoed across the hallway to my bathroom.

Cady always slept deeply. It took a wrecking ball to wake her up most days. But that didn't stop me from worrying about disturbing her.

Stripping out of my sleep clothes, I turned on the water and waited for it to warm. The old pipes in this house took forever, but it was finally habitable. I took my time washing away the residue of my nightmare. Only it wasn't a nightmare. It was a memory.

My stomach roiled, and I had to fight back the bile that surged up my throat. I shoved my head under the spray, breathing slowly and deeply. Eventually, the shakes and nausea subsided.

My fingers played across the scar that curved over my collarbone and down my side. It had faded over the past five years, but it would always be there. A reminder of hell on Earth. But also that I had survived.

I shut off the water and stepped out of the shower-tub combo. I took my time drying off and getting ready for the day. My eyes burned from lack of sleep. Not only had my nightmare woken me early, but I'd also had a hell of a time falling asleep. Images of Roan's panicked expression as he fled last night played in my head. Something had him on edge; I just had no idea what.

Taking the hairdryer into my bedroom, I finished preparations for the day. I went out to give the animals breakfast and Dory her medicine before coming back inside and making breakfast for my chick.

Maybe it was because I had extra time today, or perhaps because of my dream, but I made the meal extra special. As I placed the last berry on the plate, I grinned at my creation. There was something about forcibly turning around a day that started rough that helped me feel more in control.

I headed down the hallway and slowly opened Cady's door. A smile instantly curved my lips. My girl slept wildly: red hair everywhere, arms thrown wide, legs like a starfish. Her glittery pink nightlight made the room sparkle.

Crossing to her bed, I knelt and brushed the hair out of her face. "Morning, Katydid."

"Mmm," she mumbled, smacking her lips.

"It's time to wake up."

"Nuh-uh," she argued, still half-asleep.

"I made your favorite..." I tried enticing her.

Cady's eyes fluttered open. "Cady pancakes?"

I chuckled. "Cady pancakes all the way."

She beamed. "Today is the bestest."

I tapped her nose. "I agree. You want to eat first and then get ready?"

Cady bobbed her head in a nod, and I helped her sit up. I slid on one slipper and then the other. Grabbing her robe off the hook on her door, I got her into it.

She stumbled slightly as she made her way down the hall, and I couldn't help but laugh. Waking up was always a challenge. Chauncey hurried over to greet her, and she patted his head as she slid into her chair.

Cady grinned down at her breakfast. A stack of two pancakes made to look just like her. Raspberries for her red hair. Green grapes for her eyes. Strawberries for her mouth. Nose and eyelashes drawn on with chocolate syrup.

"I almost don't want to eat it," she whispered.

"Well, that would be a waste."

Cady giggled and cut off a bite. Then she paused. "Do you think Mr. Grizz has someone to make him pancakes?"

My heart clenched. "I don't know. He can probably make them himself."

But that was a lonely proposition, day in and day out. And I knew how that felt.

Cady's lips pursed. "We should invite him next time. Pancakes would make him less grumpy, for sure."

I choked on a laugh. My girl always told it like it was.

"I miss my glitter boots," Cady said with a sigh as we pulled up to the school.

I bit my lip to keep from laughing. "It's going to be pretty muddy out on the playground since the snow is melting. Do you want to risk ruining your favorite boots?"

They were already getting too small for her. I would have to hunt for something similar that wasn't ridiculously expensive.

"Mud does *not* go with glitter."

This time, I couldn't hold in my chuckle. "No, it doesn't."

I climbed out of my station wagon, dreading that I needed to stop by the mechanics' to get it looked at. I opened Cady's door, and she hopped out.

Catching sight of the woman walking toward me, I winced. "Morning, Katelyn," I greeted with as much warmth as I could muster.

She scrunched up her nose at me as she tossed her perfectly curled blond locks over one shoulder. "That car sounds horrible. Doesn't look much better."

I didn't let my smile dim. "It gets us from place to place."

The woman rolled her eyes, looking more like her six-year-old daughter than an adult.

Heather looked up at her mom. "Susanna and Lainey can come play after ballet, right?"

"Of course, honey," Katelyn said, ushering her daughter toward the school building.

Cady's shoulders slumped, and I had the sudden urge to deck a six-year-old. It wasn't that Cady wanted to be friends with the mean girls, but they were all in her ballet class, and they made a sport of excluding her.

I crouched low, getting to eye level with Cady. "Remember what we talked about?"

She nodded. "When people are mean, it's because they're hurting."

"That's right. They're hurting so badly they have to turn that pain somewhere else."

Cady worried her lip between her teeth. "I don't know why she hates me so much."

I wanted to lift my girl and run fast and far so no bratty classmate could hurt her again. "It's probably hard for her to see you shining so brightly."

"Cady!" Charlie yelled as he ran toward us.

Cady's face instantly transformed. "Hey!"

They were immediately lost in the chatter of everything they'd missed in each other's lives over the past twelve hours, and I knew Cady would be okay. I pushed to my feet, watching them head into school.

"Everything okay?"

I turned at Lawson's deep voice and sighed. "Heather Beasley."

He grimaced. "I wouldn't normally say this about a six-year-old, but she's awful."

"Her mom's worse."

"It's probably where she learns it from." Lawson glanced at the school. "I could have a word if you think it would help?"

I shook my head. "I think it would probably have the opposite effect."

Katelyn emerged from the school, a scowl on her expertly made-up face. But the moment she saw Lawson, she pasted on a fake smile. "If it isn't the chief of police. How are you, Law?"

Lawson fought back another grimace. "Good. You?"

"Doing just great. You know, you and Charlie should come over for dinner on Friday. Heather would love it, and so would I." Katelyn batted her eyelashes as if she were sending out Morse code.

I struggled to keep my laughter at bay.

Lawson shifted uncomfortably. "We've got plans this weekend."

Annoyance flickered across Katelyn's expression. "Another time, then."

"Maybe," Lawson said noncommittally.

Katelyn shot me a glare as she headed for her Mercedes SUV, as if it were my fault Lawson had rejected her.

"You trying to get me shanked?" I muttered.

Lawson shivered. "That woman is slightly terrifying."

"She's certainly determined."

But she wasn't the only one. Lawson had single women of all ages trying to tie him down. But in all my years in Cedar Ridge, I hadn't seen him date a single one.

"She shows up at my house with meals sometimes and tries to get an invitation to stay," he grumbled.

I winced. "Not a lot of boundaries."

Lawson shook his head. "Everything good with you?"

I nodded. This wasn't an abnormal question. It was simply the kind of man Lawson was. Checking in to make sure the people in his life were taken care of. It was what made him so good at his job.

"Everything's fine." I glanced at my watch. "I need to head out."

"You startin' early today?"

"I have to drop off my car at the mechanics'. Something's going on with one of the cables."

Lawson straightened. "Want me to grab Cady from school later?"

"You don't have to."

"I'm happy to. We can swing by and get you, too."

I glanced at my station wagon. "If you could get her, that would be a help. They're just going to look things over today so I can get the car at three, but I don't want to be late here."

"You got it. I'll take them for a snack and then drop her at your place on the way home."

"Thanks, Law. Just let me know when I can take the boys off your hands for an afternoon."

He shook his head. "You don't want my three maniacs all at once. They bring terror and destruction when they travel in a pack."

I barked out a laugh. "I've officially been warned. But I really am happy to help."

Only I knew Lawson wouldn't take it. A playdate with Charlie? Sure. But he never seemed to want to burden me with more.

"Thanks, Aspen. I'll let you know."

I gave him a quick wave and headed for my wagon. It took two tries for it to start, but the engine finally caught. I eased out of the parking lot and turned toward town.

Checking the time, I pulled over in front of the post office. I dashed inside and waved to Jules behind the desk. "How are things?"

"Boring as ever," the woman in her sixties called back.

"Boring is good," I told her.

"I think I need to get me one of those younger lovers."

I choked on a laugh as I retrieved my mail from my PO box. "Sounds like a good plan to me. Let me know how that goes for you."

"Oh, I will. In *great* detail."

I sent her another wave and headed back to my car. I quickly flipped through my mail as I went and began opening things. Electric bill. A notice from Cady's school about a play. There was one envelope with no return address.

I tore it open and tugged free a piece of paper. My blood went cold as I took in the scrawl.

You think you can take her from me? You're going to pay. In blood.

Chapter Ten

Aspen

"**Y**OU SURE YOU'RE ALL RIGHT?" THE MECHANIC ASKED as he scrubbed a hand over his salt-and-pepper beard. I forced my smile wider. "Just a little too much coffee this morning."

It was the only reason I could think of for why my hands were trembling and how I'd jumped sky-high when one of the other mechanics dropped a wrench.

Jim chuckled. "I know how that is. I gotta make sure I have me a good breakfast with protein, fat, and slow-burning carbs before I hit the caffeine."

"I'll have to remember that next time." I cast a look over my shoulder and out to the street. As if someone would be wearing a sign that read: *John sent me.*

A chill skated over my skin. It had to be him. The handwriting was too familiar. The postmark. My mouth went dry. A part of me wanted to head right over to the school, pick up Cady, and run fast and far.

"Aspen?"

Jim's voice cut into my panic, and I whirled back around. "Sorry. What'd you say?"

Concern lined his face, but he didn't give it voice. "It's gonna take me a bit to troubleshoot this baby. It looks like you've got a few things going on right now."

A heavy weight settled on my shoulders. So much for running. Not to mention the snow still covering the higher passes.

"Gotta get some new tires, too. These are bald as my pop. Don't want you gettin' in an accident with that precious cargo."

My eyes burned, and my nose stung as I mentally calculated how much this might cost. How much I had in savings, which was hardly anything. And where I could make cuts.

I swallowed the building panic. "I might have to do the work in phases."

Empathy washed over Jim's face. "Don't you worry. We'll get it figured out one way or another."

A mixture of shame and warmth washed through me. That right there was why I didn't want to leave Cedar Ridge. There was a kindness in the people here that I'd never experienced before. Sure, not all of them were sunshine and roses. But the vast majority? They cared about the people around them.

"Thank you. Can you call when you have an estimate?"

"You know I will. Have a good day. And I wouldn't hate it if you brought me back one of those bakery treats if you got some leftover."

My mouth curved, the first honest tip of my lips since I'd opened that damned letter. "You got it. Any requests?"

Jim tapped his lips with a stained finger. "I'm partial to those double chocolate muffins."

My smile widened. "Those are Cady's favorite, too. She helped me taste test to get the recipe right."

"Knew I liked that girl of yours."

I laughed. "Two peas in a pod." I glanced at my watch. "I gotta run, or I'll have an angry cook on my hands."

"Don't want that. You have a good day now."

"You, too."

I hurried out of the repair shop and into the blistering cold.

My hand slipped beneath my jacket and flannel shirt, finding the puckered skin there. The reminder that I'd made it through before and I'd do it again.

I shoved the memories down and walked toward the street. Most of the snow had melted, but it was still freezing. I picked up my pace. The Brew's cook, Zeke, would be mad as hell if I didn't hurry up. He opened for me so I could get Cady to school in the mornings, but he wasn't all that fond of people—so similar to the man who'd been haunting my thoughts lately.

I shoved images of Roan out of my mind and jogged across the street. It was early enough that the sidewalks and shops were quiet. But as I reached The Brew, I saw a few cars parked out front. I recognized most of them, but there were one or two I wasn't sure of.

The bell over the door tinkled as I walked inside, and the blast of warmth that hit me was a welcome respite from the bitter cold.

Zeke glared at me from behind the counter. "Where's your car? It's freezing out."

I smiled at his cantankerous attitude. "At the shop, getting a checkup."

He grunted. "Going back to the grill."

A light laugh rang out to my right as a blonde a little younger than me tried to cover the sound by sipping her coffee. "I gotta say, I'm glad you're back. He's not the warm and fuzzy sort."

I grinned at Elsie. "He's a teddy bear at heart. I swear."

She arched a brow. "If you say so."

"How'd the shoot go?" I asked, motioning to her open laptop with a stunning shot of the mountains. Elsie was in town for an extended stay while shooting a coffee-table book.

She grinned. "Got some good ones before the storm rolled in. I think I'll have everything I need in a few more weeks."

"But we'll miss you around here when you go," Jonesy said, lifting his mug of coffee to his white-whisker-covered mouth. "I like spending my mornings surrounded by beautiful women."

Elsie blushed. "I'll stay put if you finally agree to marry me."

Jonesy let out a guffaw as the lines around his eyes and mouth deepened. "You just name the place and time."

My lips twitched at my favorite regular's antics. He'd been in here daily since I started, and Elsie had become part of the package deal when she got to town. I had other daily visitors, but they didn't stay as long, most getting a coffee before heading to work or school. I liked being able to count on having Jonesy and Elsie to keep me company.

That spot between my shoulders started to itch. The telltale sign that someone was watching. My gaze instantly swept the room and collided with steely gray eyes. Something about them was cold. Too cold.

I swallowed hard, forcing myself to move behind the counter and ignore the stare. I was on edge. Anyone glancing my way would have me on alert.

Hanging up my coat, I shoved my purse into the cabinet. I turned around to get the register sorted and there he was, those gray eyes just as assessing as before.

My palms dampened, but I forced myself to smile at the man while taking in everything I could about him. Dark brown hair. Pale skin. Probably in his late twenties or early thirties. He wore a name-brand jacket and had a nice watch—money but not gobs of it.

"How can I help you this morning?" I greeted.

The man returned my grin, but his expression had an edge. "Tell me what you recommend."

I didn't want to take my eyes off the man, feeling like he might strike if I did. But I flicked a quick glance at the bakery case. "If you're going for savory, you can't go wrong with the cheddar and scallion biscuit. If you're in the mood for sweet, I like the orange-cranberry scones."

"Sounds amazing. I'll take one of each."

I nodded, moving to grab the tongs so I could get his items.

"You from here?" the man asked.

I couldn't help the tension that swept through my muscles. It had taken me so long to get used to the tourists' and locals' curious natures and remind myself that they only wanted to make conversation, not uncover all my secrets.

"Been here almost five years now."

The man grinned again, but I didn't see an edge to it this time. The curve of his mouth read genuine. I gave my head a little shake. John's letter was making me lose it.

The guy handed over a twenty. "You're a local, then. My buddy and I are here to do a little hiking and exploring. Any places you recommend?"

A tourist. The tension bled out of my shoulders a fraction as I made change. "There's a company in town called Vacation Adventures. They have a whole slew of guided trips you can take."

"Sounds awesome. I'll have to check it out. Thanks…"

"Aspen," I filled in.

"Thanks, Aspen. I'm Steven."

"Nice to meet you."

He took the plates from me. "If these taste as good as they look, I'm sure I'll be back."

I chuckled. "I've been warned."

As he stepped away from the counter, a woman in her sixties took his place. I fought the groan that wanted to surface as I struggled to keep my smile in place. "Good morning, Ms. Peabody. What can I get you today?"

She looked around the café before her gaze settled back on me as if hoping some juicy piece of gossip would land in her lap. "I'll take an Earl Grey tea and a bran muffin."

"Coming right up." I poured the hot water into a whimsical mug that fit with the rest of the décor of The Brew. I'd convinced the owner, Sue, to let me redecorate with a minimal budget. Cady and I had a blast hunting for finds at garage and estate sales and giving the place a new coat of paint. The result was an almost *Alice in Wonderland* look, full of color and life.

I handed Ms. Peabody her breakfast and took the exact change she gave me. There was never a tip from her.

"Did you hear that SAR rescued a man off the mountain the night before last?" she asked.

A shiver ran through me as I thought about how cold it had been. "No, I didn't."

Ms. Peabody let out a little huff, but I didn't miss the glee in her eyes. "Tourist, of course. Decided to go hiking in the snow. Got hypothermia and scared his poor wife to death. They're staying at my B&B, naturally."

I tried to stifle my laugh. She'd said it as if that garnered her some sort of prize. But I guessed when gossip was your currency, it did.

The bell over the door rang, and I glanced up to greet the newcomer. The words *Welcome to The Brew* died in my throat. Piercing blue eyes met mine. His light brown hair looked more than a little wild, and stubble dotted Roan's jaw. He carried a large bag of something, and I knew it had to be heavy because I saw his muscles bulging, even under his jacket.

Ms. Peabody pursed her lips and hurried to a table as Roan strode toward me. He had the kind of energy that ate up space and made everyone sit up and pay attention.

"Hi," I greeted. Unfortunately, it sounded more like a rush of air than an actual word.

"Brought you some deer feed but didn't see your car."

There were no pleasantries with Roan, just straight to business. I admired the authenticity of it in a way. "My station wagon's at the mechanics."

"Good." Even the word sounded like a grunt.

"Thanks for the food. You can put it in the back if you want."

Roan jerked his head in a nod and then followed me down the hall to the storage room. I opened the door and flicked on a light. "Anywhere's good."

The shelves were packed full of non-refrigerated supplies, so there wasn't much room. But Roan slid by me and dumped the food in the corner. As he stood, we nearly came nose-to-nose.

I sucked in a breath. That faint sandalwood scent was back. It swirled around me in a tempting tease. Up close, Roan had an otherworldly beauty with a sharply angled jaw and haunting eyes. A faint scar bisected one of his eyebrows, and I had the bizarre urge to trace it with my finger.

Roan's gaze dropped to my lips. "I can load it into your car later."

I forced myself to take a step back. "That's okay."

"It's heavy."

"I know, but I'm used to lifting heavy things." Hay and feed were never light.

Roan scowled. "You could hurt yourself."

I rolled my eyes. "Or I'll just get a workout in."

Roan opened his mouth to argue, but Zeke yelled from the kitchen.

"Got customers."

And the cook wasn't about to deal with people if I was around.

I hurried out of the storage room. "Thanks again."

Roan simply grunted.

I wondered if I could decipher what each one meant if I studied them hard enough. My lips twitched at the idea.

Roan hovered by the bakery case as I slipped behind it. He looked unsure, uncomfortable.

My brows pinched. "Did you need something?"

He shook his head jerkily. "You got a ride home?"

I felt something squeeze deep in my chest. "I'm picking up my car at three."

Roan frowned. "Gonna take longer than that to fix it."

"Jim isn't fixing it today. Just doing an assessment."

That frown deepened. "It's not safe to drive."

"It's safe enough for now."

Roan simply stared me down.

I fought the urge to squirm under that dark blue gaze.

"Excuse me," a patron said from the other side of the counter, and I flushed from the roots of my hair to the tips of my toes.

"How can I help you?" I hurried to fill the customer's order. When I turned back around, Roan was gone.

A flicker of disappointment rooted itself somewhere deep. I worried that spot on the inside of my cheek.

A throat cleared, and I turned back to the register.

Ms. Peabody was standing at the counter, a stern look on her face. "I didn't know you were friendly with the Hartley boy."

She said it as if Roan were thirteen instead of well into his thirties. "I'm friends with the whole Hartley family," I hedged.

I wasn't sure Roan would consider me a friend, more an annoyance, but I'd be his friend anyway.

Ms. Peabody's lips thinned. "They are a wonderful family, but Roan…you need to be careful around him. He's not like the rest of his siblings. Not exactly normal."

My spine snapped straight. "Roan is an incredibly kind and caring human being. He was here to bring me food for an injured deer that he helped me rescue. That sounds like an amazing person to me. If you want to judge him because he's quiet or a little gruff, go ahead. But don't do it in front of me."

Ms. Peabody snapped her mouth closed, her face turning red. "I was trying to look out for you."

"Maybe. Or were you trying to stir up gossip and trouble?"

The redness deepened. "I don't need this kind of attack. I'll take my business elsewhere."

I wanted to shout good riddance as she flounced out of the café, but I resisted.

A slow clap sounded, and I looked to see Elsie grinning as she did it. "Bravo. That woman is awful."

Jonesy chuckled. "Can't say I'll miss the side of bitter with my morning joe."

"But that hottie can come back anytime. He's got a great ass."

I choked on a laugh, but it died on my lips as I watched Ms. Peabody storm across the street. I couldn't imagine what it must be like for Roan to live with that kind of cruelty and judgment day in and day out. No wonder he rarely ventured into town.

But as much as I understood, it made my heart ache for the man who had to feel incredibly alone.

Chapter Eleven

Roan

THOSE GREEN EYES WERE BURNED INTO MY MEMORY—THE spark of heat in their depths. My hands clenched and flexed as I tried to shake the image loose.

No luck.

I had a feeling Aspen's eyes and those berry lips would be playing on a loop for a long time to come.

I'd almost kissed her. Came *this* close to closing the distance and tasting that mouth.

I cracked my neck as if that would rid me of the need coursing through me. Lust didn't control me. Never had.

If I felt need starting to build, I went elsewhere. Away from Cedar Ridge. There were no names. No tender touches. Just taking what we both wanted.

But those urges had come on fewer and farther between. Maybe because I'd started to feel as empty as they were. Maybe because I was too old for that shit.

Only now, I was starting to worry that I'd made a fatal mistake in not continuing those anonymous encounters. One that made Aspen's mouth more tempting than it should be.

I strode across the street, letting the cold hit me full force. I needed to fight off her pull.

The sign for Al's Body Shop beckoned me. Al hadn't been around for at least two generations, but the name remained. It was cold enough that all the bays were closed, so I made my way to the office.

A bell dinged as I opened the door, and it didn't take long for a head to pop out from the workstations. A guy who didn't look much over eighteen took me in, eyes widening.

My teeth ground together as I fought back a curse.

"Can I help you?" There was a slight waver to the kid's voice.

"Jim," was all I said in response.

The kid scurried off. Jim emerged a few seconds later, wiping his hands on a rag. "You like scaring the piss out of my guys?"

I grunted.

Jim shook his head, a smile on his lips. "I think you do. What can I help you with? Don't see your truck out there."

"You got Aspen Barlow's wagon?"

Surprise lit Jim's eyes. "Going through that heap now. It's a miracle she hasn't ended up stranded."

A muscle ticked in my jaw. "Got a ballpark of what it's going to take to get it running safely?"

His surprise morphed into curiosity. "Still working, but I'm guessing about six Gs when we're all said and done. She needs new tires, too."

That tic in my cheek intensified. "I want to cover the majority of it. Think you can come up with a story she'll buy?"

Jim leaned back against the counter for a moment, studying me. "Who is she to you?"

Wasn't that the million-dollar question? "One of Grae's best friends. She's a good woman. Works hard. Doesn't need this shit when she's got a little girl to take care of."

It was apparently the right answer because Jim jerked his head in a nod. "I'll tell her that it wasn't as bad as it looked, and if she gives me a day or two to work her in, I'll give her a discount."

I made a low sound of agreement. "What about the tires?" Everyone knew tires were expensive as hell.

"I'll tell her I got 'em off a totaled wreck. Steal of a deal."

"Hope your acting skills are good," I muttered.

Jim chuckled. "I'll sell it."

"Just let me know what I owe you when you're done."

"Will do."

I turned to leave, but Jim stopped me.

"You're a good man, Roan."

Pain lanced my chest. I didn't look back at him. Couldn't.

I wasn't a good man. I was someone who lied to my siblings. Cut myself off from my family because it was easier. But maybe I could do a little something to even the Universe's scales by helping Aspen. Even if she never knew it.

"You coming for drinks tonight?" Mindy asked, a hopeful bent to her words as she hovered near my desk.

A rough chuckle sounded from the workstation behind mine. "Don't you know by now? Roan never shows his face at social hour."

My back molar ached as it ground against another. I hated being in the damned office—too many nosy people.

I stayed focused on the paperwork in front of me. As soon as it was submitted, I was out.

But I could feel eyes on me. I glanced up.

Mindy stared down at me, a nervous smile on her lips, her eyes hopeful. "It's going to be fun. Promise."

I fought the urge to shift in my chair. "Not my scene."

A scoff sounded behind me. "And what is your scene? Stealing candy from babies?" Oscar shot back.

I ignored him, turning back to the papers in front of me. But I sensed that Mindy hadn't moved.

"We could always do something else—"

"Roan, need you in my office," a voice boomed.

I'd never been happier for my boss to call me. I didn't want to be an ass, but I had no interest in Mindy or any of my other co-workers. I rose from my desk chair and strode through the sea of desks, not making eye contact with anyone.

Rob looked up from his laptop. "Shut the door."

I went on alert. That wasn't a typical request. Our Fish and Wildlife office wasn't overly formal or secretive. I quietly shut the door and took a seat.

"Got a call about a slain animal. Deer. Want you to check it out."

My brow furrowed. "Hunter that just left it there?"

Rob shook his head. "Not that kind of death. Sounds like someone sliced it to hell. And not the kind of cuts a hunter makes."

My jaw went hard. "Where?"

"North Ridge trail, about a mile in. Had to let Law know since it's his jurisdiction. Said he'd meet you up there."

"Who called it in?" I asked.

"Hiker. Thought it was an animal attack. Just wanted us to know that it was practically on the trail. Didn't want other hikers to run into any predators."

"Could be a cougar attack," I reasoned.

"Could be, but the hiker sent a photo. Cuts look too clean to be tooth and claw."

My stomach soured, but I jerked my head in a nod and pushed to my feet.

"You want to take Mindy or Oscar with you?" Rob asked.

I just met his stare.

He chuckled. "All right, then. Good luck. Call me when you know something."

I headed into the bullpen and made my way to my desk. Mindy was still hovering.

"Got a callout?" she asked.

"Yeah."

"What is it?"

"Dead deer."

Oscar's eyes narrowed. "We don't get called out for dead deer."

I simply shrugged as I grabbed my jacket.

"I could come with you," Mindy offered. "I don't have anything on my desk right now."

"I'm good," I clipped.

Oscar choked on a laugh, and Mindy glared at him. I made a quick escape toward reception and then headed to the parking lot. The air had warmed a bit, but I still needed a jacket. Climbing into my truck, I started the engine.

It didn't take long for me to reach the trailhead since our substation was out of town. No one else was parked in the gravel lot, but I couldn't wait. An unease had settled in my gut that I needed to answer.

Grabbing my pack, I slid out of my vehicle and headed for the trail. The quiet of the mountain wrapped around me, easing some of that feral energy that seemed to take over my muscles and bones. I let the silence soothe me, disrupted only by the rustling of pine branches and the occasional bird call.

A hint of a burn took root in my quads as I pushed up the steep incline. I welcomed the fire. It reminded me that I was alive. Real. Human.

It only took fifteen minutes to reach the fallen doe. She lay half on and half off the trail, her neck bent at an unnatural angle. My stomach roiled as I took her in. Such a waste.

I didn't begrudge someone wanting to hunt if they were going to consume the meat, but I had no respect for trophy killers—the waste of life for some sort of invisible points on a tally. But this wasn't that either. This was something darker.

"What do you think?" Law called from down the trail.

I didn't stand or look back, just continued studying the deer. Rob was right. The gashes hadn't been made by animal claws. They were too precise for that. Too clean.

"A human being did this, not an animal."

Lawson cursed as he crouched next to me, looking over the doe's fallen form. "Definitely a knife."

He tapped out a text. "Got crime scene techs coming out."

"Good." I pushed to my feet.

Lawson followed, surveying the space around us. "Saw you leave right after Aspen last night."

I stiffened. It was a leading question if I'd ever heard one.

When I didn't respond, Lawson glanced my way, raising his eyebrows.

I scowled at the forest. "Her car was giving her trouble. I followed her home."

"That was good of you. Seems like you two get along."

"What is this? Tea and gossip hour?" I snarled. I didn't usually have to worry about Lawson probing, especially not when it came to women. Because the last thing he wanted was someone asking him those questions. There were too many skeletons in that closet.

Lawson held up both hands. "Just curious. Aspen's a good woman. You could do a hell of a lot worse."

"You want me to start asking you about dating prospects?"

The shutters came down over Lawson's eyes, and I instantly felt like an ass.

I cleared my throat, turning back to the deer. I wasn't sure what it said about us that we handled blood and death better than relationships, but we always had. "What do you think?"

Lawson followed my line of sight, taking in the scene again. "Those marks there?"

He pointed to the deer's neck, and I nodded.

"They're hesitant as if the attacker still hadn't fully gotten up the nerve." Lawson pointed to the deer's middle. "Those are deeper, more confident."

He looked up and met my gaze. "Our boy's getting used to killing."

Chapter Twelve

Aspen

I STEPPED ONTO THE FRONT PORCH AS LAWSON PULLED INTO my drive. Cady bounced at my side. Her excitement never dimmed when it came to seeing her best friend. It didn't matter that she'd spent all day at school with him yesterday and then had a playdate afterward.

Lawson hopped out of his SUV as I lugged Cady's booster seat toward the vehicle. "Here, let me get that." He had it out of my hands before I could argue.

"Thanks again for doing pickup duty."

"It's no problem at all. When is your car going to be ready? I'm happy to take you to get it."

"Hopefully tomorrow. But Maddie said she'd give me a ride. She's going to help me with pickup today, too." Thankfully, I had a day off from The Brew, so I didn't need to get myself to work on top of everything else.

Lawson nodded as he got the booster seat in place, Cady and Charlie chattering over him. "I'll leave the seat at school so Maddie can grab it."

"Thank you. I'm really sorry to call on you so much." Guilt

twisted deep. I was calling on all the people in my life when they had busy schedules of their own.

Lawson straightened. "Aspen, at this point, you're family. It's what we do for each other."

A burn lit behind my eyes and in my throat. *Family.* I'd wanted that for so long. Hoped Autumn and I would build it together for Cady. And it had all been ripped away. My hand slipped beneath my flannel shirt, feeling the scar there.

I should be finding a way out of Cedar Ridge. Moving Cady to a city where we could be anonymous. But I couldn't. Not when she was so loved and cared for here. I'd have to find another way. Figure out how John had found our location. Make him think we'd moved elsewhere.

"Thanks, Law," I whispered.

Concern swept over his expression. "Everything okay?"

I'd almost told him about my past a few times; he was law enforcement, after all. But something always held me back. Part of it was thinking that the fewer people who knew, the better. The other bit was that I liked just being Aspen here. Not a woman who'd been through a horrific ordeal and barely lived to tell the tale.

"I'm good," I lied. "What about you?"

I hadn't missed the dark circles under Lawson's eyes or the deepening lines of strain on his face. But I knew he'd never tell me exactly what was going on. Lawson always kept things close to the vest.

He sighed. "Just been a long few weeks." He glanced out at my pasture. "I'm worried about Luke."

Lawson's eldest son had been acting out a bit and throwing more than a little attitude toward his dad.

"I'm sorry. I can take Charlie and Drew this weekend. Maybe you and Luke can do something, just the two of you. It's probably too cold for camping, but you could rent a cabin somewhere that isn't home."

Lawson nodded, scrubbing a hand over his stubbled jaw. "I don't want to dump those two knuckleheads on you."

I smiled. "It's what family does, isn't it?"

The corner of his mouth kicked up. "You've got a point there. Let me get a feel for my caseload, and I'll let you know."

"I'm around, so you can decide last minute if you want."

"Thanks, Aspen."

Warmth spread through me. Something about giving back to the people who had given me so much helped. "Anytime."

"Dad, we're gonna be late," Charlie called from the SUV.

Lawson chuckled. "The only kid who's worried about being on time for school."

I grinned and ducked into the vehicle. I rained kisses all over Cady's face.

"Mama!" she shrieked.

"I'm gonna miss you like crazy. Promise me you're not gonna run away and join the circus."

Cady giggled. "Why would I when we have our own circus right here? All the best parts, anyway."

She had a point there.

Charlie frowned. "I don't know. I think having a trapeze would be pretty cool."

I chuckled and tickled his belly. "I'll get right on that."

"I'm first up!" he demanded.

"You got it." I gently shut the door and stepped back, but I didn't go back inside the house. I waited until the police-issued SUV disappeared completely from sight.

A pang lit along my sternum. It was always hard to watch Cady go. It didn't matter if it was for twenty minutes or twenty hours. But watching her disappear with John's letter hanging over my head? That was torture.

"We're thousands of miles away," I whispered. "We're safe."

I forced myself to turn and head inside. I grabbed my muck boots, jacket, and work gloves, and headed back out. Sliding the keys out of my pocket, I locked the two deadbolts and the doorknob, then checked each one twice.

The temptation to check them all two more times was strong.

When we first arrived in Cedar Ridge, and Cady was still a toddler, I'd ventured into obsessive territory. I'd spent my nights walking the house, rechecking every window and door countless times.

I wasn't sure when it shifted. Maybe after a couple of months of being here with no one showing up at our door or recognizing me from news coverage.

When we were in Mississippi, one reporter always seemed to find me, no matter where I hid. Oren Randal had exposed two houses, an apartment, my office, and Cady's daycare in his articles. He'd almost cost me everything all over again.

But when he hadn't found me in Cedar Ridge, I'd slowly begun to let it all go. The panic, the fear. The shadows of it still lived inside me, but I no longer let them hold me down.

Letting out a long breath, I started toward the barn. I'd already been through the feeding rigmarole but needed some solid cleaning and muck-out time.

Mabel brayed from her pasture as she kicked out at Phineas.

"That's not nice, Mabel," I called. "He just wants to play."

She raced along the fence line, and I stopped to scratch between her ears. I bent and dropped my forehead to hers. "A little kindness goes a long way, Miss Mabel."

She huffed out a breath as if to say, "*Whatever*."

I couldn't hold in my laugh. "At least you always stay true to yourself."

The sound of tires on gravel had me straightening and turning around. I expected to see Lawson's SUV, thinking Cady had forgotten something. Instead, I saw an unfamiliar van.

My stomach twisted into a painful knot. I tugged my Taser out of my back pocket and instantly checked my best escape routes. I cursed as the vehicle pulled to a stop between the house and me. And I didn't have my damned phone.

Blood roared in my ears as two figures climbed out of the van. My eyes flared as I recognized the driver—the man from The Brew yesterday morning.

I should've stuck with my first impression of him. The one that told me something was off. My time in Cedar Ridge had changed my perspective on things. I tended to give people the benefit of the doubt. Apparently, that was a mistake.

"Hello again," the familiar voice greeted.

"This is private property. I'll have to ask you to leave." My voice was even, almost calm. But the Taser dug into my palm as I gripped it.

The second man gave me what he likely intended to be a reassuring smile. "We don't mean any harm. We just need to talk to you for a minute."

"I don't care what you mean. You're on private property, and you need to leave. I've got friends on the force here, and they'd be happy to haul you in."

Lawson and Nash would do that in a heartbeat. But it would also mean I'd have to answer a hell of a lot of questions.

The first man shot me a cocky grin. "Come on now, Aspen. Don't be like that. Or should I say Tara? Tara Monroe, isn't it?"

All the blood drained from my head, and my mouth went dry. They knew. How? Had John sent them somehow?

"Quit it. You're freaking her out," the second man snapped. He turned back to me. "We didn't mean to scare you. Really. I'm Tyson. This is Steven. We're podcasters."

Nausea swept through me. Better than someone wanting me dead, but not by much. "I want you to leave. Now."

Steven rounded the vehicle and headed toward me. "We just want to ask you a few questions. We specialize in true crime."

Of course, they did. "That's great for you, but I don't want anything to do with your podcast."

"Come on now. You're the only one who was there that night besides John. Well, unless you count that little girl."

Bile surged up my throat.

"We're just trying to get to the truth," Tyson said as he crossed in my direction. "When a respected doctor goes to jail for murdering his beautiful wife, our listeners want to know what happened and why."

"What happened was announced in a court of law. I have no comment except to say get the hell off my property before I tase you both."

They stopped a few steps from me. Steven's mouth pressed into a hard line. "Not everyone's convinced the right person is in prison."

The scar that curved from my chest down my side burned as my breaths came quicker. I couldn't get a full one. Couldn't catch hold of the oxygen I needed. The memories were too strong.

A door slammed, and my gaze jerked toward the sound. I couldn't make out the figure at first. My vision was too blurry with panic. But as the large man stalked toward us, I saw fury on his face.

"What the hell do you think you're doing?"

Chapter Thirteen

Roan

THE UNFAMILIAR VEHICLE HAD TRIPPED SOME ALARMS AS I drove down Huckleberry Lane. Nothing about it was right. The fact that it was a rental. The time of day.

I'd turned up Aspen's drive on instinct, and what I'd found had me seeing red. She was backed against the fence, fucking trembling. These two assholes had her cornered, and I was about to rip them limb from limb.

The tall, lanky one whirled around, his eyes widening as I rested my hand on my gun. "We just had some questions. That's all."

"About what?" I growled.

The shorter, stockier one with black hair glanced my way. "Don't think that's any of your business."

"Aspen's my business." The words were pure instinct, through and through. "And the fact that you've got a woman alone and cornered, and I'm law enforcement, tells me it's my business."

The stocky one scoffed. "Aspen isn't even her real name."

I didn't react. I was a master at holding back emotion. But doing it now cost me. "Identification," I barked.

"No," he shot back.

"Steven," the lanky one warned, his voice low as he pulled out his wallet and handed me a driver's license.

"He doesn't have the right," good ole Steven clipped.

"You're trespassing. I could arrest you both." I glanced at Aspen, who was unnaturally pale. "You want me to?"

She shook her head. "I just want them gone."

There was no life in her voice, no fire. That simple fact made me want to kill them both and hide the bodies somewhere no one would find them. "Identification or I arrest you," I growled at Steven as I took a picture of Tyson's ID.

Steven muttered something indiscernible under his breath and yanked out his wallet. He shoved his driver's license in my direction. I took a picture quickly and handed it back.

"Leave. And if you have any contact with Ms. Barlow again, I'll be taking you in."

Steven cursed and stalked toward his van but cast a glance over his shoulder. "This story is coming out with or without you."

"Shut up," Tyson said, hurrying after him.

I didn't move until the creeps were out of sight. The second they were, I prowled toward Aspen. She was still trembling, her hand curved around something. My fingers curled around her fist, gently opening it to find a Taser.

I tried to take it from her, but she held tight. I squeezed her hand. "You're safe now. You can give this to me. Don't want you to hurt yourself."

"The safety's on," she mumbled.

I surveyed her eyes. They were glassy and unfocused. "You don't need it right now. I've got my weapon."

Aspen swallowed, her gaze still not taking me in. "I can't let go."

I dipped down so we could see each other, eye to eye. "Trust me to keep you safe?"

It was a tall order. A vote of confidence I sure as hell didn't deserve. But I asked for it anyway.

Something about my words brought Aspen's gaze back into

focus. It was as if she saw me for the first time. Her green eyes searched mine, and then her grip released a fraction.

I quickly took the Taser, double-checking the safety and shoving it into my jacket pocket. "Come on."

I guided Aspen toward the house. She went too willingly. There were no sharp, snappy comments, no digging in her heels. She simply let me push her toward the porch with a hand on her back.

We climbed the stairs, and Aspen robotically took out her keys. But when she went to unlock the door, her hand trembled too badly.

I gently took the key ring from her and went to work on the locks. All three of them. Three avenues of defense when Aspen had only stepped out to do morning chores.

I held the door open. She moved inside, making a beeline for the couch and sinking onto it. Chauncey hobbled over and laid his head on her lap. She stroked his face and neck, rubbing behind his ears.

She was too quiet. I hated everything about it. Aspen was loud: in what she wore, in her laugh, in the life that seeped from her pores. She was anything but *this*.

I sat on the other side of the couch, turning to face her. I didn't say anything, simply waited.

Aspen stared down at the dog as she petted his head in long, even strokes. "My name wasn't always Aspen Barlow."

I worked hard to keep my expression blank.

"Five years ago, I was Tara Monroe."

Something about that name tickled the back of my brain, but I couldn't place it. Then, all of a sudden, it clicked into place. "Your brother-in-law was convicted of murdering your sister. Attacking you."

The whole situation had been a media firestorm. John Carrington had claimed he'd come home from a business dinner to find his wife murdered. Said he'd grabbed a knife and reacted when he heard someone enter the house. He'd stabbed his sister-in-law by mistake—so he said.

He'd cut Aspen.

The words circled my brain as I struggled for breath. "He hurt you."

Aspen's gaze jerked up at my growled tone. She swallowed hard as she took in the fire in my eyes. "I made it out."

"Barely," I gritted out.

Her hand trembled again, and I wanted to kick myself. "A neighbor heard me scream. He stopped the bleeding. The whole time, John cried it was some horrible mistake. That he thought I was someone who'd broken into his home. Who'd killed his wife."

"But it wasn't a mistake."

Aspen shook her head, a tear slipping free. "Autumn was leaving him. He'd become controlling. Emotionally abusive. She wasn't allowed to go anywhere he didn't approve beforehand."

My fingers dug into the couch cushions as I tried to keep myself rooted in place.

"I was there to pick her up. She was coming to live with me. Taking her daughter."

More of the pieces fell into place. "Cady."

"Her name was Lucy back then. I got custody after John went to prison."

"I'm so sorry," I said quietly.

More tears fell. "Me, too. So damn sorry I didn't get her out sooner. That I wasn't fifteen minutes earlier."

I moved on instinct. Couldn't stop myself. My hand covered Aspen's, my large palm dwarfing hers. "This could never be your fault."

"I know." Her words were a harsh whisper. "That doesn't mean I don't hate myself every single day."

The urge to pull her into my arms was so strong I had to beat it back with everything I had. "I don't think your sister would want that."

A tremulous smile spread across Aspen's face. "She wouldn't. She was such a good sister."

An ache took root in my chest, digging in deep. "I'm sorry you lost her. I'm glad that fucker's in prison."

Something passed over Aspen's face. Something that had unease sliding through me.

"What?"

She shook her head. "Not everyone believes he belongs there."

I remembered that about the news coverage. Charming doctor. Good-looking. Rich. Involved in charity work. No one wanted to believe he would kill his wife in cold blood. Even with Aspen's testimony, people thought she'd gotten it wrong. That trauma had confused her, or even that she was outright lying.

"That's why you changed your name?"

Aspen worried the spot on the inside of her cheek. "People found out where I lived, where I worked. I got jumped by two guys outside my office building downtown because an asshole reporter printed where I worked. Ended up with broken ribs and a concussion."

Fury lit my veins so fast and fierce that it was all I could do to keep breathing.

"I hit my breaking point when someone tried to take Cady from daycare, saying I didn't deserve her. After that, I knew it was only a matter of time before one of us got seriously hurt."

My fingers spasmed around Aspen's as blood roared in my ears.

"A cop helped me. Walked us through the channels to get new, sealed identities. We were supposed to be safe."

My spine jerked straight. "You are safe. And we're going to make sure you stay that way."

Aspen shook her head, her red locks catching the light. "I don't have a choice now. They'll tell everyone where I am. It doesn't matter how much I want to stay. I have to disappear again."

Chapter Fourteen

Aspen

I WAS ALREADY MENTALLY MAKING MY LIST. ROAN COULD TAKE me to get my car. I'd just have to make do with whatever Jim had done on it so far. Then I'd need to pack up here. Find someone to care for the animals. I could get Maddie for that.

"You're not going anywhere."

My head jerked up at Roan's voice. It was hard and brooked no argument. "I don't want to. But I don't have a choice."

A muscle in his jaw ticked. "Of course, you do."

"They're going to publish that podcast. And even if they don't... if they found me, others can, too." I shivered at the thought that someone already had. John. It was on the tip of my tongue to tell Roan about the letter, but I'd already shared too much.

"Leaving is the worst thing you could do."

I jerked my hand from his. The loss of the contact burned, but I shoved that down. "It's smart. It's taking care of myself and Cady."

"You'll be out there alone. You have no idea how they tracked you. They could do it again. Here, you have backup. People who care."

My throat constricted. The thought of leaving Wren, Maddie, and the whole Hartley clan had me struggling to breathe. For the first time since losing Autumn, I had people looking out for me. I'd be leaving that behind.

Roan pressed on. "If you leave, you won't have anyone looking out for you. For Cady."

That was the killing blow right there. When Autumn asked me to be Cady's godmother, I'd sworn to protect her with everything I had.

"I don't know how to keep us safe," I admitted in a whisper.

"You let me help. Let Lawson help."

Everything ached, the feeling of that bit of anonymity I had slipping away. "I don't want anyone to know."

My hand slipped under my shirt, finding the raised skin. People looked at you differently when they knew. They either pitied you or blamed you.

Roan's jaw worked. "Just me and Law. I want him to give those assholes an official warning."

It was better if Lawson knew. I understood that, but it still hurt. "Okay."

Roan studied me for a moment. "You'll stay?"

It might end up being a mistake, but I nodded. "I'll stay."

Maddie glanced over at me as we drove into town. "Are you okay? You seem jumpy."

I winced. Apparently, I hadn't been circumspect in my search for the silver van as we drove. I kept expecting the two podcasters to jump out and give me away at any moment.

"I think I had too much coffee today," I lied.

She laughed. "A day off, and you still can't stay away from the stuff."

"I guess not."

Maddie was quiet for a second, but a smile played on her lips. "Looks like you can't stay away from Roan either."

I stiffened. Roan had spent the day with me. He'd checked all my windows and doors to make sure the locks were adequate. Then he'd offered to help me muck out the barn. It wasn't until just now that I realized he was probably supposed to work today.

"He was helping me with Dory," I said quickly.

Maddie looked confused.

"The deer," I explained.

"Oh." She drummed her fingers on the wheel. "He's not usually willing to be around people much. Don't get me wrong, he'd do anything for his family, but that's about it. I think that's why he ended up at Fish and Wildlife. He does better with animals."

"He's good with people, too."

The words were out before I could stop them. It annoyed me that so many people saw Roan as something other than what he was: a kind, gentle soul. A little rough around the edges, sure, but that was just the exterior.

Maddie's brows lifted. "Sounds like you're getting to know him pretty well."

"Cady likes him," I said, trying to avoid the subject.

"Well, my bestie certainly has good taste," Maddie said as she pulled into the school parking lot.

As we slowed to a stop, Cady jumped up and down, waving maniacally. I couldn't help the laugh that bubbled out of me. It was the first one since Steven and Tyson had shown up. "I think she's excited you're picking her up."

Maddie chuckled and jumped out of her SUV. Cady ran straight at her, and Maddie scooped her up in her arms. Cady giggled. "Today is the bestest. Charlie's dad took us to school, and you're picking me up. I gots all my Hartleys."

My chest constricted. This. *This* was why I couldn't rip Cady out of her life here. She'd lain down roots. Built a community. Had a support system.

Maddie squeezed her tightly. "You're the bright spot in my day, too. You ready to go?"

I grabbed Cady's booster seat and got to work installing it in Maddie's SUV.

"I'm the readiest. Charlie already left with his dad."

"Then it looks like we can hit the road," Maddie said, setting her down.

Katelyn led her daughter by us, sending Maddie and me a dirty look. I tried my best to ignore her as I got Cady settled.

"What's that woman's deal?" Maddie whispered as we headed for our respective doors.

I shook my head. "I have no idea. She's hated me since day one, and her daughter is awful to Cady."

Maddie scowled. "I forgot you'd said that. It's still bad?"

I nodded. "Unfortunately."

"It's depressing that some people never grow out of the mean-girl stage and then teach it to their children."

I sighed as I slid into the SUV. "It's exhausting."

"What's sausting?" Cady piped in.

I should've known better than to say anything around tiny ears. "Cleaning up all of Mabel's poop."

Cady giggled. "I'm not sorry I missed that."

Maddie snorted. "I bet."

Cady chattered on and on about her day as we headed home, telling us who she and Charlie had played with at recess, the book their teacher read to them, and the art project of the day. I didn't think she stopped for a breath until Maddie parked at our house.

"Can you come in and play, Maddie?" Cady asked hopefully.

"Sorry, bestie. I gotta go train a dog right now. But let's have a girls' night soon. We can do glitter manicures."

"Yes!" Cady cheered.

"Thanks again for the ride. I really appreciate you going out of your way."

Maddie just smiled at me. "I love getting a little extra time with you two. I'll be by in the morning to get you."

I tried not to let the feeling of being a burden well up. "So glad you came into The Brew looking for a job."

Maddie shot me a dirty look. "Do not make me cry, Aspen Barlow."

A laugh bubbled out of me, and I held up both hands. "I'd never."

She pulled me in for a quick hug. "Love you."

That burn along my sternum was back, spreading and taking over. "Love you, too."

But I wasn't sure I'd earned the right to say those words to Maddie. Not when I was keeping so many secrets. I released her with guilt swirling around me and forced myself out of her SUV.

I glanced around my property, a shiver cascading through me. I had the sudden bizarre wish that Roan was still here. His big, burly presence made me feel safe in a way I almost resented. I'd been going it alone for years and worked hard to ensure Cady and I were safe.

Opening the back door, I unhooked Cady's booster seat straps. "Ready for a snack?"

"Obvi."

My brows hit my hairline. "Obvi?"

She grinned. "Drew says it a lot."

I could only imagine all the things Charlie's older brother said. I only hoped Cady wouldn't accidentally drop an F-bomb in the first grade.

Cady hopped out of the back seat and ran toward the house.

"Just leave the booster since I'm driving you tomorrow," Maddie said.

"Okay, thanks. Have a great training session."

"I'm meeting with a chihuahua with aggression issues."

"Oh, boy," I muttered.

Maddie's eyes filled with humor. "He loves the wife but growls and bares his teeth whenever the husband gets near her."

I chuckled. "Have fun with that."

"I always do."

I shut the door and headed for the front porch. Checking the screen door, I pulled out the tiny piece of wood. Then I set to work unlocking all the locks. Each one sounded like a cannon going off. They used to make me feel safe. Secure. But now I felt exposed. As if a dozen of them wouldn't protect me.

Cady charged inside the moment the door was open and began her lovefest with Chauncey. I quickly closed the door and relocked it, stepping to the window to survey the drive. I watched and waited as Maddie drove off. No silver van appeared. But that didn't mean it wouldn't.

"Mama?"

I turned at the sound of Cady's voice.

Her face scrunched. "You okay?"

She was a little empath, through and through, always sensing others' emotions.

"Yeah, honey. I'm okay." I wouldn't lie and say I was good. I wasn't. But I *was* okay. We were. And that would stay true.

I let out a long breath. "You know what we need?"

Cady released her hold on Chauncey. "What?"

"Cocoa smash."

Her eyes went comically wide. "Before dinner?"

I laughed. "Sometimes, you need to treat yourself. But you have to promise me you'll eat your veggies when it's time."

"I promise! I promise!" Cady started booty shaking across the living room toward the kitchen, singing as she went. "Cocoa smash. Cocoa smash. Cocoa smash."

Warmth spread through me as I grabbed the vanilla ice cream from the freezer and the hot chocolate mix from the cupboard. I dished up ice cream and sprinkled a healthy dose of the powder on top.

"Extra on mine!" Cady begged.

I sprinkled a little more. "Go big or go home, right?"

"I always go big."

I grinned. "I like your attitude."

I smashed the ice cream and hot chocolate mix together, creating what almost looked like chocolatey soft serve. Then I handed a bowl to Cady. She took it gleefully. "Tell me the story again."

Pain struck deep, but it was an agony I always welcomed. "Your mom always had the best ideas."

Cady was curious about her mom but didn't bring her up often.

She knew Autumn was in heaven and looking over her, and that Autumn had given her all the best parts of herself. But she also knew that it wasn't safe to tell others about her mother.

Cady smiled as she took a bite of her ice cream. "Maybe that's where I get my good ideas from."

"I bet so." And it killed that Autumn wouldn't get to see that in her daughter. "I'd had a bad day at school. Some kids were mean to me." I left out that they'd been making fun of me because my clothes were too small and ragged. "I really wanted ice cream with chocolate syrup—it was my favorite—but we didn't have any syrup. Your mom tore the kitchen apart looking."

"But she couldn't find any," Cady supplied.

"Nope. There was none to be had. But she told me she was going to make me the most special dessert."

Cady grinned, chocolate all over her teeth. "Cocoa smash."

"She made up the name on the spot. Made it feel special. That was just the way your mom was. Could make the most normal day feel extraordinary."

"I wish I knew her," Cady whispered.

I slid into the seat next to her. "Me, too, Katydid. But she loved you so much. The amount of love she gave you in just a few months was more than most people get in a lifetime."

Cady stirred her ice cream, now turning to soup. "I'm kinda lucky."

I stared at the little girl I loved more than life, wondering what she meant.

"I get two of you. My mom and my mama."

My chest felt shredded. "I'm so lucky I get to be your mama."

I pulled her into my arms. "Heart explosion. I need to hug you."

Cady giggled. "It's too tight."

"Sorry, I've got too much love to give, and it's leaking out of my eyeballs."

She squirmed free. "You gotta get control of that love stuff."

I picked up my bowl of ice cream and took a bite. "Never."

A knock sounded on the door.

I was instantly on my feet, crossing the space as my heart hammered. My fingers curled around my Taser as I peeked through the little window, bracing myself. The air left my lungs on a whoosh as I took in the figure on the other side. Unlocking the deadbolts and the knob, I opened the door. "What are you doing here?"

Roan's broad form ate up the space, and the intense energy surrounding him swept outward, cascading over my skin. "You got a couch I could stay on for a while?"

Chapter Fifteen

Roan

ASPEN'S JAW WENT SLACK. SHE HAD TO OPEN AND CLOSE her mouth a few times before she could speak. "What?"

"Your couch. Gonna sleep on it for a while."

She shook herself out of her stupor. "That's not necessary."

That muscle in my cheek ticked. "Think it might be. Those two haven't left town yet."

I'd done some digging after leaving Aspen's and found out where they were staying. Took a little drive, and there was no packing up happening at their rental cabin. I would have to get Lawson involved for sure. But the idea of Aspen and Cady staying here alone in the meantime didn't sit right.

"Mr. Grizz!" Cady yelled. "We're having cocoa smash."

I grimaced as I looked down at the contents of Aspen's bowl. "What is that?"

She flushed. "It's vanilla ice cream with hot chocolate powder."

I winced. "You're gonna go into a sugar coma before you finish."

"Don't knock it until you try it."

I simply grunted.

Aspen clutched her bowl tighter. "You don't need to stay. We're fine."

My back teeth ground together. "I could get Law to put a squad car on the house."

She snapped her mouth closed.

"You're staying?" Cady said hopefully, chocolate smeared all over her face as she popped up behind Aspen.

"Depends on what your mom says." I arched a brow in challenge.

Aspen glared at me, only it didn't have the desired effect. It only made her green eyes burn brighter and her lips purse in a way that made them look too damned kissable.

"I want a slumber party with Mr. Grizz!" Cady said as she hopped up and down. "Slumber party! Slumber party!"

"Cady…" Aspen warned gently.

"It's all the sugar. They turn into little fiends," I quipped.

Aspen shot me a death stare. "Yup, Mr. Grizz is staying, and he told me he *really* wants a glitter manicure."

"YEEEEEESSSSS!" Cady yelled as she skipped toward the hall. "I'm getting my stuff right now."

My eyes narrowed on the too-gorgeous-for-her-own-good redhead. "Glitter manicure?" I gritted out.

Aspen shrugged. "Payback's a bitch." She shoved a bite of ice cream into her mouth. "And you don't get any ice cream," she mumbled around her bite.

A little of the chocolate dribbled onto her lip. My gut tightened as images of me licking chocolate off all sorts of places filled my mind.

"I'm trying to help," I growled.

A bit of that anger and frustration melted away, and Aspen's shoulders slumped. "I know. I'm sorry. I just—we're used to taking care of ourselves. Having someone in our space isn't normal."

An invisible fist ground against my sternum like a mortar and pestle. I hated the defeated cast of her words. I'd take her fire any day. "We can't always carry our own load. Sometimes, we need help. It doesn't make us weak. It makes us human."

Those green eyes connected with mine. "What about you? Do you let someone help carry your load?"

My ribs tightened around my lungs, making it hard to breathe. "I have."

Aspen arched a brow. "Why am I finding that hard to believe?"

Because she saw way too much.

Aspen sighed as if disappointed that I wouldn't let her in, but she let me off the hook. "How do you know the podcasters haven't left?"

I shifted in place. "Did a little digging. Found out where they're staying. Took a drive."

"Digging?" Aspen pressed.

"I know a thing or two about computers." It was a skill I kept quiet about, but it had come in handy more than once.

"Legal things?"

My lips twitched. "Doesn't matter if no one knows you're doing it."

Aspen grumbled something under her breath. "The last thing I need is you getting arrested because you're trying to look out for me. Your family would never forgive me."

"My family would pat me on the back and tell me *good job*."

She frowned. "You really think that?"

"I know that. They get that sometimes you have to color outside the lines to do what's right." Hell, they'd help if I let them in on what was going on.

Aspen worried that spot on the inside of her cheek. "Just don't get caught, okay?"

"I'm too good to get caught."

She rolled her eyes. "Men. Always so cocky."

"There's cocky, and then there's knowing what you're doing."

Aspen's eyes flared, filling with liquid fire.

Oh, hell. That was not what I needed to see. I forced my gaze away to break her hypnotic spell and cleared my throat. "Didn't see any signs of Steven and Tyson packing up."

Aspen toyed with the hem of her flannel shirt. "They're going to publish the podcast."

"I'm talking to Lawson first thing tomorrow. He'll give them a more forceful warning. He might want you to get a restraining order, as well."

"That won't stop the media from spewing bullshit. Trust me, I know."

That grinding feeling was back in my chest. I understood a little of what she'd been through. Knew what it was for people not to believe you. To turn against you. But I didn't know what it was to be caught up in a media storm on top of it. To have unstable people grabbing hold of the story and coming after you.

I hated what she'd endured. And even more, I detested that she'd had to go through it alone. Aspen couldn't be much older than twenty-six or twenty-seven. Five years ago, she would've been barely past college age. And she'd taken on a kid and a vicious court battle.

"Law has a way of bringing people around to his way of thinking," I assured her. And if he didn't, I'd be there to help.

Aspen bobbed her head in a nod, but I could see the anxiety eating at her. And I understood it. People's morbid curiosity was far too easily reignited. I'd seen it time and time again.

"Whatever happens, we'll deal with it."

Aspen swallowed hard. "Thank you. I don't know why you're helping me, but I'm just going to say thank you."

"You're a good person. You don't deserve this. If I can shield you a bit, I'm happy to do it."

"You're a good man, Roan," she said softly, but each word hit like a physical blow.

People around here didn't see me that way. At best, they saw me as damaged goods. At worst, someone to fear. But Aspen? She saw me as the man I wanted to be.

Cady bounded out of the back hallway. "I've got pink and purple and green and blue. The pink's my favorite. What do you want? Ooooooh, I could do all the colors! Sometimes, Miss Maddie gives me rainbow nails, and it's the bestest."

Aspen's lips twitched as she headed for the kitchen. "Have fun, Mr. Grizz."

I muttered a curse under my breath. Cady grabbed my hand, leading me over to the couch and explaining all the different colors in detail. As she chattered about what glitter shone the brightest, her mom looked on from the kitchen with amusement. That pressure returned to my chest.

Sheer panic nearly stole my breath. Nothing could happen to these two. They were lights in a world of darkness. And I knew better than most that anything could happen when people believed lies about you like the ones people believed about Aspen.

Chapter Sixteen

Aspen

"H e's still sleeping," Cady whispered, leaning over Roan.

I frantically waved her back to me. I swore, you let a six-year-old out of your sight for a second, and you never knew what they'd do.

She leaned closer, almost as if checking his breathing. Roan's lumbering exhale fluttered the hair around her face. He looked so relaxed in sleep. Peaceful. Almost childlike. I'd never seen him with so few defenses in his wakeful hours. And it made me wonder just what he was guarding against.

Cady glanced up at me, and I widened my eyes as I kept waving her over. She frowned, her shoulders slumping, but she obeyed.

"I want Mr. Grizz to have breakfast with me," she complained.

"Then you're going to have to wait a bit. Most people don't wake up at five in the morning."

Cady let a little giggle loose. "I was excited. I couldn't sleep."

Something foreign slid through me. A longing. For something I wasn't sure was in the cards for me. Watching Roan sit as Cady painted each fingernail and toenail last night, letting her talk his ear off and answering whatever out-there question she asked, had made me realize I wanted that. A partner. Someone to share the ups and downs with.

But that was impossible when you didn't let anyone in enough to truly know you.

"Okay, I'll eat now," Cady mumbled. "I'm too hungry."

I bit back a laugh. "All right. What do you want? Cheerios and bananas or Cap'n Crunch and strawberries?"

"I want the Cap'n," Cady answered.

"Coming right up." I grabbed bowls and cereal, then got to work slicing berries for us both. As I turned around, I caught sight of Pirate slinking around the couch.

It was as if it happened in slow motion. I waved a hand, trying to get the cat's attention, but she was too focused on her prey. That prey being the bare toes peeking out of the blanket covering Roan.

Pirate launched herself onto the arm of the sofa and attacked Roan's foot with a vengeance. He came awake on a shouted curse, jerking upright. The cat let out a loud hiss, not pleased to be separated from the game.

"What is that thing? A monster from the seventh circle of hell?" he snarled.

I hurried over to him, snatching Pirate into my arms. "She's just a kitten. She's still learning her manners."

Roan glared at the creature in my arms. "It looks more like that thing went ten rounds with Mike Tyson."

"She's not a *thing*. She's uniquely beautiful," I argued.

He lifted a brow as if to say: *Is that really what you're going with?*

I knew that Pirate was a little odd-looking with her one eye, half an ear, and patchy fur, but she was loved.

"Mama says looks don't matter. It's what's on the inside that counts," Cady chimed in helpfully as she munched on her cereal.

"What's on the inside is a demon. I almost lost a toe," Roan grumbled.

"Pirate just got carried away. She's sorry. Aren't you, girl?" I asked.

Pirate butted her head against my chin.

"I'm not taking any chances. Where are my shoes?"

Roan let the blanket drop, revealing that he had been shirtless underneath it. My mouth went dry as I took in his broad shoulders and muscled chest. A dusting of hair covered his pecs, trailing to a line down his abs and below.

Roan stood, bringing us face-to-face, just a breath apart. We both stilled. It was as if the world went quiet around us, and there was only him and me. So close it would only take the barest of movements to know what his lips tasted like.

Pirate swiped out with her paw, smacking Roan right across the face.

"What the hell?" he barked.

She leapt from my arms onto the couch and then darted down the hallway.

"You scared her," I chastised.

"She could've taken my eye out," Roan snapped.

"You need some cereal, Mr. Grizz," Cady said around her bite of Cap'n Crunch. "You're hangry."

I pressed my lips together to keep from laughing. "What do you think, Mr. Grizz? Would some cereal help?"

Roan scowled at me, and then a look of interest filled his face. "What kind do you have?"

"Cheerios and Cap'n Crunch."

"I haven't had Cap'n Crunch since I was a kid."

I grinned. "Captain it is. Pirates are partial to you, after all."

The scowl was back on Roan's face. "I'm going to get cleaned up."

He headed down the hall. I chuckled to myself as I headed back to the kitchen and made Roan a bowl of cereal.

"Mr. Grizz is funny," Cady said, still munching away.

"He is."

A few minutes later, Roan emerged dressed in a fresh Fish and Wildlife uniform that accentuated his shoulders and chest. I instantly dropped my gaze to my cereal.

The chair between Cady and me slid out, the legs dragging against the wood floor.

"Are you gonna help more animals today?" Cady asked.

"I'm not sure yet. Maybe," Roan said as he took a bite of cereal.

I glanced at him out of the corner of my eye. His light brown hair was a little wild, swooping across his forehead. My fingers itched to get lost in the wavy locks.

Cady peppered Roan with question after question. He never lost his patience with her or got annoyed. Instead, he asked what her favorite animals were and if there were any she wanted but didn't have.

An ache settled in my chest as I watched the two of them. I wanted this for Cady. But it wasn't something I was sure I could ever give her.

"All done," she chirped.

Her voice snapped me out of my swirling thoughts. "Teeth and outfit time. You want some help?"

Cady shook her head. "I can do it. Can I wear my glitter boots today?"

There was so much hope in that question.

"I think we'd better wait one more day. There's still a lot of mud out there." Or there had been when I slipped out to feed the animals this morning. Dory's wounds were already healing. I had a feeling she'd be good to go in a matter of days.

Cady pouted. "I hate mud. It ruins everything."

"It just means you'll appreciate your glitter boots that much more tomorrow."

Cady slid off her chair and started singing *Tomorrow* from *Annie* as she headed down the hall.

"She's definitely got a flair for the dramatic," Roan said.

I chuckled. "I predict theatrical productions in our future."

His gaze roamed over me, heating each place it touched. "What's with the glitter? Everything with you two is covered in it."

My cheeks flamed. "Cady has always loved it."

"What about you?"

"She likes to make sure I have my sparkles."

Roan was quiet for a moment, simply staring at me. "And you give her what she wants."

I shrugged. "Something as simple as this that makes her happy? Why wouldn't I? It makes her feel like we're connected."

He swiped his thumb back and forth across the stubble below his bottom lip. "She knows you're not her birth mom."

It wasn't a question. And I shouldn't have been surprised that Roan had put the pieces together. He always saw a little bit more than everyone else.

"She understands she has two moms. She calls me Mama and Autumn Mom. She also knows that her mom has to be a secret."

"She knows what happened to her?" Roan's voice grew rougher with his question.

I shook my head. "Not really. She knows someone took Autumn away. The older she gets, the more she reads between the lines."

"She's gonna want to know more."

I let out a breath. "I know. I never want to lie to her. It's about choosing my words carefully."

Roan nodded slowly. "You're an amazing mom."

My throat burned. "It's been trial by fire, but I'm learning. And I love her like crazy."

"Anyone can see that."

His words were a balm. I often doubted that I was enough for Cady. That I could be all she needed.

Our eyes locked and held for a beat, then two. An understanding swirled between us.

"I'm going to talk to Lawson about everything this morning, but I'd like to loop Holt in, too," Roan said, making a swift subject change.

I jerked upright. "No."

He lifted a brow. "He's still part owner of Anchor Security, his company back in Portland. He can get an amazing system in place here in no time. And he can do recon on Steven and Tyson."

I shook my head rapidly. "I don't need a security system, and after everything with my car, I sure as hell can't afford one. And Law can look into the podcasters."

"Holt will keep it to himself."

"I don't want anyone else to know. It's hard enough that you're going to tell Law. I just—it makes people look at me differently. And the more people who know, the easier it'll be for it to get out, even if they don't mean to slip up."

It was already sending me into a panic that Roan knew. The fact that he was so quiet helped. He wasn't a chatterbox. Didn't get loose lips.

Roan sighed. "Fine. We'll start with Law."

"Thank you," I breathed.

His steely blue gaze met mine. "Just want to make sure you're safe."

My breath caught in my lungs. I couldn't inhale or exhale. I'd wanted that for so long, someone to care what happened to me. If I lived or died. If I was all right. And here Roan was, handing that care to me as if it were the easiest thing in the world.

The gift was dangerous. Because all I wanted was more.

Chapter Seventeen

Roan

GRAVEL CRUNCHED UNDER MY TIRES AS I PULLED TO A stop in front of the hillside house. It looked complete from the outside, but I knew from talking to Holt and Wren that they still had a ways to go on the inside. That finishing work could take forever.

It was early, but a couple of the construction crew's vehicles, and Holt's fancy-ass SUV were around. I turned off my truck and hopped out.

Holt was talking to his friend, Chris, who was also the contractor on the project. He glanced at me with a grin. "What do you think?"

"Looks good."

Holt shook his head, a smile still in place. "He's so verbose."

Chris chuckled as he extended a hand to me. "How ya doin', Roan?"

"Good."

Chris just grinned wider. "I'll see you inside, Holt."

Holt sighed as he turned to me. "You know, most people ask how the other person is."

My brow knitted. "I hate small talk."

"I'm well aware." He shook his head again. "So, what's up that required a seven a.m. meeting?"

I toed a piece of gravel with my boot. "You still got the hookup with Halo security systems?"

Holt's eyes flared. "Sure. Anchor uses them for all our jobs. I can call Cain if I need to place an order for components. What do you need?"

I hesitated for a moment. "I want to put in a system at Aspen's."

That grin was back on Holt's face, but it was more mischievous this time. "You two seem to be spending a lot of time together."

"It's not like that. I'm just helping her out with a few things. She's a good woman." Too good for the darkness that swirled around me.

Holt's smile slipped. "Everything okay?"

I jerked my head in a nod. I wouldn't tell Holt without Aspen's go-ahead. I couldn't do that to her. "She just lives a ways out of town. Has a kid. She should have a system."

"You're right. I can call and get the order in today."

"Send me the bill," I told him.

Holt arched a brow.

I sighed. "She can't afford it. You know it's no big thing for me to cover it." It wasn't for any of us. The fact that our dad had sold his outdoor gear company had left my siblings and me with healthy trust funds. And I never knew what to do with mine.

He clapped me on the shoulder. "I'll get the parts at cost and help you install."

"Thanks." I shifted on my feet. "Keep this between us until I can tell Aspen."

Holt barked out a laugh. "You didn't ask her if it was okay?"

I worked my jaw back and forth. "She didn't seem all that open to the idea."

"I'd better get started planning your funeral."

I scowled at him. "It'll be fine."

He just grinned. "Whatever you say."

"I gotta go meet Law," I grumbled.

"Hope to see you alive later," Holt called as I headed for my truck.

I ignored him.

Then he shouted again. "I love the pink glitter nails, by the way."

My family were a bunch of assholes. Lovable assholes, but assholes all the same.

I climbed behind the wheel and headed down the gravel road. It only took me a few minutes to make it into town. Since it was early, I snagged a spot in front of the police station.

The young officer behind the desk looked up and swallowed hard as I walked in. "Morning, Mr. Hartley."

I jerked my head in a nod and headed for the bullpen. Wren stood in the dispatch area, stretching her back and rubbing her pregnant belly. Concern washed over me.

"You okay?" I asked, voice low.

She turned with a smile on her face. "I'm good. Apart from the fact that this little girl feels the need to kick me in the kidneys every five minutes. I'm predicting a soccer player."

A small smile curved my mouth. "An all-star, for sure."

Wren laughed. "What are you doing here?"

"Got a meeting with Law. He in yet?"

She nodded. "In his office." A concerned look passed over her face. "I'm worried about him. I don't think he's sleeping much. He needs help."

I didn't think so either. Between a rash of tough cases and raising three kids alone, he was up against more than his fair share of a load. "I'll try to talk to him."

Wren let out a huff. "Good luck with that. Every time I try, he brushes me off."

I squeezed her shoulder. "You're a good sister-in-law."

Her eyes gentled. "Not yet, but soon."

I chuckled. "Fair enough."

Turning from dispatch, I maneuvered through the sea of desks and headed toward Lawson's office. Nash looked up from his box of donuts. "What are you doing here?" he asked through a mouthful of pastry.

I grimaced. "Don't speak with your damned mouth full."

Nash rolled his eyes and swallowed. "Priorities."

And that would always be food. I moved to take one, and he smacked my hand.

"I've only got half a dozen," he clipped.

"You're gonna get heart failure at forty."

Nash leaned back in his chair, patting his stomach. "Never. I'm fit as a fiddle."

I just shook my head. "I gotta go talk to Law about a case."

"Let me know if you need the real MVP in there with you. I'll have it solved in no time."

I snorted and headed for the chief's office, knocking on the closed door.

"Come in," Lawson called.

I opened the door and stepped in, closing it behind me.

"Hey. I've been combing through the evidence team's report on the slain deer. There's not much, other than a knife definitely made the cuts."

I lowered myself into a chair opposite him at his desk. "I've got the word out with Fish and Wildlife and the Forest Service to be on the lookout for anyone acting out of the ordinary."

Lawson nodded, and the light caught the circles under his eyes that seemed darker than just a couple of days ago.

"You okay?" I asked.

Surprise lit his features. "Sure. Why?"

"No offense, but you look like shit."

Lawson grimaced. "Just a lot going on right now."

"There's been a lot going on for the past year."

He sighed. "I know. I'm gonna get some help."

"Help?"

Lawson wasn't one to lean on anyone. It was as if he saw asking for help as being a burden, even though he was always ready to give it to others.

"I started looking for a nanny."

My brows flew up. "Seriously?"

He shrugged. "The kids have a million activities now, and it's not like I can trust Luke to keep an eye on the other two."

There was a pain in Lawson's voice at that admission. Whatever hormones Luke had stumbled into as a teenager had been giving his old man a hell of a time.

"It's not a bad idea. I guess I'm just surprised you're willing to do it," I said.

Lawson shrugged. "Desperate times call for desperate measures."

"Let me know if I can do anything."

"I will."

But I knew he wouldn't. I guessed all of us Hartley siblings carried baggage and secrets.

I shifted in my seat. "Wanted to run something else by you."

Lawson leaned back in his chair. "Shoot."

"Need it to stay between us."

Lawson instantly went on alert. "Is this about—?"

"No," I cut him off, knowing what he was going to ask. "It's about Aspen."

His eyes flared in surprise. "What about her?"

"For starters, her name wasn't always Aspen Barlow. It was Tara Monroe."

It took Lawson a few beats before shock spread across his face. "Holy hell."

"I know," I said, voice low. "You remember the case?"

He nodded. "There were some crazy conspiracy theories around it. People who thought she lied about the husband attacking her."

My jaw went rock-hard. "Idiots."

Lawson grunted in agreement. "The blood spatter on his clothes clearly showed he was the assailant."

"But people hated thinking the charming doctor could do something like that."

Lawson shook his head. "I can't imagine what she's been through." He studied me thoughtfully. "I've known her for years, and she's never said a word. You've only known her a matter of days, and she opened up."

I shifted uncomfortably. It wasn't a question, but it called for an answer, nonetheless. "It was happenstance, really."

The words felt like a lie, but I let them stand. I took Lawson through everything Aspen had endured, and by the time I stopped talking, he looked about ready to tear his office apart.

"What the hell is wrong with people?" he snarled.

"My thoughts exactly."

Lawson scrubbed a hand over his face. "What do you know about the podcast?"

"From what I can tell, they've got a big audience. Almost half a million followers on their social accounts."

"Shit," he grumbled. "You think they heeded your warning?"

"Nope. Drove by their rental cabin on my way into town. They're still there."

Lawson stared at me for a beat. "And how'd you find out where they were staying?"

I shrugged. "Not really important."

He sighed. "Roan."

"I'm not asking you to use the information in a court of law."

"I know, but—"

"All you need to worry about is giving them an official warning that sends them packing. If they don't listen, I'll play bad cop."

Lawson frowned. "But you're not a cop."

"Okay, I'll play *if you don't get your sorry asses out of here and never bother Aspen again, you'll live to regret it.*"

Lawson was silent for a long time as if choosing his words extremely carefully. "This has to bring up things for you."

I stiffened. "It's not about that."

"It might not be, but that doesn't mean it won't stir up some demons. A chunk of this town believed you did something horrible."

"I'm aware," I gritted out.

Memories battered at the walls I'd constructed in my mind. *A fist connecting with my jaw. A boot slamming into my ribs. Fighting to stay conscious.*

"Roan, I know it messed with you."

My throat burned. But he *didn't* know. None of my family did. Lie after lie. They'd simply built on each other.

Instead of coming to and telling someone what had happened, I'd half-crawled to the doctor and said I'd taken a fall while mountain biking. The doctor had been skeptical, but since I was over eighteen, there wasn't a damned thing he could do. My medical records were confidential.

My parents were such a wreck about the shootings and Wren, they hadn't even questioned my story. My siblings were much the same. There was a brief moment when I thought Lawson might've known there were things I wasn't saying, but he never pushed.

I stared my brother dead in the eyes. "Trust me. I know it twisted me."

More than he would ever understand. I never saw their faces. Had to walk around town wondering who it had been. Still wondered. Every single person I came across was a suspect. It wasn't just the physical injuries. It was the psychological stuff.

I swallowed down the burn coursing up my throat. I wouldn't let what happened to me happen to Aspen.

Chapter Eighteen

Aspen

MADDIE AND CADY BELTED OUT THE LYRICS TO *SHAKE It Off* as we pulled into the elementary school parking lot. Neither of them was particularly on key, which just made me smile wider.

Maddie came to a stop and turned down the stereo. "You ready for an awesome day?"

"The awesomest," Cady said with a grin.

"That's my bestie. We shake off the haters." She held out a hand for a high-five.

Cady slapped her palm against Maddie's. "Think Taylor Swift likes glitter?"

"Duh," Maddie said.

I chuckled, hopping out of the SUV and letting Cady out.

Katelyn walked by with Heather in tow. "*Still* without a car?"

I forced a grin. "I really appreciate just how much you look out for me, Katelyn."

Katelyn's haughty smile faltered. It was almost as if my back-handed compliment had short-circuited her brain. She huffed out a breath and stormed toward the school.

"She's grumpy *all* the time, not just when she needs a snack," Cady piped in.

I laughed and pulled her into a hug. "Some people are just unhappy, Katydid."

She tipped her head back so she could look up at me. "It's a lot more fun being happy."

"I agree." I kissed the top of her head. "Where's Charlie?" Usually, we got here at the same time.

Cady frowned. "He had to come early today because his dad had to work."

I mirrored Cady's frown. Lawson could've dropped Charlie off with me instead of sending him to the school's early care program. "Well, you'd better go find him. He's probably been missing his best pal."

That was all Cady needed. She took off running, her pink glitter backpack slapping against her back.

Once she disappeared, I hurried to Maddie's SUV and slid inside.

"What did the queen bitch have to say?"

I grimaced. "Some snarky comment about me still not having a car."

"That woman needs a life," Maddie mumbled as she headed out of the lot.

"You aren't wrong. How are things with Nash?"

A soft smile spread across her lips as she glanced down at her ring glimmering in the morning light. "Really good."

"Love seeing you happy like this," I said softly.

"Do not make me cry. I'll boob punch you."

I snorted. "I've been officially warned."

She pulled into the lot at the body shop and parked, looking over at me. "I want you to have this kind of joy."

"I'm happy. I've got Cady and the animals and amazing friends."

Maddie studied me for a moment. "Don't you want more? A partner? Ridiculously hot sex?"

I choked on a laugh. "I don't know, Maddie. I'm not sure I'm built for it. It's not the easiest for me to let people in."

But memories from last night and this morning flashed in my mind. Stolen seconds with Roan. His tenderness with Cady.

Maddie was quiet for a moment. "You ever going to tell me why that is?"

My stomach twisted like a tightly wound ball of yarn. "It's not important."

Maddie reached over and squeezed my hand. "If it has marked you like this, it's important. And I'll be here to listen whenever you're ready to share."

I swallowed the saliva pooling in my mouth. "Thank you."

I didn't deserve her friendship, but I was grateful for it all the same.

"Got your back. Always."

I glanced over at her. "Same goes. Even when Nash steals the last of your ice cream."

Maddie barked out a laugh. "Us doing battle over the last of the ice cream is something *no one* wants to get in the middle of."

"Consider me warned." I opened my door and climbed out, rounding to the back passenger seat. I unhooked Cady's booster seat. "Thank you so much for carting us around the last two days."

"Please, I got Taylor Swift sing-alongs and promises of glitter manicures. I'm a happy camper."

I laughed. "You and Cady are a match made in heaven."

Maddie grinned at me. "She's my girl."

I adored how my friends loved her. "See you later."

Maddie gave me a wave as I shut the door and started toward the office. Footsteps sounded on the pavement, and I jerked.

The younger mechanic stopped in his tracks. "Sorry, ma'am. I was just gonna take that for you and put it in your wagon."

I sent him a wobbly smile. "Guess I'm a little jumpy this morning. Thank you."

"It's no problem," he said, taking the booster seat. "I've got a little sister who still uses one of these. I'm an expert at taking them out and putting them in."

"It is a science."

He chuckled. "First time I tried, I was cussing up a storm."

"You and me both."

He laughed as he jogged back toward an open bay.

I let out a breath. "Get it together," I whispered to myself.

The electronic bell dinged as I opened the door. Jim looked up from the reception desk. "I'm just finalizing your paperwork. Good news is that it wasn't nearly as bad as it first looked."

The tension that had held me captive for the last few days released a fraction. "Really?"

"Really. We got you a new set of tires and fixed those corroded cables. Just cleaned up everything here and there."

"How much do I owe you?" I braced.

Jim scanned his sheet. "With the discount for letting me take my time and the used tires, the total comes to six-fifty."

I blinked. I thought for sure the work would be in the multiple thousands. "That's it?"

He bobbed his head in a nod. "That's it. Jake's bringing it around front now."

I pulled my wallet out of my purse and found my debit card, handing it to Jim. "Thank you."

"Anytime."

I studied the mechanic for a moment. Why did I have a feeling he was cutting me a deal that was a little too good?

"Four-letter word for a creepy crawler's home?" Jonesy called.

"Dirt," Elsie answered without looking up from her computer.

I grinned as I rounded the counter with my coffeepot. These were my favorite days. The ones in our slower months when it was just the regulars. It felt like spending the day with old friends just shooting the shit.

Elsie looked up as I refilled her mug. "You are an angel on Earth."

I chuckled. "If only everyone were so easy to please. How are the photos coming?"

Elsie flipped her computer around. "What do you think?"

I sucked in a breath. The image was incredible. It was of a path through the forest, but the way she'd done the exposure made it moody and alluring. It pulled you in and didn't let go.

"That's amazing. I can't wait to order the book."

Elsie nibbled on the corner of her thumbnail. "I've still got a few more spots to shoot."

"I'm gonna miss you around here when you go."

She glanced out the window. "I'll miss it here, too. There's something about the peace."

"I know. Most places don't have it."

Jonesy held up his mug for a refill. "I think she just needs to move here. Make it her base of operations."

Elsie chuckled. "I gotta get a real job after I finish this book. Sadly, the payout for photography books isn't the greatest."

"You should think about staying. There's a bunch of galleries in town that I'm sure would love to show your stuff," I said.

She seemed to mull it over. "Maybe."

The bell over the door chimed, and I turned to greet the newcomers. When Steven and Tyson strolled in, the words died on my lips. My mouth went dry, and I gripped the coffeepot tighter.

Tyson spoke first. "We just want to talk. Hear your side of the story."

"You need to leave." My voice didn't give away the fear that had begun to take root, and I was grateful for that.

"Not talking just tells us you have something to hide," Steven said with a sneer.

The handle of the coffeepot dug into my palm. I wanted to bean him with it.

"This is a privately owned business. We have the right to refuse service to anyone. Leave. Now." My voice vibrated a bit, but it could've been fury.

"The story's out there," Steven said snidely. "If you don't want to talk, we'll just *fill in* the blank spots."

Elsie's chair scraped back. "She asked you to leave."

Steven's eyes narrowed on her. "This is none of your business."

"You're making it everyone's business by making a scene in a public place," Elsie shot back.

Steven turned back to me. "Your buddies know you're a manipulative liar? That you cost a man his life? His daughter?"

My mouth went desert-dry as blood started to roar in my ears.

The bell on the door jingled, the happy sound so contradictory to what was happening in front of me.

Footsteps reverberated on the hardwood, but I couldn't look away from the two men in front of me. As though if I took my gaze off them for a single second, they would strike.

A throat cleared. "Steven Christensen, Tyson Moss."

Lawson's voice made a little of the fear slip away.

They both turned to face him. At the sight of his uniform, Tyson's eyes went wide, panicked. "We were just talking to her."

"I think *harassing* is a better word, and that's a criminal offense," Lawson shot back.

Steven scoffed. "We've got freedom of the press."

Lawson looked at him like he was a moron. "That allows you to publish articles without fear of retribution. But even that has its limits. Like when you publish out-and-out lies."

Anger lit in Steven's gray eyes. "It's a man's story. He's not allowed to speak his truth?"

My stomach cramped in a vicious twist. They'd spoken to John. And at least Steven had been taken in by him. That charm had always been John's best weapon. Oren Randal, the reporter back in Mississippi, had been taken in the same way. It'd nearly cost me everything.

Lawson shrugged. "I'd just be real sure your past is squeaky clean before you go around trying to expose others'. People might start taking a closer look at *you*."

The threat hummed just below his words. But everyone heard it.

Tyson grabbed Steven's arm. "Let's go, man."

The dark-haired one's eyes hardened on Lawson. "Shouldn't be shocked a pig's trying to silence me."

"Just trying to keep you from bothering my citizens."

Tyson dragged his friend toward the door, whispering under his breath.

The moment the door closed, I started to shake.

"Are you okay?" Elsie whispered.

I nodded numbly. "Sorry about that."

"I'm gonna take her to get some tea," Lawson said, moving closer.

Elsie flushed. "Oh, yeah. Of course."

Lawson guided me into the kitchen and began pulling cabinets open until he found what he needed. A few minutes later, he was shoving a warm mug into my hands. The scent of lemongrass teased my nose.

"I think we have grounds for a restraining order," he said evenly. "You might not get a permanent one, but I'm guessing a judge would give you a temporary one."

I concentrated on the warmth seeping into my palms. "But then everything would be on the public record."

"It would."

I held the mug tighter. "No. It's not worth it."

Lawson sighed, leaning back against the counter. "I can have another conversation with them tomorrow if they don't leave, but they seem pretty damned determined to release this podcast."

"Roan filled you in?" I asked, already knowing the answer.

Lawson nodded. "Wish like hell you would've told me long before now."

I winced. "I'm sorry. I—"

He held up a hand. "I get having secrets. I'm just glad that you told Roan. That he's helping. I think you two are good for each other."

"I didn't exactly tell him. He showed up when Steven and Tyson were at my house."

Lawson arched a brow. "And you couldn't have talked your way out of it? I find that hard to believe."

He was right. I'd been recognized before. I'd play dumb, come up with a million and one excuses, and *always* talked people around to my side. But I hadn't with Roan.

The truth was, I'd wanted to tell him. To open up to someone and let all the burdens go. But I hadn't gone to a friend. To Maddie, Grae, Wren, or Lawson. I'd gone to Roan.

And I was terrified about what that meant.

Chapter Nineteen

Roan

ANNOYANCE HAD PRICKED AT ME ALL DAY, MAKING ME surlier than usual. I'd snapped at Mindy and had bitten Oscar's head off until everyone finally gave me a wide berth. It wasn't their fault.

It was mine. And Aspen's.

She wouldn't stay the hell out of my head. I kept thinking about her at the most inopportune times. Like when I should've been finishing up paperwork. Or while meeting with my boss.

Sometimes, it was a niggling worry, me just needing to know if she and Cady were all right. Other times, it was a flash of red hair and the gleam of those green eyes—or worse, the way she smelled. A smoky cinnamon with a sweetness I couldn't place.

I hadn't missed the hint of attraction I'd seen in those green depths—a look I definitely did not need to see.

I banged a fist against my steering wheel as I stared out at the forest surrounding the Fish and Wildlife office. I needed to get a grip. I'd never struggled with control before. I kept more emotions in check than anyone else I knew. But then again, I'd never been normal.

Turning on the engine, I put my truck in reverse and backed

out of my spot. My cell rang as I turned out of the parking lot, so I hit the button on my steering wheel to answer. "Hartley."

"It's Law. We've got another one. Cougar this time."

My gut twisted. "Where?"

"Meadowrun trail, half a mile from the south trailhead."

I cursed. "Getting bolder."

That trail was closer to town. The kill closer to the parking lot and people. I'd hoped the deer was a one-off. Some freak passing through. But we weren't going to get that lucky.

"I know," Lawson said, voice low. "Can you come take a look?"

"I'm already on my way. Probably take me ten to get there."

"See you soon."

I hung up without saying goodbye. Pleasantries always felt like a waste of time. A falsity. I had no place in my life for that. I wanted raw and real. To know where I stood with people, not wondering if they would turn around and stab me in the back.

Turning onto the road that would take me closer to town and the trailhead, I tapped a beat on my steering wheel. A cougar wasn't exactly easy prey to pin down. And they were heavy. Unless the unsub had lucked out and shot one right on the trail, they'd have to move it. And that took effort.

I made the ten-minute drive in six, anxious to get to the scene and see what we were dealing with. Several other vehicles were in the lot, and I recognized Lawson's SUV parked off to the side. I pulled in next to it.

Jumping out, I grabbed my pack and headed up the trail. The voices reached me before the sight. But what I saw turned my stomach.

The majestic animal had been torn apart. I bit the inside of my cheek to keep my temper in check.

Lawson strode toward me. "I do not have a good feeling."

"Who called it in?" I asked.

"Another out-of-town hiker. The mayor is tweaked, and so is the town council. They don't want anything that could mess with tourist season."

"Good thing it's about to be winter," I mumbled.

Lawson shook his head. "That's not good enough for them. They want this person found and locked up."

I did, too. Just not for the reasons our small-town politicians did. Sometimes, I wondered if anything was more important than tourist dollars in their eyes.

"The hiker see anything suspicious?" I asked.

"Nope. She ran like hell the minute she saw it. Nearly had a panic attack."

I didn't blame the woman. The scene was grisly, to say the least.

A figure near the fallen animal straightened, and my eyes flared in surprise.

"Roan, good to see you. Wish it was under better circumstances." Dr. Miller snapped off his gloves, disposing of them in a trash bag.

"I thought it might be helpful to have a vet's take," Lawson explained.

Dr. Miller glanced at my brother. "I wish you would've called me about the first victim. It would've been helpful to see it, as well."

"Sorry, Damien," Lawson said. "We weren't thinking this had the potential to turn into a serial."

That was true with the deer. Now, it was blind, dumb hope. And hope was a death sentence.

"Can you tell us anything?" I asked.

Dr. Miller nodded. "The cougar was caught in a trap and then shot. The body was mutilated postmortem."

"Small mercies," I muttered.

"Trapping's illegal on state land," Lawson said, a muscle under his eye fluttering.

"Doesn't mean people don't do it," Dr. Miller said. "I've seen several animals who were caught in traps."

"People are assholes," I grumbled.

"They certainly can be," Dr. Miller agreed. "I'm no crime scene expert, but from the photos you've shown me of the deer, I'd say it's likely the same person. The cuts are in the same places. Only these are deeper."

Lawson scrubbed a hand over his stubbled jaw. "Getting more comfortable with it."

"That'd be my guess." Dr. Miller glanced at his watch. "I have to get back for a patient."

Lawson extended a hand. "Thanks for coming out on such short notice."

Dr. Miller nodded as he shook the proffered palm. "Happy to do what I can to help. Please let me know if there's another victim."

"I will," Lawson assured him.

Dr. Miller stopped near me. "Question for you."

I just stared, waiting.

He shifted on his feet. "Do you know if Aspen is single?"

It was as if someone had jabbed a hot poker through my chest. My hands fisted as I fought off the shock of pain. "She's got a lot going on right now and doesn't need guys giving her trouble. Leave her alone."

Each word vibrated with fury, and Dr. Miller's eyes flared. "Not in a place to date. Got it."

I glared at him.

"All right, then. I'm gonna head out." He hightailed it down the trail.

The moment he was out of sight, Lawson barked out a laugh. "Hell, Roan. Pretty sure you just made the vet crap himself."

I turned my glare on my brother. "You think Aspen needs someone messing with her head right now?"

A little of the humor fled Lawson's expression. "No, she doesn't. But she could probably use a partner. Someone who has her back. Someone to share her burdens with."

That burn in my chest lit again—some dead part of me trying to flare back to life.

"But it seems like you've been playing that role pretty well the past few days."

My back teeth ground together. "That's not what this is."

Lawson stared me down, dead-on. "If that's the case, then you shouldn't care about a good man showing interest in her. Have never heard anything but great things about Damien. Maybe I'll invite them both over for dinner and get the ball rolling."

"Law…" I growled low.

His lips twitched. "Just think about why you hate the idea so much."

I didn't want to think about it. Didn't want to admit what it might mean. Couldn't.

"I gotta bring you up to speed on something else," Lawson said, interrupting my spiraling thoughts.

"What?" I snapped.

"Went to The Brew this afternoon to talk to Aspen."

I stiffened.

"The podcasters were there, hassling her."

Fury lit in my veins. "Why. Didn't. You. Say. Anything?" I could barely get the words out.

"I was going to call you but then got word about this." Lawson gestured to the scene.

"You should've told me the second I got here," I clipped.

The image of Aspen trembling on her couch flashed in my mind. Was she scared now? Alone? How had she been when Lawson left?

"I knew you'd freak, and I needed your head in the game when you got here. Aspen's fine. I told her we would meet after she picks up Cady and Charlie from school."

"You wanted my head in the game?" I gritted out. I was going to kill my brother.

Chapter Twenty

Aspen

CHARLIE AND CADY RAN OUT OF THE DOUBLE DOORS, holding hands and giggling as if there was no one else in the whole world but them.

"Don't you think that's a little inappropriate?" Katelyn sneered.

I had to close my eyes for a moment and breathe. It had been the longest day in recent history. I'd been confronted with a shirtless Roan this morning—my dry spell making itself abundantly known—a full day at work, the run-in with the podcasters, talking with Lawson, trying to smooth things over with Elsie and Jonesy, and attempting to concoct a story they would believe without outright lying.

I did not need bitter, bitchy Katelyn on top of it all.

"I think their kind of friendship should be celebrated, don't you?" I asked, casting a look in her direction.

Her casual perfection made me cringe at my sweater and faded jeans. Katelyn pursed her lips. "They're holding hands. They're too young for that."

"They're kids. It's completely innocent."

Katelyn scoffed. "I shouldn't be surprised you're condoning this behavior. You were what? Twenty when you had her?"

I stiffened. The judgment wasn't entirely new. I was twenty-seven now, twenty-two when I'd taken custody of Cady. But I looked a little younger, and whatever piece of glitter Cady had stuck on me today didn't help that fact.

I plastered on a wide smile. "Katelyn, you're too kind. I love that you think I look so youthful."

Her jaw dropped, and I turned to greet Cady and Charlie. "Hey, you two."

"Hi, Miss Aspen," Charlie greeted.

"How do you feel about coming home with us this afternoon? Your dad and uncle are going to meet us there."

I heard a sound of annoyance come from Katelyn's direction as she stalked away.

Charlie grinned widely. "That would be awesome!"

Cady jumped up and down while keeping hold of his hand. "Is Mr. Grizz gonna be there?"

A prickle of something passed through me. "He is."

"This is the best day EVER!" she cheered.

"Come on, kiddos. Charlie, I've already got your booster in the car."

"Aw, man. I keep telling Dad I don't need one no more."

I bit back a chuckle. "I'm afraid it's the law, and it wouldn't be very good if your dad didn't follow the law since he's the chief of police."

Charlie's shoulders slumped. "I guess."

Cady tugged on his hand. "We can decorate your booster. I put pink glitter and stickers on mine."

He looked at her thoughtfully. "Could we do frog stickers?"

"Totally," Cady said.

"Okay."

That being settled, I got the two of them situated in the back seat. "Ready to rock and roll?"

Charlie grinned. "You got cookies at your house?"

I twisted in my seat. "Do I look like an amateur to you?"

His little brow furrowed. "What's an am-am-a-teur?"

"Someone who doesn't know what they're doing. A beginner."

He grinned again. "Nope. You make the best cookies and muffins and scones *ever*."

"Thanks, Charlie. That just made my day."

"It'll make my day if I can get some of those cookies."

I laughed as I pulled away from the curb. "I've got cookies, but I was thinking we could do some experimenting in the kitchen after I chat with your dad and uncle. I'm working on a new recipe."

"Is it a yummy one?" Charlie asked skeptically, not sure he wanted to give up on cookies.

"Mama's recipes are always yummy," Cady told him. "Well, other than when she makes broccoli. This isn't broccoli, is it?"

God, these two were good for the soul.

"No broccoli. I wanted to make double chocolate peanut butter cup muffins."

Silence reigned in the car for a beat.

"That sounds freaking awesome!" Charlie cheered.

"It's like my favorite but better," Cady echoed.

"I'm glad I've got your vote," I said as I turned onto Huckleberry Lane.

The two of them talked in a rapid-fire language I didn't have a prayer of understanding. I caught the occasional mention of a type of candy or a dessert, but that was it. But the chatter and joy warmed my heart. It was the perfect balm after a trying day.

I pulled into my drive, spotting Lawson's SUV. But when I saw Roan's truck next to it, my heart rate ratcheted up. "Get a grip," I muttered to myself.

The second the car was in park, and the engine was off, the kids were unbuckling and climbing out. I hurried to follow them, catching sight of Roan and Lawson emerging from the barn. The kids ran toward them.

"How's Dory?" Cady called.

Roan's lips curved the barest amount. If I didn't make a habit of studying the man, I likely would've missed it. "She looks really good. Bet she'll be able to go home in another few days."

Cady's expression dropped. "I'll miss her."

Roan's face gentled. "I bet you'll see her around. And you'll be so happy knowing she's back with her family."

Cady bobbed her head in a nod as she looked back at me. "I'd be real sad if I had to be away from my mama."

My heart squeezed.

Lawson gave me a chin lift. "You've got even more than the last time I was here. An emu?"

I gave him a sheepish smile as I cast a quick look at Emmaline in a pasture with a few of the goats. "She needed a place to go."

Lawson shook his head. "Can't wait to see what shows up next."

"I think I want a grizzly bear next," Cady piped in.

Lawson choked on a laugh. "I think Roan might have to arrest you then."

Cady glanced up at Roan. "Arrest me?"

Roan's lips twitched. "Bears aren't meant to be domesticated. They could hurt you without meaning to."

Cady's mouth pressed into a firm line. "Not if we're friends, and he's had a snack."

I squeezed Cady's shoulders. "How about we get *you* a snack before you start taking us out one by one?"

She giggled and turned around to fake nibble on my arm. "Tastes just like Cap'n Crunch."

I laughed and led the way to the house. At the top of the stairs, I reached for my little piece of wood in the doorframe, unlocked the deadbolts and doorknob, and ushered everyone inside.

Chauncey lumbered toward us, and I gave him a quick pat as I held the door for him to go out and do his business.

Roan eyed the space suspiciously. "Where's the demon?"

Lawson's brows hit his hairline. "The demon?"

"You ever meet that one-eyed creature from hell?" he challenged.

Chauncey lumbered back up the steps and inside. I locked the door, even though the house was full of people. Some habits were hard to break.

"My cat. He's scared of a poor, innocent cat," I informed Lawson.

His eyes filled with humor as he turned back to Roan. "You're scared of a cat? You work with the most dangerous wildlife in the county, and a cat did you in?"

"That so-called *cat* nearly took my toe and my eye," he grumbled.

"That just means Pirate likes you," Cady said.

"She could like me a little less," Roan muttered.

"Can we go play in my room?" Cady asked.

"Don't you want a snack?"

She shook her head. "I wanna show Charlie my new game."

"Okay. But let me know if you guys get hungry."

Charlie glanced over his shoulder. "We're still making the chocolate peanut butter muffins, right?"

"You know it," I promised.

As the two kids disappeared down the hall, I turned to the men dwarfing my living space. "Can I get you something to drink? I've got coffee, tea, water, and juice."

"Wouldn't say no to tea," Lawson said.

The fact that he drank tea was always a surprise to me. His masculine energy seemed in opposition to it.

I glanced at Roan in question.

He moved past me into the kitchen. "I'll get everything. What do you want?"

I blinked in surprise. "Tea's good."

Sitting at the battered kitchen table, I watched Roan move around my kitchen as if he'd lived in this house all his life. I shouldn't have been surprised. He was an expert watcher and could pick up the tiniest details in a split second.

As the kettle heated on the stove, I turned to Lawson. "What's the plan?"

Lawson leaned back in his chair. "Roan didn't think the word I had with Steven and Tyson was strong enough, so we stopped by their cabin on the way here."

My gaze flicked to Roan as he gently pulled mugs from my cabinet. He paused as he took in the illustrations on the outside.

Bright pink hearts on one. A rainbow between two clouds on the other. And a Pegasus on the last.

He just shook his head and returned to his task. But something about those large, callused hands dwarfing the mugs Cady had painstakingly picked out made my heart squeeze.

I forced my focus back to Lawson. "How'd the second conversation go?"

His expression was carefully blank, and that blankness put me on edge. "They've been informed they are no longer allowed on the property of The Brew or your home. If they go against that official warning, they'll be arrested."

"Can't imagine they took that well," I mumbled.

Roan slid the Pegasus mug in front of me. "They don't have to like it. They just have to obey it."

I studied Roan's rainbow mug as he sat. "Is that hot chocolate?"

A hint of red hit Roan's cheeks as he shrugged. "I like hot chocolate. Just not on top of ice cream."

Lawson dunked his tea bag in and out of his water. "I'll have officers keeping an eye out for them."

I stiffened. "I don't want anyone else to know."

Lawson's expression gentled. "No one here would believe the nonsense some of those conspiracy theorists spout."

I pressed my palms against the sides of the mug, trying to let the heat ward off the dark memories that wanted to break through. "You don't know what it was like," I whispered. "People were awful. Some just stared with pity, but others were cruel. Someone dumped an entire iced coffee over my head. Another person who came into my office for a meeting started screaming at me that I was a liar and a whore." And everyone had known where to find me, thanks to Oren Randal.

I stared down at the swirling liquid as those memories pressed— memories of how things had gotten so much worse.

A hand landed lightly above my knee and squeezed. My gaze flew to Roan's, but he didn't move.

"We're not going to let that happen to you here," he vowed.

"You can't stop it. No one can. Not if everyone knows the truth."

Lawson blew out a breath. "Okay. I'll tell my people those two were hassling you at The Brew and I want to keep an eye out. That's the truth, just not all of it."

I swallowed hard and nodded. "Thank you."

Roan gave my thigh one more squeeze and then released me. I missed his heat the second it was gone. I wanted to beg him to bring it back. Needed the steady pressure that seemed to somehow ground me amidst my swirling thoughts.

"We need to figure out how they found you," Lawson said.

I nodded, my gaze dropping to my darkening tea.

"Has anyone else found you here?" Lawson asked.

My blood ran cold, my muscles winding tight. "I got a letter."

The air around me went electric.

"What kind of letter?" Roan growled.

"Not the warm and fuzzy kind," I said.

"Was it signed?" Lawson asked.

I shook my head. "No. But I know who sent it."

"Who?" Roan demanded.

"John. The man who killed my sister."

Chapter Twenty-One

Roan

RAGE PULSED THROUGH ME, PUNCTUATED BY AN ICY, stabbing fear. Neither was an emotion I welcomed. Hell, I didn't welcome feelings of any sort. Nothing extreme. I lived for the slow and steady, the calm.

Right now, I was anything but those things.

"Why the hell didn't you say anything?" I snarled.

Aspen reared back, and I knew I should've taken more time to reel in my emotions.

"Dial it back a notch," Lawson warned.

"This is something we needed to know," I gritted out.

Lawson released his hold on his mug. "When did you receive the letter?"

"A couple of days ago at my PO box."

My jaw clenched. "Which means he knows where you are."

Aspen's hands trembled as she set her tea down. "He's in prison. It's not like he can show up here. If he planned to expose me, he would've done it already. He wouldn't have given me a warning."

She let out a shaky breath. "John has always gotten a thrill out of letting me know his reach is long. He sent me flowers at my work.

Chocolates I'm allergic to at home. He wants me scared, however he can manage it."

"How do you know the letter was from him?" Lawson asked.

I was envious of my brother in that moment. How easy it was for him to keep his cool. To remain measured, thoughtful, and calm.

"I know his handwriting," Aspen explained. "Christmas cards, paperwork, crossword puzzles."

Because the devil had been someone living inside her family, not some stranger attacking from the outside.

"Do you still have the letter?" Lawson asked.

Aspen nodded.

"I'd like to take a look."

She pushed her chair back and stood. I didn't miss the shakiness in her limbs. That only made me want to gut the man more. Rip him limb from limb. I felt a desperate, clawing need to know that Aspen was safe and he couldn't torment her anymore.

"Can you handle this?" Lawson asked, voice low.

My gaze jerked away from the hall and toward him. "Of course, I can."

"You sure as hell aren't acting like it."

My back teeth ground together. "She should've said something."

"Maybe. But you don't need to bite her head off because of it."

I gripped the table, the worn edge biting into my palms. "I know."

Lawson sighed. "Take a walk if you need it. There's no shame in having to pull it together."

I glared at him. "I'm not going anywhere."

"Fine, but you need to wipe that look off your face."

"What look?"

Lawson picked up his mug of tea. "The one that says you're about to go on a murder spree, taking out anyone who looks at Aspen wrong."

I bit the inside of my cheek and then forced a smile. "How's this?"

Lawson blinked a few times as he stared at me. "You look like a feral clown or something. Pretty sure that's going to give me nightmares."

I socked him in the arm.

"Hey, don't hate on me because I told you the truth."

Footsteps sounded on the hardwood, and I tried to find that mask again. The one that allowed me to keep everything I was feeling on the inside.

Aspen slid an envelope in front of Lawson. "Here."

He pushed back from the table. "I want to grab gloves and an evidence bag really quick."

Aspen winced. "I didn't even think about the fingerprints thing."

Lawson squeezed her shoulder. "It's okay. You didn't know what was inside."

He headed through the living room and out the front door, leaving Aspen and me in silence.

She wound her way around the table and slid into her chair again, not saying a word.

"Are you okay?" I asked softly.

She looked up, studying me for a moment. "I like you better when you're not hiding."

I blinked. "What?"

Aspen drew a circle in the air that encompassed my face. "I like authenticity better than fake politeness."

I swallowed hard. "I scared you."

She shrugged. "You startled me. There's a difference. You were angry. Because you care. I like that better."

I moved on instinct, covering her hand with mine and gripping it tightly. "I was fucking furious. Almost decked Law when he told me what happened at The Brew. Want to kill that waste of space in prison and do it slow. There's so much anger in me it nearly burns me alive. And it's always been safer if I keep a lid on it."

Aspen's green eyes stayed locked with mine as I spoke. She didn't waver, didn't look away, not even for a second. "You have to let it out. If you don't, it'll eat you alive."

She wasn't wrong. I'd been letting it devour me for so long I was used to living in the agony. "I don't trust myself to do that."

"Because people already look at you like they should be scared," Aspen surmised.

No one had ever guessed that or understood it. "Some part of me wonders if they were right to be afraid."

Aspen flipped her hand over, lacing her fingers through mine and squeezing the blood out of my palm. "They couldn't be more wrong. You're a good man, Roan. Maybe the best I've ever known. You hide that gentle goodness beneath mountains of armor. But that doesn't mean it's not there."

A burn lit in my throat, making it impossible to speak.

The screen door slapped against the frame, and Aspen pulled her hand from mine. I instantly missed her touch. It felt like I'd lost the best gift I'd ever received.

Lawson's steps slowed as he approached. "Everything okay?"

Aspen laughed. It was light and airy, everything the situation wasn't. "Just obsessed podcasters, letters from the man who tried to kill me, and mean-girl moms and daughters. Your typical everyday happenings."

I frowned at her. "Mean-girl moms and daughters?"

She waved me off. "A story for another day."

"I'm glad you're keeping your sense of humor," Lawson said, snapping on gloves.

I wasn't so happy about it. It made me worry that Aspen wasn't taking things as seriously as she should be.

"Better laughing than crying. Both release endorphins, you know," she explained.

Lawson carefully examined the envelope before opening it. "I didn't know that."

"If you need to let go, watch a funny or sad movie. Laugh or cry and release it all."

"I'll remember that," Lawson said as he pulled the sheet of paper from the envelope and deposited the envelope in one evidence bag.

Slowly and methodically, he unfolded the letter. I wanted to rip the paper from his hands to read the words. He laid it on the table, and I stared at the letters.

You think you can take her from me? You're going to pay. In blood.

That fury was back, burning through me. But the icy-cold fear won out this time. This wasn't someone writing to express regret or even anger. This was someone hell-bent on vengeance for what he saw as a wrong.

My vision tunneled as memories assailed me.

"You think you're gonna get away with this, you little bitch boy?" a man's voice sneered as his boot crashed into my ribs.

"Fuckin' pigs might not be doing shit, but we will," another snarled.

Something cracked across my skull, and everything went black.

A hand squeezed my arm, bringing me back to the present. Aspen was there, worry filling her expression. I blinked a few times and cleared my throat, trying to shake it off. "He should be having his incoming and outgoing mail examined, shouldn't he?"

Lawson nodded. "But inmates have a way of finding work-arounds. Nothing is foolproof."

"We need to call the warden at his prison." My voice was even, as if the memories I battled had deadened everything inside me.

"Gonna do that as soon as I get back to the office, but I'm guessing he'll be gone for the day. It's a few hours later in Mississippi."

And what could happen overnight? How many letters could John sneak out? How many plans could he set in motion?

Aspen glanced at my brother. "Why don't you leave Charlie here? You can grab him on your way home."

"You don't need an extra kid underfoot," he argued.

"Charlie's a joy, and I did promise the kids they could help me with some recipe experimentation. But I should warn you, he'll probably come home hopped up and covered in chocolate."

Lawson chuckled. "He's come home covered in far worse."

"Then we're good to go," Aspen said with a smile.

It amazed me that it was authentic. We were looking at a threat from the man who had tried to end her life, and here she was, smiling about inventing recipes with two six-year-olds.

"Thanks. That gives me a few hours before I need to pick Drew up from practice and get Luke from his friend's." Lawson slid the letter into a second evidence bag and sealed it. "I'll get these to the station and filed, but I'll do it myself so there aren't any curious eyes."

Aspen nodded. "Thanks, Law. I know keeping this under wraps is tough, but I appreciate it."

"I'll do whatever I can to help." He gathered his things and headed for the door. "See you later, Charlie Bear," he called.

"Bye, Dad!"

Aspen followed Lawson and locked the door as it closed.

I turned, watching her make her way back to me. "How do you do it?"

Her expression turned puzzled. "Do what?"

"Laugh with everything that's going on and truly mean it?"

She rested a hip against the table, looking down at me. "Everyone has their struggles, but sometimes I think those who have gone through the worst are the ones with the deepest ability to find joy, even in moments of hardship and heartache."

I stared at Aspen, taking in her beauty and letting it fully hit me for the first time. It wasn't just her gorgeous red hair, piercing green eyes, and lush lips. It was the light that radiated out of her, casting a glow on everyone and everything around her.

Truly seeing that for the first time? I knew one thing.

I was completely screwed.

Chapter Twenty-Two

Aspen

I LEANED BACK IN THE UNCOMFORTABLE PLASTIC CHAIR AND watched girls in various shades of tutus and leotards twirl across the room. I loved watching Cady dance. It wasn't that she was insanely gifted; it was the sheer joy that surrounded her while she did the thing she loved the most.

But my mind kept drifting today. Back to the man who had stolen way too many thoughts. To the one who'd slept on my lumpy couch yet again. I'd awoken to cussing about a demon cat and laughed into my pillow.

Roan had scowled at me when I emerged in my fluffy robe and slippers. "That cat needs a muzzle," he'd said.

I'd just nodded and told him I'd look into it, knowing I never would.

The truth was, I loved his cranky scowls just as much as I enjoyed when his expression lightened. Because those glowers, grimaces, and glares just meant that the lip twitches and chuckles hit that much harder when they came.

Movement from Cady's pink glitter tutu caught my eye. She executed a spin, but she didn't have her typical beaming smile when she stopped. And her eyes were red as if she fought tears.

I instantly straightened, going on alert. Heather and her two awful sidekicks were snickering together as they sent looks in Cady's direction. Anger and worry surged inside me.

The ballet teacher clapped her hands. "That's it for today. I'll see you tomorrow. Make sure you get lots of practice."

Cady made a beeline for me, and I crouched low, pulling her into a hug. "What happened, Katydid?"

"Nothing," she mumbled. "Can we go home?"

"Of course." I slid on her winter coat and helped her with her boots. I'd talk to her once we were home, and she wasn't at risk of falling apart in front of her classmates. But that didn't stop me from throwing a death glare at Katelyn and her daughter as we headed out. I wanted to slip some serious ex-lax into their drinks.

I bundled Cady into my station wagon and slid behind the wheel. I kept glancing in the rearview mirror at my girl. She just stared at her hands, not saying a word. The sight had tears burning the backs of my eyes. The only time she was ever this quiet was when she was sick.

My insides twisted into an angry pretzel. I'd been trying to teach her to rise above, but that obviously wasn't working. I needed to have a conversation with Katelyn, but I feared it would only make things worse.

Turning into our drive, I saw Roan's truck in the distance. Something in me eased. Reassured me, even with all that was going on.

I pulled to a stop in front of the house and climbed out, helping Cady from the back seat. She trudged up the steps and waited for me to unlock the door. When we got inside, Roan was sitting on the couch, Chauncey curled at his side.

Everything in me warmed at the sight. At his mere presence. I loved the thought of him letting himself in with the key I'd loaned him. Of him letting Chauncey out and giving him scratches. Of him waiting for us.

I loved it all. A little too much.

Cady slid her coat off, hanging it up.

Roan grinned at her. "Hey, Tiny Dancer."

Cady's lower lip began to tremble, and then she flew at him.

Roan's eyes widened in surprise as he caught her, tutu and all.

Cady burst into wild, racking sobs. I expected Roan to freeze, unsure what to do with the ball of emotion in his arms. Instead, he simply rocked her back and forth, rubbing a hand up and down her back and whispering nonsensical things to her as she cried.

I crossed to them, lowering myself to the couch as Cady's sobs lessened a fraction. Roan's eyes collided with mine, and I saw so much pain in his—sympathy for my daughter.

"What happened?" he whispered gruffly to Cady.

She didn't answer right away, then sniffed. "Heather's so mean. She said my tutu is cheap and pathetic. That I'm embarrassing and will never be a ballerina."

Roan stiffened, gripping Cady a little tighter. I watched as he struggled to keep his breathing even. "You know she's just saying that because she's jealous, right?"

Cady looked up at him. "She hates me, and I never did anything to her."

Roan brushed the hair away from her face. "You're nice to everyone. And I bet everyone at school and ballet likes you."

"Not her, Susanna, and Lainey," Cady grumbled.

Heather's friends, I mouthed to Roan.

"They don't like you because everyone else does. They have ugliness on their insides, and it means they'll never have what you do," he explained.

"What do I have?" Cady asked.

"You've got a light in you. Same one your mama has. And I bet your mom had it, too."

Cady's eyes shone as her lip trembled again. "You know about my mom?"

He nodded. "I heard she was super special, and I know she gave that to you."

I squeezed her hand. "Roan's right. Your mom had the best light.

Brighter than anyone could imagine. And I think you're gonna be just the same."

Roan jerked his head in a nod. "You can't let anyone steal that light. Can't let anyone dim it. No matter how hard they try. Because that light's magic."

Cady blinked up at him. "Magic?"

"Definitely. It can heal hurts and make people feel safe and loved. You shine that light on as many people as possible. Even those mean girls. You don't have to be friends with them, but you just keep shining. Don't let them know they affected you at all."

Cady nibbled on her bottom lip. "I don't know if I can pretend when they're that mean."

"You gotta replace the words in your head. When they say something mean, you turn it into the best compliment ever," Roan said.

She scrunched her nose. "Like how?"

Roan shifted her on his lap so she could see his face better. "Let's say someone tells me, 'You're the ugliest person I've ever seen.'"

Cady straightened. "You're not ugly. You're handsome. Like a real-life prince."

He chuckled, the sound skating over my skin in a pleasant shiver. "Well, that's what I would tell myself they really said. I just replace the words in my head. Then you smile at them real big and say, 'Thank you so much.' It confuses them."

Cady giggled. "I bet." The laughter died away. "Doesn't it hurt your feelings when people say mean things?"

"Every now and then when I'm already having a hard day. But most of the time, I realize they don't really know me. I only care about what my family thinks about me. What the people *I* care about think."

She straightened on his lap. "We're your family now, too, and we love you a whole lot, Mr. Grizz."

Cady threw her arms around Roan in a tight hug. His Adam's apple bobbed as he swallowed. "Love you, too, Tiny Dancer."

My eyes burned, and my nose stung. *I will not cry. I will not cry.* I said the words over and over in my mind.

Cady released Roan and hopped off his lap. "I gots to get out of my leotard, and then can we have double chocolate peanut butter cup muffins, Mama?"

I swallowed the fire in my throat. "I saved a few just for you."

"Yes!" She booty-shook out of the living room and down the hallway toward her bedroom.

A smile tipped my lips. That was a little kid for you. It was the end of the world one minute, and as though nothing happened at all the next.

I turned back toward Roan to thank him for all he'd done and was met by a wall of fury. He'd kept it carefully restrained while comforting Cady, but now it was out in full force.

His breaths were more labored, his fists clenched. "I am two seconds away from driving over to that brat's house and showing her mean."

Chapter Twenty-Three

Roan

Aspen's eyes widened in shock as she gaped at me. Then she burst out laughing. I'd heard her laugh before, but not like this. It was full-out, completely uninhibited, and wrapped around me like a warm embrace.

Tears filled her eyes as she struggled for control. "Let's try to hold off on the child terrorizing, okay?"

My lips thinned at the reminder of Cady sobbing in my arms. "Someone needs to teach her a lesson."

Aspen's expression softened. "I don't disagree, but I'm not sure that person is you."

It would be if that girl didn't leave Cady alone.

"This been going on long?" I asked.

Aspen toyed with the fringe on one of her throw pillows. "Heather has never been especially fond of Cady, but it got worse when they all started ballet."

A muscle in my jaw ticked. "Have you talked to her parents?"

"It's just her mom in the picture, Katelyn Beasley."

I winced. That woman was a piece of work. She was always trying to snag one of my brothers. As they'd paired off, she'd set her sights on Lawson, who had no interest whatsoever. "You try talking to her?"

Aspen went quiet, her fingers tangling in the pillow's fringe.

"Aspen?" I pressed.

Her gaze lifted to mine. "She's not my biggest fan."

My back teeth ground together. "What. Do. You. Mean?"

"Nothing. It's not a big deal."

I lifted a hand, brushing the hair away from her face. My thumb traced across her pulse point, the rough pad such a contrast to her petal-soft skin. "Mean-girl moms," I muttered, remembering Aspen's words from the other day.

Aspen swallowed hard. "It's nothing I can't take."

Her pulse jumped beneath my thumb.

"I can feel when you're lying."

Aspen's eyes widened, and she licked her lips. "She's a total bitch. It's no wonder her daughter's awful. She insults my car, my clothes, my parenting. I doubt she'd hear anything I had to say regarding her daughter's behavior."

I struggled to keep the anger from my face. "Jealous."

Aspen snorted. "I think it's more that she's deeply unhappy. She has to tear everyone around her down so she feels better about herself."

I was sure that was part of it. But not the whole. Not even close. "You don't see how bright you shine."

She looked up at me, confusion swirling in those green depths.

"Everyone around you sees it. You have this pull. Makes people want to be in your orbit. People like Katelyn will never have that. Too much ugliness in them."

Aspen's breaths grew shallow as her gaze dropped to my lips.

Fire flared in my veins—a need so powerful it almost stole my breath.

She was close, just a breath away. One tiny flicker of movement, and I could know what it was like to drown in her taste.

"I'm ready!" Cady called as she charged down the hallway. "Can I go see Dory before I have my snack?"

I jerked my hand away from Aspen as if I'd been burned. And I had in a way. Had no doubt that simply feeling her skin would leave scars.

Aspen ducked her head and rose. "Sure thing, Katydid. Get your coat. It's cold out there."

I moved on instinct, following Aspen. Her pull still had a hold of me, and I wasn't sure that would ever change. I needed to keep my distance. Rebuild those walls. But for the first time, I didn't want to.

I slid on my boots by the door, and Aspen stopped close, zipping up her jacket. "You need a coat, too."

"I'm good," I grunted.

She huffed out a breath. "What? You're a mountain man impervious to cold?"

"No, he's a grizzly bear!" Cady said, jumping up and down.

I chuckled and hauled her into my arms, tickling her sides. "What'd you call me?"

"A grizzly bear!" she yelled between shrieks and giggles. "Big and tall and grumpy and always hungry."

I grinned as I set Cady on her feet. "That's fair, I guess."

She slipped her little hand into mine. "Let's go."

My chest gave a painful squeeze. She had no idea what her simple acceptance meant to someone like me. The power of it.

Cady tugged me outside and toward the barn as Aspen locked the door behind us. "Do you think Dory will miss us when she goes?"

"I bet she'll miss you."

We'd all been careful to keep our distance other than to give Dory her medicine twice a day. I hoped like hell that meant she'd be able to be reintroduced to the wild.

Cady tugged on the barn door, but it only moved an inch. I reached above her, sliding it open.

"Thanks, Mr. Grizz."

My lips twitched. "Anytime."

We moved inside. Most of the animals were still in the pastures, but a few were in the stalls. As we walked down the aisle, something flashed out and hit me in the arm. "What the—?" I caught myself just before I dropped an F-bomb in front of a six-year-old.

"Emmaline," Cady chastised. "That's not very nice."

She moved toward the emu, but I caught her by the back of the shirt. "I'm not sure that's a good idea."

I glared at the bird. That thing could take a chunk out of Cady.

She just grinned at me and shook off my hold. Before I could stop her, she moved up to the emu's stall, and the bird dropped its head to her shoulder, almost like it was hugging Cady.

"Emmaline just wants her cuddles," Cady said, stroking the bird.

"I'll be damned," I muttered.

I felt Aspen stop alongside me, simply watching her daughter.

"She's got that same light you do. Even the animals feel it," I said quietly.

"She's more special than I could ever dream of being," Aspen whispered.

I tipped my head down to look at her. "You both are. One day you'll see that."

Aspen's throat worked as she swallowed.

Cady released the emu and started down the aisle again, taking my hand and tugging me along. "Will you check her wounds?"

I didn't know as much as Dr. Miller, but I knew enough.

Cady climbed up on the tack box to peek into the stall. "She's sleeping," she whispered.

I glanced inside. The deer was curled up, giving us a good view of her side. "She's almost completely healed. Looking great."

Cady sighed, resting her chin on the side of the stall. "I'm happy for her, but I'm gonna miss her something awful."

That pressure in my chest was back. How could anyone be mean to this little ray of light?

I turned to Aspen. "Let me take Cady to her next dance class."

Her eyes flared. "Is there going to be a bloodbath if I do that?"

My mouth stretched into a grin. "I'm the town pariah for a reason. Everyone's terrified of me."

Finally, that terror would come in handy.

Chapter Twenty-Four

Aspen

I WIPED DOWN TABLETOP AFTER TABLETOP AS I MOVED AROUND The Brew. Normally, I'd lose myself in the music playing faintly in the background, but I couldn't stop hearing Roan's words in my head. *"I'm the town pariah for a reason. Everyone's terrified of me."*

I hadn't had a chance to challenge that statement because Cady had interrupted, wanting to take Mr. Grizz out to see her goaties. But I couldn't forget the words. I hated that Roan felt so looked down upon by the people around him.

An ache had taken root at hearing the words and hadn't left since. I wanted to help and change things for Roan, but I didn't know the first thing to do.

The bell over the door jingled, and I looked up to see Elsie heading inside. I smiled in greeting. "Hey, how was it today?"

She grinned back. "Freaking awesome. I got some really great shots. But it's cold as hell when you get higher up in elevation, even just a little bit."

I nodded, heading behind the counter. "It doesn't take much. You want something warm to drink?"

"Please. I'd love some tea, whatever you recommend. You never steer me wrong."

"Anything to eat? Zeke is gone for the afternoon, but we have a few pre-made sandwiches." I inclined my head toward the refrigerated section of the bakery case.

Elsie perused the options. "I'll take that chicken salad."

"Coming right up."

As I worked to gather her meal, Elsie watched me closely. The focus made me twitchy, and I braced for whatever was coming.

"You doing okay?" she asked softly.

I stiffened but didn't allow myself to stop moving as I plated her sandwich. "Oh, yeah. I'm fine."

Elsie toyed with the corner of the counter. "What did they want? I know you said it was a family issue…"

Her words trailed off, but I heard what she didn't say. Elsie knew I wasn't telling her the whole truth.

I focused on keeping my breaths even. In for two, out for two. I did it over and over as I searched for words that wouldn't be a lie but also wouldn't reveal the whole truth. "They wanted a statement on a case my family was involved in years ago. I didn't want to give one."

Elsie's jaw went slack in surprise. "They were reporters?"

"Podcasters."

"And you'd already asked them to leave you alone," she surmised.

I nodded. "They haven't been great at taking no for an answer."

Elsie's expression hardened. "I'm so sorry. If you ever want to talk about it or need me to give someone a knee to the balls, just let me know."

I snorted. "I appreciate it. I wouldn't mind taking the asshole one out."

Her lips twitched. "The stocky one, right? He seemed like a real piece of work."

I slid the sandwich and tea across the counter to her. "Understatement."

Elsie pulled out a twenty and handed it to me. "Guys like that are the worst. But I guess it just makes us appreciate the good ones, right?"

Heat hit my cheeks as the memory of Roan's thumb stroking my neck flashed in my mind. "Right," I mumbled.

A smile stretched across her face. "You're blushing."

"I am not." I totally was.

Elsie laughed. "Is it the chief of police?"

"Lawson?"

She nodded.

"No. He's just a friend. Our kids are the same age and best friends."

"Gotcha," Elsie said. "Then who?"

"No one, I swear. I guess I'm just wishing I had that." Not a lie. Nothing had happened with Roan, and I wasn't sure it ever would. Or if I could go there even if he was willing.

She met my gaze with a kind smile. "One day you'll get everything you deserve. There's no way the Universe won't come through for you."

"Thanks." I moved to hand Elsie her change, but she waved me off.

"Keep it for the tip jar."

She was too generous when I knew she was struggling to make ends meet herself, but I didn't argue. I'd send her home with extra cookies when she left.

As Elsie grabbed an empty table, the bell over the door jingled again, and a familiar face strode inside.

"Afternoon, Dr. Miller," I greeted.

He smiled at me. "Damien, please."

I nodded. "Damien."

"How does the doe seem? I was going to see if I could stop by later today and give her a checkup."

"She's healing nicely. Roan said he thinks she'll be ready to be released soon."

A flicker of surprise danced across Damien's expression. "Roan doesn't usually do follow-ups with his finds."

I shrugged. "We're friends, so he was already around."

Damien nodded thoughtfully. "I admire anyone who can make it through that steely armor."

I chuckled. "He certainly doesn't make it easy. I think I have Cady to thank, mostly. Once she decides someone is going to be her bestie, she doesn't give up."

Damien grinned. "She seems like quite the character."

"Understatement of the century. So, what can I get you?" I didn't remember Damien ever coming in previously, and my past meant I was usually pretty good at remembering faces.

He surveyed the menu and then the bakery case. "What do you recommend for an afternoon snack?"

"Hmm. The orange-cranberry scones are always a favorite. And we've got a new double chocolate peanut butter cup muffin on the menu."

Damien nodded, his gaze on me instead of the bakery case. "An orange-cranberry scone sounds perfect."

"Coming right up. Would you like that for here or to go?"

"To go. I need to get back to the clinic."

I slid the scone into a bag and handed it to him. "That will be five fifty."

Damien pulled out his wallet and handed me a ten-dollar bill. "I actually had another question for you."

"Shoot," I said.

"Could I take you to dinner sometime?"

I stilled, sheer panic flashing through me. "Oh. I, um. I'm not really looking to date right now. My life is, uh, complicated, and—"

Damien held up a hand, a gentle smile on his face. "Don't sweat it. Roan warned me not to ask, but I had to try."

My jaw went slack. "Roan told you not to ask me out?"

Damien nodded, his lips twitching. "He was pretty firm about it, actually."

"Oh," I said, not sure what else to add.

"Seems to be quite protective of you," he went on.

That heat was back in my cheeks as I handed Damien his change. "We're good friends."

Were we, though? I had no clue what Roan and I were in his mind.

"Seems like a bit of an extreme reaction for a friend."

I worried the inside of my cheek. "He looks out for Cady and me."

Damien shoved a few dollars into the tip jar. "Always good to have someone looking out for you. I'll see you around, Aspen."

He headed for the door, and I just stared after him.

As the door closed behind him, Elsie made bug eyes at me. "Are you crazy? That man is gorgeous, and he's a vet."

I shrugged. "I just don't feel a spark."

"Maybe you need to get your spark radar examined."

I snorted and turned to grab my rag to continue my cleaning, but I couldn't help hearing Damien's words ringing in my ears. *"Roan warned me not to ask, but I had to try."*

Now, what the heck did that mean?

Chapter Twenty-Five

Roan

"THIS IS BAD," NASH MUTTERED AS HE STARED AT THE poor, mangled bobcat that lay across the trail.

"This was rage," Lawson said, a muscle fluttering beneath his eye.

I turned away from the fallen animal, unable to take the carnage anymore. Nothing could be gleaned from the body. Not until Dr. Miller arrived and we had test results back from the techs currently scouring the crime scene.

I started back down the trail, knowing my brothers would follow. Their footfalls sounded behind me, confirming as much.

It took less than a minute to reach the trailhead. Even bolder than the last scene.

"Can we get in someone's car? I'm freezing my balls off," Nash muttered.

Lawson beeped the locks on his SUV. I climbed into the front passenger seat while Nash got in the back, and Lawson hopped into the driver's seat.

"I swear it gets colder every year," Nash said, rubbing his hands together.

Lawson turned over the engine. "Or you're going soft."

Nash glared at him. "Just because I don't want to lose my swimmers doesn't make me soft."

Lawson chuckled, but the sound died as he glanced back at the trail. "I don't see how we still have nothing."

We had less than nothing. None of the hikers ever saw someone hanging around the deceased animals. None of the Fish and Wildlife or Forest Service officers patrolling the area had seen anything suspicious. And there was no evidence except some hairs from previous animal kills on the blade.

"We know they're linked," I said.

"That's not enough to point us in a direction," Lawson argued.

Nash scrubbed a hand over his stubbled jaw. "Maybe we need to approach this from a behavioral standpoint instead of an evidence-based one."

Lawson turned in his seat to look at Nash. "Say more."

"We need to figure out what the crime scenes tell us about the perpetrator. Can you call that profiler friend of yours?" Nash asked.

Lawson winced. "Ex-profiler. He doesn't work for the bureau anymore."

"So?" Nash pushed. "It's not like he lost all his knowledge when he left. He might be able to provide some insight."

"I can try, but Anson wanted to leave that life far behind."

My brows pulled together. "Why?"

Lawson had mentioned how good Anson was at his job on more than one occasion in the past. Had said no one understood the criminal mind better. They used to discuss cases all the time.

Lawson squeezed the back of his neck. "He had a case go bad. Really bad. It marked him."

Nash winced. "That's rough."

Lawson jerked his head in a nod. "I'll make the call. If he refuses, I won't push."

"All you can do is ask," Nash agreed.

"In the meantime, I'm going to ask Rob to increase the officer presence and see if he can make a request with the Forest Service, too," I said. Maybe we could catch this prick in the act. But the state and national forests around Cedar Ridge were vast, and it would take a hell of a lot of officers.

Lawson tapped his thumb on the console. "It's worth a try."

"Somebody must have seen something," Nash said. "Kills like these…the person would be covered in blood."

I grunted. "Not everyone wants to get involved."

Nash shook his head. "If you saw someone coming down the trail looking like Carrie after the prom, you wouldn't call the cops?"

"Of course, I would. But not everyone thinks that way. Some people want to avoid contact with the police at all costs," I pointed out.

Lawson continued his drum beat on the console. "We might need to consider a reward for information."

Nash groaned. "Everyone and their brother will come out of the woodwork then. The last time we did a reward, I had to listen to a woman talk for almost an hour about how aliens had landed in Cedar Ridge and were body snatching people."

My lips twitched. "The truth is out there."

Nash glared at me. "Just keep the damn probes away from my butthole."

I choked on a laugh.

Lawson just shook his head. "I'll make sure you have phone duty when the reward goes up."

"Rude," Nash shot back.

I glanced at my watch. "Crap. I gotta go."

"Where?" Nash asked.

"Gotta take Cady to dance and stare down some tiny bitches."

The SUV went silent around me.

Nash blinked at me a few times. "What did you say?"

"Some girls are being mean to Cady. She's a good kid and doesn't deserve to be picked on."

Lawson groaned and pinched the bridge of his nose. "Please don't do anything that means I get called to the ballet studio."

I shrugged. "I'm just going to let it be known that I'm watching. That's all."

"What you mean is that you're gonna give them that serial-killer smile, right?" Nash asked.

"Maybe."

Lawson groaned again. "At least take Charlie with you. Maybe he can keep you in line."

It actually wasn't a bad idea. Not that my nephew would stop me from doing what I needed to do, but I could have a conversation with him about looking out for Cady, too. "Sure."

I opened the door and slid out.

"Roan," Lawson called.

I grunted.

"Don't give the girls nightmares for the rest of their lives, okay?"

"Only if they deserve it."

I grabbed Charlie's booster seat and headed for my truck. It didn't take me long to get from the trailhead to the elementary school. When I pulled to a stop and hopped out, Cady flew at me.

"Mr. Grizz!"

I hauled her up and onto my hip. "How was your day?"

"Pretty good."

A throat cleared, and an older teacher gave me a wary look. "Can I see your identification, please?"

"This is Mr. Grizz. He's me and Mama's bestie, and he's taking me to dance today," Cady informed her.

The woman's mouth thinned as she waited for me.

I set Cady on the ground and pulled out my badge, handing it to her.

She took her sweet time examining it as if it might be a fake. Finally, she handed it back. "All right."

"I'm picking up my nephew, as well. Charlie Hartley."

Charlie bounded up. "You are?"

I clapped him on the shoulder. "You're coming to ballet with Tiny Dancer and me."

His face scrunched. "I don't gotta wear a tutu, do I?"

"Only if you want to, bud," I said.

The teacher huffed. "We got a call about that." She acted as if she was annoyed she couldn't have me arrested.

"Thanks for *all* your help," I said with a mock smile, and she scurried off.

"She doesn't check when Miss Maddie comes to get me," Cady said thoughtfully.

I bet she didn't. Because Maddie was all sunshine and rainbows. I was…not.

"Where's your booster seat, Tiny Dancer?" I asked.

She pointed to a stone wall. I grabbed it and got it installed in my truck. Helping the kids up, I checked that they were securely fastened in their seats. "Ready to hit the road?"

Cady nibbled on her lip. "We don't have to go to dance. Maybe we could get ice cream instead."

Anger burned brightly in my gut. Those mean girls had made Cady not want to do her favorite thing. That stopped today.

"How about this? We go to dance and *then* get ice cream."

She still looked unsure.

I squeezed her shoulder. "We can't let the meanies win. Because if we do, they'll just keep doing it. Not only to you but to other people, too."

Cady nodded slowly. "I don't want them to be mean to other kids."

Such a pure heart.

I held up my hand. "Let's do this."

Cady slapped me a high-five. "Let's do this."

I shut the door and rounded my truck, grabbing a bag from the back. In a matter of seconds, we were heading for the dance studio on the edge of town. I pulled into an empty spot and helped Cady and Charlie out.

Cady grabbed her bag and ran toward the building. "I gotta change."

"Hold up, Tiny Dancer. I got you something." I handed her the shopping bag from the local sporting goods store.

She peeked inside and gasped. "For me?"

I nodded. "The woman at the store said they should be your size."

Cady pulled out a sparkly pink leotard and gaped. "These are the fancy ones."

My chest ached for her. Cady deserved the best, and if it was within my power, I'd make sure she had it. "I thought you'd like the sparkles."

She beamed and threw herself at me. "You're my favoritest ever!"

I chuckled, patting her back. "You'd better hurry and change."

Cady released me and ran into the locker room.

Charlie watched her go and then looked up at me. "Sparkles are her favorite."

"I've figured that one out."

He was quiet for a moment and then looked at the studio. "Heather and her friends are being mean to Cady again, aren't they?"

I nodded. "Do they do stuff at school, too?"

"Sometimes. But not when I'm around."

I let out a huff. Of course, not. One of them probably had a crush on my nephew and knew he would have Cady's back.

"I need you to do me a favor," I said.

Charlie nodded.

"I want you to stick close to Cady for a while. I'm gonna try to make sure those girls don't mess with her anymore."

"You got it, Uncle Roan. We're together like all the time because she's my bestest friend."

I chuckled. "Glad to hear it."

By the time we stepped inside the dance studio, Cady was emerging from the locker room in her new leotard and a glittery tutu. She grinned at me and handed me her bag.

"Knock 'em dead, Tiny Dancer."

Her smile widened, and she bobbed her head in a nod.

The small sea of women along the wall stared at me, mouth agape as I approached. I ignored all of them except for Katelyn Beasley. I flashed her a glare that should've sent her into the ice age.

She snapped her mouth closed and averted her gaze.

"That's meanie number one's mom," Charlie whispered.

"Thanks, bud."

I leaned against the wall, crossing my arms over my chest and scanning the kids in the class. It was mostly girls, but there were also a couple of little boys. "Which one is Heather?" I whispered to Charlie.

Charlie's nose scrunched up, and he motioned to a little blonde in the corner, talking to two other girls. She full-on sneered at Cady as Cady found her place among the dancers.

Anger surged, and I cleared my throat. The dancers looked my way. But my gaze was locked on meanie number one. The moment she saw my focus on her, she blanched. Her gaze flicked to Charlie.

I cast a quick look in his direction and saw that he was mirroring my exact pose and glaring at her. Heather's face heated, and she quickly averted her eyes, turning back to her friends. They kept right on talking, but this time, the glances were cast at Charlie and me.

The class began, and I kept a close eye on the mean-girl trio. Every single time I saw a sneer or caught a whispered comment, I'd clear my throat and pin them with a stare. Halfway through, it stopped altogether.

I saw Cady visibly relax. But it was more than that. She came alive. It was clear she absolutely loved to dance. The sheer joy on her face was a sucker punch to the solar plexus.

Cady spun and twirled, leapt and twisted. I wanted to give the girl her own damned studio by the time she was done. It all made her so happy.

"She's so good," Charlie whispered.

I wasn't sure that any of the kids in this class could be classified as *good*. They were way too young. But Cady had that light in her that made her shine.

I clapped him on the back. "The best."

Cady ran over and launched herself at me.

I caught her with a chuckle. "Tiny Dancer, you are incredible."

She beamed. "Really? You think so?"

"You're the best one," Charlie said.

She turned that smile on him, and I worried we might be in trouble in ten years.

"Thanks, Charlie." Cady moved her focus back to me. "Can you come to every class?"

My brows lifted.

She leaned in close. "They weren't nearly as mean today."

My back teeth ground together. "I'll come anytime you want."

"You're the best, Mr. Grizz."

"Roan," a voice cooed. "I didn't know you knew Cady."

I stiffened as I turned to take in Katelyn Beasley. She was made up to the nines, and there was no denying she was beautiful, but there was an emptiness beneath the beauty that made me cringe.

Cady twisted in my arms to look at Katelyn. "Mr. Grizz is my best friend after Charlie, and he doesn't like meanies."

Katelyn's jaw dropped, but she quickly closed it. "Well, no one should like mean people."

"She means he doesn't like *you*," Charlie said. "I see you be mean to Miss Barlow all the time, and Heather made Cady cry. We don't want anything to do with you."

Katelyn forced a laugh, but it was beyond strained. "Kids, right?"

I stared her down. "I'm going with what they said."

I bent, keeping Cady in my arms, and grabbed her bag. "You ready to go, Tiny Dancer?"

She grinned down at me as Katelyn spluttered in the background. "This is the best dance class I ever had."

Chapter Twenty-Six

Aspen

"I T WAS THE *BEST*!" CADY SAID AS SHE TWIRLED AROUND the kitchen.

I looked up from the chili I was stirring and glanced at Roan, who watched my daughter with a hint of amusement on his face. God, he was a good man. There was no feeling like watching his tenderness around her.

"Mr. Grizz is going to take me all the time so the meanies aren't mean," she added.

My brows lifted at that. "Is that so?"

Roan shrugged. "I don't mind."

I filled bowls as his words hit me in the chest. I'd been in this alone for so long. No help. No one to share the load of both the good and the bad. Getting a taste of it now almost hurt.

The buzzer on the oven dinged, and Roan moved. "I'll get it."

He grabbed oven mitts and pulled out the rolls. He didn't ask where anything was. He already knew. He lined a bowl with a towel and placed the bread inside.

Something about the simple task had me fighting tears. I quickly turned away and got to work, placing the bowls on the dinner table. "Cady, what do you want to drink?"

"Milk, please!"

"Roan?" I asked without looking, as if the sight of him so fully *living* in my space was too much to bear. What would happen when he left? Would everything feel empty? It probably wouldn't be long. Steven and Tyson had stayed away, though I'd caught sight of Steven watching The Brew from across the street.

"Milk's good," Roan said, his voice gruff.

I turned my focus to the milk. I poured three glasses and set them on the table.

Cady slid into her chair but bounced up and down. She talked about dance and school and how Dr. Miller said Dory could be released tomorrow. I didn't know how she ate her dinner between her stream of chattering, but she did.

"Can I please be excused? I want to go practice my pirouettes," she asked with a smile.

I nodded. "Take your bowl to the sink, please."

Cady hopped off her chair, dropped her bowl in the sink, and headed for her bedroom.

Then it was just Roan and me.

I took the napkin from my lap, folded it carefully, and placed it next to my placemat. "Thank you for what you did today."

Roan leaned back in his chair. "It was nothing."

I shook my head. "It was everything to her. To me."

Roan's blue gaze bored into me. "People like Katelyn, her daughter, they just need to know you're not alone. That people are paying attention."

I swallowed hard. "You think it'll work?"

I didn't give a damn about Katelyn and her snide comments toward me. I cared about Cady. What bullying and cruelty could do to her mental health. I wanted to nip it in the bud before she got to middle school, and there were things like social media and real crushes.

Roan was quiet for a moment. "I'm gonna keep showing up. They'll know that I'm paying attention. Gonna tell Law to do the same when he's around. Katelyn wants in his pants, so she might shape up for that reason alone."

I choked on a laugh. "You're throwing your brother to the wolves?"

Roan's gaze locked with mine. "I'd do anything for you."

"Still and quiet, right?" Roan asked.

"Quiet like a mouse," Cady whispered as she leaned against me.

We stood at the back of the barn. All the animals other than the ducks were out in the pastures so we could have that quiet.

Roan had the barn door open as wide as it would go. All the stalls were closed, so there was only one path to the outside.

Slowly, he opened Dory's stall and stepped inside.

The doe eyed him suspiciously. She'd filled out with all the food she was getting here and would be in good shape for winter. She pawed the ground, keeping her distance from Roan.

He moved incredibly slowly, nothing sudden or startling. Just easing her bit by bit toward the stall's entrance.

Dory looked from him to the open door and back. She sniffed the air, took a step, then another one. Her head poked out of the stall, and Cady squeezed my hand hard.

Dory halted, unsure if she wanted to leave her sanctuary. At least with where she was, she knew what to expect. She had no idea what was outside.

Roan simply waited, giving the deer time to get accustomed to the idea.

Her head lifted again, revealing the little patch of white on her neck. Her ears twitched, and she stepped out into the aisle. Then she froze, staring at Cady and me.

I sent her every loving kindness I could think of. Silent messages that everything would be okay. That she was healed now. Safe. That she could be free.

I swore something passed over the doe's eyes. Then she turned and trotted down the aisle and into the early morning sunshine.

We followed after her, watching as she bounded down my drive and into a field across the street. Tears gathered in my eyes as Cady wandered down the driveway for a better view.

Roan stopped beside me, glancing down and taking in my falling tears. He lifted his hand and used his thumb to wipe away the moisture. "What are these about?"

"I just want her to be okay," I whispered.

Roan's hand tracked down, squeezing the back of my neck. "My Tender Heart."

My breath hitched. At the nickname. At the claiming of sorts.

He lowered his head and pressed his lips to my forehead. "She has a fighting chance because of you."

"Mama!" Cady yelled. "She found her friends!"

Roan released me, moving toward Cady. But it took me a beat to get my legs to work. As if the brush of those lips had short-circuited my brain. Finally, I forced myself forward.

Cady pressed into Roan's side. "Do you see them?"

"I do," he said gruffly.

In the field across the road, a band of six deer gathered. One nosed Dory in greeting, and a fresh wash of tears found me.

"Mama, why are you crying?"

"I'm happy, Katydid. We got Dory back to her family."

"We did, huh?" she mumbled.

"Not bad for a pre-school activity," I said.

Cady groaned. "Do I have to go to school?"

My brows rose at that. "You love school. And Charlie will be so sad if you're not there."

"I know, but it won't be nearly as cool as this."

Roan chuckled. "Who knows, maybe you'll find a new animal friend at recess."

Hope lit in Cady's eyes. "We did find a frog once."

"See, more adventures to be had. Now, we need to get going or we'll be late," I said.

Roan helped me get Cady into my station wagon with her backpack in tow. As I closed her in, I looked up at him. "Thanks. For all your help and—"

"You don't have to keep thanking me," he grumbled.

My lips twitched. "Maybe I like thanking you."

Roan only grunted. "Text me. Let me know how the drop-off goes."

I read the subtext beneath his words. He wanted to know if Katelyn gave me any trouble. "I will. See you tonight?"

He jerked his head in a nod. "Drive safe."

I climbed behind the wheel and headed down the drive. There was a war waging in my chest cavity, hope and fear dueling it out in epic proportions. My fingers gripped the wheel tighter as I turned toward town.

I wanted to let myself sink into the warmth that was having Roan in my life. Not to question what this was or what would happen. But that was impossible when I'd lived through what I had. When the person I loved most had been ripped away. It made me doubt that the good things had the power to stay.

Turning into the parking lot, I realized Cady had been talking the entire drive. I winced. Mother of the year over here.

As I pulled to a stop, I caught sight of Charlie waiting by one of the teachers. "Looks like you've got company."

Cady grinned, unhooking her booster seat straps. She was already out and headed for Charlie by the time I rounded the car. He waved at me and grabbed her hand, leading her toward school. Leaving me in the dust.

The teacher smiled. "Those two are a love story in the making."

I laughed. "You might be right there."

I just hoped it had a happy ending.

Climbing back into my car, I headed for The Brew. There were more cars parked out front than usual, and I cursed. Zeke would not be happy dealing with all the customers alone.

There must be a tour group in town. They came through

occasionally, led by outdoor guides who put the groups up at the B&B or Caden's family's resort, The Peaks, if the trip was fancier.

I hurried out of my car and toward the front door. The bell rang as I stepped inside.

The moment the door closed behind me, people were on their feet. Flashes went off, and microphones were shoved in my face.

"Tara, do you still claim that John is guilty?"

"Do you regret your testimony?"

"Where is Lucy?"

My breaths came in quick pants as the crowd surrounded me, black spots dancing in my vision.

I'd been found.

Chapter Twenty-Seven

Roan

I DRUMMED MY FINGERS AGAINST THE STEERING WHEEL AS I sat parked just out of view at the trailhead. We were all spending time at various spots we thought might be likely stomping grounds for the unsub. But my thoughts were a million miles away.

I glanced at my phone for the millionth time. Still nothing from Aspen. It wasn't like her to say she'd do something and not follow through. She'd had plenty of time to drop Cady off and get to work by now.

Worry gnawed at my gut. I reached for my phone to call her, but the device rang before I could even unlock it. Lawson's name flashed across the screen, and I hit accept.

"Hey," I greeted.

"We've got a problem."

That worry in my gut turned to panic. "What?" I growled.

"Those assholes released the podcast. Aspen got to work, and a dozen reporters were waiting for her. Apparently, they sent it to the press yesterday afternoon, hoping to get more coverage."

I spat out a stream of curses as I started my truck. "Where is she?"

"In my office. She's okay but shaken up. I sent Grae to get Cady, just in case. She's going to give her and Charlie a fun skipping school day."

That grinding sensation was back along my sternum. Grae would take care of Cady, I knew it, but God, I wanted to string those podcasters up by their entrails. "I'm on my way."

I hung up without another word, needing to focus on the road. On getting to Aspen.

Gravel spit as I took a tight turn and pressed the accelerator. I made the ten-minute drive in five, tires squealing as I pulled into a parking spot in front of the station.

I yanked my keys out of the ignition and charged toward the front door. It slammed against the wall, and the officer behind the desk jumped.

"M-Mr. Hartley."

I didn't even glance his way, just strode toward the bullpen. Cops read my murderous expression and moved out of my path as I stormed toward Lawson's office.

My brother's door was closed, but I didn't bother knocking. I swung it open to find Aspen on Lawson's couch, her arms wrapped around herself, staring at her lap. She looked so damned small. Vulnerable.

Law moved to my side. "Take a breath. You don't want to freak her out any more than she already is."

I struggled to keep my breathing under control as I crossed the small room. Aspen didn't look up when I approached or when I took a seat next to her.

"Tender Heart," I whispered, slipping a hand under her red hair.

At the touch, she twisted, sliding onto my lap and burying her face in my neck.

I froze. Didn't move. Didn't breathe.

Then my arms closed around her, and I held on tightly. As if my arms could protect her from the nightmare waiting outside these walls.

Aspen didn't cry, didn't speak, she didn't make a damned sound. She just held on.

Lawson studied us with curiosity.

"How bad?" I asked.

He winced, and I had my answer. "Story's been picked up by national news outlets."

"My face will be everywhere," Aspen whispered. "We'll never be safe."

My arms tightened around her. "You're safe. We're gonna keep you that way."

"You can't. You never know who'll turn against you."

Everything in me churned and twisted. I knew what that felt like. Too much. Looking over your shoulder, not trusting anyone.

I stroked a hand down her back. "The attention will fade. Media will move on."

"They never move on," Aspen mumbled.

Her speech was slightly slurred, and I knew the adrenaline crash was kicking in. I glanced at Lawson. "I need to get her home."

He jerked his head in a nod. "You parked out front?"

"Yeah."

"Give me your keys. I'll move your truck around back. Fewer eyes."

My teeth ground together, but I handed my key ring to my brother.

He was gone in a flash, leaving me alone with Aspen. I breathed in her smoky cinnamon scent. I let it calm the most feral parts of me. And then I stood, keeping her cradled in my arms.

"I can walk," Aspen said sleepily.

I pressed a kiss to her temple. "Just let me take care of you. I need it."

"Okay." She turned her face into my neck, squeezing her eyes closed.

The moment I emerged from Lawson's office, Nash was at my side, a worried look on his face. "What do you need?"

"Can you get the back door?"

"Sure." He strode toward it. "Mads is freaking out."

I bet everyone in town was losing their minds.

"Just tell her to give Aspen some time."

Nash nodded as he opened the door. "Call or text if you need anything at all. We can bring food. Whatever."

"Thanks, man."

Nash met my eyes. "We've got your back. Both of you."

That burn had returned. The one that reminded me just how much my family cared and how much I'd hidden from them.

I forced myself to ignore the regret coursing through me and strode toward my truck. Lawson opened the passenger door, and I lowered Aspen to the seat. She blinked up at me, almost as if she were drugged. I pulled the seat belt across her body, a hint of cinnamon tickling my nose.

Straightening, I carefully shut the door and turned to Lawson and Nash. "Text me updates?"

"Of course," Lawson agreed.

I headed for the driver's side of the vehicle and slid in. Aspen barely reacted. A muscle in my cheek ticked. I wanted to end every asshole who'd put her through this torture. Every person who had thrown her most painful moments in her face.

Starting the engine, I backed out of the parking spot and pulled out of the lot. It was then that I saw the reporters milling about at the end of the block. Lawson must've forbidden them from coming on department property, but they were still waiting for their pound of flesh.

Thankfully, they didn't notice Aspen in my passenger seat as we drove by. The trip to her house didn't take long, but I tensed as we climbed Huckleberry Lane. Vehicles lined the road—average cars and news vans alike.

A few choice curses slipped free, and I wished my windows were tinted. "Duck down," I said, reaching behind Aspen's shoulders.

"Huh?" she mumbled.

"Reporters. Duck."

She paled, letting me guide her so she was folded over at the waist.

Thankfully, Lawson had thought ahead, and a squad car was already parked at the mouth of Aspen's drive. Clint, one of the department's long-standing officers, leaned against the hood. He lifted his chin, motioning me by as reporters swarmed.

Even through the windows, I heard their invasive questions, and Clint yelling at them to step back or he'd start putting people in zip ties.

I pressed the accelerator, flying down the drive. At least Aspen's farmhouse blocked us from the road a bit. I pulled to a stop and turned off the engine. "You can sit up," I said softly.

She glanced up at me and then slowly straightened. There was so much sorrow in those beautiful green eyes. "This is never going to end."

I slipped my hand under her hair, squeezing the back of her neck. "It will. It might take some time, but it'll fade." I'd make sure it did. "Let's get you inside."

Aspen nodded slowly, unfastening her seat belt.

I slid out of the truck, rounding the vehicle to help her. She moved a bit jerkily as she climbed the steps, and my worry for her intensified. I slipped the key she'd given me into the top deadbolt, unlocking it and the two other locks. I held the door open as she went inside.

Chauncey was on his feet in a flash, ambling over to us.

"I'm going to let him out real quick," I said.

Aspen nodded. "I'm going to go lie down. I don't feel great."

No one would after an adrenaline crash like that. "Okay. I'll come check on you in a minute."

She didn't even acknowledge my words, just stumbled toward the bedroom.

I clenched and flexed my fingers, trying to find an outlet for my anger that wasn't me putting a hole through a wall. I grabbed a leash from the hooks by the door and whistled for Chauncey.

"Can't risk you running off after one of those reporters. Though I wouldn't mind if you took a bite out of them."

Opening the door, I took the dog to a bit of grass for him to do his business and then guided him back into the house. As I unhooked his leash, I listened. I didn't hear anything, so I headed for the back hallway.

I hovered outside the door I knew was Aspen's. Even with all the nights I'd spent in this house, I hadn't ventured inside her bedroom. It was a no-go zone in my mind.

Swallowing, I knocked lightly. There was no answer.

I turned the knob and eased the door open a fraction. The space wasn't at all what I expected. Instead of bright colors and loud prints, it was muted pinks and grays with a hint of gold here and there.

Stepping inside, I took Aspen in. She was already burrowed under the covers, but she wasn't asleep. She just stared up at the ceiling.

I crossed the distance between us and lowered myself to the bed. "Can I get you anything?"

She shook her head.

I bit the inside of my cheek, searching for something to say. I wasn't good with words. Always said the wrong thing. But I couldn't leave Aspen alone in her head either.

"There's no glitter."

Aspen's gaze shifted to find me. "Huh?"

"Your bedroom. There's no glitter. You usually have it somewhere. A hair tie or headband. The stars on your coat. Shimmer in a sweater."

Her lips curved. "Cady hasn't infiltrated my décor in here."

"You're an amazing mom."

Aspen swallowed hard. "I didn't protect her from this."

I took her hand, squeezing. "That's not on you. It's on those bloodsucking vultures."

"I'm scared she'll somehow hear that it was her dad who hurt her mom."

"We're going to do everything we can to make sure that doesn't happen. I'll have Law call the school and talk to the principal."

Aspen nodded, her eyes drooping. "Thank you."

"Get some sleep. I'll get you something to eat when you wake up."

"Okay…" But she was already dropping off before she could finish her sentence.

I didn't move right away. Couldn't. I just watched Aspen breathe. Let a little of the feral energy coursing through me ease with the even inhales and exhales.

But the worst of the darkness still swirled inside me. Worry and fear surged and fed it. Terror that I could lose this woman who'd come to mean everything.

I leaned back on the porch swing as I stared out at the pastures. How often had I watched Aspen and Cady move around their property, feeding the animals, grooming them, playing with them? I'd thought for sure there was no way the joy on their faces could be real.

Now, I knew it was. But more than that, I knew it was there despite everything they'd been through—loss and betrayal and pain.

One of the donkeys kicked out as the other got too close. A goat sharing the field didn't take too kindly to that and charged donkey number one—the one Cady called Mabel.

I shook my head and glanced at my watch. Aspen had been asleep for over five hours. I'd checked on her three times, watching her chest rise and fall to ensure she was all right. But even telling myself over and over that she was fine didn't help.

I forced my gaze back to the fields, trying to find some of the peace I used to get watching Aspen and her animals. But too many demons circled to find true relief.

The door behind me squeaked, and I looked up to see Aspen

shuffling out in oversized sweats. She frowned at me. "It's freezing out here."

I shrugged. "I like watching the animals." My gaze swept over her face. "How do you feel?"

"A lot better. Sorry I freaked out on you."

"You didn't."

"I went all…" Aspen lifted her hands above her head and made circular motions.

"You've been through a lot."

She studied me for a moment. "Are you okay?"

"Why wouldn't I be?"

Aspen closed the distance between us and lowered herself to the swing. "Oh, I don't know, maybe because you look like you want to tear someone's head off."

My back teeth ground together. "I hate that these jackholes are putting you through this. Hate that they're putting you at risk."

Just voicing it had fear clawing at my insides.

Her hand covered mine. "It's freeing in a way."

"Freeing?"

She nodded, looking out at the pasture. "Don't get me wrong, I'm scared. I think part of me always will be. But I've been hiding for so long, worried about people finding out who I really am. Now, they know. It's all out in the open."

"You don't have to hide anymore," I surmised.

"No. I'll still have to be careful and figure out ways to shield Cady as much as possible. But I'm ready to stand my ground. We've built a beautiful life here, and I'll fight for that."

Seeing a bit of her fire and strength reemerge soothed something in me, but the terror still ate away at my insides. "You're going to be okay."

"Why don't you look like you believe that?"

I cursed the fact that Aspen was always so damned perceptive. "I do."

She was quiet for a moment and then gripped my hand tighter. "Grae told me what happened when you were younger. That you were a suspect in Wren's attack. That people in Cedar Ridge turned against you. This has to bring a little of that back. If you want to talk about—"

"I don't," I snapped.

Aspen stilled but didn't let go of my hand, didn't let my temper or scowl scare her off the way it did with others. "If you don't talk to me, talk to someone. Don't let it take you under."

Pressure built down deep. So much of it, it felt like I might combust. "I don't want anything to happen to you."

I felt her stare boring into my face, carrying a million silent questions with it.

"Got jumped when it all went down."

Aspen's hand spasmed around mine. "Grae didn't say anything about that."

"She doesn't know."

"Because she was younger when it happened?"

I shook my head, keeping my gaze on the animals in the pasture. "None of my family knows."

Aspen sucked in a sharp breath. "Why?"

"They had enough going on. Holt and Grae were a wreck with Wren in the hospital. Nash felt guilty as hell because he'd made Holt late on his way to meet Wren. Lawson was new on the force. My parents were just trying to keep us all afloat."

"But how could you cover up something like that?" she whispered.

I shrugged. "Told the doctor and them I'd fallen off my mountain bike. Doctor didn't believe me, but I was over eighteen. He couldn't do a damned thing."

"You were alone in it."

I turned at that, searching Aspen's gorgeous face. "The same way you were."

She threaded her fingers through mine. "You never reported it?"

"I couldn't see who it was. They got me from behind on my way home. I had a house in town back then. One of them hit me so hard on the head I blacked out. Think that's what saved me. Not any fun to beat on someone who's unconscious."

Aspen paled. "Roan…"

"I was fine. Concussion. A few broken ribs, broken arm. Eye swollen shut. Black and blue."

Her fingers tightened their hold. "But you had to live not knowing who hurt you. The cops got the guys who hurt me when that reporter leaked where I worked. They got some serious jail time. You haven't had any closure. That has to be terrifying."

My jaw worked back and forth. "I'm careful. I watch my back. I'm good."

"You aren't good. You've completely isolated yourself from the rest of the world."

"It's better that way. Easier."

"For who?" Aspen challenged. "You must get lonely. And the rest of the world misses out on the gift you are."

I scoffed. "Doubt the rest of the world sees it that way."

The pads of her fingertips pressed into the back of my hand. "Don't. You're an amazing man. I see it every day. You have a gentleness in you unlike anything I've seen before. You just hide it under layers of scowls and glares."

"Tender Heart…"

"I see you, Roan. The way you are with Cady. With the animals. With me. And I have a feeling the incredible things I've witnessed are just the tip of the iceberg."

I turned, taking her in fully for the first time since she'd walked outside. Her beauty was staggering, but it was so much more than skin-deep. She could soothe a ravaged soul with her presence alone.

Aspen moved then, closing the distance and pressing her mouth to mine. The shock of the contact had my lips parting and my tongue moving of its own volition. No matter how dangerous I knew it was, the need for her was too great. Her taste exploded in my mouth, heaven and hell all wrapped into one. But I knew I'd happily go down in the flames.

Chapter Twenty-Eight

Aspen

ROAN WAS EVERYWHERE—HIS HANDS TANGLED IN MY HAIR, his heat surrounding me. His taste took me under.

He pulled back, eyes wild. "Aspen," he croaked.

"Don't," I whispered. "Please, don't take it back." I didn't think I could handle it if he stole this kiss from me.

"Never." The single word was a guttural oath. His hands framed my face. "I'm not any good at this kind of thing. People. Emotions."

I looked up into those blue depths. "Seems like you're doing a pretty good job to me."

I wanted him to laugh, forget he'd pulled away, and lose himself in me again. Instead, he searched. Those eyes of his probed and tested. "I don't want to hurt you. I wouldn't mean to, but I could."

My hands fisted in his shirt. "Yes, you'll hurt me. Just like I'll hurt you. But if we care about each other, we'll mend it. We'll learn to do better the next time."

A muscle in his cheek fluttered like crazy. As if a silent war raged within him that I would never get to see.

I pressed a hand against his chest, over his heart. "No one has ever made me feel as safe as you."

Roan's Adam's apple bobbed as he swallowed. His hand trailed down, his thumb tracing the column of my neck. "Sometimes, I think you hypnotized me. Can't stop thinking about you. Even when I should be thinking about anything else."

Heat flared, hope rising along with it.

"I used to watch you."

My brows pulled together at that.

Roan flicked his chin toward the mountainside covered in trees. "My cabin's up that way. Looks out over this farm. Even before I met you, I'd sit on my balcony and watch the red-haired woman with her daughter. Always so happy. So patient. So full of *life*. I thought you couldn't be real."

His thumb trailed lower, then he pressed a hand over my heart. "But here you are, this living, breathing thing. A walking temptation."

"Give in," I whispered.

Roan's eyes sparked. "You don't know what you're asking."

"Then show me."

He moved so fast I didn't see it coming. One second, I was on the porch swing. The next, I was in Roan's arms. My legs went around his waist on instinct as he strode into the house.

The door slammed behind us, and Chauncey lifted his head from his dog bed in question.

"Lock," I breathed.

Roan took one step backward, flipping the top deadbolt, and then he was moving again. His long strides ate up the space. He didn't kiss me as he moved, but his gaze was like a physical caress, stroking and teasing.

He made it to my bedroom in a matter of seconds, shutting the door behind us. He lowered me to the floor so slowly it was almost painful. My core pressed against the long, thick ridge in his pants, and I almost whimpered.

"Need you to be sure."

I looked up into his face, infusing every bit of certainty I could into my voice. "I'm sure."

Roan stroked his thumb across my pulse point. "Need control."

I swallowed against the dryness in my throat. "Okay."

That thumb trailed over my chest and down my sternum. His fingers twisted in the hem of my sweatshirt. "Arms up."

There was a grit to his voice, a need, and it had heat pooling between my thighs. I obeyed.

Roan slowly peeled my sweatshirt off and tossed it to the floor, leaving me in my sleep camisole. His eyes flared as he drank me in. "So pretty."

I let my arms slowly fall, soaking in Roan's stare.

His finger traced my nipple through the delicate fabric. It peaked and tightened. "Fuck. Look at that response. So beautiful. So perfect."

My heart sped up as need pulsed low.

"Can I have this?" Roan asked, his fingers toying with the strap of the tank top.

I nodded.

"Words, Tender Heart. I need the words."

"Yes," I breathed.

The camisole was gone in a flash, joining my discarded sweatshirt on the floor.

Roan stepped back, towering over me and taking in every inch of my bare skin. He stilled in front of me, looking at the scar that ran along my collarbone and down my side. I fought the urge to turn and cover myself, but before I could, Roan bent.

His lips trailed across the raised flesh. "I'd do anything to take away this pain."

"Roan." His name was a hoarse whisper.

"Anything," he echoed.

Tears stung my eyes as Roan's fingers followed his lips. He wasn't scared of my damage. It didn't make him flinch. He took me exactly as I was.

He kept moving, circling me, stopping behind me, and tracing a finger down my spine. "Smoother than I ever could've dreamed."

"Roan…"

He pulled me flush against him, my back to his front. I could feel the need pulsing between us, his hardness nestled against my ass.

Roan slid a hand beneath the waistband of my sweatpants and under my panties. I let my head fall back against his shoulder, breathing hard.

His fingers slid down, exploring. Wetness gathered between my thighs. He cupped me. "This heat. Could burn a man alive."

My core clenched at his words. "Roan…"

"Patience."

I pressed my thighs together, tightening around his hand, trying to give myself more pressure, more friction. Just…*more.*

Roan pinched my thigh, making a tsking noise. "Behave."

I twisted my head and bit his neck.

He chuckled, the sound only driving me higher.

"You're mean," I chastised.

Roan's fingers were back, teasing and toying. "I warned you. But you said you were sure. Changing your mind?"

"Never."

"That's my girl," he whispered in my ear, his teeth nipping the lobe as two fingers drove inside me.

I did whimper then. There was nothing I could do to stop it. Those long digits stroked and twisted, bringing me higher and then backing off. It was a glorious torture, and I only wanted more.

"Please," I begged.

"Tell me what you need."

"More," I breathed.

"Be. Specific." Roan's fingers curled.

My mouth fell open on a soft mewl. "That. You. Inside me."

Roan's hand was gone in a flash. Then he sank to his knees, taking my sweatpants and panties with him. He tapped my left leg. "Lift." Then my right. "Lift."

Then, my slippers and every last stitch of clothing were gone. I lowered my hands, feeling the need to cover myself somehow.

"Don't," Roan clipped.

I stilled.

"You're the most breathtaking thing I've ever seen. Don't hide an inch of that beauty from me."

My hands fell to my sides, and I breathed deeply.

Roan's hand traced up my leg to my ass. He gripped it hard. "Perfect." He nipped the globe. "So damn bitable."

A shiver coursed through me, one of heat and need.

He shifted, coming around in front of me but still on his knees, his gaze locked on the apex of my thighs. "Knew you'd be beautiful."

Roan's thumb parted me, and he leaned forward. His tongue flicked across my clit, and I nearly lost my balance. Roan's arm came around my legs, holding me steady. "Still."

I couldn't get a single word out, but I nodded. Roan grinned against my core. His tongue circled that bundle of nerves as his fingers drove inside me. Each swipe of his tongue nearly sent me over the edge. But it was as if he knew what would take me there and wasn't ready for that quite yet.

"Please," I whimpered.

"Need to come?"

"Yes." I was past shame in begging. I just needed release, escape from the pressure building inside me.

Roan added a third finger, pressing on that spot inside as his lips closed around my clit. He sucked deeply, and pinpricks of light danced across my vision. My thighs shook violently as my walls clamped around him. Nonsensical sounds slipped from my lips.

Roan teased out each wave of pleasure. Just when I thought it was over, another surged until my legs finally gave out.

He scooped me up, depositing me on the bed and grinning down at me. "Like that afterglow on you."

My entire body tingled, but it was the mischievous smile on Roan's face that nearly did me in. "Need *you*."

Roan stepped back, his fingers going to the buttons on his shirt. "You've got me."

I gulped as he tugged his undershirt free. I knew Roan was a large man but seeing all that muscle in the flesh nearly had me swallowing my tongue.

"Like the view?"

My eyes met his. "Could look at you forever."

His expression softened as he kicked off his boots, and his fingers went to the button on his pants. "Seems like a waste of time to me." He stilled for a moment. "I don't have a condom."

My mouth went dry. "I'm on the pill to regulate my periods. And I've had a checkup."

"I have, too. And it's been a long time for me."

There was something about that. The trust he gave me, the way he let me in. This was more than sex.

"It's been a long time for me, too," I whispered.

Roan moved in a flash, jerking free the rest of his clothes and then striding toward me. My breath hitched as his big body covered mine. My legs encircled his waist, his tip bumping against my entrance.

Those endless blue eyes sought mine. "You still sure?"

My hand lifted to his stubbled cheek. "Always."

It was all Roan needed.

He slid inside on a long glide. My eyes fluttered closed at the stretch—so much delicious pressure.

"Need those eyes," Roan growled.

My lids flew open.

His expression was almost pained. "There she is."

With that, he began moving. My fingers dug into his shoulders as he thrust deeper, picking up speed. Everything built all over again, quicker this time.

"Torturous heaven," he gritted out.

My back arched, bringing Roan deeper, and he cursed. It set something free in him—that wildness in Roan finally loose.

He took me.

Each thrust was deeper than the one before. Wave after wave of sensation crashed into me, tears gathering in my eyes. It was almost more than I could take.

"One more, Tender Heart. Come with me." Roan's thumb found my clit, circling and then pressing.

I clamped down around him on a cry, the vise grip taking him with me. Roan drove into me again and again. We spiraled together in frenzied need.

Roan collapsed, rolling to his back and taking me with him as he still pulsed inside me.

I struggled to catch my breath. "That was…"

"Fucking awesome?"

That startled a laugh out of me.

"Please don't," he groaned. "You're going to kill me."

I tried to stop but still grinned against his neck. "For as quiet as you are most of the time, you're surprisingly verbose during sex."

He grunted.

"Back to your talkative self, I see," I groused.

Roan flipped us again, sliding out of me, his hand lifting to my face. "Never felt anything like that, what we just had."

My heart stutter-stepped, and I struggled to breathe. "Me either."

I opened my mouth to say something else, but a car door slammed outside. My gaze flew to the clock, and my eyes widened in panic. "Cady."

Chapter Twenty-Nine

Roan

I HAD NEVER SEEN SOMEONE MOVE WITH THE SPEED ASPEN did. She flew off the bed, frantically searching for her discarded clothes. "Oh, my God. I'm going to mother jail. What if we hadn't locked the door? She could've walked in."

I couldn't help it. I chuckled.

Aspen glared at me. "This isn't funny. Would you get dressed?"

My lips twitched, but I sat up, trying to figure out where my clothes had gone. "No one's going to break down the door."

"Men," she huffed, pulling on her sweats.

A knock sounded on the front door, and Aspen jerked upright. "Crap, crap, *crap!*" She whirled on me as she tugged on her sweatshirt. "You get dressed. I'm going to hold off Cady."

I nodded, pressing my lips together to keep from laughing. Aspen was talking about Cady like she was a tiny dictator.

She charged out of the room, and I quickly got dressed and slipped into the bathroom to pull myself together. By the time I finished, I heard voices in the living room.

"Who were all those people, Mama? Mr. Caden made me play a disguise game, and I put his coat over my head when we drove in. He's so silly."

My gut twisted at her innocent words, but I was grateful my sister's fiancé had thought quickly on his feet. The last thing we needed was a photo of Cady getting out to the media.

"Mr. Grizz!" Cady flew at me, and I hauled her into my arms.

"Hey, Tiny Dancer. Did you have fun with G and Caden?"

She nodded her head enthusiastically. "The mostest! We got to go to the stables at the resort and go riding. On a *school day*." She sighed. "I wish I could do that every day. And then Miss Grae took us to get cheeseburgers and milkshakes. I got strawberry, and it was the yummiest."

"Sounds like a pretty epic day." I glanced at Caden. "Thanks for your help."

He nodded, studying me as if I were an alien. "Of course." He paused for a moment. "Crowd outside is getting bigger."

I set Cady down. "Hey, can you get your new board game set up in your room? Then you, me, and your mom can play."

She grinned up at me. "Totes." Then she took off down the hall.

"Totes?" I asked.

Aspen shook her head. "Drew is teaching her all sorts of lingo."

Caden snorted. "Might want to be careful there."

She winced. "Hopefully, he's mindful of little ears."

Caden shifted, glancing from Aspen to me and back again. Aspen's cheeks heated, and she twiddled her fingers. He cleared his throat. "If you guys need a more secure place to stay, you're welcome to take one of the cabins at The Peaks. We have tight security, and no press is allowed onsite without explicit permission."

"Thank you, Caden," Aspen said softly. "I really appreciate that. But we've got the animals, and Cady has her routine. I want to try to keep things as normal as possible."

He nodded. "I get that. But if you change your mind, the offer's always there."

"That's really kind of you."

"I'm sorry for what you've been through. I can't imagine. If you need anything at all, please let us know," Caden said.

Aspen's throat worked as she swallowed. "You're not mad I didn't say anything?"

Caden's expression softened. "We all have our secrets—the things that are hard to share. The only reason we'd want to know is so we could help."

Aspen's eyes misted. "And G?"

I hadn't realized how nervous Aspen was about keeping this secret until right now. Her fingers twisted so hard her knuckles bleached white, and I saw her breaths coming quicker than normal.

Caden's lips twitched. "I won't lie. You'll probably be getting a visit from her sooner rather than later. She's dealing with a mix-up at the resort right now. Otherwise, she would have been here with me. But she loves you. She only wants to make sure you're safe and okay."

"She's just going to be nosy and pushy about it," I muttered.

Caden chuckled. "Roan isn't wrong."

Aspen worried her lip. "She'd be right to be pissed at me."

"She's not," Caden assured her. "I promise."

Aspen nodded, not looking completely convinced.

"I gotta get back to the resort." Caden glanced at me. "Walk me out?"

I instantly went on alert but nodded, following him to the door.

We headed out into the chilly afternoon air and moved toward Caden's G-Wagon. He paused by the driver's door, twirling his keys around his finger. "What's the deal with you two?"

I stiffened. "None of your damn business."

Caden's eyes flared. "Not trying to be an ass, but that woman's been through a lot. You haven't exactly been the relationship type."

I didn't say a word, simply stared back at him.

Caden sighed. "Gigi's losing her mind worrying about Aspen. She's freaking out about the press, the crazy ex-brother-in-law, Aspen's mental health. She's going to be protective of her right now."

A little of the tension bled out of me at that. Caden had my sister's back, and I couldn't begrudge him that.

My jaw clenched and unclenched. "I like them. Both of them. They make me feel…like I belong."

And for someone who'd never truly felt that way, the feeling mattered.

Caden stilled, pain slicing through his expression. "Roan. You do belong. You're family. Your sister loves you like crazy, and so do the rest of your siblings. Your parents, too."

I toed a piece of gravel with my boot. "I'm different. I don't fit."

"Different doesn't mean you don't fit. It just means you make the puzzle that much more interesting. Grae and your family gave me a place to belong when I needed it the most. I couldn't want anything more for you than to feel that."

He clapped me on the shoulder. "If Aspen gives you that? Hold tight and don't let go."

That grinding sensation was back along my sternum. I didn't have words for Caden, but he seemed to understand. He just clapped me once more on the shoulder and climbed into his SUV.

I stood there for a moment, staring out into the fields surrounding the farmhouse.

Don't let go.

I didn't want to. But fear that I'd screw it up dug in deep. Or worse, worry they'd be taken from me.

My gut twisted in a vicious squeeze. I shoved down the fear and turned back to the house.

As I walked inside, Aspen stilled, mid-pace. "What did he say?"

"He was trying to give me the big-brother staredown, which is hilarious since he's younger than me."

Aspen's brow furrowed. "About Grae?"

I shook my head. "About *you*. He was basically asking me my intentions."

Aspen's jaw went slack. "What?"

I chuckled. "You've got lots of people in your corner, Tender Heart. Just need to take a moment to really see it."

Her expression went soft, and a hint of humor entered her eyes. "What *are* your intentions with me?"

I moved in closer, wrapping an arm around her waist and pulling her close. "Lots of this." My mouth took hers, my tongue stroking deep. I'd just had her, yet that fire lit in my veins. The need for more. For everything.

Aspen broke away, struggling to catch her breath. "You need to be registered as a dangerous weapon."

My lips twitched.

Aspen's fingers twisted in my shirt. "I want to take things slow around Cady. I've never introduced anyone to her before."

"I get that. We can go as slow as you need to, as long as you're not kicking me out."

Aspen's gaze shifted to the side.

I pulled her tighter against me. "What?"

She forced her focus back to me. "I like having you here. But sometimes I worry I like it too much."

Beautiful pain spread through my chest—agony and bliss all wrapped into one. "I'm here for as long as you'll have me."

"Mama! Mr. Grizz! Come oooooon!" Cady called.

A smile spread across Aspen's face, hitting me center mass. "Come on, let's go get our butts kicked by a six-year-old."

"I think I had too many meatballs," Cady mumbled, holding her tiny belly.

Aspen shook her head, but a smile played on her lips. "I warned you five might be too many."

"But they're soooooo good."

I squeezed her shoulder. "I feel your pain. I think I might've overdone it, too. We need to walk it off. Maybe do a few laps around the living room."

Cady slid off her chair and grabbed my hand, tugging me to my feet. "We can march like we're in the army. Charlie always wants to play soldiers, so I'm good at marching."

I couldn't hold in my chuckle as Cady strutted toward the couch, bringing her knees up ridiculously high with each step. Chauncey lumbered to his feet and barked, thinking it was a game. The noise sent the demon cat skittering out of her hidey-hole. She launched herself onto the couch with a loud meow.

A knock sounded on the door, making Chauncey bark louder. It startled the cat, and Pirate flew off the couch toward the nearest person. Me. Her claws dug into my shirt and my damned chest. I cursed. Loudly.

"Ooooooh, Mr. Grizz. That's a no-no word. You're gonna have to do an act of kindness to pay that one off," Cady said, still marching.

I peeled the cat off me, glaring at it as Aspen opened the door. She stepped back, motioning Lawson in. "Welcome to the zoo."

His eyes flicked to me and then to the beast in my hands. "Is that a one-eyed cat?"

"It's a demon from the fiery pits of hell." I set Pirate down, and she ran down the hall.

"That's another one, Mr. Grizz. Be careful, or you're gonna get extra chores," Cady warned.

My brother chuckled. "You gotta keep him in line, Cady."

She let out an exasperated sigh. "I'm trying. It's not easy."

Lawson pressed his lips together to keep from laughing outright.

Aspen shut the door. "Is everything okay?"

Lawson turned to her. "I need to borrow Roan for a minute about a case. Not yours," he assured her.

My skin prickled as I saw something pass across Lawson's expression. Something ominous.

"Oh, of course." Aspen motioned to Cady. "Come on, Katydid. Let's pick up your room while they talk."

Lawson turned, glancing at Aspen again. "I heard from an Evan Kemp in Jackson."

She stilled in the hallway. "He's the police officer who helped me get a new identity."

"Seems like a good cop," Lawson said. "He wanted to make sure you were okay. That we were looking out for you."

A soft smile spread across her face, and a hit of jealousy landed in my gut. "He would. I'll text him and let him know I'm all right. He doesn't have my new number."

Lawson nodded. "He's going to be my point of contact at the Jackson PD, so I'll keep him up to date."

"Thanks, Law." Aspen placed a hand on Cady's back and guided her forward.

"Aw, man. I always miss the good stuff," Cady grumbled as she followed Aspen down the hall.

Lawson chuckled. "That kid is hilarious."

I nodded, my lips twitching. "She is."

He studied me for a moment. "Are you…smiling?"

I instantly wiped the grin from my mouth. "Shut up."

Lawson slapped me on the shoulder. "Happy for you, brother."

I scowled at him.

"Unfortunately, I'm about to steal a little of that happiness."

My entire body went on alert. "What?"

Lawson shifted in place. "Just got a call. Body was discovered. Human this time. And the death wasn't accidental."

Chapter Thirty

Aspen

I PICKED UP A RIDICULOUS NUMBER OF STUFFED ANIMALS scattered across the floor as Cady chattered away. But my focus was on the men in the living room. It was as if it'd hit me for the first time that even though Roan worked for Fish and Wildlife, he was still a law enforcement officer. He carried a gun. He could be hurt.

"What do you think, Mama?" Cady asked, breaking into my spiraling thoughts.

"Sorry, Katydid. Can you say that again?"

"I'm gonna be a ballerina on the weekends and a game warder during the week."

My mouth curved. "You mean a game warden?"

She threw her hands out wide. "That's what I said."

A knock sounded on her door, and I quickly opened it. Roan filled the space, his expression stormy.

"What happened?" I whispered.

A muscle popped in his jaw. "Someone was killed. Might be tied to a series of animal deaths." Roan pitched his voice low so Cady couldn't hear.

I sucked in a sharp breath. "Oh, God."

"I need to go to the crime scene."

"Of course."

"The girls and Holt are coming over to hang with you until I get back," Roan said.

"They don't need to do that," I argued.

"Please." Roan slipped his hand beneath my hair and squeezed the back of my neck. "I won't be able to focus if I know you're here alone."

And he needed that right now.

"Okay," I said softly.

He leaned forward and pressed a quick kiss to my forehead. "Be back as soon as I can."

My throat tightened. "Please, be safe."

"Always," he assured me.

"Where ya going, Mr. Grizz? Gotta help another deer?" Cady asked.

"Not tonight, Tiny Dancer. Gotta help Lawson with something."

She nodded as if that made all the sense in the world. "You're a good brudder."

Something passed over Roan's expression—pain or guilt, I wasn't sure. He ignored her statement and instead said, "Take care of your mama."

"I always do," Cady shot back.

We followed Roan to the door just as my friends piled onto the porch.

Grae held up a bottle of wine and pointed it at me. "You are in big trouble."

I winced.

Wren shoved Grae. "Don't freak her out." She strode toward me and wrapped me in a tight hug, even with her pregnant belly between us. "I'm so sorry for everything you've been through."

"I'm sorry I didn't tell you," I whispered.

She just squeezed me harder. "You don't have anything to apologize for."

Wren released me, and my gaze immediately went to Maddie.

She was the person I was closest with. I'd never forgive myself if I hurt her.

Maddie moved quickly to me and pulled me into another hug. "I knew it was bad. I just didn't know how bad. I hate that you've been in this alone."

My eyes burned. "I wasn't, though. I had all of you."

"If you make me cry…" Grae warned.

"Oh, crap," Holt muttered. "I don't know if I'm cut out for this estrogen fest."

Wren smacked her fiancé. "You cried the last time we watched *Little Women*."

"Whatever," he muttered, his gaze cutting to me. "The alarm components for your house should arrive in the next couple of days. We'll get it installed ASAP."

My brows pulled together. "What do you mean?"

Holt grimaced. "Roan didn't tell you that he asked me to order an alarm system?"

"No, he conveniently forgot," I said, pinning Roan with a stare.

He just shrugged. "You needed one."

"Well, I'm guessing I can't afford whatever fancy-A one Holt just ordered."

"It's a friend's company," Holt interjected. "He gives them to me at cost, and Roan and I work for bakery treats."

I just scowled at Roan. "We will be talking about this later."

Grae let out a low whistle. "Someone's in trouble."

"Who?" Cady asked. "Who?"

Grae bent to Cady and stage-whispered, "Roan."

Her eyes went wide. "Uh-oh, Mr. Grizz. You gonna get grounded?"

Everyone laughed.

Roan just shook his head. "Lawson and I have to go. You guys all set?"

Holt jerked his head in a nod. "I got 'em covered."

"Thanks," Roan said. His gaze cut to me, and I saw so much promise in those blue depths. Then, he was gone.

As the door shut, Grae turned to us. "We need some epic girl talk." She glanced at her brother. "Could you play with Cady for a little bit?"

Cady grinned. "We could play tea party, Mr. Holt. It's really fun. I make the best tea!"

Holt winced and glanced at his fiancée. "You owe me for this. Favors for a week."

"What kinda favors?" Cady asked.

Grae snorted. "Real special ones I don't want to know anything about."

Maddie smirked, and Cady just looked confused.

"Come on," Holt said. "Fix me some of this tea."

Cady squealed and ran down the hall, Holt striding after her.

"We need cups," Grae instructed.

I grabbed glasses from the kitchen. "Wren, do you want anything nonalcoholic to drink?"

She shook her head. "I'm good. If I drink anything, I'll have to pee every two seconds, and I don't want to miss anything."

Nerves bubbled up as I grabbed three glasses. I returned to the living room, placing them on the coffee table.

Grae immediately popped the cork with a wine opener she'd brought and started pouring, but she conveniently skipped herself.

I lowered myself to the couch next to Maddie. "You don't want wine, G?"

Her eyes shifted to the side.

Wren jerked upright. "Grae Hartley."

She winced. "I might be knocked up."

"Might be?" Maddie squeaked.

A smile of sheer joy spread across her face. "Okay, I'm most definitely preggers."

Wren burst into tears. "We're going to have babies together. They'll be in the same grade just like we were."

Grae's eyes shimmered. "It's going to be the best," she whispered.

Wren stood and wrapped Grae in a hug. "I'm so happy."

"Me, too."

Pressure built behind my eyes as Wren released Grae. "This is the best news. I needed this today."

Grae shot me a grin. "We can thank Caden's super sperm for that one."

Maddie snorted. "I don't need those kinds of details."

Grae just shrugged and turned to me. "How are you? Really?"

Maddie squeezed my thigh. "You don't have to talk about anything you don't want to."

"The H-E-double-hockey-sticks she doesn't," Grae argued. "I need to make sure she's safe."

"I am," I told her. "At least as much as that's possible."

Wren rubbed a hand over her belly. "I'm so sorry about your sister."

My throat burned. "She was amazing. The best mom ever."

Tears filled Wren's eyes again. "I know she's watching over you and Cady, so grateful for what an amazing mom you are to her girl."

"Thank you," I croaked.

Grae fanned a hand in front of her face. "It's too early for tears." She turned to me. "Are you *really* okay?"

I swallowed hard. "Most of the time, yes. I'm sorry I didn't tell you. I just—it felt easier this way. Safer. If I didn't tell a soul, then no one would ever know."

"Except someone found out," Maddie said softly.

"I don't know how. I got a threatening letter from John, and then the podcasters showed up."

Grae jerked upright. "What threatening letter?"

I winced and recounted the anonymous threat.

"I think you and Cady should move in with Caden and me," Grae said the moment I finished.

"Caden already offered, and I appreciate it. I really do. But I don't want to uproot her. Routine is so important at this age. And Roan's staying here—"

"Wait, what?" Wren asked, shock filling her voice. "Roan is staying at your house?"

I nodded slowly, heat rising to my cheeks. "He has been since the podcasters showed up."

"Roan doesn't even stay at his parents' on Christmas Eve when everyone else does," Maddie said. "Says he can't handle not having his own space."

"I didn't know," I mumbled, the heat flaring in my face.

Grae's eyes narrowed on me and then flew wide. "Holy cannoli, you're banging my brother."

Chapter Thirty-One

Roan

GRAVEL CRUNCHED BENEATH MY TIRES AS I PULLED INTO the parking lot. It was already crowded with vehicles: evidence techs, police cruisers, even the coroner's van. I scanned the surrounding forest. The dark branches and sweeping quiet were in such opposition to what currently teemed inside.

Lawson and I climbed out of our vehicles at the same time. His face looked just as grim as I was sure mine did.

"This trailhead is farther out than the other two," I told him—something he already knew. But my true question was hidden in the words. *Why?*

Lawson scrubbed a hand over his stubbled jaw. "I'm guessing the unsub is a little less brave when they have a human victim."

My gut churned. Hadn't our town seen enough death and darkness?

"Another hiker called it in?" I asked.

Lawson shook his head. "Forest Service. They've had an increased presence just like Fish and Wildlife."

It was then that I saw the guy sitting on a log, a cop I recognized giving him a bottle of water. He wore the Forest Service uniform but couldn't be more than twenty. Twenty-one tops. A kid. His hand shook as he took the water bottle, taking a small sip.

Lawson led us in that direction.

The kid looked up and swallowed hard. "Chief Hartley."

"Brian. You doing okay?"

Brian's cheeks colored. "Lost my lunch."

Lawson lowered himself to a boulder so he was at eye level with the kid. "Did the same thing the first time I worked a case with a body. It's completely normal."

Brian jerked his head up and down in a staccato nod.

"Think you could walk me through it?" Lawson asked.

He was so good at this—the people stuff. Letting others know he cared. That he was with them. It was a gift I'd never have.

Brian's throat worked as he swallowed. "My boss is having us all work different trailheads right now. We're supposed to walk a mile and a half in and then back out, then go to the next one."

It was smart. All the bodies had been found within a mile of the trailheads.

Brian stared down at the water bottle, his hand tightening around it. "I'd already done four others today. Nothing. I just wasn't expecting it."

"Were there any other vehicles in the parking lot when you pulled in?" Lawson asked.

Brian shook his head.

"Did you see signs of anyone else on the trail?"

"No," he answered. "Nothing until I saw *her*."

My gut soured. I hadn't known anything about the victim until right then. But it was a she. It made it more real then, knowing that.

A muscle in Brian's jaw ticked. "It was so bad. Never seen anything like it. Just…awful."

Lawson squeezed the kid's shoulder. "Need you to think really hard. When you were walking back out, did you see anything?"

"I-I don't know. I was kind of in a daze. Had to step off the trail to puke. Made the call on my sat phone. And then I just…waited. I almost thought maybe I'd imagined it. Like I got dosed with something and was hallucinating."

I'm sure he wished that was the case. Poor kid would have nightmares for the rest of his life. He'd signed up to work in the wilderness, not discover dead bodies.

Lawson gave him another squeeze. "We've got mental health services. Want you to take advantage of that."

Brian looked up. "I don't need—"

"Do it," my brother urged. "You don't want something like this getting a hold. Don't want to start looking to booze—or worse—to dull the memories. Face it. Get help. Get healthy."

He nodded slowly. "Okay."

"Good." Lawson slapped him on the back and stood, giving his officer a look that told the cop to stay with the kid. The guy nodded.

Lawson started toward the trail, and I followed, turning on my flashlight. I didn't need the light to hike by. I'd trained my eyes to adjust over the years and could navigate most of these woods blindfolded and with my arms tied behind my back.

But tonight, I didn't want to miss anything. Evidence could be anywhere.

"You take left. I'll take right," Lawson said, flicking his light on.

We moved slowly up the path, taking our time. My flashlight beam swung by brush and trees, rocks and fallen logs. But I didn't see anything out of place. The forest was just as it should be.

But someone had tainted it. Brought evil into a place that had always felt like my respite. Just the knowledge of that had me pissed as hell.

I'd spent so much of my youth escaping here. The trees and creatures had always welcomed me. Never judged or mocked. They embraced me.

Voices sounded up ahead, making me take my focus off the ground in front of me. Lights shone brightly. It almost seemed like the kind you'd find at a stadium. But this was no football game.

Nash turned as we walked up. There was none of the typical

amusement on his face. His brows were pinched, his jaw set hard. "It's bad."

I didn't need his warning to know that. Someone was dead. That was enough.

Yet still, the first sight of the body pulled me up short. The woman was young. In her early or mid-twenties. But there was no life in her, no vitality. Her skin looked almost gray. And her body had been torn to hell. Vicious slash marks and stab wounds. So much rage.

"Luisa," Lawson said in greeting to the coroner.

She looked up, her tanned skin a shade paler than normal. "Law."

"Any guesses how long she's been out here?" he asked.

Luisa's lips pursed as her gaze traveled back to the body. "It's colder than normal for this time of year. That muddies things. But I'd guess it's recent. This afternoon, maybe. I need to check the temps hour by hour for a better estimate. But based on marks on the body, she was killed elsewhere and moved here."

Lawson nodded, his jaw clenching. "That helps."

Dr. Miller stood nearby, but his gaze remained focused on the fallen woman and her stab wounds. As though he could stitch them back together with sight alone if he stared hard enough.

"Thanks for coming out, Damien," Lawson said.

The vet forced his eyes toward my brother. "Of course. These wounds are a little different. Deeper. But there are too many similarities for it to be a coincidence."

Lawson glanced at Nash and me.

"He's angrier," I said. "Maybe he knows the victim?"

Nash pulled an evidence bag out of his pocket. "Got her ID. Marci Peters from Montana."

I tapped my fingers against the side of my thigh. "I don't recognize her. Tourist?"

"Most likely," Lawson agreed. "I'll have an officer call around to the local hotels and rental companies, see if we can figure out where she was staying."

"There's a large lump on the back of her head. Some blood," Luisa said. "She was struck from behind. Probably unconscious before she hit the ground."

"Small mercies," Nash muttered.

I didn't disagree. At least she hadn't felt the torture that came afterward.

Lawson stared down at the woman for a moment. "We were right."

Nash sent him a quizzical look.

"Someone was practicing," Lawson explained.

My back teeth ground together. "That means they won't stop here."

Chapter Thirty-Two

Aspen

THE BED DIPPED, AND I JERKED UPRIGHT, COMING OUT OF a sound sleep. I reached for the Taser on my nightstand, but a hand clamped around my wrist.

"Just me."

My entire body sagged at Roan's voice. "Hell. Are you trying to give me a heart attack?"

He pulled me against him. "Sorry. Didn't know you had some of that demon cat in you."

I frowned in the dark. "Pirate isn't a demon. She's just playful."

"Tell that to my almost decapitated toe."

"So dramatic."

Roan nuzzled his face into my neck, breathing deeply.

My body began to come alive, but I shut that shit down fast. "Cady's down the hall."

"I know," he whispered, his voice gruff. "Just need to hold you for a few minutes."

My hands closed around his arms. "Was it bad?"

"Young woman's dead. That's always bad."

My fingers gripped him harder. "You okay?"

"I've got you in my arms."

"That's not an answer."

Roan's hold tightened around me. "If you're in my arms, I'm always okay."

My heart jerked inside my chest. Large neon letters spelling *DANGER!* flashed in my head. But instead of pulling away like I should have, instead of telling Roan to go back to the couch, I burrowed deeper into his hold.

And let sleep pull me under, feeling safe for the first time in years.

"You had a slumber party without me?"

Cady's affronted voice had me jerking upright and my eyes going wide. Roan was a little slower on the move, not having years of parental quickness on his side. Kids trained you fast. That first plaintive wail after a nightmare. The first slight gagging noise that said they were about to throw up all over their bed.

But apparently, my reflexes had dulled just enough because I hadn't heard Cady's door open, her tiny feet pitter-pattering along the hardwood, or my door opening. She glared at us, hands on her hips. "That's not fair."

Roan pushed up against the pillows, his tee pulling tight across his muscled chest and light brown hair in haphazard disarray. "Tiny Dancer…"

She huffed but flew at us, launching herself onto the bed and burrowing between us. "Next time, I get to come to the slumber party."

Roan pressed his lips together to keep from laughing as his eyes met mine.

It's not funny, I mouthed at him.

"We weren't having a slumber party, Katydid. Roan was just checking on me and fell asleep."

Roan snorted, and I fought the urge to smack him. Hard.

"I still wanna have a slumber party. We can do face masks and glitter nails and hair braids."

Roan's face scrunched. "I am not doing face masks."

I grinned. "Come on, I think you'll look really cute in the princess one, don't you, Cady?"

She giggled. "That one's the best. It leaves your face all shimmery after."

Roan groaned. "It's bad enough I'm catching grief at work for the glitter on my nails."

I choked on a laugh.

Cady tipped her head back so she could look up at Roan. "They don't think it's pretty?"

He clamped his lips closed. "They, uh…it's not my usual look."

Cady nodded knowingly. "You need more pink in your outfits."

I couldn't hold in my laughter this time.

Roan lifted on one arm, staring down at Cady and me. "Is she laughing at me, Tiny Dancer?"

Cady giggled. "I think so."

Roan shifted, grabbing me and tickling my sides.

I shrieked and twisted. "No! I'm too ticklish!"

Chauncey let out a low woof that said he wanted in on the fun.

Roan's fingers lit along my sides, making me squeal so loud I probably woke the animals in the barn. His hand fell away, and he wiggled a finger in his ear. "Hell, you're gonna break an eardrum."

"Bad word, Mr. Grizz," Cady chastised.

"Sorry, Tiny Dancer."

I blew the hair out of my face and sat up. "You're both traitors."

Cady giggled again.

I tickled her sides, and she shrieked.

I grinned down at her. "Payback."

"I'm gonna get you when you least expect it," Cady shot back.

"Well, why don't you pick out your outfit for the day first? I think you can do glitter boots today."

That was all it took. Cady leapt from the bed and charged out of the bedroom.

Roan slipped his hand behind my neck, pulling me to him.

"Morning breath," I warned.

"Don't give a damn."

My chest constricted as Roan's mouth took mine in a slow kiss. As he pulled back, he rested his forehead against mine for a moment.

My fingers fisted in his tee. "I don't want Cady to get confused."

"Does she seem confused?"

I worried the inside of my cheek. "No. But she could be later when you're not staying here anymore."

Roan's fingers tangled in my hair, and he tugged the strand back so I had to look at him. "I'm not going anywhere. You may not need someone with you twenty-four-seven, but I'm still going to be around. A whole hell of a lot."

The corner of my mouth kicked up. "I'd like that."

"Good," Roan said with a grunt.

I pressed my lips together to keep from laughing. "Your sister figured out that, uh, something is going on between us."

Figured out was an understatement. Grae was practically bouncing off the walls with glee.

Roan groaned. "Of course, she did. I'm never going to hear the end of it."

My brows pinched in confusion.

"She was always trying to set me up with friends or telling me to get out there and date. I always said I didn't want to. That I wasn't built for it."

I pressed a hand against the ridges of his abdominals. "What changed?"

"You," Roan said.

I shoved at his chest. "You say you're not good at the relationship thing, but I think you're too good."

Roan chuckled.

"I've got it picked out!" Cady yelled.

I swung my legs over the side of the bed. "Duty calls."

I got to work getting Cady dressed and then myself. I would

try to brave The Brew today. Lawson had promised to station an officer at the door to turn away any media. I had to try because if I couldn't work, my little savings account would be depleted in no time.

Cady tugged me down the hall. "Something smells really yummy."

My brow furrowed. It did smell delicious. I came to a stop just outside the kitchen. The table was set, and each place had some sort of amazing scramble, fruit, and toast.

"YUM!" Cady shouted, hopping over to her chair.

"You made breakfast," I said, my nose stinging.

Roan shrugged. "You need more than sugary cereal to keep up your energy for the day."

When was the last time someone had made me breakfast? It was probably Autumn. Tears gathered as I tried to shove them down.

Roan was in my space in a flash. "Hey. What's wrong?"

I swallowed down the emotion clogging my throat. "No one has taken care of me in a long time."

His expression softened as his hands cupped my face. "Tender Heart."

"Thank you," I whispered.

"I'd do anything for you."

Everything burned in the best kind of way.

"Stop acting funny and eat," Cady said around a mouthful of food. "It's gonna get cold."

That startled a laugh out of me, and I grinned. "She's right. Can't waste this amazing meal."

And amazing it was. We stuffed ourselves silly as we laughed and talked. Roan insisted that he would be driving us to and from work and school. He'd cleared the part-time schedule with his boss. Apparently, he had so much vacation time he could leave the country for two months and still be fine.

As we made the drive into town, warmth spread through me. Having someone to do the little things with, like dropping Cady off, made everything just a little sweeter.

Roan turned into the school parking lot. "Ready to knock 'em dead, Tiny Dancer?"

"Duh!" she shot back.

"That's what I like to hear." He pulled up in the drop-off line and hopped out. I followed, nerves pricking me. I was sure word about my real identity had made the rounds to a good chunk of the town by now.

I tried to focus on Cady as she told us all about her and Charlie's plans for the day while Roan got her out of her booster seat.

Movement caught my attention, and I looked up. Katelyn flounced toward the school, tossing her blond hair over her shoulder and glaring in our direction.

It was a dumb move. Because if anyone could glare, it was Roan. His head lifted as if he sensed her look, and the stare he leveled on her would've made me piss my pants.

Katelyn tripped over her feet, quickly righting herself and hurrying inside.

I snorted. "At least I don't have to listen to her anymore."

Roan grunted and then crouched low. "I want you to stick close to Charlie today. If Heather or those other girls pick on you, just pretend you can't hear them. It'll drive them crazy."

Cady smiled and threw her arms around Roan. "Thanks, Mr. Grizz."

The urge to cry was fast and strong, but I forced it down. Cady released him, hugged me, and then ran for the school.

I looked up into Roan's beautiful eyes. "You're a good man. The best man I've ever known. Don't ever let anyone tell you otherwise."

Chapter Thirty-Three

Roan

ASPEN'S WORDS HAD ECHOED IN MY HEAD ALL DAY. *"You're a good man. The best man I've ever known. Don't ever let anyone tell you otherwise."*

My throat worked as I swallowed, trying to clear the ache there. It was impossible because that ache was everywhere. A pain that only came from coming back to life.

How long had I kept it all turned off—every heightened emotion and feeling? It had helped keep out the bad, but also locked out the good. Until Aspen.

She'd changed everything before I'd even known her name. Those little glimmers of hope and light as I watched her from my cabin perch. As I saw her kindness play out in front of me.

I turned into the police station parking lot. It was more crowded than normal. There were a couple of county sheriff vehicles, Fish and Wildlife, and Forest Service. Seemed Lawson had called everyone in for a meeting of the minds.

I snagged a parking spot in the back corner and headed around front. As I opened the door, the officer behind the desk looked up. "They're in the conference room."

"Thanks," I said with a nod.

The shock on his face was blatant. I cringed. How much of an ass had I been over the years that a simple *thanks* warranted a dropped jaw and wide eyes?

A varied group milled around the conference room. Groups weren't my favorite thing. There was a reason I'd chosen to live most of my life in the wilderness. But I didn't have a choice.

Taking a deep breath, I stepped inside. My boss, Rob, moved in my direction and clapped me on the shoulder. "How are you holding up?"

The urge to scowl was so strong. I hated the idea of anyone in my business, but I knew Rob was asking because he cared, not because he was being a nosy asshole.

"Good. Thanks for letting me work half-time for a bit."

The corner of Rob's mouth kicked up. "You're saving me from having to pay you a ridiculous amount of overtime." The amusement left his expression. "You need any help, just let me know."

I gave him a rough nod. "Appreciate it."

The sheriff called Rob's name, and he turned to answer. I took that opportunity to slink into a back corner, hopefully hidden by the majority of the crowd. Most people gave me a wide berth. They didn't try to talk to me because they knew I didn't do polite chitchat.

That didn't apply to my siblings, though. Nash elbowed his way through the crowd, a bakery bag in hand. He squeezed in next to me, looking annoyed. "Why'd you have to find the most cramped spot in the entire room?"

I gave him a bland look. "You didn't have to stand here."

"Of course, I did. Who else is going to mock Lawson's authoritative voice with me?" Nash pawed through his bag and pulled out a donut.

I snagged the bag from him.

"Hey!" he protested.

I grabbed a glazed donut from the bag and handed it back. "Should've stood elsewhere."

"It's a damn good thing I brought extras," he grumbled.

My lips twitched.

"Holy hell. Was that a smile?" Nash gaped at me.

My mouth went flat again. "Shut up."

"Aspen must be a miracle worker, man."

"Nash…" I warned.

He munched on his donut. "We need to get her into political office. She could broker world peace in no time flat."

I had no doubt.

"All right, everyone," Lawson said as he strode to the front of the room. "Let's get started."

Nash and I shared a look. Lawson's voice always went an octave deeper when he had to speak in an official capacity.

"I appreciate you all coming," he continued.

Muttered acceptances of the welcome rumbled.

"I want to go through what we've got so far. Vic is Marci Peters, twenty-three years old, from Montana. I spoke with her parents last night. She was doing a solo backpacking trip around the Pacific Northwest."

"Stupid," one of the officers muttered. I thought his last name was Hall.

Lawson sent him a quelling look.

I got the officer's point, though. Hiking alone wasn't the smartest move. Anything could happen out there, from a sprained ankle to an animal attack to something twisted like this.

"Marci arrived two days ago. She got a room at the motel at the edge of town and planned to do some day hikes around the area."

"Anyone at the motel see her talking to anyone?" Clint asked, his notepad out.

Lawson nodded. "Spoke with the manager. Sally said Marci was the friendly type, the kind that never met a stranger."

Just like Aspen. Warm. Welcoming. And that had likely gotten Marci killed.

"Officers will be interviewing the guests today. Trying to see if anyone paid her especially close attention."

Sheriff Jenkins nodded. "We get confirmation yet if the knife wounds on the vic match the animal kills?"

Lawson shook his head. "Not yet. Luisa is doing the autopsy today, so we should have that information by tonight."

"If they match, then this was most likely random," Nash added.

Lawson glanced in our direction. "Likely. Anything about her could've caught the unsub's eye. The way she looked, something she did, the simple fact that she was alone."

And if we didn't know why she'd been chosen, it made searching for the perp much harder. As discussions continued, no one said the one thing we all knew: We needed another human victim to find a pattern.

"Okay, I think that's it. Let's all keep in close contact throughout the day," Lawson said. "I'll send out a memo as soon as I get the report from Luisa."

But we all knew what it would say. The chances of those knife wounds not being a match were slim to none.

Everyone began filing out of the room, but Lawson motioned to me. "How's Aspen holding up?"

"As good as can be expected." My lips twitched. "Helped that you ticketed every reporter on Huckleberry Lane."

Nash grinned at our brother. "Abusing police resources for Roan's babe? I like it."

Lawson shrugged, but there was a hint of humor in his eyes. "There's no parking on that road. It's too narrow. It could prevent emergency vehicles from passing safely. I'm just enforcing the law."

"Well, they're gone now, and they haven't come back," I informed him.

"Good. They're still crawling around town, though. I've got an officer stationed outside The Brew, but you might want to pick her up around back. Don't let them get a photo if you can avoid it."

I jerked my head in a nod. "I'm heading there now so we can go pick up Cady."

Nash shook his head. "It's like someone kidnapped our brother and replaced him with a pod person. He's all domesticated and shit."

Lawson smacked Nash upside the head. "Like you aren't?"

They began to bicker back and forth, and I took that as my

cue to leave. I slipped out of the conference room, made my way through the bullpen, and headed outside. It was cold, but the sky was clear, the sun glittering on the lake across the street.

I rounded the building to head for the parking lot, but my steps faltered as I took in two figures waiting just off police department property. I hadn't seen Steven and Tyson since their episode revealing Aspen's new identity and location came out. I hadn't wanted to. I didn't trust myself.

Now, I knew that had been the right move. Fury surged inside me as I stalked toward them.

Tyson paled a fraction, but Steven? He looked like he got a charge out of my anger. An ugly grin spread across his face. "Well, hello, officer."

"Hope you're watching your step," I growled.

"We don't need to watch shit," Steven shot back. "We've got freedom of the press."

"That freedom doesn't carry to your personal lives. I hope neither of you has made any mistakes. I got a brother who can find anything, and since you decided to ignore the warnings of law enforcement, I'm going to let him unearth everything he can find about you."

I'd text Holt the second I got into my truck and have him sic Anchor's tech team on these two.

Redness crept up Steven's throat. "You can't threaten us. We're press."

I snorted. "You're wannabe reporters who don't have real jobs. And that wasn't a threat. It was just a friendly heads-up as to what's about to happen."

Steven surged forward, but Tyson caught his shirt and hauled him back. "Shit, man, don't hit him."

Damn, I wished he would've gotten in a shot. Because then I could've thrown his ass in lockup.

I shook my head and started toward my truck. "Keep him in line, Tyson."

Steven snarled and cursed. "We've got so much dirt on your

precious girlfriend it's not even funny. We're going to ruin her, and you won't be able to do anything but watch."

I forced myself to keep moving, not to give the asshole what he wanted. But it cost me. Because I wanted to remove every threat to Aspen from this Earth—and do it permanently.

Chapter Thirty-Four

Aspen

THE BELL OVER THE DOOR JINGLED, AND I FOUGHT THE urge to groan as Janice Peabody walked inside. I'd thought I wouldn't have to see her for a few weeks after our tiff over how she talked about Roan. But the triumphant smile on her face told me my time was up, and this visit wouldn't be pleasant.

The café had been slammed all day. I didn't blame people for being curious. It was a natural reaction. But I did blame them for treating me like a monkey at the zoo.

There had been a steady stream all morning and into the afternoon. They'd order a drink or treat and then blatantly stare at me as I worked. It made me want to pull on a monster Halloween mask and shout *boo*.

Thankfully, an hour or so after lunch, things calmed down. My regulars like Jonesy and Elsie came in, and Zeke finished his shift. I could breathe again.

Until now.

Janice strode toward the counter, a cat-that-got-the-cream smile on her face. "Aspen. Or do you prefer Tara?"

I jolted at the use of my old name. Just those two short syllables made my stomach cramp and memories threaten.

I did everything I could to keep any reaction off my face. "What can I get you, Ms. Peabody?"

Annoyance flickered across her face. "I just was curious if you felt bad for lying to all of us for *years*."

Jonesy lumbered out of his chair. "Janice…"

I held up a hand to tell him I had this. "I didn't lie to a single one of you."

Janice's brows pulled together. "You lied about your name. About where you're from. About what you did."

"I've got a legal driver's license that says my name is Aspen Barlow. Not a lie. I never actually answered a question about where I'm from; I avoided talking about it. Also, not a lie. And unless you were in that house where I was chased with a goddamned knife and *stabbed*, then I'd back the hell off—also not a lie."

Janice's mouth fell open.

Jonesy started a slow clap.

I let out a long breath. "And now, you can leave and never come back."

Red hit Janice's cheeks as she sputtered. "You can't kick me out. You don't own this coffee shop."

"No, I don't. But I am the manager, and Sue has given me permission to ban whomever I see fit. That's you and the vile bullshit that always comes out of your mouth."

"Well, I never—"

"Shut it, woman," Jonesy snapped. "And get your booty movin' on out of here."

Janice glared at him. "Your family won't be welcome in my establishment anymore when they come to visit."

"They don't want to stay there anyway. Grae got them a discount to stay at The Peaks. They're gonna be livin' in the lap of luxury instead of having to deal with your oversalted eggs."

"I do *not* oversalt my eggs," Janice huffed.

Jonesy shooed her toward the door. "Maybe you're losing your sense of taste along with your good sense in your old age."

Janice didn't even try a comeback for that one, she just stormed out.

Elsie's gaze jumped from the door to Jonesy to me and back to the door. Her jaw was slack, and her eyes wide. "That was…"

"A buncha bullshit," Jonesy muttered and turned back to me. "You okay, darlin'?"

I opened my mouth to say something, but no words came out.

He made his way back to me. "You're shakin'. Why don't you sit down?"

Elsie leapt to her feet and hurried over to me. "Come on."

I shook my head. "I'm not sad," I said quietly. "Not scared."

Jonesy eyed me carefully. "Then what are ya?"

"I'm pissed," I muttered.

He barked out a laugh. "Now that I can get behind. That woman is a piece of work."

"Understatement of the century," I grumbled.

Elsie's lips twitched. "You need water or anything?"

"What I need is a shot of whiskey."

She grinned. "I could get behind that. Maybe we need a night out on the town."

I sighed, leaning against the counter. "Maybe once things calm down. Sorry about the drama."

She waved me off. "Please, this is the most excitement I've had all week."

I chuckled. "Well, I hate that I removed your source of entertainment."

Jonesy snorted. "I can do without that busybody. One of these days, she's gonna look around and realize she has not one friend in the world."

Elsie frowned. "That's sad."

"It is," I agreed. "But she's gotta start to feel those consequences, or she'll never change."

Something flashed across Elsie's eyes. "People rarely feel consequences these days."

I studied her for a moment. It wasn't the first time I'd had a hunch that Elsie had been through some things. It was the tiny things she let slip and the shadows in her eyes. But I never pushed. I knew from experience that would only make her bolt.

"You know what we need?" I said.

Jonesy's bushy gray eyebrows lifted. "What's that?"

"Double chocolate peanut butter cup muffins on the house."

He grinned, patting his stomach. "I'd never say no."

I glanced at Elsie. She forced a smile, clearing those shadows. "I do love chocolate."

Plating muffins for all of us, I sent them back to their respective tables. We all chatted as I worked on cleaning tables, grabbing bites of my muffin in between. Jonesy told us story after story about his childhood in Cedar Ridge. The time when he and his friends stole a boat and took it for a joyride. When they toilet-papered their principal's house.

I sent him a chastising look. "I had no idea you were such a troublemaker."

"It's how I stay young," he said with a charming grin.

I snorted. "It's how you get away with anything."

The bell over the door jingled, and Officer Smith poked his head in. "Is it all right if I use your restroom? That coffee you gave me was a little too good."

I motioned him in. "Of course. It's right down the hall."

He disappeared, and I started to head back to the counter, but the bell tinkled again. I turned to greet the newcomer—and felt all the blood drain from my face.

"Hello, Tara," the man said.

He was at least ten years older than me, his dark brown hair silver at the temples now, but I'd never forget his face. His photo had been printed beneath byline after byline. Ones that questioned whether the cops had found the right person. Ones that called my mental state into question. And worst of all, those that called me a manipulative liar who was jealous of my sister's happiness.

"Get out," I croaked.

Oren Randal just grinned. "That's not any way to greet an old friend, is it?"

Images flashed in my mind. Him shouting horrible questions at me as I ran from the courthouse to a waiting police cruiser. Him waiting outside my office, my home. Never giving me a moment's peace. Telling everyone who would listen where I lived, worked, and spent any time.

My breaths came faster as my body remembered the feeling of constantly looking over my shoulder. Of never feeling safe.

"Get out, or I will tase your ass and get you thrown in jail," I growled.

Oren's eyes flashed. "Wouldn't be the first time you tried to ruin a man's life, would it?"

Roan's imposing figure appeared behind Oren. I hadn't even heard him come in.

"Back away from her before I rip your spine out through your nose."

Chapter Thirty-Five

Roan

MY HANDS FISTED SO TIGHTLY I WOULDN'T HAVE BEEN surprised if I broke a knuckle. The reporter's words swirled in my head, making spots dance in front of my eyes. *"Wouldn't be the first time you tried to ruin a man's life, would it?"*

The guy's head jerked in my direction, and he paled. It was a smart reaction. There was enough fury running through me to snap his neck in a single breath.

But then he made a dumb move. He ignored that flight response and went for false bravado, straightening his shoulders and trying to appear taller. He wasn't successful.

"I was having a conversation with the woman. It's still a free country, isn't it?"

"Sure. You're free to make your choices, just like I'm free to snap your arm in three places before I break your nose," I snarled.

The man's jaw dropped. "You all heard that. He threatened me. I'm going to have you arrested."

Jonesy began to whistle. "The only thing I heard was you intimidating a woman who asked you to leave her establishment."

The reporter's face turned beet red. "I have a right to ask my questions."

I prowled toward him. The rage swirling inside me was a living, breathing thing. A monster hungry for blood. "You don't have any rights. And you sure as hell don't have the right to terrorize an innocent woman with your fucked-up ideas."

He stumbled back a step, then another. "It's the truth. I've spent more time reporting on this case than you'll ever know. I've spent time interviewing the accused. You should listen to what John has to say. He—"

I shoved the man's chest hard. "If I wanted to listen to bullshit, I'd follow you to the damned toilet."

Anger flashed in the reporter's eyes. "Careful who you ally yourself with. She'll take you down, too. Spin lies about you and ruin your life. She's a bitch, just like the rest of them—"

I struck before I had a chance to temper my response, my fist connecting with the man's nose, the punch ending in a satisfying crunch.

He crumpled to the floor in a heap, curling in on himself and cupping his face. "You broke my goddamned nose!" he howled. But his voice was all wrong.

Footsteps sounded in the hallway, and Officer Smith appeared. He frantically searched the room. "Oh, shit."

I glared in his direction. "Where the hell were you? You were supposed to be watching the door."

Aspen stepped into my space. There wasn't even a hint of fear in her beautiful green eyes. She pressed a hand to my chest. "It's not his fault."

"The hell it's not. He was supposed to be watching for assholes like this one."

"I-I had to use the restroom. I'm sorry," Officer Smith stammered.

"Get some damned Depends next time," I clipped.

Jonesy choked on a laugh, but the other woman in the café just stared at the man on the floor, clearly in shock.

The reporter struggled to his feet. "Arrest this man," he ordered Smith, still holding his nose. But the blood had leaked out, running down his face and onto his shirt. "He hit me. That's assault."

Aspen whirled on him. "You might need an MRI because your memory is obviously faulty. You tripped and hit your face on the floor."

The man gaped at Aspen, then his expression went hard. "You lying little—"

I took one menacing step toward him, and he stumbled backward. He tripped over a chair and landed on his ass again.

Jonesy let out a hoot of amusement.

Officer Smith crossed to the man, helping him up. "I'm going to have to escort you out."

The reporter jerked his arm out of Smith's grasp and stomped toward the door. "You can't hide the truth for much longer, Tara. I'm not the only one who sees."

Aspen began to tremble, and I wanted to break the asshole's face all over again.

Officer Smith followed him out with another muttered apology. I strode toward Aspen, framing her face in my hands. "Look at me."

Her eyes slowly met mine, but they were unfocused.

"He touch you?"

"No," she whispered.

"You okay?" I knew she wasn't, but I had to ask anyway.

Aspen's head bobbed up and down in my hands. "He was the worst of them."

My brows pulled together. "You know him."

She swallowed, her throat working slowly on the movement. "Oren Randal. He works for a newspaper in Jackson. When everything came out, most people believed me at first. But he never did. It was like he hated me on principle or something."

Her eyes glistened as she struggled for words. "He'd call at all hours of the day and night. If I got a new number, he'd find it. He'd show up at my house. Find me if I moved to a new place. My work. He'd ask the most horrific questions."

I wrapped my arms around Aspen, pulling her to me. "I'll deal with him," I growled.

Her hands fisted in my shirt. "No. He'll be smarter next time. He'll bait you and have someone recording. You need to stay away from him."

There was true panic in Aspen's words, her fingers so tight in my shirt I worried she'd rip it. I gripped her tighter. "Okay, Tender Heart. I'll steer clear."

She shuddered against me.

I wanted to kill the pissant for her fear alone. But I'd keep my word. I'd try to stay away. However, I'd sic my brothers on him with no apologies.

Aspen tipped her head back. "We need to go get Cady. I don't want to be late."

I nodded. "My truck's in the back lot."

"Okay." She released me and took a few steadying breaths, then turned to her two patrons. "Sorry about the adventures today."

Jonesy patted her on the back. "Don't you worry about a thing, darlin'. You just take care of yourself. Call me if you need me."

"Thanks," Aspen said, stretching up to kiss his lined cheek.

The woman I'd seen in The Brew a few times stood and slung a pack over her shoulder. She took Aspen's hand. "Please be careful. Some of these people…"

Aspen squeezed the woman's fingers. "I will. I promise, Elsie."

She didn't look convinced but nodded.

Once the customers were out the door, Aspen locked up and waved to Smith to let him know she was leaving. "Okay, I'm ready."

I wrapped an arm around Aspen's shoulders, guiding her toward the hall. She made a quick stop to grab her purse and then we headed for the back door. My heart still hammered against my ribs in a painful beat. Punching Oren hadn't done a damn thing to satiate my rage.

We came to a stop by the passenger side of my truck. Aspen turned to face me, her eyes searching. "Are you okay?"

I stared down into that questioning gaze. "You're asking me if *I'm* okay?"

She gave me a tiny shrug. "You did just punch someone in the face. I should've gotten you some ice before we left."

"My hand's fine." It ached like hell, but I didn't care. The pain only helped keep the edge off my fury.

Aspen lifted a hand and pressed it to my face. "Thank you."

A burn lit beneath her touch.

"For making me feel safe for the first time in five years."

Panic coursed through me like a wildfire taking out dry brush. I wanted to give that to Aspen. More than anything. But the fear that lived inside me said I'd fail when it truly counted.

I pressed my forehead to hers. "I'd do anything for you. Anything."

Aspen's breath hitched. "I know."

I stood there for a moment, just breathing in her cinnamon scent and letting it calm the beast that still raged inside me. After a minute, I released her and opened her door. "Let's go get our girl."

Something flashed in Aspen's eyes that looked a lot like hope as she slid into the truck.

We made the drive in less than two minutes and pulled up to the carpool line just as school was getting out. Cady ran toward my truck, and Aspen got her situated in the back.

"Mr. Grizz, we had art today, and I drew you a picture. It's of me and Dory. That way, you'll never, ever forget Dory, and this is like her telling you thank you. It's in my backpack."

My ribs constricted, squeezing my lungs. "Thanks, Tiny Dancer."

She kicked her legs up and down, glitter boots shining. "Can Charlie and I have a playdate tomorrow? There's no school."

Aspen twisted in her seat. "I don't see why not. Let me text Lawson and see if it's okay with him."

"Yay!" she cheered. "I'm gonna marry Charlie one day. Then we'll all be family."

My eyebrows just about hit my hairline. "You're too young to be thinking about marriage."

"Not *now*, Mr. Grizz. Later. When I'm old like Mama."

Aspen snorted. "Gee, thanks."

My lips twitched. "Just as long as you're not thinking of running away on us now."

"Never! I'm having way too much fun. Our slumber parties are the bestest."

Aspen glanced my way. Some of those shadows had cleared with her daughter's excitement. "Being the *bestest* is the highest compliment she's got."

"Nuh-uh," Cady argued.

Aspen arched a brow at her. "Then what is?"

She grinned. "Sharing my glitter nail polish."

I barked out a laugh. "Good to know."

When I pulled into Aspen's drive, there wasn't a reporter to be found, but Lawson still had a cruiser parked out front. I knew that was a sacrifice with the murder case going on at the same time, and I appreciated it more than I could say.

I waved to the officer as we turned in. By the time I parked, Cady was bouncing in her seat. "I gotta get out."

Aspen hurried to get Cady free and unlock the door. "Do you need to pee?"

"Nope!" Cady ran inside, and Aspen gave me a puzzled look.

A second later, Cady reemerged, putting on a helmet.

"Katydid," Aspen said. "Let's save bike riding for after your snack."

"I'm not riding my bike," she called, running toward the pasture.

We trailed after her.

"Where are you going?" Aspen yelled.

"Ms. Breaker taught us about goats today. She said this is how they play."

Cady slipped through the rails on the fence and headed straight for the four goats. They all brightened at her arrival. Then she lowered her head and ran toward one.

Aspen gripped my arm, but the goat just lowered his head in answer, and they headbutted. Cady let out a giggle as she turned to the other goat. They crashed into each other, and Cady went flying with another giggle. "I'm a goatie now!"

A laugh rumbled out of me as the third goat started nibbling on Cady's pant leg.

Aspen stilled next to me, her gaze slowly finding mine. There was wonder in those green eyes.

"What?" I asked.

"Most beautiful sound I've ever heard—you laughing."

Chapter Thirty-Six

Aspen

"AAAAAAYEEEEEE!" Charlie shouted as he flung himself off the monkey bars.

I winced as he landed with a thud. "Lawson's never going to let me watch Charlie again if I bring him back in a full-body cast."

Grae laughed from her spot next to me on the bench. "My brother is raising three boys. Almost all of whom have been in a cast at one point or another. He knows there's no stopping them."

Cady let out a higher-pitched squeal as she flew off the monkey bars like Charlie.

Roan moved as if he were going to launch himself off the bench. I grabbed his arm to stop him, and he snapped his gaze in my direction. "I don't think it's safe."

My insides went squishy in a way that only happened when Roan looked out for my girl. "She has to learn her limits."

I glanced around the park for the tenth time, checking for any sign of reporters. There was nothing. I'd tucked Cady's red hair up in a beanie, and I had mine woven tightly in a bun and covered with a ski cap.

Caden chuckled as he glanced at Roan. "I'm pretty sure you gave your parents daily heart attacks at that age."

Roan just grunted in response, and I couldn't hold back my smile.

"I'm pretty sure that means yes," I said.

Grae grinned. "It's impressive that you're already becoming fluent in his grunts."

I patted Roan's chest. "It'd be hard to have a conversation otherwise."

Grae burst out laughing.

Roan glared at both of us. "Stop ganging up on me."

I bit back my giggle. "Come on, big man. You can take it."

Roan leaned in close, whispering in my ear. "There's gonna be punishment for that later."

I shivered. "God, I hope so."

He growled low, the sound washing over me.

Grae groaned, and I quickly looked up, following her line of sight. Katelyn was heading toward the park with two other moms, their daughters in tow.

"What?" Caden asked, confused.

Grae glanced at him. "Don't you remember Katelyn from high school?"

Caden shuddered. "I think I tried to block out any memories of her. She's ruthless."

Katelyn's gaze narrowed on the four of us as she sat on a nearby bench with her friends. She tossed her blond hair over her shoulder and began whispering to her cohorts.

I didn't give a damn about her; I was worried about her daughter picking on Cady. Heather glared at Cady but then glanced in Roan's direction, swallowing hard. Instead of starting anything, she tugged her friends toward the other side of the playground. I let out the breath I'd been holding.

Grae turned to me. "Did you let Roan threaten that little mean-girl-in-training? You knew I wanted to, but you wouldn't let me."

Caden choked on a laugh. "You want to go toe-to-toe with a six-year-old, Gigi?"

Grae let out a huff. "If she's being mean to Cady, I do."

"Roan might've taken Cady to dance one day and been his usual brooding self," I told her.

Grae grinned at her brother and held out a hand for a high-five. Roan smacked her palm.

"You're both incorrigible," I muttered.

Katelyn's voice raised. "She's been lying to everyone for *years*. It's shocking that Lawson even lets Charlie go with her."

My molars ground together, but I ignored her.

Grae started to get up, but I grabbed her arm. "Don't," I whispered. "She's not worth it."

"She shouldn't be allowed to spew her bullshit," Grae growled.

"It'll only make her do it more if you say something."

Grae's mouth pulled down in a frown, but she nodded.

"You know, that podcast said she might have lied about the whole thing," Katelyn said louder. "Maybe she's the one who did it."

I glanced at Cady to see if she could hear Katelyn, but she was happily playing with Charlie, oblivious to it all.

Roan took my hand, squeezing it. "Want me to go over there?"

I shook my head. "No, let's just ignore her."

Out of the corner of my eye, I saw Katelyn's gaze narrow on our joined hands.

"It's sad, really, Roan ending up with her. He's already been through so much. The whole experience must have twisted him, everyone thinking *he* was the murderer. He's clearly unstable now. He definitely shouldn't be around children. But it's no surprise Aspen doesn't care. She just sees dollar signs."

Roan's jaw went hard as granite. But it was more than that. There was defeat in his gaze. An acceptance that this was how some of this town would always see him.

I was on my feet before I could stop myself. Roan called my name, but I didn't listen. I strode toward the three women on the bench.

Katelyn smiled triumphantly. "Aspen, how nice to see you."

"Sadly, I can't say the same. It's funny the bullshit that streams out of your mouth because, really, the only person who's sad here is *you*. If you had a shred of decency, I'd actually feel bad for you. I've tried to be kind, even in the face of your ugliness. Tried to ignore you. But sometimes a bully needs to be hit with the cold, hard truth, and that's what you are: a bully."

I sucked in a breath. "It's truly pathetic that the only way you seem to feel good about yourself is by putting others down—good people who have done nothing to you."

"He's dangerous—"

"Don't," I snapped. "The only reason I haven't broken that perfect nose is because I don't want to scare the children in this park. But if you say one more word against Roan, I will find you, and I will rectify that."

Katelyn's jaw dropped.

I turned to her friends. "Think about who you spend time with. Who you let your *children* spend time with. Her cruelty is becoming known in this town. And I, for one, wouldn't want to be associated with it."

"You're the one the people in this town should be worried about. You're probably a murderer," Katelyn spluttered.

The other two women shared a look and then glanced at Grae, Caden, and Roan. Whatever they saw there had them rethinking their life choices. They stood and motioned to their daughters.

Redness crept up Katelyn's neck. "Rachel. Perrin," she hissed. "Where the hell are you going?"

The one named Perrin turned around. "She's right. You've always been a bit of a bitch, but it's been on overload lately. I know you're bitter about your ex leaving, but pull it together."

Katelyn went completely slack-jawed. Then she turned furious eyes on me.

"Don't even think about it," I warned. "You're only going to dig yourself a deeper hole. Pull your shit together and see if you can figure out how to be a decent human being."

I felt a presence at my back, and Grae stepped up next to me. "She's right. Think about your words real long and hard. I've picked up knife-throwing as a hobby and wouldn't mind a new practice dummy."

Katelyn snatched her purse off the bench and stood. "Come on, Heather. We need to leave. This park isn't safe anymore."

"Not for the likes of you," Grae muttered.

I had to turn away. I worried if I kept watching Katelyn, I'd go after her and really break that perfect little nose. As I turned, I caught sight of Roan. I was expecting fury. Hurt even. Instead, I found his shoulders shaking as he laughed so hard that tears filled his eyes.

I gaped at him. "You're laughing?"

He struggled to get composure. "You threatened to break her nose."

"It only seems fair. You broke someone's nose for me."

Roan grinned, pulled me into his arms, and nuzzled my neck.

I breathed him in, letting his scent swirl around me. "I hate that people say this crap about you. Makes me livid when you're the best person I've ever known."

His arms tightened around me. "Tender Heart." The nickname was a gruff utterance. "I don't give a damn what they say. I give a damn what *you* say. And it seems like you'd go down into the fiery pits for me."

I tipped my head back. "I'd follow you anywhere."

"Please don't make out right now," Grae muttered. "I'm happy you two are together, but I don't need to see that."

Roan shot his sister a scowl.

Grae held up both hands. "Why don't we take Cady and Charlie for a sleepover at our house?"

"You don't have to do that," I argued.

Caden wrapped an arm around Grae's shoulders. "We'd be happy to."

Grae sent him a soft smile. "Might be good practice."

This time, Roan turned a gentle look on his sister. "Happy for you, G."

"Don't make me cry. My hormones are already going crazy," Grae sniffed, smacking him. Then she turned to the playground. "Sleepover at my house!"

The kids cheered.

Roan brushed the hair out of my face. "Now what are we going to do with an entire house to ourselves?"

I pulled my robe tighter around myself as I stepped out of the bathroom and listened. I'd expected Roan to be on me the second we walked through the door, but he wasn't. He'd taken the dog out. Made me a cup of tea. So, finally, I'd taken a shower. Now, I didn't see or hear him anywhere.

Maybe he'd gone out to the barn. I couldn't deny the hint of disappointment that flickered to life. But I ignored it and headed into my bedroom.

I came up short when my bare feet hit the carpet. Roan stood by the window, shirtless, in nothing but low-slung uniform pants. I nearly swallowed my tongue.

Slowly, he turned, his gaze heating as he scanned my body.

I didn't miss the opportunity to drink him in. The wide expanses of muscle, the lightly tanned skin, that dusting of hair that teased his chest and then disappeared in a thin trail beneath the band of his pants.

"All clean, Tender Heart?"

Roan's voice was liquid smoke and had my toes curling into the carpet as I forced my eyes to his face. "Yes."

He moved toward me like an animal stalking its prey.

"I like this." Roan's fingers twisted in the fabric of my silk robe.

"It's soft," I explained, something he already knew.

"Not as soft as this." Roan's hand slipped beneath the fabric to tease the skin of my chest.

My breath hitched.

"Softer than silk. Like a flower petal." His head dipped, and he ran his lips along the opening of my robe.

My fingers hooked into the waistband of his pants, needing something to keep me steady.

Roan's hands moved to the tie at my waist. Slowly, he tugged it free, and my robe fell open. "So damn beautiful. More beautiful than I ever could've imagined."

Heat pooled low. My nipples pebbled under his stare in the cool air.

Roan traced one peak with his finger. It tightened, seeking, searching for more of Roan's touch.

"Do you trust me, Tender Heart?"

What a loaded question for someone like me. Someone who had been through battle after battle. Who had lost it all time and again.

But I breathed deeply and told him the truth. "Yes."

Maybe that made me a fool. Maybe it made me the bravest woman in the world. But all I knew was that Roan had me, body and soul.

His eyes flared with blue heat, and his fingers found the tie. He pulled it free from the loops, draping it over his broad shoulder.

My brows scrunched, but not for long because then Roan was ridding me of the robe altogether. It fell to the floor, and he sucked in a breath. "I could stare at you forever."

His finger trailed over my core, his eyes becoming hooded. "Already aching?"

"Yes." It was as if Roan had me in some kind of truth haze.

"Let's see what we can do about that." His eyes flashed again. "On the bed."

His voice took on a snap—a demand for control.

There was a rush of wetness between my legs.

I moved slowly toward the bed and lowered myself to sit.

Roan watched me as if I were the most riveting thing he'd ever seen. "Lie back."

I bit my lip and did as instructed.

"Hands above your head."

My breaths came quicker as the pressure between my thighs built. I lifted my arms.

Roan moved to one side of the bed, his eyes locking with mine. "You sure you trust me?"

"Always."

The blue in his eyes swirled and changed. Turned heated, desperately needy, and maybe just a little bit in love.

Roan pulled the robe tie from his shoulder and secured my hands to the iron headboard. As he tugged the silk taut, my heart hammered against my ribs. Everything felt heightened.

He stared down at me. "Look how beautiful. Your back arched." His finger traced the curve. "Your breasts on display for me to taste." His lips closed around one bud, and he sucked hard.

A whimper left my lips. A zing of sensation shot from nipple to clit, and I pressed my thighs together.

"Need me?" he cooed.

"Yes," I breathed.

Roan straightened in a flash and strode to the end of the bed, unbuttoning his fly. "I had plans to tease you. To make you wait. But I need to be inside you."

There was a God in heaven.

He shucked his pants and prowled toward the bed. His hand ghosted up my thigh. "Ready for me?"

I opened my mouth to answer, but then Roan's fingers slid inside me, and all that came out of my mouth was a mewl.

He grinned. "That's my girl."

My core clamped down at the words.

Roan cursed and slid his fingers free. "You're playing with fire." A smile stretched my lips. "Not afraid to get burned."

Roan's eyes flashed, and he hooked my legs around his waist. A second later, he thrust inside. No warning, just taking. And, God, it was everything.

My eyes fluttered closed as I tried to absorb every sensation.

"Uh, uh, uh," Roan chastised. "Don't close your eyes. I want to see every ounce of pleasure you're drowning in."

I forced my lids open as Roan thrust deeper. My hands tugged at the bindings, wanting freedom to get to Roan. To feel him. But not being able to move made the rest of my body only feel *more*.

Roan angled his hips, taking me deeper. I whimpered but didn't let my eyes close.

Roan's hand slipped between us, his finger circling that bundle of nerves.

My hands held tightly to the belt, gripping it with all I had as he arched impossibly deeper. Then his finger pressed down.

There was no warning, no easing into things. I came with lights dancing across my vision and muscles jerking to attention.

Roan cursed as he emptied himself into me, and I took it all. Wave after wave of pleasure rolled through me until I simply collapsed, Roan on top of me.

I struggled to catch my breath. "I think you just gave me a stroke."

Roan pulled back a fraction, a smile playing on his lips. "I'm taking that as a compliment."

"Cocky," I muttered.

"No." He nuzzled my neck. "Just obsessed with your body. Going to make it my mission to learn every inch."

Chapter Thirty-Seven

Aspen

I TOOK A SIP OF MY COFFEE AND WATCHED MY FAVORITE presentation: the Roan breakfast show. The corded muscles of his forearms bunched and flexed as he expertly flipped an omelet. Then he grabbed the second pan and did it all over again.

It was my favorite way to spend the morning, watching Roan and listening to Cady talk about all her various plans for the day. One week had slid into two, and we were all just…holding.

There hadn't been another murder, and most of the reporters had left. Everyone except Oren and the two podcasters, Steven and Tyson. The normal news media had realized there wasn't a story here. At least not one they'd have access to. And the locals had mostly stopped staring, too. They were curious but not rude, giving me space.

Yet still, Roan stayed.

He hadn't mentioned going back up to his cabin at all. And he was no longer sleeping on the couch. Cady hadn't batted an eyelash at the change. She just liked having her best pal in close proximity.

"Whatcha starin' at, Mama?" Cady asked around bites of her eggs.

My cheeks heated. "I like watching Roan make omelets."

She bobbed her head in a nod. "Me, too. He does the flip thing, and they're the yummiest."

Roan sent a smirk in my direction as he plated our food.

"It's not nice to be cocky," I called.

"What's cocky?" Cady asked.

"It means you've got a big head," I explained.

Her nose scrunched. "Mr. Grizz's head looks normal to me."

Roan chuckled as he set my plate in front of me and kissed my temple. "See? I'm perfect."

I grunted.

Cady giggled. "You sound like Mr. Grizz!"

Roan just laughed harder.

I'd never get tired of the sound. It was deep, raw, and real, and it wrapped around me like the warmest embrace.

Those laughs were coming easier these days, too. More often. But I didn't take a single one for granted.

I took a bite of my omelet and moaned. The veggies and cheese exploded on my tongue in the perfect combination.

Roan leaned in. "Keep making those noises, and I'm gonna have to take you out to the barn before school."

My face heated as my gaze flew to his. We'd had to get creative when it came to finding time together, but I didn't care one bit.

"I like the barn," I whispered back, my voice going husky.

"I wanna go to the barn!" Cady chimed in. "The barn is way more fun than school."

I stifled a laugh and turned my attention to Cady, studying her for a moment. "Is Heather being okay?"

Cady worried her lip between her teeth, and I braced to hear what awful thing the little girl had done lately. "I feel bad for her," Cady said with a sigh.

My eyebrows hit my hairline. "Why?"

"Her friends don't play with her anymore. She's sad."

I winced. That had been my doing when I called out Katelyn and made her friends aware that the town was paying attention. "What do you think you should do?"

Cady thought about it for a moment. "I'm gonna see if she wants to play with me and Charlie at recess. If she's mean, I won't ask again, but maybe she learned her lesson. Like when you give me a conserquwence."

I pressed my lips together to keep from laughing. I didn't have to punish Cady often. I could count on one hand the times I'd had to do it this year. But she always took the fact that I was disappointed in her behavior the hardest.

"I think that would be really kind of you, Katydid."

She grinned at me and slid out of her chair to take her plate to the sink. "Kind hearts are the best hearts."

"Yes, they are." I glanced at Roan to find him frowning. "What?"

"I don't want that girl to hurt her."

My heart gave a painful squeeze. The depth of care he had for Cady reached a spot inside me I didn't know existed.

"Heather might hurt her. But Cady's strong. She's surrounded by people who love her." It wasn't just me anymore. It was Roan, his siblings, their partners, and his parents. Through them, I'd found the thing I'd always been missing: family.

Panic filled Roan's expression. "Why do you look like you're about to cry?"

A laugh slipped from my lips. "Because I'm happy."

The tension in Roan's face eased. He reached up to cup my face. "I'm glad."

"Thanks for making me that way."

"Tender Heart," he whispered gruffly. "Don't have time to fuck you this morning."

I snorted, pushing to my feet to clear our now-empty plates. "So romantic."

He smacked my butt on the way to the sink. "And don't you forget it."

"I'm ready," Cady called as she pulled on her coat.

We piled into Roan's truck and headed for school. It didn't take us long to drop Cady off. I caught a brief glimpse of Katelyn, but she mostly avoided glancing in our direction. And Heather did look a little sad.

"I feel bad for Heather," I mumbled as we headed for The Brew.

Roan flicked his gaze to me in question.

"She's a kid. She learned to be mean from her mom. It's not even her fault."

Roan grunted.

"She needs someone to show her the way."

He pulled to a stop near The Brew. "You've got eighty-two animals and a daughter. The last thing you need is to take on another kid."

"I didn't say anything about taking her on."

Roan twisted in his seat. "Know you, Tender Heart. You really gonna tell me you aren't thinkin' about bringing that little girl into the fold?"

I shrugged. "Would that really be so bad?"

"If I have to deal with her mom, it would be."

I winced. "You have a point there. I'll come up with a plan."

Roan just shook his head, and then his eyes narrowed on something in the distance. "That fucker."

He was out of the truck in a flash, and I hurried to follow after him.

Roan strode down the sidewalk and past The Brew to a narrow alley between the buildings. "Get the hell out of there before I decide someone's trying to break in and shoot."

A curse sounded, and Oren stepped out of the shadows. "I haven't gone into that godforsaken café. You can't touch me."

"That's where you're wrong." Roan took one giant step forward, and Oren stumbled back.

"Get the hell away from me."

Roan's eyes narrowed. "You're the one who keeps showing up in our lives. Think it might be time for you to get one of your own."

"People have the right to know the truth!" Oren shouted.

"Except you're not giving them the truth. It's why your paper fired you, isn't it?" Roan snapped.

I sucked in a breath. Roan hadn't shared that tidbit of information.

Oren's face heated. "I'm freelance. My narrative can't be controlled."

"Have fun publishing that on conspiracy theory websites," Roan snarled.

Oren struggled to keep his breathing under control. "People are going to see that all of this is lies from a bitter woman. Someone who couldn't handle her sister's happiness. Just you wait."

He stormed off, and I gaped.

"What is wrong with him?"

Roan sighed, moving into my space and wrapping me in his arms. "I didn't want to ruin our night, but remember when Holt called?"

I nodded. We'd been mid-game of Sorry! with Cady, and Roan had stepped out onto the front porch to talk to his brother.

"He's had his security team at Anchor doing some digging on Oren, Steven, and Tyson."

"He didn't have to do that," I mumbled.

Roan just shook his head. "He wants to help."

"You two already have my house rigged like Fort Knox."

"We do not," he argued.

"Whatever," I grumbled.

Roan squeezed the back of my neck. "Holt's team hasn't found a lot on Tyson and Steven yet, but Oren is a different story. His wife had an affair, and he found out not long before your case broke. From everything we can tell, he's turned into a hell of a misogynist. And he's active on some pretty messed-up forums."

I shivered. "And he lost his job?"

Roan nodded. "His paper didn't want him out there covering the case. They didn't think there was anything left to report on. But he wouldn't take no for an answer, so they let him go."

"That doesn't sound like a good combination of things."

"No," Roan agreed. "It doesn't."

My gaze dropped to the ground. "Is that why you've been sticking close?"

Roan took my chin in his fingers and lifted. "You want me gone?"

I swallowed hard. "No."

"Good," he said with a grunt. "Because I'm not going anywhere."

I hummed as I wiped down tables. The tune wasn't even discernible, but I didn't care.

Elsie glanced up from her computer as I came by. "You seem like you're in an extra good mood."

"I am. I'm happy."

Jonesy chuckled. "Well, that's sayin' something considering what you've been through these past few weeks."

"You know, sometimes going through the hard stuff just makes you appreciate the good things more," I said as I dragged my rag across another table.

Something flickered in Elsie's eyes that told me she understood. "There's something powerful in finding purpose to the pain."

I nodded, wondering what she'd been through. I kept hoping she might open up, but she never did. Still, she hadn't left Cedar Ridge. Maybe she was trying to find the courage to be a part of a community again.

"It's finding those little silver linings," I agreed.

Like the fact that all the events of the past month had brought Roan into my life. Into my home. Into my bed. And he wanted to stay.

The urge to giddy-squeal embarrassingly loud was strong. He hadn't said anything about officially moving in, but I wasn't sure what else, *"I'm not going anywhere,"* could mean.

The bell over the door jingled, and I turned to welcome the newcomer. Only it wasn't a customer. It was a guy who looked to be in his early twenties, carrying a massive spray of red roses.

"Aspen Barlow?" he asked.

"That's me," I said, crossing to him.

Elsie let out a low whistle. "That man of yours is not messing around."

"Thanks," I said to the guy, taking the flowers and setting them on the counter. I frowned at the arrangement. This didn't really seem like a Roan choice. He was more of a wildflowers-he-picked-on-a-hike kind of guy. But maybe I was wrong.

I pulled the card out of the holder and opened it.

RED FOR ALL THE BLOOD OF YOURS THAT SHOULD'VE SPILLED. NOW IT WILL.

Chapter Thirty-Eight

Roan

I STRODE INTO THE CONFERENCE ROOM TO FIND NASH STUFFING his face with a sandwich while Lawson combed through a file on the table.

Nash lifted his chin. "Hey, man."

I grimaced at him. "Your face is covered in mustard."

He shrugged and kept eating. "I'm hungry."

"You say that like it's a new revelation," Lawson muttered. "You're always hungry."

I lowered myself into the chair next to Nash and nabbed a potato chip.

His hand smacked down on mine. "Do not eat *my* potato chips."

"Get a grip. There are more in the vending machine," I grumbled.

"Then go get yourself some. These are my favorites. They're maple bacon. Mads orders them special for me."

I jerked my hand free and popped the chip into my mouth. "Mmm. They are good."

"You're a bastard," Nash growled.

"Children," Lawson warned. "Please dial it back before everyone else gets here. I don't want to have to stick both of you in the drunk tank."

Nash scrunched up his nose. "It smells like puke in there. I'd never be able to finish my sandwich."

I snorted. "Always has his priorities."

I moved to snag another chip, but Nash hauled the bag to his chest. "Mine."

I couldn't help it, I laughed. He looked like Gollum in *Lord of the Rings*.

Both my brothers' eyes widened, and they gaped at me.
"What?"

Lawson shook himself out of his stupor. "You laughed."

"So?" I said, a hint of annoyance slipping into my tone.

Nash studied me for a moment. "It's not that you never laugh; you chuckle sometimes. But it's not like that."

Lawson grinned. "It's Aspen. She's got him whistling a merry tune these days."

"Oh, grow up," I muttered.

Nash leaned back in his chair. "It's true. You're different. Lighter. You talk more, too."

It was probably because I was around Cady all the time. She never stopped talking. I'd gotten used to the noise instead of constant silence.

I fought the urge to squirm in my seat.

"Happy for you, man," Lawson said. "Commitment looks good on you."

I glanced at my older brother, taking in the circles under his eyes and the scruff on his jaw. "Could look good on you, too."

Lawson's face closed down. "Think I'll pass on that."

Nash popped a chip into his mouth. "It's a freakin' waste, seeing how all the single women in this town would give their left ovary for a chance at the chief of police."

He glared at Nash. "They would not."

I arched a brow at him. "I don't know about that. I've seen you with some stage-five clingers."

That glare turned to me. "I think I liked you better when you didn't talk."

Nash burst out laughing. "That's cold."

I just shook my head, but my lips twitched. "You guys were always on me to *participate, join in*. Careful what you wish for."

"Don't worry, I'm regretting it right about now," Lawson muttered.

A knock sounded on the open door, and Sheriff Jenkins stepped inside. "Afternoon."

"Bruce," Lawson greeted.

"Law," he said in return, taking a seat. "How are things around here?"

"Quiet," Lawson said. "I don't like it."

Sheriff Jenkins frowned. "I get it. That prickle at the back of your neck that says this isn't over."

Lawson nodded.

Nash set his bag of chips down. "Maybe the vet and Luisa are wrong. If the knife marks aren't actually a match, then this death could be an isolated incident. Wrong place, wrong time sort of thing."

Sheriff Jenkins let out a low whistle. "Don't be letting Luisa hear you think she got it wrong."

Lawson chuckled. "I've learned my lesson once before."

The corner of Sheriff Jenkins' mouth kicked up. "I've done the same. Won't make the mistake twice."

"It was just a thought," Nash grumbled.

"Or someone's waiting for the heat to die down before they make another move," I said.

Sheriff Jenkins glanced at me. "I'd guess that's more likely. I saw the photos of the body. This was either extremely personal or someone with a taste for killing."

I nodded and turned to Lawson. "Did you get ahold of Anson?"

Lawson's mouth thinned. "Yeah."

"Who's Anson?" the sheriff asked.

"An old friend of mine who used to be a profiler with the FBI."

Nash scoffed. "Can you call him a friend when he tells you to screw off whenever you get in touch?"

Lawson pinned him with a stare. "He went through a lot during his time with the bureau. Wants away from that world. I get it. I could just really use his insight right about now."

"I take it he wasn't eager to help?" Sheriff Jenkins asked.

Lawson shook his head. "He hung up on me."

Nash chuckled.

"Hell," Lawson muttered. "He might be broodier than Roan used to be."

I scowled at my brother. "You're an asshole."

My phone buzzed in my pocket, and I pulled it out. A text flashed on the screen.

> **Tender Heart:** *I got something at The Brew. I think it might be from John.*

I was on my feet in a flash, moving for the door.

"What the hell, Roan?" Lawson asked, getting to his feet.

"Aspen."

It was the only thing I said, and it was all my brothers needed. They followed me out the door and through the police station.

Blood roared in my ears as I shoved open the door and stepped out into the sunlight. The brightness didn't do a thing to warm the frigid ice swimming through my veins.

"What happened?" Lawson clipped.

I shoved my phone at him, and he cursed as he read the text message. "She's fine. She's at The Brew. Safe."

My gut churned. He didn't know that for sure. We had no clue what was in play.

Fury pulsed through me as I picked up to a jog.

Lawson grabbed my arm. "You need to pull it together. Going in there like this will freak her out."

I struggled to get my breathing under control, but each inhale and exhale was painful. "This asshole tried to kill her," I gritted out.

"And he's locked up in prison," Nash reminded me.

"He got out a damned letter. Whatever he sent her today. What else can he do?"

The panic reared up, nearly taking me to my knees.

Lawson's eyes widened. "You love her."

My mouth snapped closed. I wasn't even sure I knew what love was.

"You're just figuring that out?" Nash clipped. "Of course, he loves her. Roan doesn't like to spend more than an hour with anyone, and he's been living in her house for weeks."

Something shifted in my chest. A painful rearranging of muscle and bone. And as it moved, a deep knowledge settled into place.

I was in love with Aspen Barlow. Her daughter, too. And if anything happened to either of them, I'd never survive.

Chapter Thirty-Nine

Aspen

I STARED AT THE FLOWERS ON THE COUNTER. I DIDN'T WANT to touch them. Even to throw them in the trash.

I hated that John was winning. That he still had the power to terrify me. Anger surged so fast and fiercely it nearly stole my breath. And on its heels came a burning behind my eyes—the pressure of tears. But I refused to let them fall.

The bell over the door jingled, and I swung around as if John himself might walk through those doors. But it wasn't him.

Fury had carved itself into Roan's face as he stalked toward me. Most people would've taken a step back, trembled even. But Roan's anger was comforting in a way. It told me he cared.

Roan pulled me into his arms, holding me tightly. "You're okay?"

"I'm fine," I mumbled into his chest.

I could hear that others had entered the café and tried to extricate myself from Roan's hold, but he held firm.

"Need a minute."

His voice was gruff, almost pained, and my heart cracked. But I didn't move. I let Roan hold me, taking what he needed, assuring himself I was okay.

Finally, Roan slowly let me go. His hand lifted to my cheek, his thumb sweeping back and forth. The callused tip sent a shiver through me. "Need you to be okay."

"I am," I promised.

Lawson cleared his throat. "What happened?"

I turned to see him, Nash, and a worried Jonesy and Elsie. Heat hit my cheeks. The last thing I wanted was another scene at The Brew. But I guessed we were past that point. "I got those." I inclined my head toward the flowers. "But they came with a card."

Roan moved to the counter where I'd dropped the note. He let out a series of curses that deserved an award. "How?" he gritted out.

Nash pulled out his phone and started texting. "I'll have someone bring some evidence bags and gloves."

"God, I hope there are prints," Lawson said, pulling out his own phone. He tapped a few things on his screen and held it out between us.

It rang a few times before a woman picked up. "Cedar Ridge Floral and Gifts, how can I help you?"

"Hey, Nan. It's Law. You fill an order for red roses to be delivered to The Brew?"

"Sure did. There a problem?"

Lawson glanced at Roan, whose muscles were strung so tightly it was a miracle he hadn't ripped something. "How'd that order come in?"

"Mail, actually. Someone sent cash and their own card. Card was sealed. Said it was a surprise for an old friend. What's going on?"

"You still have the envelope?" Lawson pressed, not answering her question.

Nan was quiet for a moment. "I don't think so. Came in yesterday. We've taken the trash out already."

Roan's jaw clenched, his teeth grinding.

"I'm going to send someone over to check. Okay?"

"All right, Law," Nan agreed.

"And put a hold on any flowers going to Aspen Barlow," Lawson said.

"You need to tell me what's going on," Nan pushed.

"You watch the news lately?" he asked.

"You know I don't want to fill my head with that garbage. I watch my soaps, and that's it. Plenty of drama there."

Lawson shook his head. "We'll explain when we stop by."

"All right, then," Nan agreed and hung up.

"Probably the only person in Cedar Ridge who hasn't seen your face everywhere," Nash muttered and typed on his phone. "I'll tell Clint to head over."

"Who doesn't check the damned card?" Roan growled.

I turned, pressing a hand to his chest. "It's not her fault."

Roan pulled me against him again. I could feel his heart beating against my cheek.

Lawson looked at Jonesy and Elsie. "Did you guys see anyone suspicious around the time the flowers were delivered?"

Jonesy shook his head. "No, but I wasn't paying real close attention."

As Lawson turned to Elsie, her gaze dipped, and her cheeks heated. "It was just us in the café. I didn't see anyone outside," she mumbled.

Lawson, oblivious to Elsie's reaction, shifted his focus back to me. "You notice anyone who shouldn't have been here?"

I frowned. "You think it could be someone here?"

Roan's hold on me tightened as if he could shield me from the entire world.

"We need to look into every possibility. You've gotten a lot of media coverage over the past couple of weeks," Lawson said.

"Oren was waiting outside this morning," Roan growled. "And those two damn podcasters are still here."

Nash's eyes flared. "Is Oren also dead at this point?"

"Not yet," Roan gritted out.

"Not helping, Nash," I chastised.

He sent me an apologetic smile. "Sorry, but that dude is just asking to end up in a shallow grave somewhere."

I turned in Roan's arms so I could face him and framed his face in my hands. "Look at me."

He didn't at first.

I pressed more firmly against his cheeks, feeling the stubble biting into my palms. "Roan."

His head dipped, his eyes meeting mine. But he was somewhere else. I stretched up onto my tiptoes and kissed him. I put everything into the kiss, trying to reassure. To comfort.

When I pulled away, *my* Roan was there again.

He pressed his forehead to mine. "Tender Heart."

"Don't do that," I whispered.

"Do what?"

"Disappear on me."

Roan pulled back, searching my eyes. "I'm with you. Always."

"This is making me all sorts of uncomfortable because I feel like you're about to go find a closet to bang it out," Nash muttered.

Lawson smacked him upside the head.

"Hey!" Nash rubbed the back of his head. "That hurt."

Lawson's phone rang, and he glanced down. Tapping the screen, he put it to his ear. "Hey, Nan. You remember something?"

Lawson's expression went stony. "Thank you. Just leave it on a table. Don't touch it again. Clint's coming over to your place now."

He disconnected and shoved his phone into his pocket.

"What?" Roan demanded.

Lawson looked at us. "She found the envelope the order came in. There was no return address, but there was a postmark. Jackson."

"John," I whispered. I hadn't been sure about the handwriting this time, but now we knew.

And just like always, even when he was locked up, he found a way to reach me. To hurt me. But this time, he wouldn't settle for torment. He wanted blood.

Chapter Forty

Roan

I EASED THE PORCH SWING BACK AND FORTH AS I STARED AT the dark fields and forests. The quiet shadows had always been a comfort. A blanket of nothingness that soothed.

But not tonight.

Everything in me was still churned up. It was all I could do to hide it from Cady. But Aspen saw it all. She always did.

Lawson had put a call into the prison to see about locking down John's privileges and talked to Evan at the Jackson PD. The problem was, we didn't have hard proof it was Carrington. Just that it was *someone* in Jackson. The best the warden could give us was that he'd have guards keep a closer eye on John.

I knew that wouldn't actually happen. They were already stretched thin. And keeping eyes on prisoners twenty-four-seven was impossible.

The hinges on the door squeaked as Aspen stepped out. She pulled her long coat tighter as she made her way to the swing. "Aren't you freezing?"

I shrugged. "I don't really feel it." It was a miracle I felt anything at all.

Aspen lowered herself to the seat next to me and nestled close.

It was one of the things I loved about her—how she always burrowed deep. It didn't matter if I was in a piss-poor mood or not. Nothing kept her away.

She looped her arm through mine and dropped her head to my shoulder. "I'm worried about you."

That was her, too. Honest. Straight to the point. Always caring about others.

"Tweaked me," I admitted, gazing at the starry sky.

"Me, too," she said quietly.

"Hate that. Hate that he still has ways to get to you after everything you've been through."

"Lawson said the guards are keeping a closer eye. Maybe they'll catch something," Aspen said hopefully.

I tugged her closer to me. "Always looking on the bright side."

"It's better than the alternative, don't you think?"

I shrugged. "I think it's good to be prepared for what might come. And it's not just John. I went to the site Oren's been posting on. Read the comments section of Steven and Tyson's podcast. There are some seriously messed-up people out there."

Aspen was quiet for a moment. "People who think I lied about John."

That grinding sensation was back in my chest. "I know what can happen when people get stuck on a wrong idea. You could get hurt—"

"I've already been hurt," Aspen said, cutting me off. She pressed her hand over her scar. "I was almost killed." Her green eyes bored into mine. "I've been harassed and attacked. And guess what? I'm still here."

Fear dug in its ugly claws. "Nothing can happen to you," I whispered, my voice turning gruff.

Aspen reached up, her hands framing my face again. "It already has. I was alone and made it through. I have no doubt that I'll make it through again with you at my side."

Fire lit in my veins. "How do you have that kind of belief in me?"

"Because I see you, Roan. After you almost scared me to death coming out of a blizzard like the abominable snowman, I realized that all that gruff exterior was just trying to hide the most gentle core."

"Tender Heart…"

"It's true. I hate that you hide your true self from everyone around you. It's time you let them see."

My ribs tightened around my lungs, making it hard to breathe.

Aspen's thumbs stroked across my cheeks. "Stop hiding. There's no reason for it. You're the most amazing man I've ever known."

Those three little words teased my tongue, but fear kept me from setting them free. "Don't know what I did to deserve you."

A smile pulled at her lips. "I am a pretty awesome catch."

I chuckled, and a bit of the pressure in my chest released. My lips brushed against hers. "You are."

The kiss deepened. My tongue stroked in, teasing and toying. I'd never get tired of that taste. It burned through me. Made every nerve ending stand at attention.

Aspen moaned into my mouth, and my dick twitched.

Her pull was so strong, so fierce. I'd never fight it off. And I didn't want to.

I moved then, hauling Aspen so she sat on my lap facing the fields.

"Wha—?"

I cut her off with a nip to her ear. "Stay still. Think you can do that for me?"

She squirmed on my lap, and I groaned.

"Don't make me spank you."

She squirmed again.

I chuckled, but the tone was darker. "Like that idea?"

"Maybe."

I grinned and trailed my lips down her neck. "Want to feel you come on my fingers, but you have to be very quiet."

Aspen's breaths turned to short pants, punctuating the air. "Yes."

My grin widened. I unzipped her coat. The sound echoed like a cannon in the quiet night.

I slipped a hand beneath the waistband of her sweats, then into her panties. The groan was back on my lips. "This heat could give third-degree burns."

I cupped her, and Aspen pressed into my hand with a whimper. "Still," I commanded.

She listened.

That ready acceptance had my dick straining against her ass.

My fingers slid inside, and Aspen's mouth fell open on a pant. "You feel like heaven."

I pumped my fingers in and out, stretching and twisting, relishing every flutter of her core. It was like figuring out all the colors you could paint with. Which twist and flick brought her higher. What tempo made her quiver.

A third finger slid inside, and Aspen let another whimper free. The sound wrapped around my cock and squeezed.

I thrust in and out, faster and faster, as Aspen's legs started to shake. My thumb found her clit and pressed.

She bit back her cry as she clamped down so hard on my fingers that I'd likely have bruises. "That's it. Give it all to me."

Her head tipped back, her lips parted, and she rode every crest and wave. I pulled each swell of pleasure, over and over, until she collapsed against me.

I slowly slid my fingers from her heat and licked them clean.

Aspen jerked upright. "You did not."

My lips twitched. "My favorite flavor."

Her jaw dropped, and she hopped to her feet, pulling me up and tugging me toward the door.

"Where are we going?"

Aspen shot me a grin over her shoulder. "You had your fun, it's only fair I get mine. And my bathroom has great insulation."

Chapter Forty-One

C ADY BOUNCED UP AND DOWN IN HER BOOSTER SEAT.
"They're going to bring bugs and snakes and lizards and
all sorts of things."

I fought a shiver at the word *snake* but tried to hide it. Cady
loved *all* living things, and I didn't want to change that for her.

"What do you think will be your favorite?" Roan asked from the
driver's seat as he turned into the elementary school parking lot.

"Hmm," Cady said thoughtfully.

My gaze slid to my phone again. I'd gotten the alert two minutes into the drive, and my stomach had been in knots ever since.
Steven and Tyson's podcast had a new episode.

I worried the inside of my cheek as I stared at the title they'd
given it. *Who's Lying Now?*

"Lizard!" Cady shouted, breaking into my thoughts. "But I heard
he's gonna bring a dragon."

My brows lifted at that. "A dragon?"

Cady and Charlie had been beyond excited for The Bug Guy to
visit their classroom, but dragons seemed extreme.

Roan chuckled. "I bet he has a bearded dragon."

I turned to glance at him. "That sounds dangerous."

"No, they actually make great pets," Roan informed me.

"Maybe we'll get one of those next, Mama. I want a dragon."

I pinched the bridge of my nose where a headache was building. "I think we've got a full house right now, Katydid."

"We'll see," she singsonged.

Roan just laughed harder.

"Stop it," I whisper-hissed.

He pulled to a stop in the pickup line and bent to kiss me. "You'd never say no to an animal in need."

Cady giggled. "Don't do that in front of Charlie. He doesn't like kissing."

Roan grunted. "It's a good thing. If that changes, you let me know."

"Okay, Mr. Grizz," Cady said, unbuckling her straps.

I jumped out of the truck and helped her down, then bent to give her a quick squeeze. "Love you. Have the best day."

She smacked a kiss on my cheek. "You, too, Mama!"

Then she was gone, running for the doors of the school.

I watched her go for a moment before turning back to the truck. How long did we have before I had to tell her the truth about her father? How long until she would be aware of all the articles and podcasts and *Dateline* specials?

I opened the door and climbed inside. Roan watched me as I buckled my seat belt and then pulled away from the curb, not saying a word. But instead of heading straight to The Brew, he pulled to the side of the street in front of a gallery that hadn't yet opened.

"What's wrong?"

I stared at my hands in my lap. "New podcast episode."

Roan cursed. He unbuckled my belt and pulled me closer to him. "You don't have to pay any attention to that noise."

"Cady will hear it all one day. That's what I hate the most."

He sighed. "We'll be there to help her through it when the time comes."

My heart rate ratcheted up. *We.* God, I wanted that. Nothing felt like too much with Roan by my side. Somehow, his gruffness soothed the worst of any situation.

"Are you going to listen to it?" he asked softly.

"Probably," I admitted. It was like a car wreck I couldn't turn away from. One I needed to shield Cady from however I could.

Roan plucked the phone from my lap. "Then we listen together."

He tapped a few buttons on the screen, and the now-familiar intro music began to play.

"*Welcome to Twisted Lies, The True John Carrington Story. I'm Steven.*"

"*And I'm Tyson.*"

"*Today, we've got a special guest joining us,*" Steven said. "*A reporter who has covered this case from the beginning, Oren Randal.*"

My stomach dropped, and Roan slid his hand into mine, weaving our fingers together.

"*Welcome, Oren,*" Tyson greeted. "*It's great to have someone who's been with this case in real time.*"

"*It's a pleasure to be here,*" Oren said. "*We need people like you keeping this case in the forefront because I don't think we have the right person behind bars.*"

I gripped Roan's hand tighter. All I could think about was the implications of Oren's casual words. If John ever got a retrial, this could poison the jury pool. Cady could hear this, possibly causing her to question things, not to mention it could make everyone in my day-to-day life look at me differently.

"*I'm glad to hear you say that,*" Steven cut in. "*I'm not even saying that Tara Monroe meant to lie. She could've been traumatized by finding her sister. By being accidentally stabbed. Her mind could've automatically decided John was the killer, even though there's a very plausible case for him not being involved.*"

Oren scoffed. "*Oh, I think she lied on purpose. I think she was jealous that Autumn loved John so much. That they had this happy life she wasn't all that involved in. She saw a chance to get some payback for John stealing her sister away and took it.*"

"*I don't know,*" Tyson said. "*We got copies of the forensics reports this week, and that blood evidence on John was pretty damning.*"

There was silence for a moment.

"You seriously think she's telling the truth?" Steven asked, shock evident in his voice.

"You saw the photos," Tyson said. *"How do you get that kind of blood on you? It looked like spray."*

"He loved his wife," Oren cut in, voice tight. *"He said time and time again that he held her after he found her."*

"But that doesn't explain—"

Steven cut Tyson off. *"It does explain. If you lift someone with those kinds of wounds, blood is going to get everywhere. I can't believe you're starting to fall for her sob story. She's a manipulative—"*

I hit stop on my phone. "I can't listen anymore," I croaked.

Roan hauled me into his lap, cradling me to his chest. "Don't. They don't have any damned evidence. It's just the same half-cocked conspiracy theories."

Tears burned my eyes. "I can't imagine how scared she was. I told her I'd always have her back, always be there for her. And when she needed me the most, I didn't."

"Aspen." Roan brushed his hand over my hair in soothing strokes. "You fought for her every step of the way. You're still fighting for her. For the girl she gave life."

I let out a hiccuped breath. "I miss her."

"Of course, you do." He pressed his lips to the top of my head. "Tell me about her."

"She's the one who invented cocoa smash."

I could feel Roan's mouth curve against my hair. "You mean that instant cavity in a bowl?"

A laugh burst out of me. "She invented it when I wanted ice cream with chocolate syrup after a bad day, but we didn't have any. It's way better anyway."

"Sounds like a really good sister."

"She was the best," I whispered. "We didn't have a lot growing up. It was just my mom and us. Mom couldn't seem to hold down a job. Sometimes, we got lucky, and she could scrounge together enough money for an apartment. Other times, it was a shelter or our car."

Roan's grip on me tightened.

"I was okay, though, because I always had Autumn. She made sure I was all right. Safe. Warm. Fed."

"She was more like your mom."

My throat burned. "Yeah."

We were quiet for a moment, Roan just holding me tightly and soothing the worst of the hurt.

"I think that's why she stayed with John longer than she should've. Because she wanted the family we never had. She was so desperate to give her daughter a good life."

Roan cupped my cheek, tipping my head back. "But now you're giving Cady that good life. Look at how loved she is. How full of magic her life is. *You* did that."

I swallowed, trying to clear the ache in my throat. "I've tried. So damn hard. But things really soared when your family came into our lives."

The Hartleys had given us so much. Cady's best friend. Women who had become like sisters to me. Kerry's motherly nurturing and care. Nathan's sweet gruffness. Holt's, Nash's, and Lawson's brotherly ways. And Roan.

He had become the greatest gift of all.

Roan brushed his mouth against mine and then pulled back. His gaze bored into mine. "You've given me more than I ever could've imagined. Even before I knew you, you were this spark of light in the shadows. But being in your orbit? It's so bright it casts out everything else."

I pressed a hand to his chest, feeling the steady beat there. It wasn't an *I love you*; it was so much better. It was raw and real and…Roan.

The woman stared at me for a beat too long as I offered her the bills and change in my hand. My stomach twisted. I didn't recognize her as a local and hoped like hell she wasn't a reporter.

She licked her lips as she took her change from me. "I'm so sorry about what happened to you," she whispered. "Know that you're believed."

Her eyes shone, a glimmer of tears there as her gaze connected with mine.

My throat tightened. There was an understanding in her expression. Something that told me she'd seen the effects of abuse in one way or another. "Thank you. I can't tell you what that means."

She nodded and shoved the change into the tip jar. "Stay safe."

"I will."

And then she was gone.

A weight lifted off my shoulders, something I'd carried for years. And all it took was one stranger telling me she believed me.

"You okay?" Jonesy asked from his usual table.

I cleared my throat and shot him a smile. "I'm good. Better than good, actually."

Elsie's lips twitched. "That got anything to do with the big, burly man in your bed?"

I snorted. "It doesn't hurt."

"I bet." She grinned and turned back to her computer, getting to work on editing her newest batch of photos.

I frowned at the computer screen. "You're still holding off on going up into the mountains, right?"

Elsie sent me a sheepish smile. "I went on some trails yesterday—but close to my cabin, I promise. There haven't been any more incidents, so I think it's fine."

I pinned her with my best motherly stare. "You should at least wait another week or two. And bring a Taser and bear spray when you go."

She grinned at me. "I promise I'll bring both."

"Thank you," I said, letting out a breath.

I turned to grab my rag and cleaning spray. Tackling the bathrooms was my least favorite task at The Brew, but someone had to do it. And it was better to get it done while things were quiet.

As I stepped past the pantry, I heard the squeak of hinges. I turned, but it was too late. A hand clamped over my mouth, and someone jerked me back into a broad body.

"Listen, you little bitch. You're going on the record and telling everyone you're a lying sack of shit. You're going to recant your testimony and finally give John his freedom," Oren snarled, his breath hot in my ear.

I moved on instinct, my elbow jerking back in a hard thrust. I'd watched countless self-defense videos on YouTube and practiced the moves until I knew them by heart, but I'd never actually used them.

Oren grunted, his hand loosening around my mouth.

I twisted, my hand coming up in a palm strike. Unfortunately, he managed to dodge the worst of it, so it only pissed him off.

Oren's fist struck out, catching me across the cheek.

I saw stars for a moment, but the adrenaline kicked in as he grabbed for my shoulders. My knee jerked up on instinct as I yelled.

Oren collapsed to the floor with a cry as Elsie and Jonesy ran into the hallway.

"What the hell happened?" Elsie asked, her eyes wide.

That was when I started to shake. "I think I broke his balls."

Chapter Forty-Two

Roan

L AWSON LEANED AGAINST THE COUNTER OF THE SPORTING goods store on the outskirts of town. "Has anyone coming through seemed off at all?"

The woman behind the counter stared blandly at him. "Law, I answered all these questions the first time you came by."

"I know, Meg," Lawson soothed. "But we're talking to everyone a second time, just to see if anything new shakes loose."

She grunted. "We get plenty of oddballs. Tourists who have no business being out on those trails, kooks who think the world is going to end any day now coming in for supplies, and then just your everyday out-there folks who like hunting a little too much."

Lawson sighed. "You know what I mean, Meg. Someone who put you on edge."

"You got time for a list?" she asked as she brushed her salt-and-pepper hair out of her face.

"They'd need something to help them move a body. Tarps and rope, maybe. Could've bought a knife, too," I said.

Meg's eyes narrowed a fraction. "You think this is some sicko who'll strike again?"

Lawson's mouth pressed into a firm line. He hated when people gossiped about an investigation, and the look on Meg's face told us she was going to do just that. He pinned her with a stare. "We don't want to cause alarm. Right now, we think this was an isolated incident, but we still need to find out who did it."

"Of course, you do," Meg huffed. "Can't imagine letting my girl head out backpacking alone. That's a recipe for disaster."

"Not everyone knows what you can meet out on the trails," Lawson said.

Meg shook her head. "Poor thing." She was quiet for a moment. "I can't think of anyone I pegged as a murderer. No one bought all three of those things. But countless folks have bought one. I can pull invoices and make you a list, but it'll take me some time."

Lawson nodded. "Appreciate it. Just give me a call when you're ready, and I'll send someone to pick it up."

"Will do. You boys stay safe out there," she ordered.

"Always do," Lawson said with a smile.

I followed my brother out of the store and toward his SUV. "Can't exactly arrest someone because they bought a knife or rope."

He shook his head. "No, but it gives us a starting point."

I guessed that was better than anything we had so far. We had exactly zero leads. No one had seen a damned thing when it came to Marci Peters. The fact that a woman could simply disappear and then show up sliced to hell put me on edge.

We climbed into Lawson's SUV, and I turned to him as he started the engine. "What's next on your list?"

He was about to answer when his phone rang. Lawson pulled it out and pressed it to his ear. "Hartley."

His face went stony. "How long ago?" A pause. "On my way."

He tapped the screen and tossed his phone into the cupholder.

"What?" I asked as he pulled out of the parking spot and stepped on the gas.

"Don't freak out on me."

Every muscle in my body tightened. "Those words don't exactly help."

Lawson winced and glanced my way. "Oren Randal attacked Aspen at The Brew. She's fine, though."

Those muscles seized as a tremor cascaded through me. "If she was attacked, she's not fine," I ground out.

Images flashed in my mind, each one worse than the previous. They spun into memories. The feel of a boot cracking my ribs. A blow to the head.

"Roan, I need you to breathe, or I'll have to pull over," Lawson warned.

"Keep driving," I snapped.

"She's okay." He stole a glance at me. "I'm not sure this fixation on Aspen's safety is healthy."

I wanted to deck my brother. He didn't get it. Didn't understand. "I just need her to be all right."

"And she is."

"Won't know that until I see her."

"Okay," Lawson muttered.

He flicked on his lights and pressed the accelerator. A second later, we were pulling up in front of The Brew as two officers jogged down from the station.

The second Lawson hit the brakes, I was out of the SUV and running for the door. I jerked it open and stormed inside.

"Back here," Jonesy called.

I stalked toward the back hall. Only a piece of me recognized the man on the floor. The piece that wanted his blood. But I only had eyes for Aspen.

Her body trembled as she leaned against the wall. Her cheek was red and swelling.

I crossed to her in three long strides, my hands hovering over her cheeks, needing to touch her but not wanting to hurt her. "Aspen."

"I'm okay."

But she wasn't. Aspen's voice trembled just like the rest of her.

I pulled her gently into my arms, needing to feel the rise and fall of her chest against mine. "Where does it hurt?"

She swallowed hard. "Just my cheek. He surprised me. I don't know how he got in. But I got him pretty good."

I glanced down at the man cursing and writhing on the floor. He'd been hog-tied with something.

"Are those…aprons?" Lawson asked.

Elsie blushed. "It was all that was around."

"Quick thinking. I like it." He turned to Clint and Officer Adams. "Can you get this piece of garbage up and book him for assault?"

"With pleasure," Adams said, bending down to replace the aprons with cuffs.

"Everyone's going to know you're a liar. They'll come for you," Oren screamed.

"He's crazy," Aspen whispered as Clint and Adams tugged him down the hallway.

I forced myself to pull back and look at Aspen's face. "I think we need to take you to Doc and get you checked out, just to make sure you're okay."

She shook her head but winced. "It's just a shiner. It'd hurt worse if anything was broken."

I scowled. "You don't know that."

Aspen sent me a pleading look. "I don't want to go to the doctor. I just want to go home."

Lawson studied her for a moment. "You lose consciousness at all?"

"No. I didn't even hit the floor."

My gut twisted. Aspen had been in this hall fighting for survival. Alone.

"Roan," she whispered.

My gaze jerked to her.

"Stay with me."

I knew what she meant. Stay in the here and now. Don't let myself get pulled into the past. Into memories she knew could drown me.

I pressed my forehead to hers. "I'm with you, Tender Heart."

Aspen let out a long breath. "Good. Then you can listen to me tell Law how I broke the asshole's balls."

I wanted to laugh because I knew it was what Aspen was going for. But I couldn't quite get myself there.

As she recounted every moment of the encounter to Lawson, my body strung tighter. Oren Randal was clearly unstable and obviously fixated on Aspen. It was a recipe for disaster.

Lawson moved to the back door and motioned to an evidence tech. "Grab a photo of this and see if you can get any prints. Someone tampered with the lock."

I glared at the door. "We're getting you better locks and an alarm system here."

"Roan—"

"Don't," I snapped. "I'm doing everything I can not to lose it right now. Please just let me do what I can to make you safe."

Aspen pressed a hand to my chest and stretched up onto her tiptoes. Her mouth took mine in a long, slow kiss. "Okay. Just promise me you won't get lost in the woods. That you'll stay with me."

The woods of my mind could be a dangerous place. It was easy to spiral there. But I had Aspen and Cady to fight for, so I'd always come back.

"Not going anywhere," I promised.

"Good," she said with a pat to my chest.

Lawson cleared his throat. "Gonna need to take a few pictures of your face now, and then again after the bruises develop."

"Not now," I gritted out.

Aspen squeezed my arm. "It's okay. I can do it."

But I didn't miss the tremor in her hand as it dropped from my arm. She'd likely been photographed after John's attack and now battled with her memories.

The evidence tech, who didn't look older than twenty-one at most, held up his camera. "Just look into the lens."

The camera flashed, and Aspen jerked.

I let out a curse.

Lawson squeezed my shoulder hard. "Keep it together."

The tech eyed me skeptically. "Look to the left."

Another flash and jerk.

"To the right."

Bright light and twitch.

"That's enough," I barked. "I'm taking her home."

"That's all I need," the tech said softly.

Aspen turned to face me, worry etched into her expression. "The worst is over."

"You don't need to comfort me," I growled. "I should be taking care of you."

Her lips twitched. "You are kind of like a grizzly bear with a thorn in his paw right now."

Lawson snorted, pulling out his phone as it rang. "She's not wrong there." He tapped the screen. "Hartley." His entire demeanor changed as he listened. Then his gaze shot to mine. "There's another body."

Chapter Forty-Three

Roan

"**S**TOP SNARLING," LAWSON SAID AS HE TURNED ONTO THE back road.

"I'm not snarling," I snapped.

He shot a look in my direction. "You're practically spitting and muttering things under your breath."

I turned to look out the window. "I didn't want to leave her."

Lawson was quiet for a moment. "I get it, man. But she's going to be fine. Mom's clucking over her like a mother hen, and Dad's keeping an eye out—not that he needs to because Oren's locked up."

"Don't say his name," I growled. The asshole's face filled my mind, stirring a fresh wave of rage. I knew he wouldn't be in lockup forever. He'd make bail and be free to come after Aspen again.

"I've already got Clint on the restraining order. Oren'll be served before he gets out. He comes close, we'll get him."

I just grunted. It wasn't good enough. Nothing would be.

"If you can't get your head in the game, it's better if you're home," Lawson said low.

I glared at him. "Name one time my head hasn't been in the game. We're not at the crime scene yet. Get off my back."

Lawson snapped his mouth closed, his hands tightening on the wheel. "I've never seen you like this."

"Because I've never cared about anyone like this before," I muttered.

He glanced at me before returning his focus to the road. "You're going to have to figure out how to deal with all the stuff coming up. I don't know if it's about what happened around the shooting or—"

"Don't," I said quietly. "I'm fine."

"You're not," Lawson argued. "I can see you winding tighter and tighter. I know it's new for you, having feelings like this, but I don't want it setting you back."

"How would you feel if you were in my shoes? Your person being attacked. People spreading vicious lies about her that could lead to anyone acting out. Would you just shrug and turn it off?"

It killed that they'd seen me do that before. When shit hit the fan for all my siblings, I'd been able to keep going. But Aspen had unlocked something in me, and I couldn't put things back in the bottle.

A muscle under Lawson's eye fluttered. "Well, I don't have a person, do I?"

Shit.

"That's not how I meant it."

He huffed out a breath, his fingers stretching around the wheel. "I know you didn't. But if I'm honest, it's one of the reasons I don't. Having three kids I love more than life is hard enough—knowing what's out there, all the things that could hurt them. I can't add more to that plate."

I bit the inside of my cheek. Lawson's ex had messed with his head in ways I wasn't sure he'd recover from. And he blamed himself for a lot of the shit that was hers and hers alone. But he wouldn't be able to hear that now. He never could.

"Sometimes, it's worth the risk," I said quietly.

As twisted up as I was currently, I'd never give up a single moment with Aspen and Cady.

Lawson's jaw clenched, making that muscle twitch again. "Not for everyone."

He pulled into a spot at the trailhead and shut off the engine. The parking lot was already teeming with vehicles and various forms of law enforcement. There was a presence from CRPD, Harrison County, and Fish and Wildlife.

I slid out of the SUV and shut the door. Whoever this was had been impatient this time. The body was right in front of the map and welcome sign.

My gut roiled at the sight. The body wouldn't be identifiable by facial features.

This was pure rage.

Nash grimaced as we approached. "Never seen anything like it, and I hope I never have to again."

"I take it we don't have an ID?" Lawson asked.

He shook his head. "Luisa and the techs are working now, but we'll have to confirm with dental records if he isn't in the system."

He. That was all we knew.

Lawson jerked his head in a nod. "I've got the print scanner in my SUV if you want to grab it." He handed Nash the keys.

"Male. That's a hell of a different type," I muttered.

"Also, they didn't drag him up the trail. Either it was heat-of-the-moment, or the unsub was too angry."

"He was definitely angry," I said, inclining my head toward the decimated body.

Lawson's hands clenched and flexed. "Understatement. Hopefully, he was pissed enough to leave some evidence behind."

"Got it," Nash called as he jogged back.

As we approached the body, Luisa looked up and shook her head. "Gotta stop meeting like this, Chief."

"I don't disagree. Any idea on time of death?"

"I'm guessing sometime late morning," she answered.

"Same knife?" I asked.

Luisa glanced my way and grimaced. "There's too much damage

to the body for me to know from visuals alone. I need to get him back to the morgue."

Hell. This was beyond bad.

"Can I run a print?" Nash asked.

Luisa nodded, motioning him over. He made a conscious effort not to look at the worst of the gore, and I didn't blame him. This would give everyone who saw it nightmares for weeks.

Luisa lifted a single finger and pressed it to the electronic pad. Nash repositioned the scanner a few times to guarantee a complete image, then pulled it back.

One of the techs offered him an alcohol wipe.

Nash thanked him and cleaned the screen. "Let's see if we can connect to cellular."

We weren't that far out of town, so hopefully, it would work.

We all waited as Nash stared at the screen. A minute later, a ding sounded. My brother's jaw went slack. "Holy shit."

"What?" Lawson barked.

Nash turned the screen around, and a driver's license photo and name appeared.

Tyson Moss. Steven's podcast partner.

Lawson guided his SUV down the mountain toward the rental Steven and Tyson had been staying in. "Dumb luck or related?"

It was the question I'd been asking myself since the ID came in. I wanted it to be dumb luck. It was a small town, after all. There were a limited number of potential victims.

But something niggled at the back of my mind. Something that said there were no coincidences in life.

"When they broadcasted Aspen's location, they could've brought anyone here. Someone who liked John for all the wrong reasons," I said. My fingers twitched. I'd already texted Holt and asked him to head to Aspen's. I needed more eyes on her until we figured out how everything was linked.

Lawson's jaw worked back and forth. "Exactly what I'm afraid of."

"We also need to take a longer look at Oren Randal."

Lawson's gaze flicked to me. "You think he's capable of this?"

"I wouldn't put it past him. There's a real sick rage there."

"You're right. I'll do some more digging."

He flipped on his blinker and turned into the long drive we'd been down before. The familiar van was parked in front. Lawson pulled in behind it, and we climbed out.

Lawson rested a hand on his weapon as we approached the house. I did the same. Neither of us said out loud that we could be walking up on anything. We didn't need to.

I lifted my hand and knocked.

No sounds came from inside.

I knocked again.

"Keep your fuckin' pants on," Steven shouted as footsteps sounded.

A second later, the door jerked open. He looked like hell—hair sticking up at every angle, dark circles under bloodshot eyes.

The moment Steven saw us, he scowled. "I haven't broken any damn laws, so get off my property."

"Not actually your property," I muttered under my breath.

He started to close the door, but Lawson put out a hand to stop it. "We need to talk to you about Tyson."

Steven's scowl deepened. "What'd that prick tell you?"

My brows lifted at that. "Trouble in paradise?"

"He's a fuckin' traitor. We had a thesis for our podcast. We were going to get John's case overturned. Then we'd have movie deals and book tours. We'd be set. And then he was all, *'But what if she's telling the truth?'* Who gives a damn? So, I punched him. It barely landed. I can't believe he called you assholes."

"He's dead," Lawson said.

Steven reared back. "The fuck you say?"

"Tyson is dead. We found his body two hours ago."

"Y-you're wrong. I saw him this morning. I—there's no way."

"I'm sorry, Steven."

I had to give it to Lawson, he sounded like he meant it. And he probably did. The guy might've been an asshole, but he didn't deserve to die.

"How?" Steven rasped.

Lawson took a breath. "We'll get to that in a second. I need to ask you a few questions to get a timeline. When did you last see Tyson?"

"Around ten a.m.," Steven mumbled.

Lawson nodded. "Where was he headed?"

"I'm not sure. He said he was going into town."

"And what did you do after you two parted ways?" Lawson pressed.

Steven's gaze jerked to Lawson. "How'd he die?"

"I'll fill you in as soon as I've got this timeline down," Lawson said calmly.

"I'm not answering another question until you tell me how," Steven grumbled.

"He was murdered," I said, not an ounce of emotion in my voice.

Steven paled as his gaze jerked from Lawson to me and back again. "You think I had something to do with it?"

Lawson held up a hand. "We just have to get a timeline. Cover all our bases."

"Bullshit," Steven spat. "I've seen how this works. You guys try to pin it on the innocent guy just to get the case off your docket."

"We're not—"

"Fuck off, pig. You want to talk to me? Call my lawyer. I have one since you've been giving us so much trouble." Steven slammed the door in our faces.

I turned to Lawson. "That went well."

Chapter Forty-Four

Aspen

I WRAPPED MY SWEATER TIGHTER AROUND MY BODY AS I SWUNG back and forth on the porch swing, watching Cady talk Nathan's ear off at the fence line. She couldn't have been more excited to have the three of us pick her up from school. She hadn't batted an eye at my story of hitting my face on a cabinet at work. I didn't make a habit of lying to Cady, but this was one instance where she wasn't ready for the truth.

The hinges on the door squeaked as Kerry opened it, balancing two mugs in her other hand. She smiled as she headed toward me. "I thought some hot cocoa might be in order."

My nose stung at the kindness, the caretaking. My mother hadn't been very good at that, too busy simply trying to keep her head above water.

I took the mug and wrapped my hands around it. The warmth seeped into me, both from the beverage and the thoughtfulness. "Thank you."

Kerry lowered herself to the spot next to me on the swing. "How are you feeling?"

I opened my mouth to say *fine,* but Kerry cut me off. "*Really* feeling."

I gave her a sheepish smile. "The ibuprofen helped, but my face is still throbbing a bit."

Lines of worry deepened in Kerry's face. "How about that beautiful brain and heart?"

"A little overwhelmed," I admitted.

She patted my thigh. "I can only imagine. You know I'm here if you ever need to talk. Need someone to watch Cady so you can have some time to process. Anything."

My eyes burned, and I struggled to swallow. "You aren't mad I lied to you?"

I hadn't seen Kerry and Nathan since the podcast came out, and the moment they appeared at The Brew to take me home, the nerves had set in.

Kerry's eyes widened. "You did no such thing."

I blinked a few times.

"I do believe your name *is* Aspen Barlow according to the US government. So you didn't want to open up about a painful past… We all have things that are hard to talk about."

The tears began to leak out then. "Kerry."

She put her mug on the porch and did the same with mine, then wrapped me in a tight hug. "Sweet girl. You've been through more than anyone should ever have to."

The tears came faster then. There were no sobs. Just silent rivers of emotion tracking down my cheeks as Kerry rocked me. How long had it been since I'd had this kind of motherly affection? I honestly couldn't remember.

"I hate that you've been carrying this alone for so long," she whispered. "But you're not alone anymore. We've got you."

A hiccuped sob escaped me.

Kerry rubbed soothing circles on my back. "Just let it out. You've been holding too much in."

"It feels like if I let go, the pain will never stop."

"I know, but if you don't, it will drown you. Take you to a dark place you won't ever come back from."

So, I let myself cry, secure in Kerry's embrace, feeling a true sense of family for the first time since I'd lost Autumn. I wasn't sure how long the tears lasted, but I slowly came back to myself. To the moment. And I felt…lighter. Exhausted and wrung out, but lighter.

Kerry brushed my hair away from my face. "There you go. A good cry does wonders."

My mouth curved. "Sorry about the unload."

She waved me off and handed me my hot cocoa again. "You don't have a thing to apologize for. You need to let it free. And you should keep doing it or everything will just build up again."

I traced the heart design on the mug. "I talk to Roan."

He was the first person I'd felt safe enough to share things with. Something about the gentleness he'd had with the deer had made him that for me. But over the past couple of weeks, I'd worried about putting more on his shoulders. I could see the stress in him, the worry—not just for me and Cady but also about the case he was working.

A light shone in Kerry's eyes. "He's different since he met you."

I stilled.

"Smiles more. Laughs. I didn't realize how silent he'd become until I heard him *really* laugh again." Her breath hitched. "You gave me my boy back, and I'll love you forever for that."

Tears welled once more. "Please don't make me cry again. I'm gonna get dehydrated."

Kerry laughed. "All right. No more tears. But tell me, do you love him?"

"Yes." The answer was instant and sure.

"He know that?"

I leaned back on the swing. "We haven't said the words, but I feel it every day. In everything he does. And I hope he feels the same from me."

Kerry squeezed my knee. "I know he does. But do yourself a favor. Give each other the words. They bind you in a way. Remind you of all the things they encompass."

"I don't want to scare him off," I admitted. "Or put any pressure on him."

Kerry laughed again. "You think that boy of mine scares easily? Let me tell you, he doesn't."

But that wasn't exactly true. Parts of Roan had been terrified since the town turned against him, since his attack. It was why he'd hidden so much of himself. His family deserved to know all of him. Because the broken and damaged pieces made him beautiful. They gave him his kindness and empathy for the creatures that were often overlooked. Made him fiercely protective and loyal. Made him love so deeply.

I wanted his family to get to know *that* Roan. And more than anything, I wanted Roan to feel fully seen by them.

Tires sounded on the gravel, and I looked up to see a line of cars headed up the driveway. I blinked a few times.

"I'd say word has gotten around," Kerry muttered. "Prepare yourself for incoming chaos."

Chaos was exactly right. Holt and Wren climbed out of their SUV, Lawson's three boys piling out of the back. Grae and Caden pulled in next to them. And Maddie in her SUV after that.

They were all out of their vehicles in a matter of seconds, and it took even less time for my girls to make it to me. Grae hauled me out of the swing and wrapped me in the tightest hug. "I'm so glad you're okay," she whispered, emotion thick in her voice.

Maddie's arms wrapped around both of us. "Me, too."

Then Wren was there. "Move over, G, my belly doesn't fit."

Grae laughed and scooted. I wasn't sure how long we stood there. I let their love pour over me. I didn't care that Oren had attacked me. That I would have one hell of a shiner. Because in that moment, I felt more at peace, at home, than I ever had in all my days.

Chapter Forty-Five

Roan

As I turned onto Huckleberry Lane, I noticed both Lawson's and Nash's headlights following me. I groaned. All I wanted was to go to what I thought of as home. To wrap myself around Aspen and make sure she was okay. To listen to Cady tell me all about the many adventures of her day.

But I should've guessed that Lawson and Nash would also want to check on them. I turned onto the drive and grimaced at all the vehicles in front of the farmhouse. Scratch that. My entire family had decided they needed to make sure all was okay.

I parked at the end of the row and slid out of my truck, heading for the door. I opened it to laughter. Everyone was piled on every available surface.

I scowled as I took them all in.

Grae caught my look and burst out laughing. "Someone is *not* happy we're here."

Maddie grinned and waggled her eyebrows. "I think he was hoping for some *alone* time with Aspen when he got home."

My scowl deepened.

Nash smacked me upside the head as he passed. "Don't glare at my girl."

Cady launched herself off her chair and ran toward me. "Mr. Grizz!" She leapt in the air, and I caught her, balancing her on my hip. She pressed her little hand to my stubbled cheek. "Why so grumpy?"

Everyone hooted at that.

I loved my family, but sometimes I wanted to kill them.

"It's a little *loud* in here," I told her.

Cady giggled. "We're having fun."

"Yeah, Mr. Grizz," Grae called. "You should try it sometime."

I shot her a glare and moved through the throng of people. There was only one other person I wanted to see. I pinned Holt with a stare, and he instantly rose from the spot on the couch. I lowered myself and Cady to it.

"Mr. Grizz, we invited Heather to play at recess, and she was *nice*."

My brows lifted, a bit of anxiety swirling in my chest. The last thing I wanted was that kid hurting Cady.

Charlie scrunched up his face. "She wasn't that bad. She doesn't like frogs, though, so we can't be best friends."

Lawson chuckled at that. "It's good to have priorities."

"But also to give people second chances," Aspen said, ruffling Cady's hair. "Proud of you, Katydid."

She smiled as she clambered off my lap and called to Charlie about getting out her new game.

I turned to Aspen. My hand lifted, ghosting across the deepening bruise on her cheek. "You should be resting."

Her beautiful mouth curved. "This is way better."

Something shifted in my chest. Gratitude for my interfering, nosy family. That they made my girl feel loved and cared for. I leaned forward and pressed my lips to her forehead.

"Oh, schnitzel," Grae muttered. "I'm going to cry."

Caden chuckled and pulled her tighter against him in the over-stuffed chair. "Gigi."

"It's the freaking hormones," she muttered.

Wren laughed. "Welcome to my world."

My dad looked around the room, surveying its occupants. "What's the latest?"

It was then that I realized he was checking for kids. None of them were here. Cady and Charlie had taken off for her room, and I guessed Luke and Drew were playing video games in Aspen's tiny office at the back of the house.

Lawson frowned, his gaze shifting to Aspen. "Not good."

She stiffened next to me. "What?"

I wrapped an arm around her. "The victim was Tyson Moss."

Aspen sucked in a breath.

"Who's that?" my mom asked.

Wren sent her a worried look. "One of the podcasters."

Lawson kept his focus on Aspen, something in his expression telling her to brace herself. "We need to consider the possibility that someone who likes killing came here because of their fascination with John's case."

"Oh, God," Aspen whispered.

"Hey," I said, cupping her uninjured cheek. "None of this is your fault."

"People are dead," she said, the words barely audible. "Animals, too."

"Because of someone who's seriously messed up in the head. Not because of you."

Aspen nodded, but her eyes glazed.

"I think we need to consider asking Holt's company for a security detail," I told her.

That pulled Aspen into the here and now. "I don't know. Having strangers following us would scare Cady."

"We can explain it to her."

Aspen's brows pulled together as she stared out the front windows. "It's like there's no good choice. One scares her; the other puts her at risk."

I couldn't take the pain in her voice, anything but that. "We can figure out another way."

Lawson nodded. "We can station an officer at the school and

keep one at The Brew. Roan, Nash, Holt, or I can drive you wherever you need to go."

Gratitude swept through me at my brother jumping in to help.

"What about me?" Caden groused.

"You got a concealed carry permit I don't know about?" Lawson asked.

Caden scowled at him. "Fine."

Aspen scanned the room. "Thank you. For keeping us safe. For making sure Cady has the life she deserves."

I pulled her to me. "Nothing's going to happen to either of you." I knew my voice held a hint of desperation, but it couldn't be avoided.

Aspen's head tilted back, and she lifted her hands to frame my face. "It's not going to happen again. We'll be okay."

Holt's gaze narrowed on the two of us. "What's not going to happen again?"

"Nothing," I muttered.

Aspen dropped a hand to my chest and whispered, "Tell them. It's time."

Everything in me constricted. I knew this secret had built a wall between me and my family. Created a darkness that ate away at me. Until I'd seen Aspen. She'd reminded me of all the good there was in the world. Helped me fight off the darkness before I even knew her name.

I pulled back, searching Aspen's eyes. I saw nothing but acceptance in her gaze. She'd be there for me either way.

My dad shifted on the other sofa. "What's going on, Roan?"

I swallowed, my throat going dry. I turned to see all of them staring expectantly.

Aspen wove her fingers through mine, squeezing.

"I lied about something," I said. My voice was calm and even, nothing giving away the war going on inside me. That calmness had always been my protection. My mask.

I stared down at my hand linked with Aspen's, the point of

contact grounding me. "Remember when I had my mountain bike accident?"

The energy in the room shifted, everyone going on alert. Every single person aside from Aspen had been affected by that time. Wren had almost died. Holt had almost lost the love of his life—Grae her best friend. My parents had been a wreck. It was Lawson's first murder case. And Caden, Maddie, and Nash had all been trying to support the people they loved.

"Of course," my mom said. "You were in bed for weeks. I still think we should've taken you to the hospital."

I swallowed the bile in my throat. "It wasn't a bike accident."

Dad's gaze turned alert. "Then what the hell was it?"

"I got jumped. Didn't see who they were. It was late in the day, already getting dark. They got me from behind. Thought I was the one who'd helped kill all those people."

It hurt to say the words. Nearly burned me alive to set them free. And it was then that I knew just how much this had weighed on me. The price I'd paid all these years. How it had made me retreat further and further until I'd almost ceased to exist.

"What?" Mom whispered.

"I didn't want you to know." My voice was a husk of a rasp.

"Roan," she choked. "You were black and blue from head to toe. You had a concussion and broken ribs. Someone did that to you?"

"Who?" Dad demanded. "You must have seen something."

"I didn't," I said, trying to find that calm again. "I have no clue who they were, and I don't want to know."

"Why the hell not?" Nash demanded. "They need to pay for what they did. They could've killed you."

I let out a stuttered breath. My feelings on what had happened had changed since I'd met Aspen and come to know her light. I wasn't constantly wondering who'd stuck the knife in my back; I simply felt sorry for them. "I don't want to put a face to that hate. Don't want to know who in my community could've been cold enough to do that. But what I do know is that they have to live with it. With the fact that they attacked someone innocent. It likely tortures them. That's enough."

"It's not enough," Grae choked out, tears filling her eyes. "You changed. I thought it was just being a suspect, but it was this."

I couldn't lie to her and say I hadn't. Because I had.

"But it made him the amazing man he is today," Aspen said softly, her voice breaking through the crackling energy in the room. She looked around, meeting everyone's eyes. "It made him kinder than anyone I know. More empathetic. It made him want to care for creatures who need our love and protection. It made him fiercely protective of every single person he cares about. What he went through was horrible. But Roan turned all that ugliness into the most beautiful thing I've ever seen."

Grae cried harder. She slid off Caden's lap and crossed to me, pulling me up. Then she threw her arms around my middle. Grae had always been tiny but fierce. And her grip now was that of someone four times her size. "I love you. More than you'll ever know."

"I love you, too, G," I whispered. "I'm okay. I promise."

Her gaze flicked to Aspen. "Because she helped you heal."

I couldn't lie. That *was* a huge part of it. Aspen showed me how our worst moments could become our greatest strengths.

As Grae released me, Holt stepped in. So much swirled in those familiar blue eyes. He hauled me into a hug. "I'm so sorry. I was so lost in what I was going through. I couldn't see that you were hurting."

"Holt," I choked out. "You nearly lost the person you love most in this world. You didn't need to be worried about me."

"You're my brother." There were tears in his voice. "You never should've dealt with it alone."

Wren had tears tracking down her face as she squeezed my arm. "We should've done more to protect you. I tried to tell them you didn't have anything to do with it. I should've tried harder."

"Wren…" I pulled her into a hug. "You were healing from being shot. It's a miracle you had it in you to tell them what you did."

Each member of my family hugged me in a way they hadn't in

years. And for the first time, I really let them. We all needed it. I knew that much.

Lawson stepped into my space, his gaze hard. "You should've told me."

"I didn't want anyone to know."

"I was a damned cop," he growled.

I took his shoulders, squeezing hard. "Not everything is your responsibility."

"I could've done something. Got camera footage. Found witnesses," he argued.

"Law. I'm okay."

His dark eyes blazed. "I've seen you battling something these past weeks, so on edge with everything happening to Aspen. It was more than just being worried for her. It was terror."

I let out a rush of breath. "I know what it's like when people turn on you."

Lawson cursed.

"I have to battle with that knowledge. But it helps that my family has stepped up for her in every way. Helps me trust that she'll be safe."

The muscle beneath Lawson's eye fluttered. "The way you should've been safe."

"I'm not going to say I regret it," I told him. "Because it brought me to where I am. Here. Now. And even with the shitstorm swirling around us, this is the happiest I've ever been."

I let my older brother really see that. I didn't hide beneath a mask of calm nothingness. I let him see the fear but also the sheer joy.

The problem was, being this happy meant I had more to lose.

Chapter Forty-Six

Aspen

"S HE'S OUT," ROAN SAID SOFTLY AS HE SLID INTO BED NEXT to me, Chauncey snoring in his dog bed on the floor.

The only light in the room was from my bedside lamp. I turned onto my side so I could see Roan fully—his sharply angled jaw, those hypnotizing blue eyes. I surveyed every millimeter of him. "How are you doing?"

His family had stayed until Cady's bedtime. I didn't blame them. I would've wanted to stick close after Roan's admission, too. We'd ordered pizza and made ice cream sundaes. It had all helped, but I knew Roan had to be exhausted.

He traced a finger over my deepening bruise. "I should be asking you that."

"You're the one who let loose a decade-old secret. I need to know how you really are. Not the pretty answer just to make me feel better."

Roan's lips twitched. "Like I've been run over by a truck."

I brushed the hair away from his eyes. "Are you glad you did it?"

He stared down at me. "Yes. I hate that it's causing them pain. But for the first time, I feel like there isn't a wall between us."

My fingers trailed down to his neck. "They'll get to really *see* you now. That will be a gift. But it's going to take you all some time to process."

"I know. And I'll give them that time."

My mouth curved. "It might require some conversation, and I know those aren't always your favorite."

He grimaced, and I couldn't help but laugh.

"It'll be a stretching exercise for all of you."

Roan pulled me into his arms, burrowing his face into the crook of my neck. "I wanted to come home to you and Cady. Instead, everyone under the bloody sun was here."

"Made me feel loved," I admitted.

"Then I guess I'm glad," Roan grumbled.

I couldn't help it, I laughed.

"Are you laughing at me?" he asked, affronted.

"Can't help it. You're funny."

"I'll show you funny." Roan dove in to tickle my sides.

I bit his shoulder to keep from waking Cady.

"Ow! That hurt," he clipped.

I bit him again. "That's what you get."

Roan's eyes heated. "If you want to talk punishments—"

"Mama!" Cady yelled. "Nightmare!"

We were both on our feet in a flash, all heat vanishing. Roan was out the door and down the hall before me. The second he opened her door, Cady flew at him.

Roan cradled her in his arms, rocking her back and forth. "It's okay, Tiny Dancer. I've got you."

"There was a monster under my bed, and he was trying to get me," Cady sobbed.

"No monsters are gonna get you when I'm around," Roan said, his voice gruff.

My heart squeezed painfully. This man was everything I'd ever wanted for my girl and so much more.

"Look, I'm doing a check, Katydid." I bent and peeked under the bed. "Nothing here but a few stuffed animals."

"Y-you're sure?" she asked.

"Totally positive."

Cady burrowed deeper into Roan's hold. "Will you stay with me for a while?"

"Always, Tiny Dancer. As long as you want."

Elsie winced as she strode toward the register. "Should you be working today? You look a little rough."

I gave her a wan smile. "Gee, thanks."

"Sorry. I just meant your shiner. And you seem a little tired."

I sighed. I felt like I'd been run over by the same truck Roan had. "Cady had a couple of nightmares last night, and it took us a while to get her down."

"I'm sorry," Elsie said. "Is she okay?"

"She was a little sleepy and cranky this morning but hanging in there. Hopefully, she goes down early tonight."

"Let me know if I can do anything," Elsie offered.

"Thanks. I really appreciate it. Now, what can I get you?"

"I'll take one of those chocolate peanut butter cup muffins. You've got me addicted."

I laughed as I grabbed the muffin. "I love to hear that."

Elsie handed me a few bills. "Keep the change."

"Thanks," I said, adding the extra to the tip jar.

I lost myself in the rhythm of customers. The sun was out, and things were busier than they had been lately. It wasn't just Jonesy and Elsie filling seats. A handful of tourists, locals on their lunch breaks, and a mom out with her infant were also in. But Officer Hall stayed perched outside to ensure we had no unwanted patrons.

The hustle and bustle were a welcome break. It helped to distract me from everything else that was going on. One hour bled into two, and people came and went in a steady flow.

A curse sounded from the kitchen, and I winced. "You okay, Zeke?"

"Need you to watch the stove or take out the trash," he called back.

I did not want to be responsible for ruining whatever Zeke was cooking. "I've got the trash."

He was right. It was full to bursting and needed to be taken out now. I lifted the bag and swore it weighed more than I did. It took me two tries to tie it off, but I finally succeeded and swung it over my shoulder.

I unlocked the new deadbolt Holt had installed on the back door and stepped into the alley. The forest behind us meant I was greeted by birdsong and the wind. At least the breeze kept down the smell of the dumpster. I pushed the lid up and threw the bag in.

As I turned to head back to the café, movement caught my eye. But I was too late.

Something struck the side of my head. Blinding pain flashed, and I fell. I hit the ground hard, groaning. I tried to sit up, to do anything, but a boot stomped down on my neck.

"Time for you to get yours, bitch," a voice growled.

A needle plunged into my arm, and the world started to melt away. I tried to scream, call for help, yell for Roan. But every word was stolen from my lips. And then there was nothing at all.

Chapter Forty-Seven

Roan

"**H**OW DO WE HAVE NOTHING?" I SAID, SLAMMING MY pen down on the pad of paper.

Lawson and Nash eyed me warily. Nash scooted his box of donuts toward me. "Need something to eat?"

Lawson's lips twitched.

"It's not fuckin' funny," I snarled.

Lawson just rolled his eyes, not put off by my bellow. "Sorry, but any time Nash *offers* to part with food, you know you're in a bad way."

"I panicked," Nash defended. "I don't want him going over the edge and punching us both."

I grabbed the box and flipped it open. "Just for that, I'm taking the Boston Cream."

"Hey! I was saving that one."

"I know. That's why I'm taking it."

Nash turned to Lawson. "You're right. I think I liked him better when he just brooded silently."

I took a huge bite of the donut in answer.

Lawson chuckled, then patted Nash on the back. "I'll get you some more tomorrow."

"I wanted it today," Nash grumbled.

Lawson just shook his head. "I think you'll survive." He leaned back in his chair at the head of the conference table. "Let's go over everything from the beginning."

I groaned. "We need to interrogate Steven."

The podcaster had retained a lawyer—one who ordered him not to answer any of our questions this morning. We'd gotten nothing.

"It's not like that prick will tell us a damned thing," Nash muttered.

"I put a call in for the visitor logs from John's prison. I want to see just how often those two got together," Lawson said.

"Oren Randal, too," I added.

The reporter had made bail late this morning after being served with a restraining order. Lawson had Clint and Adams tailing him at a distance to make sure he obeyed it. Another two officers were sitting on Steven's rental cabin, but they hadn't seen any signs of movement, and his vehicle was still in the drive.

"I want to take a closer look at *anyone* who had a lot of contact," Lawson said.

Nash pulled the box of donuts back in his direction. "I think we need to get posters up at all the trailheads. Ask people to call in if they see any suspicious behavior. Maybe a hiker saw something and they just don't know it."

"Not a bad idea," I said.

Lawson tapped his fingers on the table. "I didn't want anyone to panic."

I pinned him with a stare. "I think we're past that. Two people are dead."

His jaw tightened. "Point taken."

Lawson shouldered everything, including the weight of the entire town. He didn't want to frighten a soul if he didn't have to.

Nash glanced at our older brother. "Word has already gotten around to most everyone. This will warn those who haven't heard to be careful on the hiking trails."

"All right. I'll have something drawn up."

A knock sounded on the conference room door, but the person on the other side didn't wait for an answer. The door swung open, and Wren appeared, one hand on her pregnant belly, her face pale. "Abel's on a call from The Brew. Aspen's missing."

Everything in me stilled. The air in my lungs seized. I must have heard her wrong.

My ears rang as Nash and Lawson leapt to their feet. Nash was at my side instantly, hauling me up, his expression full of concern. "Roan."

The sound of my name had me jerking out of my haze, and then I was moving. I shoved aside chairs and bolted for the door, Nash and Lawson on my heels. I didn't stop for a damn thing as I booked it out of the station and down the sidewalk.

All I could see was Aspen's face in my mind. That stupid glitter headband from Cady. The way the light in her green eyes danced when she gave me hell. How they went soft when she told me she saw the best in me. The way they heated when I knew she wanted more.

I hauled open the door to The Brew, making the bell jangle in a weird, off-kilter way. Everyone's gaze shot to me.

Officer Hall, the cook, Zeke, and Jonesy were huddled together in the hallway as customers milled about the café. I stalked toward them. "What the hell happened?"

Their heads snapped up.

Zeke paled, guilt filling his expression. "She took the trash out. It was taking forever, so I finally went out to see what the issue was, and she was just...gone."

"You let her take the trash out *alone*?" I growled.

Nash took hold of my arm. "Breathe, brother."

I shook him off and shoved past the dick who'd let Aspen outside by herself. Jerking the door open, I scanned the alley and the woods. There was nothing.

I yelled her name. Still no sound.

Lawson, Nash, and I fanned out, our eyes on the ground, looking for signs of anything as we walked toward the dumpster.

My gaze caught on something on the cement. *Was that oil?*

I crouched low, touching a finger to the ground. As I brought my hand up, my stomach pitched and roiled. Blood.

"Law," I choked.

He was by my side in a flash, a curse on his lips. "We don't know anything. Keep breathing."

But I couldn't. Aspen had always told me I made her feel safe—for the first time in years. But I'd failed her. I'd promised her I had her back, and she'd been out here alone.

My ribs tightened, my breaths coming in quick pants. But all I could do was stare down at my hand. The blood. *Aspen's* blood. The stain would be with me forever.

"Didn't tell her I love her," I rasped.

"Roan," Nash said quietly.

"It freaked me out, knowing I felt that way, so I didn't give her the words."

And now, I might not get the chance.

Chapter Forty-Eight

Aspen

MY MOUTH FELT LIKE COTTON, FUZZY AND DRY. My eyelids fluttered, flickers of light bursting into my vision. Everything hurt as if I'd been caught in a riptide and banged against the rocks several dozen times.

It took more than a few tries to bring my surroundings into focus. They were blurry at first like I had on glasses that didn't belong to me.

Then I saw it. A simple, one-room cabin. A tiny kitchenette. A small sitting area. A bed.

And a person tied to a wooden chair next to me.

My stomach dropped as bile surged. Everything came together in a kaleidoscope of memories. Taking out the trash. The noise. Being hit on the head.

Someone injecting me with something—drugs, obviously.

"Steven?" I croaked.

His eyes were wide as he jerked against his bindings. His wrists were secured to the arms of the chair, and his ankles to the legs. There was some sort of scarf or bandana tied around his mouth so he couldn't speak, only make muffled grunting noises.

What the hell is happening?

Then I saw what held me to my seat: zip ties at the wrists and ankles. That bile was back, panic hot on its heels.

"Who has us?" I whispered.

Steven's eyes bugged wider as he tried to get out a name, but I couldn't decipher it.

I tugged on the zip ties, checking their strength. They bit into my flesh with a sharp sting. I winced and muttered a curse.

My gaze swept the room, zeroing in on the windows at the front of the cabin. All I could see were trees, nothing that gave me a clue as to where we actually were.

I leaned forward in my seat, trying to balance on my feet. I wondered if I could get free if I broke the chair. Wiggling from side to side, I tested the furniture's sturdiness. It seemed pretty well made. Maybe if I threw myself backward?

A noise sounded from outside. Footsteps on gravel? Or something being dragged?

My stomach cramped as I set my chair back on the floor. The door flew open, and a figure filled the space. They were backlit by the afternoon sun, making it hard to see.

They took a step inside, pulling a rolling duffel behind them. And as they did, a gasp slipped free. "Elsie?" I choked.

A sneer spread across her lips. "Do you know how tired I am of being called that stupid fucking name? Almost as tired of having to listen to your constant woe-is-me act. At least you had decent baked goods at the piece-of-shit café."

My jaw went slack. It didn't make sense. Elsie was kind. Thoughtful. She'd had my back with the podcasters. She'd helped me secure Oren. But there was none of that kindness in her now.

It was as if she'd completely morphed in front of my eyes. The slightly jumpy woman with the warm smile was gone. There was only a snake now.

She laughed. "What's the matter? Cat got your tongue?" She inclined her head toward Steven. "This one couldn't shut up. Finally had to gag him."

Nausea swirled as my mind raced. I tried to put things in order and figure out what I needed to do. The countless YouTube videos I'd watched flashed on repeat.

"Never let them get you to a secondary location."

Well, that ship had sailed. But then another instruction stuck in my head.

"Stall. Buy yourself time so you can get out."

Maybe if I could figure out what the hell her motives were, I could talk my way out of this.

I swallowed, trying to clear away the worst of the dryness. "What should I call you then?"

Elsie dropped the duffel. "Iris."

As I studied the woman, taking in her blond hair and piercing blue eyes, I found the name fit her better than Elsie.

"What's in the bag?" I asked.

She laughed. "I'll give it to you. You're calm under pressure." Her laughter died. "Maybe that's how you convinced the cops you weren't a delusional liar."

My breath caught. Steven's presence had basically told me what this was about, but Iris's words confirmed it.

"I didn't lie."

Iris stormed toward me, her hand fisting in my hair and jerking my head back. "You won't get away with that here. You're going to tell the goddamned truth if it's the last thing you do."

She released me with a snap. The shock and pain had tears welling in my eyes as I struggled to catch my breath.

"How did I lie?" I croaked.

Iris's fingers clenched and flexed as if she were trying to keep herself from wringing my neck. "John told me how jealous you were of him and Autumn. That you couldn't stand that she was finally happy. That he'd given her everything she ever dreamed of. You knew he didn't kill her, but it was your chance to finally stick it to him."

Her ramblings sounded so much like someone else I knew. "Is Oren helping you?"

She cackled. "That moron? Hardly. He's a woman-hating piece

of garbage who can't write to save his life. He can't be counted on for anything." Iris's lips curved. "But John said he was a good tool to keep making you pay in the short term."

Fear and rage warred deep within me. John had always been a puppet master, great at pulling strings to get what he wanted. He'd do whatever he could to hurt me with whatever he had at his disposal.

Iris bent and unzipped the duffel. I half-expected her to pull out weapons. Instead, she removed audio recording equipment. Two microphones. Assorted wires. A laptop.

"The acoustics in here aren't ideal, but good ole Steven's just gonna have to deal. Right, Steve?" she asked.

He went pale but nodded slowly.

"You gonna keep your trap shut if I take that gag out?"

He nodded again.

Iris crossed to him and jerked the scarf free.

Steven sucked in several ragged breaths. "Water?" he rasped.

Iris rolled her eyes. "So dramatic. But I guess we can't have our star host dehydrated."

She crossed into the kitchen and toward a case of bottled water.

I glanced in his direction, whispering. "Were you working with her?"

"No," he hissed, his voice low. "I'd never seen her until that day at your coffee shop. She stopped by my cabin and said she had a tip for the podcast. She drugged my damned coffee."

I couldn't read any deception in his words, but I wasn't about to trust the jerk. "Does anyone know you're missing?"

He shook his head. "I don't think so. My lawyer should realize it tomorrow when I don't make our meeting."

But tomorrow would be too late.

"She's fucking crazy," Steven bit out.

"I heard that," Iris singsonged. Turning around, she glared at Steven. "It's not nice to call me crazy. Not when I've been so kind to you. I'm going to put your silly little podcast on the map."

"I-I appreciate that," he stammered. "But I'll have to be in town to upload. There's no Wi-Fi up here."

It was a smart play. Maybe Iris was unhinged enough to take the bait.

She tsked at him. "Don't get ahead of yourself, Steve. We need to record our episode first." She turned to me. "It's your first interview. Feeling nervous?"

I swallowed hard. "Not really feeling like an interview."

Iris's gaze went hard. "Well, I'd get in the mood. You're going to finally admit every single thing you did to ruin John's life. You're going to help set him free."

The way she said his name turned my stomach. It was like a physical caress.

"You know John well?" I couldn't hide the slight tremor in my voice.

A dreamy look spread across Iris's face. "Of course, I know him well. We're engaged. When he gets out of prison, we're going to get married."

Oh, shit.

That dreamy look vanished, replaced by pure hatred. "But you have to admit all your lies for that to happen."

Sweat trickled down my spine. "I didn't lie, Iris. I don't know what John has been telling you—"

The slap came out of nowhere, so hard the metallic taste of blood filled my mouth.

"Shut up, you whore! He warned me. Warned me you'd try to talk me around to your lies. But I'm stronger than that. I'll never believe you. You're going to tell the truth."

Iris pulled a knife from the waistband of her jeans. The blade glistened in the streaming sunshine. "I'd be happy to motivate you if you need it. It would be my pleasure."

Chapter Forty-Nine

Roan

THE BREW AND THE BACK ALLEY TEEMED WITH PEOPLE. Evidence techs from CRPD and the county were combing every inch of the place, but they weren't saying anything helpful.

Nash looked up from his phone. "Mom and Dad are getting Cady from school."

My gut twisted. Cady. How could I face her? What the hell would I tell her?

Lawson seemed to read my mind, squeezing my shoulder. "One thing at a time. We don't need to tell Cady anything just yet. Hopefully, Aspen will be home before Cady knows anything is wrong."

That grinding sensation was back along my sternum like the gears of a bike that hadn't been properly oiled. "We have no clue where she is. Who took her."

"I'm getting the camera feeds now," Holt said. "We'll see if anything's there."

Nash nodded. "There has to be something. It wouldn't make sense for the perp to wait in the alley all day. There'd be no guarantee Aspen would go out there."

"They had to be in The Brew," I said quietly.

"Or keeping a close eye from outside," Lawson agreed. He turned to Holt. "Did you put anything in on the front of the building?"

Holt sent him a withering look. "Do I look like an amateur to you?"

But there weren't enough cameras in the back—just one that caught Aspen heading for the dumpster. And then nothing. Whatever had happened was just out of sight.

"Okay," Holt said. "I found when Aspen goes into the kitchen and heads for the back door."

I crossed behind him, watching the feeds from several cameras at once.

"We need a list of folks who leave in the next sixty seconds," he muttered as he watched it play out.

There was only one figure who slipped out the door.

"Who's that?" Nash asked.

My back teeth ground together. "Her name's Elsie. She's a regular. Aspen said she's a photographer taking nature pictures of the area."

Holt looked up. "She's a tiny thing. You really think she could take Aspen down? The other victims?"

"If she had the element of surprise," I said.

"I'm gonna run her. You know her last name?" Lawson asked.

I shook my head. Why the hell hadn't I asked when I met her?

"We'll get it. You know where she's staying?"

I thought back, trying to remember if Elsie or Aspen had said anything. Then I stilled. "She had a Cedar Ridge Vacation Adventures pen. She's either staying in one of their rentals or went on one of their trips."

Lawson was already hitting a contact on his phone. "Hey, Jordan. Need your help. We've got a suspect in a missing persons case. First name, Elsie. She had one of your pens."

There was a pause. "Thanks, man. She at one of your rentals?" Another beat.

Lawson motioned for Holt's computer. "Driver's license would be great." Lawson typed letters and numbers into a database. "Appreciate it. Call me if you hear from her." Then he hit end on his phone.

We all waited in silent expectation.

"Elsie Jones went on a private hiking trip with Noel. Said she wanted to scout some spots for photos. They make copies of the driver's licenses of all trip participants."

Lawson hit search on the database, and a little swirl of color appeared on the screen as we held our breaths. Then an error box appeared.

This license is not valid.

I cursed. "A fake."

"Hold on," Lawson said. "He texted me a photo. Let me make sure I didn't get it wrong."

He pulled up the image, reading off the numbers. It was a match.

My stomach plummeted. "This was planned." For way longer than we ever knew. Because Elsie was a staple at The Brew before I even met Aspen.

"What the hell is going on?" Nash muttered.

"I'm texting this to my contact at the prison. I want to see if he recognizes her," Lawson said, his fingers flying over his phone's screen.

My throat grew tighter with every second that passed. As if I could feel Aspen slipping away. What hell was she living through right now? Was she even still breathing?

Holt stood, his hand clamping on my shoulder. "Don't go there. I know it's where your mind wants to live, but you can't let it. We're going to find her." He let out a shuddered breath. "She changed you. Brought you back to us. Not gonna let you lose her now."

My eyes burned like they'd been dunked in battery acid. "You can't promise that."

"The hell I can't. You helped me get Wren back when I thought I'd lost her all over again. The Universe will help me repay that debt. Just gotta keep the faith, brother."

I wanted to. God, did I want to. I let my eyes close and drifted back to months ago. When I sat on my balcony and saw that flash of red hair. The way I swore I could catch her laugh on the wind as she hoisted her daughter into the air. How she soothed her animals with the gentlest touches. The way she cared for everyone around her. She was light and hope, and I would hold on to that with everything I had.

"Holy hell," Lawson muttered.

My eyes flew open. "What?"

"Her name is actually Iris Morton. She visited John in prison every week for over a year. Those visits stopped three months ago."

"When she came here," I growled.

"Running a search now," Holt clipped, moving instantly to the laptop. His fingers flew across the keyboard, and then they simply stopped. "I've got something. She's been flagged in the system. Restraining order from her ex-husband. She tried to kill him."

Chapter Fifty

Aspen

I COULDN'T TAKE MY EYES OFF THE KNIFE, THE WAY THE silver gleamed in the sunlight. I could only wonder one thing. "Did you kill them?"

My voice didn't even sound like mine. It was empty. Devoid of all emotion. Like a robot's. Not someone asking whether the person in front of them had committed cold-blooded murder.

Iris's mouth stretched into a smile as she examined the knife. "I studied the case so closely. Wondered what it would take to do that to someone. Wondered if *I* could do it."

The urge to vomit was so strong, but I forced it down. "Did John tell you to kill those people?"

Her gaze snapped to me. "John is a good man. He would never."

He'd simply unlocked something in Iris.

"You killed Ty," Steven choked.

Iris glared at Steven. "He deserved so much worse than what he got. I heard him on your show. Lying about how the blood evidence meant John was guilty. He had to pay."

A smile stretched across her face. "No one thinks a little thing like me could ever hurt anyone. I told him I needed to talk to him alone. That I had information on the case, but he couldn't tell anyone I was giving it to him."

She laughed. "So gullible. Met me right at the trailhead. It was nice not to have to drag his ass anywhere. Kept ruining my tarps having to do that. But I bet he regretted our little rendezvous."

"You fucking bitch."

Iris struck out with her knife, slashing Steven across the chest.

He cried out, thrashing in pain. The cut didn't look lethal, but it wasn't shallow either.

"Do *not* call me a bitch." Iris's eyes flashed, rage swirling in their depths. "My ex tried that once and lived to regret it."

My heart hammered against my ribs as Steven struggled for breath. It wouldn't surprise me if he passed out. That kind of pain could easily be too much for a person.

Iris wiped the knife on her jeans, the blood smearing across the denim. "There's really no need for name-calling. Especially when I'm about to get you a goddamned Pulitzer."

I could see it then. She legitimately believed in this alternate dimension she'd created for herself.

"How did you meet John?" I asked. I needed to know. Had to understand how this had all come to be. And maybe, just maybe, I could buy enough time for Roan to find me.

Just thinking his name had me fighting tears. His face filled my mind: his gruff snarl, the twitch of his lips, one of those rare and precious smiles. I loved them all. Loved that each one made me appreciate the other. But most of all, I loved how deeply he cared. How he gave that care to the people and creatures around him without wanting to claim a second of glory for himself.

I wanted to tell him that. Wanted to see those blue eyes when I said those three little words.

He'd given me so much—a true family. A sob lodged in my throat as Cady's face swirled in my memory: her beaming smile and shining green eyes. What would happen to her if I died? Who would take care of her?

"I saw him on the news," Iris said dreamily, jerking me out of my spiraling thoughts. "His interview with Oren Randal. How could you not see his pain? His grief?"

I'd give it to her. John had been convincing in that farce. He'd somehow managed to dredge up actual tears as he stared into the camera and said, *"I did not kill my wife. I have no idea who did, but they stole everything good from my life because it means I've lost my daughter, too."*

That had been the turning point. The time when people wondered if I was too traumatized or spiteful to remember things correctly. They'd explained away the blood evidence. The timelines. So many had simply believed him.

"I wrote to him first," Iris said. "Told him I'd do whatever I could to help. We became...friends."

Except John didn't have friends. He had people he used.

"I sent him money for the commissary. Books. Magazines. Finally, he asked me to visit."

I tugged on my restraints, praying they'd magically loosened. "And you fell in love?"

She sent me a quelling look. "Not right away. We understood each other. We'd both been hurt. We supported each other. Listened."

"And he sent you here?" I pressed.

Iris's jaw tightened, her teeth gnashing together. "I came on my own. He just wanted me to get the truth out of you so he could be free. Scare you a little bit. But I knew you needed worse."

"Boiling baby bunnies and killing a bunch of people isn't exactly getting the truth," Steven mumbled.

"Don't make me slit your throat before it's time," Iris growled.

I expected Steven to panic or pale, but he just stared at her. Maybe he'd realized what I had. She had no plans of letting us walk out of here. Or maybe his temper would always get the best of him.

"Thought you needed me for an interview," he taunted.

Iris moved to the duffel and crouched. "I can always run the interview myself," she said, pulling out a gun.

My mouth went dry. The knife was bad enough. A gun felt more final somehow—a quicker end.

Steven bit back whatever retort was on his lips and simply glared.

"That's better," Iris said with a smile.

She shoved the knife back into her waistband but kept hold of the gun. A reminder, maybe. She pushed the table where she'd placed the audio gear toward us.

"We really need to get moving. Time's running out. I hear ole Cedar Ridge is crawling with cops."

A flicker of hope lit somewhere deep. Roan was one of the smartest people I knew. He'd figure this out. He'd find me. I just needed time.

I'd spin a hell of a story if it got me that. If it bought me a chance.

Iris positioned the microphones in front of Steven and me, then connected them to her laptop. "I don't have your intro music, but I can add that later. What's important now is the inter-view." Her eyes narrowed on Steven. "Help me clear John's name."

Steven snorted. "I'm not doing a damn thing for that asshole. He's been treating me like a puppet for six months."

At least this little adventure had opened someone's eyes.

Iris pushed to her feet. "He has given you *everything.*"

"He told me where his sister-in-law was hiding out. That's it. I should've known when he said he'd turned someone in the court system that the dude was bad news."

Iris's breaths came faster and faster. "*I* turned him. I had to sleep with that disgusting piece of trash to get information on Tara's new identity." She closed her eyes and slowly exhaled. "But I'll do anything for John."

My stomach roiled. How many people had John twisted?

Steven started laughing, but it was the maniacal kind. The type that told me he was losing it and quickly. "Lady, if he's whor-ing you out to get what he wants, get a clue. He doesn't love you."

Iris moved in a flash, raising her hand. There was a deafening pop.

Steven screamed as blood bloomed on his shoulder. "You fucking shot me!"

"You're lucky I didn't put a bullet in your brain," Iris seethed. She turned to me, gun still pointed. "Start talking or I'll give you a hole to match his."

Chapter Fifty-One

Roan

HOLT'S GAZE TRACKED BACK AND FORTH ACROSS THE screen. "There's not a lot of information to go on here. Wait. I've got some notes from the original police file."

I struggled to swallow as Holt read. Every second felt like agony.

"Iris found out her husband was cheating on her and stabbed him with a kitchen knife," Holt said, still scanning the screen.

"Holy shit," Nash muttered.

I couldn't breathe. Aspen was in the hands of someone incredibly violent who had been in close contact with the man who'd tried to kill her.

"Roan?" Lawson asked carefully.

"We need to find her," I croaked. A million different scenarios flew through my head, none of them good.

"Already looking," Holt assured me. "Under her alias and legal name. I'm guessing she has a rental. Someplace removed." His fingers stilled on the keyboard. "Bingo."

I moved in a flash, taking in the address on the screen. I knew the area. Removed was exactly right. There were no other homes. No cell phone reception. No Wi-Fi. A place you could get away with anything because no one could see or hear you.

I was moving before I even realized it, running for the door.

Someone called my name, but I didn't stop. Footsteps followed me, and I knew it was my brothers having my back. But I didn't pause to acknowledge them. All I could think about was Aspen.

Her name was a whispered chant in my head—a form of prayer. As though if I said it over and over, she would be okay.

"My SUV," Lawson yelled as we reached the parking lot at the back of the police station. "I've got gear in the back."

I made a beeline for the passenger side as he beeped the locks. We climbed in within a matter of seconds.

Lawson started the engine.

"I called it in. Backup's en route. They'll wait on the main road," Nash said as he buckled his seat belt.

He knew better than most how delicate these situations could be. One wrong move, and Elsie, or whatever the hell her name was, could be spooked. And then anything could happen.

Lawson flicked on his lights as he pulled out of the lot, but he didn't hit his sirens. He pressed down on the accelerator. "Holt, you gotta stay in the SUV."

"The hell I do."

"You're not law enforcement," Lawson growled.

"I signed that piece of paper. I'm a consultant," he argued.

"That doesn't cover this sort of thing, and you damn well know it," Lawson shot back.

Nash clapped him on the shoulder. "Give Law a break. He's going to have an aneurysm with all the rules he's already breaking."

Because I shouldn't be here. Shouldn't be part of an operation trying to get the woman I loved out of harm's way. I wasn't a cop in this town. Law enforcement, sure, but not under Lawson's jurisdiction. But he hadn't even suggested I should stay back. He knew it wouldn't have gotten him anywhere.

Lawson flicked off his lights as he turned onto the road that led to the cabin. When we reached the long drive, he pulled behind some trees and threw the vehicle into park.

We hopped out instantly, closing our doors as quietly as

possible. We moved to the back of the SUV, and Holt pulled the hatch open. Lawson handed all of us but Holt vests. We checked our weapons, and Lawson retrieved his long-range rifle.

He glanced at Holt. "Bring them up to speed when they get here."

Holt jerked his head in a nod. "Don't do anything stupid and get yourselves shot."

Nash's lips twitched. "I'd never do that."

Holt smacked him upside the head. "You get one more hole in your body, and Maddie'll kill you herself."

Nash winced. "You've got a point there."

"Let's move," I gritted out. There was no time to waste. We could be too late as it was.

That thought had everything in me constricting. It was hard to walk, to breathe. I didn't want anything to do with a world without Aspen.

"We stick to the trees, see what we're dealing with. Then, we go in," Lawson instructed.

Nash and I both gave quick nods and followed Lawson's lead. It took us less than two minutes before the cabin came into view. But those one hundred and twenty seconds felt like a lifetime.

A navy SUV was parked out front, but everything was quiet—too quiet.

Lawson moved in closer, up to the very edge of the tree line. We circled until we reached the first set of windows. They looked in on a kitchen and through to a—my breath caught.

Aspen.

Tied to a fucking chair.

Her face was black and blue from Oren's attack, and now she had a split lip. Shock ripped through me as I saw Steven tied to the chair next to her. I could only get a glimpse of Iris. A flash of her blond hair. Her arm. The gun in her hand.

Nash cursed. "Second hostage is shot."

I hadn't even noticed the blood blooming on Steven's shoulder.

"We need to move," I growled.

"Let me see if I can get a shot from the front," Lawson said.

"She could see you," I argued.

Lawson was already moving. "I'll stay covered."

We followed the edge of the trees, and Lawson crouched low, getting into position. He let out a slew of curses. "I don't have it."

A crack lit the air as though lightning had struck without any hint of a storm.

I didn't think. I simply moved. Running for the cabin with everything I had.

I hauled open the door. Steven cried out in pain, more blood oozing from his good shoulder.

Iris's head jerked in my direction. Her eyes went wide. "No! She doesn't get to be happy. She has to pay!"

Iris raised the gun and pointed it at Aspen.

I didn't think, I simply dove.

Iris screamed, the sound so loud and deranged that it nearly pierced my eardrums. "No! She has to die!"

She was strong for such a little thing, and I struggled to grab hold of the weapon.

A crack sounded, and the world went sideways.

Chapter Fifty-Two

Aspen

ROAN GRUMBLED SOMETHING UNDER HIS BREATH FROM HIS spot on the couch next to me.

I shifted, my brow furrowing. "Is your shoulder hurting?" I asked, my voice barely audible above the laughter and chatter in the room.

"No," he grumbled. "It's fine."

"Don't glare at me. You were shot."

A muscle in Roan's jaw flexed. "Grazed."

"You needed twenty stitches," I snapped back.

Thankfully, that was all he'd required. My life had stopped the moment the gunshot sounded. It wasn't until I saw Roan still moving and pulling the weapon from Elsie's grasp that I'd started to breathe again.

"I'm fine," he muttered. But he sounded anything but as he scowled at the rest of the people in the room.

Everyone was here: Nathan and Kerry. Holt and Wren. Nash and Maddie. Grae and Caden. Lawson and his boys. Cady was in heaven, and so was I.

"They've been here forever," he mumbled.

I pressed my lips together to keep from laughing. "That's why you're glaring?"

"I'm not glaring."

I raised an eyebrow at that. As much as Roan smiled and laughed more, big groups for long periods of time would never be his thing.

I leaned in. "Roan. I was kidnapped. You were shot. Cut them some slack. They want to make sure we're okay."

We were all piled into my tiny house, and Kerry had made so much food we'd never eat it all. Thankfully, Roan's and my injuries were mild, but the hospital had wanted us to stay overnight just to be safe. Luckily, Cady just thought she was getting a fun sleepover with Nathan, Kerry, and Charlie.

But now we were home. Iris was in jail. Steven had made it through surgery. Oren had been charged with assault. And John had lost all visitor and communication privileges. Lawson's source at the prison told him that John was already losing his mind at not having contact with the outside world.

It wasn't justice, not truly, because it wouldn't bring Autumn back. But Cady and I were safe now. And that was the only thing Autumn would truly care about. I had to hope our safety meant she was finally at peace.

It would take time to heal, but we would be okay—better than okay.

Roan pulled me tighter against him. He hadn't stopped touching me since the moment he found me. Not even in the hospital. The nurses had finally given up and just let us share a bed.

I pressed a hand to his chest. "I'm okay."

He nuzzled my neck. "I know. It's just going to take a little while for the rest of me to believe it."

My heart ached at that. The whole ordeal had impacted Roan more than me. I was sure I'd have nightmares for a while, but I had always known Roan would come. No one made me feel safer or more loved. I didn't need the damn words.

Roan stood, hauling me up with him.

"What are you doing?" I asked.

"Need to show you something," he said.

"Now?"

"Is this your way of telling us you want us to leave?" Holt called, his arms around Wren's pregnant belly.

"No, I know I'm stuck with the lot of you for the foreseeable future," Roan grumbled.

Grae laughed. "Good thing you're aware. I was thinking we could have a pretty epic slumber party tonight."

"Yes!" Cady cheered. "I want all the slumber parties."

I laughed, and Roan groaned. He started tugging me toward the door. "Let's go before they all move in."

I grinned at Cady. "Be back in a minute, Katydid."

"Okay, Mama." But she was already distracted by something Charlie was showing her.

Roan guided me out the door and toward his truck.

"We have to drive to this something?"

He opened the passenger door and helped me in. "It's not far."

I slid in and fastened my belt. The air was cold and smelled like snow. I wouldn't have been surprised if we got a few inches tonight.

Roan got behind the wheel and started the engine.

"Are you going to give me any clues?"

He grunted and shook his head.

The reaction only made me smile. Too many people for one day.

Instead of turning toward town, he went in the opposite direction. He guided his truck up Huckleberry Lane until we reached a gate with several cameras. He rolled down his window and punched in a code.

"Is this your property?"

He nodded. "Bought it not long after my attack. Made it as secure as I could. No one's ever been up here but me."

And he was letting me in. The simple action had tears gathering in my eyes.

As the gate slid open, my gaze searched for the house. It took a minute for it to come into view. A simple but gorgeous A-frame cabin. With some snow, it could've been a Christmas card.

"It's beautiful," I whispered.

"Thanks," he mumbled, pulling to a stop.

Roan slid out and came to help me. He took my hand and led me up the walk to the front door. He slid a key into one lock after the other and then guided us inside.

The space was minimalistic, but the walls had gorgeous photographs of nature and animals. There was also a massive stone fireplace and a back wall that was all windows.

I gasped as I headed for it. His view was jaw-dropping. You could see all of Cedar Ridge. The town, the lake, the beautiful mountains surrounding us.

Roan slid open the door and ushered me out onto the balcony, shutting it behind us.

I instinctively moved toward the railing, wanting to take it all in.

"This is where I first saw you."

I looked up at the sound of Roan's voice, right into those beautiful blue eyes.

"It was just a flash of red." His lips twitched. "I was annoyed at first. I never saw the old guy who lived there before you. It was like I had this whole mountainside to myself."

My mouth curved.

"But then I saw your kindness. The animals you added, one after another. How patient you were with your daughter. At times, I swore a light shone straight out of you."

My heart jerked in my chest as my breaths came quicker.

"You were the light in the shadows. A glimmer of hope when I felt like all mine had been burned out. I think maybe I loved you even then."

My lips parted with a sharp inhale. "You love me?"

Roan wrapped his arms around me. "With every ounce of my being. Didn't think it was possible. Didn't think I was capable. I know I won't do it exactly right—"

I pressed a hand to his chest. "You do it perfectly."

Those blue eyes shone. "I love you, Tender Heart. That's never going to end."

"I love you, too." My voice broke on the words. "Never thought I'd get this. You've given me everything. Safety. Acceptance. A family."

"You gonna give me something in return?" Roan asked.

"Anything."

He inclined his head over the balcony. My gaze followed, and the tears were instant. Everyone we loved was out in my drive, holding up a massive handmade banner. Each letter had been painted and decorated, most likely by Cady and Charlie.

MARRY ME?

My gaze shot back to Roan's, tears spilling over. "You wanna marry me?"

"I want to be yours in every way I can. Want to be your husband. Father to Cady and any babies you'll give me. Everything you'll let me be."

"Yes," I whispered. A single syllable, not nearly enough for what I wanted to say, but all I could get out.

He slid a diamond band onto my finger. It looked like glittering leaves woven together. The most perfect ring for me. One that wouldn't bang up against things as I worked with the animals or at the café. One that reminded me of the peace we'd both found in the nature around us. One that was a blend of him and me.

I stretched up onto my tiptoes, my mouth hovering over his. "You already are everything to me."

Chapter Fifty-Three

Roan

ONE MONTH LATER

"M AMA," A LITTLE VOICE WHISPERED ON THE OTHER side of the bed.

Cady was trying to be quiet, I'd give her that. But it was more of a whisper-shout, her excitement bleeding into her voice.

"Mmm," Aspen mumbled, pressing her backside into me as she shifted.

I fought the urge to groan at the sensation. I mentally recited SAR procedures in my head.

"I gots to show you something," Cady whispered louder.

I squinted against the early morning light filtering in through the bedroom windows. "What's going on?" I grumbled.

"We gots to go," Cady urged.

"The wedding isn't for hours, Tiny Dancer."

She bounced on her tiptoes, a ballerina through and through. "Not the wedding. Something else. You have to see."

"You can keep sleeping," Aspen told me as she sat up.

I blinked a few times, shoving up against the pillows. "No, I'm up."

Movement caught my eye, and I tried to shift, but it was too late.

Pirate launched herself from her spot on our dresser and onto my damned head. Her claws dug into my hair and scalp. I spit out some words I really hoped Cady didn't remember.

"Demon cat," I growled as I pulled the thing off me.

She swiped at my nose.

"Shit!"

Then the damned cat headbutted my chin and started purring.

Cady and Aspen promptly burst out laughing.

"See, she loves you, Mr. Grizz," Cady chirped.

I stood, setting the cat on the bed. "Well, her love's toxic."

Aspen stifled another giggle and turned to Cady. "What did you want to show us?"

Her eyes brightened. "Come on!"

Aspen grabbed my robe as I picked up a sweatshirt.

"I can't believe she's up. She didn't fall asleep until after ten," I mumbled as we followed her out the door.

Aspen shrugged. "Big day. She's excited."

I wrapped an arm around her and brushed my mouth across hers. "You ready?"

"Would've married you the day you asked."

A burn lit in my chest—the best kind of pain.

Cady opened the front door and stepped out onto the porch. There was a light dusting of snow over everything, a sight I'd never get tired of. "Dory came. She brought her family."

I followed Cady's hand as she pointed. And there Dory was, surrounded by her herd. That burn deepened and spread. You could never be sure if the ones you helped would make it, but she had. And she'd come to show us that she was okay.

I lifted Cady into my arms. "See those two little ones?"

Cady nodded.

"I'm pretty sure those are her babies. They're sticking pretty close. She probably had them last spring."

Cady's eyes went wide. "I bet they missed her so much when she was gone."

Aspen slipped under my free arm. "But think how happy they are now that they're all together."

A smile spread across Cady's face. "I bet they're the happiest. Just like us."

The burn flared deeper. My girls. I wasn't sure how, after everything, I'd gotten this damned lucky.

Aspen looked up at me, her eyes glistening with unshed tears. And I knew she felt the same way.

"Love you, Tender Heart."

"Love you, too," she echoed.

"I love you both. And Dory and Mabel and Emmaline and—"

A horn sounded, cutting Cady off and making all the deer head off in the opposite direction. Grae's SUV pulled to a stop in front of us, and she, Maddie, and Wren jumped out.

"It's wedding day!" Grae yelled, doing some sort of shimmy shake.

I frowned at her. "Isn't it a little early?" I wanted time with my family before we had to deal with all the people. It was a small wedding, but it had still grown to more than I wanted to deal with. I would only do this for Aspen. She'd insisted on Jonesy attending, but I'd drawn the line at inviting Dr. Miller, who continued to care for all the animals. I wasn't having a man who'd asked her out at our wedding.

"Early?" Maddie asked. "We need all day to prep. It's girl time. You need to get."

I jerked back. "It's my house."

At least it was for the moment. We'd cleared everything out of my A-frame so we could do a major expansion on the home. We were going to combine our two properties so we could have the view and our animals.

"Not today, it's not," Grae singsonged.

Wren patted me on the shoulder. "Holt's heading up to The Peaks to meet the rest of the guys. Caden's got them putting on quite the breakfast spread for you."

"Whatever," I grumbled.

Aspen stretched up onto her tiptoes and pressed her lips to mine. "See you at the altar?"

I smiled against her mouth. "I'll be the one saying I do."

"This collar is making my neck itch," I muttered.

Holt chuckled. "At least she didn't want you in a tux or even a tie."

"Small mercies," I mumbled.

We were all in navy suits and white shirts. Nice, but not stuffy. Given we were getting married at Caden's fancy-ass resort, things could've been a lot worse. But I'd give it to Aspen, the room she'd picked was perfect. An all-glass conservatory full of plants that looked out at the mountains—just enough space to fit our twenty or so guests.

Nash popped some sort of appetizer into his mouth. "You can get married anytime if these are the snacks Caden provides."

Caden snorted. "We need an extra food budget just for you."

Nash patted his stomach. "I'm a growing boy."

"Yeah, your gut's growing," Caden shot back.

Nash glared at him. "I'll have you know I still have a six-pack. But you look like you're getting a little soft."

"Let's hit the boxing ring tomorrow so I can show you how soft I am."

Holt shook his head. "At least the black eyes will be *after* the wedding photos."

The door to the suite burst open, and Lawson hurried inside. "Sorry I'm late," he muttered as he ran a hand through his already disheveled dark hair. But it was more than his hair that looked out of sorts. It was him.

"You okay?" I asked.

He jerked his head in a nod. "That interview with the nanny candidate went longer than expected."

"How'd it go?" Holt asked.

The first few interviews had been disasters: a woman who acted more like a drill sergeant, one Lawson had said spent more time coming on to him than answering questions, and another who had only seemed interested in Lawson's cable package and snack selection.

Lawson swallowed, his throat working as his hand flexed. "Good."

Nash arched a brow. "That's all you're giving us? You sound like Roan used to."

"Yeah, man. At least give us another hilarious interview story," Caden said. "I've been living for those."

"She's nice. I hired her," Lawson said.

Holt sent the rest of us a quizzical look. "What's her name?"

"Hallie." Lawson cleared his throat. "We've actually met before. A long time ago."

My brows rose at that.

"Where?" Nash asked.

A knock sounded on the door. "I'll get it," I said.

Crossing the room, I pulled it open and froze.

Aspen stood in the hall, creating an image that would be burned into my brain for all eternity. She was always beautiful, whether working at The Brew, mucking out stalls, or simply laughing. She could steal my breath anytime. But this was something different.

Her red hair was curled in loose waves around her face, and whatever she'd done with her makeup made her green eyes pierce straight to my soul. And the dress...

I'd never given a damn about a dress until this one. The straps were a see-through gauzy fabric that made it seem like it was being held up by nothing at all, dipping into a V at the front, showing just a tease of the swells beneath. It hugged her body and then flared out at the waist in layers of delicate fabric with flowers embroidered on them.

"Tender Heart," I croaked.

The corner of her mouth kicked up. "You like it?"

"Never seen a more beautiful sight."

"Roan," she whispered, emotion clogging her throat.

"Mama, now?" Cady asked at her side.

It was then that I finally took in my Tiny Dancer. She wore a dress similar to her mom's but in a pale pink with larger flowers.

Aspen grinned. "We were supposed to do this *after* the ceremony, but someone didn't want to wait."

Cady bit her lip and tugged on her mom's arm. Aspen bent, and Cady whispered in her ear. "What if he doesn't like it? What if he doesn't want to?"

I crouched low, taking in the box in Cady's hand. "You know I'm gonna love whatever you give me because it's from you."

Cady's eyes got glassy, but she still looked a little unsure.

Aspen crouched, too, the fabric of her dress swirling around her. "Sometimes, we just gotta be brave, Katydid. It can feel scary to show people just how much we love them, but Roan loves you right back."

"To the moon and the stars, Tiny Dancer," I said.

Cady looked at me, hope in those green eyes. She slowly handed me the box.

I carefully undid the ribbon and opened the lid. There was a stack of papers inside. I scanned the first few lines, and then my gaze jerked to Aspen. "Is this what I think it is?"

Aspen's eyes filled. "We went to see a lawyer in town, and he helped us with the paperwork. You just have to sign, and then we file."

"You wanna be my real dad, Mr. Grizz?" Cady asked.

The burn of tears built in my eyes. "Nothing would make me happier, Tiny Dancer."

She flew at me then. I stood, lifting her into the air, then wrapped Aspen in with us. "Not sure how I got so lucky with these girls of mine."

Aspen pressed her lips to my throat. "Love you, Roan."

"In this life and beyond," I whispered back.

Epilogue

Aspen

TWELVE YEARS LATER

I PACED BACK AND FORTH ALONG THE FOYER OF OUR HOME. The space had seen so much life. Racing through it to get to the car when my water broke the first time. The boys' first steps. Photos of Cady's first school dance. Roan carrying Chauncey to the car when we had to say goodbye and then welcoming a new three-legged puppy he'd brought home six months later.

We'd seen a million ups and downs in this home and the beautiful life we'd built. But I wasn't sure I'd ever been this nervous.

My pacing picked up speed as I worried the corner of my thumbnail.

"What's your deal, Mom?" Max asked from the couch, not looking away from the TV that housed his precious video game.

"Yeah," Max's twin brother, Colin, echoed as he hit a series of buttons on the controller. "You went wired after Dad called."

Lewis looked up from his book at his spot by the window. "Everything okay?"

I nodded like one of those bobblehead dolls. "Everything's fine."

Max snorted. "Your voice gets all high-pitched when you lie."

"It does not." I winced as my tone went shrill.

Colin burst out laughing. "The only time she was worse than this was when she had to tell Dad that Cady had her first date."

I grimaced at the reminder. Roan had not taken his baby girl growing up well. It helped that we'd have our three boys for a few more years, but Cady was getting ready to fly the nest.

Lewis's brows lifted. "Cady isn't getting married, is she?"

That had the twins' gazes shooting to me.

"No, no, no. Nothing like that," I promised. My girl was eighteen. Way too young to be thinking about that.

The sound of tires crunching on gravel had my nerves ratcheting up another few levels. My hands fisted as my palms went damp. A car door closed. Then there were footsteps outside.

He'd texted from the post office on his way home from his SAR meeting. Much to his chagrin, the community's perception of him changed once people started seeing him with Cady. They saw the gentleness I had from that very first meeting. Now, he was constantly asked to serve on volunteer committees, sports teams, and everything in between.

The door swung open, and Roan filled the space. It didn't matter if it had been twelve minutes or twelve years, I never tired of looking at my husband—his broad shoulders and muscled form, gorgeous face, now with a few lines from smiling and laughing, and his hair peppered with gray. But those blue eyes stayed the same.

"It came?" I whispered.

Roan closed the distance between us and handed me the envelope.

It looked like any business envelope, except the top of the return address read *American Ballet Theatre*. My fingers rubbed circles on the paper. "It's thin."

It hurt to even say the words. My girl had fallen in love

with dance. She'd been enamored with it from the moment she started, but as she'd gotten older, it had become clear that not only did she love it, but she was also incredibly talented. She'd done classes, camps, and even a special summer program in New York.

The American Ballet Theatre was her dream. And I wanted my girl to have all her dreams, even if it meant losing her to the other side of the country. But this envelope? I worried it was about to dash all those hopes.

Roan squeezed my shoulder. "Let's just see what it says before we borrow trouble. Where is she?"

"Where do you think?" I asked.

Cady processed everything through dance. The good and the bad. But it was especially her outlet during times of anxiety. When we'd told her the whole truth about John, she'd locked herself in the studio for weeks until she had a hold of the feelings she needed to talk about. She did the same when we lost Chauncey. When she'd fallen in love. When she'd suffered her first heartbreak. And knowing that she should be hearing back about her audition for the company at ABT had her pretty much dancing around the clock.

Roan's lips twitched, and he wrapped his arm around my shoulders. "Come on," he said, plucking the envelope from my fingers and guiding me toward the stairs. "Don't burn down the house," he called to the boys.

"If you chill Mom out, we'll be angels," Max yelled back.

Roan chuckled. "Holding you to that."

We descended the staircase to an area Roan had built just for Cady. I couldn't help but take in the space as we stepped into the room. One wall was entirely mirrored with a ballet bar across it. The opposite wall was all windows with a view of Cedar Ridge. It was magical, and Cady had wept when she saw it.

Just like I'd wept when he told me he'd covered the repairs on my car all those years ago and when he surprised me by buying The Brew for me. Roan loved to spoil his girls.

Classical music filtered out through speakers as Cady spun across the floor. I might never know the name of each move, but I knew that Cady made me *feel* with each bend, twist, and leap.

As she twirled again, she stopped right in front of us, grinning and breathing heavily. "Hey. Is it dinnertime already?"

"No," I began. "I…I mean your dad…I mean we—"

Roan squeezed my shoulder and handed the envelope to Cady. "This was in the mail."

She took it slowly, staring at the return address. "It's thin," she whispered.

Roan ducked his head so he could meet Cady's eyes. "Tiny Dancer, no matter what's in that envelope, you are incredible. You've achieved more than most people could ever dream of. But you also found what you love. What lights you up. Nothing and no one can take that away from you. You'll shine that light wherever you end up."

Cady's eyes glistened, and she threw her arms around Roan. "I love you, Dad."

"Love you, too. Know you're going to do great things."

As she pulled back, she held his eyes. "Thank you for always believing me. For spending a summer in New York, even though you hate big cities. For always having my back. For being my dad when you didn't have to be."

Tears pooled in my eyes, spilling down my cheeks.

Roan cleared his throat, his eyes glistening. "Greatest privilege of my life, you choosing me to be your dad."

Oh, God. The gift of these two was more than I'd ever be able to repay.

"Open it," Roan said softly.

Cady took a deep breath and tore into the envelope. She pulled out the paper and unfolded it. Her eyes scanned back and forth and then shot to us. "I'm in."

Roan hooted, hauling her back into his arms. I burst into more tears. Roan pulled me in, too. "My girls."

I just cried harder, which only made Cady laugh.

"You really got her going this time," she said with a smile.

Roan hugged us both tightly and then brushed his lips against mine. "My Tender Heart."

"Thank you," I whispered.

"For what?"

"For giving us everything," I said, the words barely audible.

"It's you," Roan uttered, his voice low. "You're the light in the shadows. Always have been. Always will be."

Acknowledgments

Now for my favorite part of any book, the acknowledgments. I love taking a moment to think back on the writing and editing of a book, what was going on in my life, and who helped me reach the finish line. Getting to THE END is a marathon, and it's not always easy. But it's those tougher books that make you that much more grateful for the people in your life.

First, in my writerly world. Sam, I'm so thankful that this writer world brought us together because I honestly don't know what I'd do without you. Thank you for walking through all the life and authorly things with me. Your friendship is the greatest gift. Rebecca, thank you for helping me figure out just how Roan's story would play out. I'm pretty sure I sent you hours of voice memos on this one, and I'm incredibly grateful you didn't block me on your phone. Forever grateful for you! Laura and Willow, thank you for being a constant ear and source of laughter. Your friendship is on my forever list of gratitudes. Elsie, thanks for letting me turn you into a prison pen pal murderer. Little has brought me more joy. But more than that, thanks for always having my back and being the best friend. Amy, thank you for sprinting, reading a million blurbs, and just generally being such a source of light in my world. I'm so lucky to have so many amazing friends in this community. You all know who you are. I'm so thankful to have you in my corner!

Second, in my non-writer world. My STS soul sisters: Hollis, Jael, and Paige, thank you for making me feel like the most supported and celebrated human on this planet. I always feel seen and cherished, thanks to you. Love you to the moon and back.

And to all my family and friends near and far. Thank you for supporting me on this crazy journey, even if you don't read "kissing books." But you get extra special bonus points if you picked up one of mine, even if that makes me turn the shade of a tomato when you tell me.

To my fearless beta readers: Crystal, Elle, Kelly, and Trisha, thank you for reading this book in its roughest form and helping me to make it the best it could possibly be! And an extra thanks for loving Roan so much!

The crew that helps bring my words to life and gets them out into the world is pretty darn epic. Thank you to Devyn, Margo, Chelle, Jaime, Julie, Hang, Stacey, Katie, and my team at Lyric, Kimberly, Joy, and my team at Brower Literary. Your hard work is so appreciated!

To all the bloggers who have taken a chance on my words… THANK YOU! Your championing of my stories means more than I can say. And to Jess, Monica, and Paige, especially, I'm so grateful for your support, but more, your friendship. This book world (and my world) are extra awesome because you three are in it! To my launch and ARC teams, thank you for your kindness and support, and for sharing my books with the world. An extra special thank you to Crystal who sails that ship so I can focus on the words.

Ladies of Catherine Cowles Reader Group, you're my favorite place to hang out on the internet! Thank you for your support, encouragement, and willingness to always dish about your latest book boyfriends. And especially for your excitement about Roan. You're the freaking best!

Lastly, thank YOU! Yes, YOU. I'm so grateful you're reading this book and making my author dreams come true. I love you for that. A whole lot!

Also Available from
CATHERINE COWLES

The Lost & Found Series
Whispers of You
Echoes of You
Glimmers of You
Shadows of You
Ashes of You

The Tattered & Torn Series
Tattered Stars
Falling Embers
Hidden Waters
Shattered Sea
Fractured Sky

The Wrecked Series
Reckless Memories
Perfect Wreckage
Wrecked Palace
Reckless Refuge
Beneath the Wreckage

The Sutter Lake Series
Beautifully Broken Pieces
Beautifully Broken Life
Beautifully Broken Spirit
Beautifully Broken Control
Beautifully Broken Redemption

For a full list of up-to-date Catherine Cowles titles, please visit
www.catherinecowles.com.

About
CATHERINE COWLES

Writer of words. Drinker of Diet Cokes. Lover of all things cute and furry. *USA Today* bestselling author Catherine Cowles has had her nose in a book since the time she could read and finally decided to write down some of her own stories. When she's not writing, she can be found exploring her home state of Oregon, listening to true crime podcasts, or searching for her next book boyfriend.

Stay Connected

You can find Catherine in all the usual bookish places…

Website:
catherinecowles.com

Facebook:
facebook.com/catherinecowlesauthor

Catherine Cowles Facebook Reader Group:
www.facebook.com/groups/CatherineCowlesReaderGroup

Instagram:
instagram.com/catherinecowlesauthor

Goodreads:
goodreads.com/catherinecowlesauthor

BookBub:
bookbub.com/profile/catherine-cowles

Amazon:
www.amazon.com/author/catherinecowles

Twitter:
twitter.com/catherinecowles

Pinterest:
pinterest.com/catherinecowlesauthor

9 781951 936464